Walls

A Novel By R.T. Donlon

Corinne,

Thanks for the support!
Hope you like it :)

To the love of my life—my wife.
You've stuck with me through it all.

PART ONE

THE CITY

1

His knuckles pressed white against the handlebars of the motorbike. The air smelled of burning souls and fresh forestry—a strange combination, but it seemed to be normal in these times. The engine screamed with speed down the deserted highway and, for the first time in a long time, Henry felt courageous enough to risk his life. He could see the quiet metropolis in the distance, rising up into the colorless sky. He had finally come to terms with his destiny. This place would be the last he would ever see.

A murderous tingle ran through his veins. He kept his eyes glued to the road, catching glimpses of the barricading walls reaching like musclebound arms into the sky. They had nowhere to go, but the sheer sight of them forced a sense of fear to rise to the forefront of his mind. He wondered if he was doing the right thing—risking his life to rescue Shanna—or if it was all just a futile attempt at chivalry. One that he would regret after it was all too late.

We'll find out soon enough, he thought.

Miles passed. The motorbike squealed and spurted heavy, mechanical noises and uncomfortable vibrations into the afternoon. It possessed the power to drown out any irreparable thoughts running through his mind, yet even in its oil-fueled rage, Henry could not pry his mind away from the memories of Shanna, who, as far as he knew, was still inside that empty house, in the middle of the city, with a broken ankle. He wished he had never left her. He wished he could take it all back, but wishful thinking, along with many other things, was a thing of the past.

He allowed his mind to drift. He remembered the smell of the deserted apartment as he walked her over to the far corner of the room and let her fall gently to the dusty floor. It was a murky smell—something dank and

3

mysteriously stagnant—like a swamp in wet season. The building had been boarded up and locked, but Henry had discovered a way in through a loose wooden board on one of the back windows. Shanna was shivering, harder than he had ever seen her shiver before.

"I'll find help," he had said. Thoughts of panic ran like gazelles through the empty crevices in his mind. He had been inching towards the door seemingly without notice.

"No!" she yelped. "Don't leave me here."

"I'll be back. *I promise.*"

He had never wanted to leave her in the first place, but he knew it was the only way. He convinced himself that he would return with help, accompanied by someone with the strength to carry her out of the city, or with someone who could at least mend the broken bones in her ankle. But in all honesty, he had never been too certain that he would be able to locate someone with those types of skills, especially now.

In times like these, Henry thought, *it's every man for himself.*

He remembered the tears running down the skin of her cheeks. He had wiped them away cautiously, brushing the back of his hand against the side of her face. He kissed her forehead, looked her straight in the eyes once more, told her how much he loved her, and walked straight out the door. It was a moment he would never forget—mainly because of his lack of reciprocity, but also because of the ripping feeling in his chest and the pools of guilt that had haunted him every night since.

But he *had* promised to return. And he would live up to that promise no matter what it took. So here he was, days later, riding towards the overrun city of Boston, from whence he came, with nothing but Shanna—and the Dead—on his mind.

The dry, blubbering sounds of the motorbike continued its rattling below him—increasingly worse now—sighing and coughing as if it were having a heart attack, yet even in the midst of it all, its last few dying spurts inched Henry closer to his fate. It weaved in and out of the abandoned veins of the Interstate slowly now, chugging, hacking. He hadn't reached the walls north of Lynn just yet, but he could see the shadows looming across the line of buildings in the distance, close enough now to smell the stagnant rotting flesh emanating from inside the city limits. It was worse than when he left. An acute and potent stint of panic flooded his mind.

Please keep her safe, he prayed, but not sure to whom.

He imagined her tear-stained face—the image he had clasped in his mind since leaving her—and hoped that his rescue would not come too late. He dug his grip harder into the motorbike's handles, adding incentive to push the machine forward, but the action provided nothing more than a warbling, delayed cough. It lessened until he could almost feel the bike deflating underneath him. Somewhere on the dashboard, he knew a small glowing 'E' was shimmering, alerting him of an empty fuel tank.

"Great," Henry mumbled.

The day was still hazy, even in its waning hours, burnt with the heat of its prescient summer light. Henry welcomed the darkening, brisk evening as would a lost traveler. Of course, he wasn't lost, but Boston was no longer a place to travel and something told him he would regret this moment—wishing away the heat. He looked up into the sky, peered into the afternoon sun and sighed, letting the motorbike crawl across the asphalt and come to a complete, halting stop. He swiveled his leg to the left so that he no longer straddled the seat, letting the motorbike fall to the road in a sequence of clanking metal noises until one, louder tumultuous *thud* led to the complete silence of another fallen vehicle in a graveyard of others.

His legs would have to carry him from here.

When Henry reached the city limits, the sun had already begun its descent into darkness. Through the wall he could hear the harsh breathing of the rising Dead. Dusk was a shift change for the countless bodies, crawling from the city sewers and subway lines, like rats, into the city streets, the disappearing sun a comfort from the pain that came from its burning light. Even from where he stood, still distant enough from the walls themselves, he was certain they could smell him, even through the thick cement that barricaded him. The thought of it sent a lone, biting shiver down his spine.

He reached into his pocket and brought a dirtied radio to eye level. He flipped a minuscule switch that powered the fragile box and watched the lime-green powered light flicker in and out of consciousness. The batteries had been running low for some time now and a frequented worry that its power would soon run out kept him pessimistically vigilant. He shoved one side of his earbuds into his ear and dangled the other helplessly at his side.

A strong, female voice projected through the static airspace, clearing the frequency for a few short minutes. Henry smiled at the gentility in her voice—it comforted him somehow, reminding him of Shanna in many ways—but cringed, too, at how vulnerable each syllable truly sounded. Perhaps that was the reason he looked forward to these few, brief moments every day. It was a way to connect without connecting. It suppressed the guilt of losing her. "*The Dead like dark and musty places, like sewers and subway lines,*" the voice projected. *If you are stuck in the city and somehow listening to this program, stay inside until morning. I repeat: Stay inside until morning."*

She spoke in urgency, as if the entire world was falling apart. He stared at the silent streets in front of him. Exile and desolation covered the landscape like blankets. She wasn't wrong. What used to be bustling highways and back-end roads were now nothing more than glorified sidewalks, yet the message looped every evening at exactly the same time—a sign that even worry was an artificial glimpse into the truth of the city. When the woman's voice cleared once again to static, he clicked the radio off and shoved the headphones back into his pocket.

Nothing has changed, Henry thought. *This goddamn city is lost.*

He reached the outer city walls as the sun faded into remnants of already used light. The buildings crept higher into the sky like shadowy, towering Goliaths aching for violence. It had been a long walk, longer than Henry had wanted to travel, and his feet now ached with a dull, senseless pain. It was done. He fell to his knees, closed his eyes, and allowed his mind to drift into the darkness that filled the dense air. There was no time to rest—not here, not until Shanna was safe. He opened his eyes again and forced them to edge the crest of the barricading walls. He wondered how he could ever muster the strength to climb such a monstrous thing, let alone dodge certain death, face-to-face with the Dead.

"No ladders on this side," he mumbled to himself, remembering the construct he had used to escape from inside the city only days before. "How the hell am I going to do this?"

He knelt there for several more contemplative minutes, breathing steadily, until his eyes caught a flash of movement to his right. A flicker of metal and light broke against the darkened buildings across the road. *It could be anything*, he thought. *Don't freak out.* Slowly, he rose to his feet and ceased his breathing. If one of the Dead had somehow escaped, he would hear the groans from far enough away, but even then, they were dangerous. He would have to be careful. He kept quiet, stepping slowly towards the movement, his heart racing in fluttered beats.

From the backpack at his shoulders, he pulled a baseball bat. He gripped the handle of it tightly, wrapping his fists against the polished wood of the handle in a half-ready cocked stance. It was an appearance, he imagined, that would seem awkward to an onlooker, but it was the safest position, for him, to be in. If anything jumped out of the impending darkness, he could clock it hard with one, violent swing. His forearms tensed, his biceps bulged, and he could feel his pulse throbbing in his fingers now. He shuffled skeptically into the asphalt garden ahead.

The faintest noise echoed in the darkness, like scurrying without the shuffling, and cocked the bat even further behind his shoulder, twisting his torso enough to ensure damage, if needed, to whatever was hiding in the abyss. Honestly, wasn't that all that mattered?

Another glimpse of movement ripped Henry into a battering of nervousness. The street from where the movement had come was now empty, but Henry could still feel a presence, as if he was in a crowded room, surrounded by people who wanted him dead. A drain trickled into a sewer catch—drip by drip—from one of the last of the still functional, but abandoned buildings. The silence now felt almost torturous. The moon's gray light wasn't helping, pouring into the alley like a hazy steam rolling away into a careless chasm of space. He moved forward by a step, tenuously, with his hands shaking. Several minutes passed. The quiet stung Henry's ears with strenuous tension. He kept the bat close to his shoulder, holding it still, swiveling his head in each direction, analyzing what he could of the landscape. The emptiness offered nothing but a cold, harsh feeling of doom.

Then, in a cold whisk of air, cold metal felt angry against the back of his skull.

"Don't move or I *swear* I'll put a bullet in your brain."

The voice was deep, but not typically powerful. It ran like needles through Henry's ears. The barrel of the gun steadied against his head, almost cataclysmically smooth, but still a symbol of dark deviance. *Out of all the ways to die*, Henry thought, *I'm going to die by the hands of a goddamn looter.*

"There's no need for this. *Please*," Henry lowered his voice to match that of the man's, "I'm not going to hurt you. Take my things. Take it all."

Henry dropped the backpack and the baseball bat, allowing it to *thud* against the tar.

"Anyone who actually *wants* to climb into that cesspool is a *crazy* bastard," the man whispered. "Tell me. Why should I trust you?"

The man's voice held a subtle Hispanic nuance—one that felt more comforting than expected from a situation like this. Henry tried to convince himself that this was a sign that he would not die tonight, but the gun at his head told him otherwise.

The walls hissed. Henry pictured hundreds of bodies pushing against the cement on the other side of the wall, wanting to satisfy their most animalistic cravings—consuming fresh meat caught in their grinding, ceaseless teeth.

Henry tried to casually shift his weight to his other foot, but the man caught the action and jabbed the gun harder into the skin protecting his brainstem.

"What are you doing here anyway?" he asked.

Henry sighed before answering.

"M...My girlfriend," said Henry, bowing his head. "She's waiting for me in the city."

There was a hesitation, then a laugh, loud enough to start another wave of hissing and groaning from across the barricades, brewing an unsteady current of tension between the two men.

"Let me get this straight," the gunman giggled sinisterly. It flooded Henry's ears more like the sound of gurgling. "You're climbing the walls of a city overrun with thousands, *if not millions*, of zombies wanting nothing more than to eat you alive, just to tell your girlfriend you love her?"

Henry felt the pressure of the hardened metal against his neck release. The gunman backed away, scratched his head with the barrel of the pistol, still giggling in staggered and repeated drones of laughter. Tones of cigarette use rasped the man's voice. The moon had completely vanished behind a string of blackened clouds now, leaving nothing but darkness to consume them both.

Henry turned, still not able to decipher the man's features through the black.

"And all you have to defend yourself is a *baseball bat?*"

The man had now holstered his gun, clearly embracing the idea that Henry was not a threat.

"Your name?" Henry questioned, changing topic.

It was the only phrase he could push from his mouth. A sour guilt formed as a lump in his throat.

"Quintero," he replied.

Henry dropped his eyes to his feet, analyzing the man's mud-soaked shoes, then glanced up at the moonlight, again, soaking the street. It was in this moment of silver lighting that Henry caught his first real glimpse of the man beside him.

His high cheekbones showed some signs of aging, but his body appeared to be in peak physical condition. His eyes were a shady brown, the whites were mildly bloodshot, and sunken into his face. Along his waist rested a belt holstering four pistols. Ammunition straps wrapped around his right shoulder, resting against the sawed-off shotgun dangling from his back in a makeshift sling. His black hair was slicked back and forgotten.

He dressed entirely in black—from his leather jacket and shirt to the second belt that held his jeans around his waist. The jacket fit not too tightly, but snuggly around his biceps. The sleeves funneled downward past his triceps and wrapped around his wrists in a tight, conical fashion. He stood at an angle with most of his weight against his left foot.

Henry wondered why Quintero had bothered to stop him at all.

"So now you know *my* name," Quintero continued. "Yours?"

"Henry," he spoke through crackled syllables. "Please, you *have* to let me find her. If she's alive…"

Quintero shook his head and folded his arms into each other. The muscles bulged against his chest.

"*No one's* alive in there, man. The Dead have ravaged everything. It's suicide, *especially* at night."

Quintero's words sent a blistering chill down Henry's spine. A knot formed in the back of his throat, forcing him into a muted mush of frustration and sadness. He could feel the guilt tightening his neck, noosing him at the metaphorical gallows of regret. In no way would Henry allow this one man to stop him from finding Shanna. He had returned for this and this only, so if he could not save her, he had made up his mind a long time ago that he would die trying.

Quintero noticed the sudden dip in Henry's eyes, bent down, and picked the bat up from the street. He had seen this type of expression in people before—one of exponential determination, of immediate reprisal. In fact, Henry was starting to remind him of a younger version of himself. *Damn,* he thinks. *This kid. He's gonna kill me.* But innocence and all, the gunman was beginning to realize that Henry was something more than just a lovesick fool. Somewhere deep inside—somewhere only Quintero could see—the kid possessed the grit, the gristle needed to make it behind the walls.

That alone changed his mind.

Henry kept his head lowered, staring at the confetti asphalt, thinking. The sounds of the Dead ceaselessly dragging their miserable bodies amplified.

"Hey," the gunman spoke, snapping into a wildly cynical grin while deepening his voice into sincerity. He held the bat at arm's length and by the barrel, beckoning for Henry to reach for its handle. "I'm guessing I can't convince you to leave? Save yourself before it's too late?"

It was the first time Henry had broken even the slightest smirk since the Infection. The choice was made. They would enter the city after all—together. He didn't know what had caused the sudden change of heart in Quintero, but he certainly was not going to ask. He reached out and clasped the bat in his fist, swinging it into his right hand. Quintero ripped a pistol from its holster.

"I like you, Henry. I don't know why, but you're alright."

He cocked the weapon, made sure the silencer hadn't shifted, and walked towards the city barricades.

"Well," Quintero spoke. "If you're jumping in, I sure as hell can't sit and watch."

2

"We can't climb over at night," said Quintero, his jaw barely moving as he spoke. "They'll be on us in minutes."

The two men walked towards the wall, ignoring the thoughts of what lurked behind it.

"The Dead come out of the sewers and subway lines at night. It's like they can sense when the sun is gone or something."

Henry clutched the baseball bat tightly, white-knuckling the wood. His face sunk. The thought of the Dead left a void somewhere deep within him—something he felt he could never get back.

"Not all of them," Henry corrected. "They still walk the streets at day, too. I fought them off when I left."

"You mean you *already* escaped from this hellhole once?"

Henry nodded.

"If *you're* out, then why is your girlfriend still in there?"

"She broke her ankle," Henry explained. "We never would've made it if I brought her with me."

Quintero cleared his throat softly.

"So you think it's gonna be easier *now*?"

Henry shrugged, mostly from lack of words. He thought back to his escape. The dents in the bat were proof of its violence. He had swung it maliciously many times—over and over—in an effort to ward off the Dead, but, of course, they continued their targeted shuffling toward him, most of the time with their jaws sloughed open, drooling at the sight of fresh meat. The sheer number of them, he remembered, grew wildly before his eyes, like waves of corpses crashing into the streets. He remembered how it felt to crack into a forehead or snap a jaw, but the worst of it all was, by far, the groaning—the murderous grunting, echoing and wailing.

Quintero's pistols shimmered in the moonlight. The gunman raised them against the night, snapping another clip into place. While the Dead amplified fear in Henry, the gunman seemed nothing but calm and collected, as if he were a tour guide, merely showing off the newly renovated outer city limits. It was an awkward feeling to be in the presence of such professionalism, yet Henry embraced it all the same.

"Here's the plan. We go in through the subway lines. There shouldn't be much action down there at this time of night," the gunman explained.

"But aren't they blocked?" Henry asked.

He now felt like a child tagging behind his father. The surrounding darkness made it difficult to find landmarks, let alone anything of recognition. Only the wall barricade stood clear against the moonlight, but even its shadows created such a contrast that the rest of the outskirts soaked into blankets of thick black. He exaggerated his strides just to keep up with Quintero, but found himself breathing too hard and too fast already. *It's going to be a long trip if I can't even keep up with him,* Henry thought. *Just calm down.*

"They are," Quintero replied, "but I know a way in—the old *Breakers' Circle.*"

Quintero whispered those last words with hot breath, accentuating the fact that that particular name was to be kept an ongoing secret. Henry had no idea where the Breakers' Circle was located, but instantly shook off the confusion and raised his eyebrows to signal artificial surprise. He didn't care. If the plan led him to Shanna, then it only seemed logical, although the Breakers' Circle sounded like a dungeon—a dark, morose cavern where only bad things happened. There was a particular anxiety working its way through his veins at the thought of it. He didn't like the feeling at all, yet he decided he would just follow and listen anyway. The man *did* seem to know what he was doing.

The darkness wrestled with Henry's vision for about twenty more yards until the protruding subway entrance abruptly shimmied into view. A slew of dead-bolted chains coupled the several blocks of wood, securely locking the slabs of metal doors. Attached by a single string hung a dirtied, gritty sign facing the left corner of the entrance, reading: NO ONE IN, NO ONE OUT in large, orange, spray-painted letters. It swung freely at an angle in the foul, picked-up breeze.

Henry tried the door.

"It's locked," he confirmed. The expression on Quintero's face suggested this was assumed.

"Follow me," the gunman spoke, pointing the pistol in his left hand towards a nearby utility shack. It rested only two hundred feet from where they stood, eclipsed by a strange mixture of shadows and silver tones of moonlight. Even after squinting, Henry could only make out the shack's brittle lining. The outline, however, was enough to cast judgements. How would this help him reach Shanna? An empty shack? They approached it quickly, Henry realizing its doors were padlocked, as well—similarly to those at the subway stairwell's entrance. He peered at the gunman with a furrowed brow. How do locked doors mean access to the city? Had Quintero not known this?

But the gunman wasn't walking toward the doors. His eyes focused on the far right corner of the building's frame where a chunk of wood had come loose. Its rot exposed a dark expanse in the shack's interior.

"Here," whispered the gunman. "We enter here."

Quintero forced the slab of wood to the side and held it tense against the shed's vinyl siding. He squeezed in first, followed quickly by Henry, releasing the rot and snapping it back into place. It rang like a muffled gunshot, echoing and ebbing through the thick air, pulsating the quiet like an earthquake. A new wave of hissing erupted from opposite the wall and, immediately, Henry's skin crawled with disgust. He somehow felt closer to them now in this closed-off room, vulnerable, afraid.

Quintero propped himself upward, noticing Henry's demeanor almost instantaneously.

"You'll need more balls than that, kid," Quintero grumbled. "You can't be scared or you'll die in there."

Henry nodded, but knew that apathy—the kind Quintero exuded so well—also meant no mercy, something he just couldn't seem to break. To survive would mean to break his moral code, to understand that the Infection changed the city for the worst. He would have to adapt. He knew this. And if he failed, the resolution was desperately simple—he would end up dead, just like the rest of metropolitan Boston. *Dead.*

He squinted through the darkness, peering about. The room was unavoidably small—the kind of cramped that induced acute claustrophobia, panic attacks, and rapid heartbeats—and emanated the rotten stench filtering through the subway lines below. *Just outside*, he thought to himself, *there is a mob of starving, filthy psychopaths wanting nothing more than to tear out my throat.*

"Hope you didn't wear your Sunday's best out here," Quintero cracked, prying up a few floorboards from his knees. "Smells like shit down there."

The descending ladder felt grimy against their hands. Quintero dropped in first and splayed out, pistols outstretched. A sudden scurrying of rats and insects resonated down the underpass, but dispersed as quickly as they had come. Quintero paid no attention to these noises. He listened for something else. Blackness covered the tunnel in every direction. No groans. No wailing. For now—in the musky silence of the corridor—it seemed the coast was clear, so the gunman clicked the safeties into place and slid the guns back into their respective holsters. "Let's go," he said.

"Are you *sure* this is the safest way into the city?" Henry asked. The fear came in waves, sending his heart into a flurry of palpitations.

"Positive," the gunman replied. His voice rang with an elusive, superior confidence in the reverberating cavern ahead. Quintero's jacket made the frictional noise as leather does when it's pressed against itself. In an odd way, it relaxed Henry enough to press forward, drowning out the sound of dragging bodies from above. He tried not to think of Shanna as one of them, as one of the Dead, but the idea—as brutal as it seemed —was not entirely farfetched.

Quintero was right, though. The subway tunnels were nothing short of empty and expansive, stretching for miles into the distance. Only the occasional stagnant zombie entrenched the railway tracks with their torsos shred in two. Clean slices, as if each body had been there since the start of the Infection when the trains had made their rounds into and out of the city. The two men would pass them on the farthest side, watching as the Dead's milky eyes followed them with the bloodthirstiest of intentions, scouring and snorting the air for the pungent odor of fresh meat. They stayed far enough away to avoid them easily.

After several minutes, Quintero turned suddenly, stopping Henry in his tracks. In the dark, he could barely see Quintero pressing his index finger up against his mouth in an effort to keep him silent. Up ahead, as Henry strained to see, were a dozen of the Dead meandering about, slowly grazing each other, and breathing quickly and autonomously with tremendous force. These were not the *just born* types. Those would be stumbling and collapsing on each other. These seemed more methodical, not by much, but enough to decipher which from which. All Henry could make out were hazy, blurred figures swaying their shoulders in slow, dramatic movements.

Quintero reached to his waist with both arms and brought the pistols to his face.

"Stay here," he spoke in full volume.

The Dead broke stride at the sound of his voice, propelling themselves toward the two men. Henry took in a staggered breath, harnessing the gurgling rise of fear in his throat. There were a dozen rapid *pops* each followed by its own quick burst of light. Suddenly, the urge to panic flushed from Henry's mind. All that was left in him was emptiness—no longer an urge at all—but a need only to progress, to fight to keep going, survival. Henry watched Quintero's eyes burst with adrenaline in the inconsistent flash-lighting, focusing on each pull of the trigger. The slap of a fleshy body colliding with soiled ground coupled each muffled blast.

Twelve shots. Twelve kills. And then there was silence.

"We should be good," Quintero said, breaking the quiet between them. The smell of gunpowder and lead filled the tunnel. Henry eased the quick pumps of his heart, now mixing with the focus of adrenaline, scouring his body like a virus. He felt extraordinarily alert. Was this what it felt like to kill? He understood the *need* to kill those disgusting things, but not for himself, not for Shanna, but for a fresh start, for a new beginning. *Vengeance*, he thought. *Take this city back.*

The two men moved forward, shuffling through the dark of the subway line, over lifeless bodies and the maze of cement and brick that seemed to bleed at their feet. Above, the dragging of limbs grew louder.

"Where did you leave the girl?" Quintero asked.

"At the corner of Congress and Lowell. It's the brown, stilted complex."

He stopped for a moment, hesitating, then continued. "The people who lived there were *nuts*."

Henry chuckled, but the attempt at humor failed when he heard the monotone grunt from the gunman. Suddenly, he wished he hadn't been so quick to crack the joke.

He hadn't *really* met the family, but remembered them clearly, seeming as though they were a relatively obvious bunch. There were eight of them—three boys, three girls, the mother, and the father. They walked the streets of Boston by day with ragged cardboard signs in outstretched arms, pinning their propaganda against the backdrop of the metropolitan buildings. The words REPENT: THE END IS NEAR splattered against the signs in neon paint across their gritty surfaces. By night, while their children slept, the couple played quiet jazz music at a nightclub only a few blocks down from Lowell Street. They made enough in tips to survive on bread and water, but usually nothing more.

The mother let her dreadlocks grow out into wild, matted cyclones knotted to her scalp. She was not overly attractive, but possessed the adorable type of face and pearl-dipped smile that tends to lift spirits. Henry liked that about her. Couple that with a fit, slightly fragile frame and you suddenly have a woman intriguingly stuck in physical limbo. He remembered how her freckles rolled across the bridge of her nose like army ants at work, how her green eyes caught the sun and glimmered into emerald, algae-filled ponds. She happened to be the one person in the entire city to which Henry took notice...well, besides Shanna, of course. Through the hustle of city life, she alone stood out and, although she hardly ever wore anything revealing, Henry couldn't help but imagine the curves of her waist, the rise and fall of her breasts as she breathed, the golden hue of her skin.

He wondered if she had turned into one of the Dead yet.

Henry mockingly named her the "hemp goddess" the day of the Infection. Shanna had laughed at *that* one.

"The hippie of the decade," she giggled, intertwining her fingers in Henry's as they strolled the sidewalk home. "How can they be so naïve?" she spoke, brushing her shoulder against his. Her eyes reflected the golden shine of her hair. *What was it about eyes that he remembered so clearly?* "The end of the world is nothing more than a silly hoax."

Wrong.

Within the next few hours, the family up and left, leaving everything they owned behind. Only a torn piece of paper taped to the front door offered any indication of why they had left. It had been scribbled in black ink, quickly, yet diligently—GOOD LUCK AND GOD BLESS. GONE TO SAFETY. They knew something was about to happen—something no one else knew. Henry passed the house later that morning and noticed the loneliness of it firsthand. Their abandonment dug a hole in his mind, dumping a sense of eeriness into it like a child scooping mud into a pale. He glanced up at the boarded windows and thinning paint and shivered a deep, core-chilling shiver.

It turned out they had been right all along. All of it.

"Lowell is another couple of blocks from here," Quintero murmured. He pointed ahead in the darkness.

Whispering was annoying, but they couldn't be certain if the darkness would reveal any more of the Dead beyond their limited vision. "The subway lines don't reach that far."

Henry gulped. The sound rushed like thunder down his throat, popping in his ears. He stepped cautiously ahead, but the deepening sensation in his chest forced his legs to buckle. "If the subways don't run to Lowell," Henry asked, "then how do we get to the house?"

Somewhere above them, a faint trickling of water seeped through the street, near ground level. Little specks of moonlight seeped into the stagnant air, illuminating the acerbic wisps of dust they kicked up as they moved. The shuffling and groaning was now a constant fixture, amplifying against the damp acoustics of the tunnel. Henry peered up at the dripping ceiling, suddenly worried.

Not only did the ceiling feel more fragile down here, but the subway floor felt increasingly slimy against his feet, probably slippery with the mess from days—maybe weeks—of excrement, bodily fluids, and rotting flesh congealing into seeping tributaries amidst a labyrinth of cracked cement. The dust they kicked up was no longer the dry type, but sour, fecal clouds. The smell hadn't registered until the men's first encounter with the Dead, but now, Henry's eyes watered as he drew each shortened breath. He inhaled through his mouth and exhaled through his nose, but even that couldn't diffuse the odor. Nausea ascended to the base of his throat, bubbling there, and constricting his abdomen so that the feeling would stay.

"We have to find an empty street," Quintero whispered, continuing the conversation. "With a little luck, maybe the gunfire attracted them that way." He pointed back towards the mess of mangled bodies no longer in sight.

"You mean we have to go up *there*?" Henry asked. His eyes peered up towards the ceiling. He already knew the answer.

"Like I said," Quintero continued. "Grow some balls, kid."

Without expression or response, the two men maintained a brisk stride. Henry retreated slightly, trailing Quintero only by a footstep or so, but enough to confirm he had definitely lost the battle of words just a minute prior, resigning to the role of *follower* rather than *leader*. *Think of something else,* he thought, refusing to allow fear to creep so easily into his mind once again. He tried to envision a memory not clouded by the Infection, but couldn't seem to focus. Instead, he found himself rocking the baseball bat between the middle finger and thumb of his right hand, persuading himself into a vague sense of optimism about the nearly impossible task lurking in the not-so-distant future.

"Up ahead," Henry pointed. "That's the Hancock stop. We're only about five hundred feet from the house."

Quintero halted, glaring at Henry, scratching his head with the barrel of one of his four pistols. For some strange reason, the moonlight forcing its way into the tunnel made the gunman appear less contrived, stronger. His eyes now sat like hidden gems against his darkened skin.

"You sure about that?" Quintero sighed. "Once we go up there, we can't go back. If we're too far away, we're nothing but easy meat."

The thunder of Henry's gulp, again, quivered in his eardrums. If anything, the idea of leaving the tunnel put knots in his stomach, arising that not uncommon feeling of nausea that continued to boil at the base of his throat. Yet he was certain in this realization. If there was a place to surface into the city, Hancock Street was it. He closed his eyes momentarily and envisioned the landscape above him writhing with the Dead, moving like worms through the sea of streets. The image was not a pleasant one, but forced his heart rate to peak. *Great,* he thought, but he would need the adrenaline.

Quintero took the first steps toward the open station—now in shooting range—pistol drawn with his finger tense against the trigger. His eyes examined the scene. He turned the corner and, immediately, the walls broke into smeared, ruby-red stains and splattered gunshot fissures— earthquake-like chasms splintering into the cement. Around the corner, a dozen motionless bodies sprawled headfirst against the station floor.

This wasn't a fight, thought Henry. *This was an execution.*

A caked pool of blood rested at the base of each skull, clearly consistent with gunshot wounds to the head. Quintero hunched over and nudged the rotting skin of the closest corpse with his foot.

"They're dead alright," he said, still quietly. "But they turned before they were killed. They're still fresh. Whoever did this was pretty efficient."

Henry shifted his eyes back to the bodies. Each one rested shoulder-to-shoulder with the next, perfectly positioned like the clean-up after trench warfare. He wanted to avert his eyes, but couldn't. What he *really* wanted to do was throw up.

The low rumble of the ventilation system just beyond the turnstiles kicked its way to power—still functioning amidst the failing city—and generating a sickly resonating echo, breaking the otherwise intense silence filling the raunchy space. Something felt off about the shadowed area ahead, tainted in the flickering fluorescence, like a man trapped in the layer of an angry dragon. It felt thick, impending.

Quintero crept forward first, placing one foot in front of the other in slow, efficient steps while Henry followed behind. He tried not to shiver in the mix of damp cool and fear (he knew Quintero wasn't), but still, the tremors filled the inner workings of his muscles. Then suddenly, along the opposite wall, Henry caught a glimpse of a thin stream of moonlight washing over a narrow, blood-splattered stairwell. *A tap of luck or an omen of danger?* he asked himself, but he tapped Quintero on the shoulder anyway, as though mulling over the question would only further daze the situation. "It's the exit," Henry said, but the look in the gunman's eyes proved he had already put the pieces together.

Quintero was already halfway down the corridor before Henry heard a sharp *tick* from behind him and turned toward the darkness, pushing a shimmy of nerves up his spine. A part of him expected some sort of gripping, bloody hand to emerge from the shadows, but nothing reached for him. He was alone in the silence. *But was he?* He couldn't be entirely certain from where he was, but he stood with his neck cocked for several seconds, suddenly afraid. *You're paranoid,* he thought to himself. *There's nothing down here.*

Guns sprawled at the gunman's sides, the metal of the barrels flickered like silent firecrackers in the fluorescent lighting. They walked cautiously, controlling each monotonous step toward the end of the line, until Quintero stopped, breathing in silence, keeping his eyes focused ahead.

The sheer sight of them caught Henry off-guard, almost as if he was staring at a watercolor painting that had just come to life. Thousands upon thousands of the Dead lined the darkened space, fighting against the growing tide of stagnant bodies at their feet. Whatever Henry thought before, he now knew, without a doubt, the city was lost—taken by the unforgiving hoards that wobbled and hissed in front of him. The shadows blurred their shapes, but the worry of individual zombies didn't matter any longer. This was a *mob* of grueling groaners—bodies aching for meat and violence. There was no telling what they were capable of. The two men could only stand and wait to make their next move.

Another loud *tick* filled the corridor, as if someone had sounded an alarm. The mass of bodies, as if on cue, began grunting and screaming and pushing their way through each other. Hundreds of body parts and patches of skin ripped and sloughed from appendages as the bodies shifted, dispersing another bout of potent, rotten flesh odor to the men's noses. The sheer force of the mob crashed like a tsunami wave breaking at its highest crest. And just like that, they were gone—down the subway line and out of sight.

The two men stood stiff in the new deafening quiet.

"I've never seen that before," Quintero whispered, pausing before saying what he really wanted to say. "It's like they're working *together*."

Henry couldn't think too much into it. His sinuses already hurt from focusing into the black. His eardrums bulged from the waves of hot blood pulsing through them, so he just nodded, creased his forehead, and furrowed his brow to keep his eyes from closing.

"I don't know," he finally managed to say. "You're right, though. Something's going on down here."

But Henry noticed there was something different about Quintero in this moment. He peered on in puzzlement, noticing the gunman's shoulders tightening, his face emptying into a hollow, sickening white, his eyes, like his pistols, shimmering black, expanding pupils covering the color in his eyes. Yet it wasn't these things that caught Henry off-guard. It was the fact that Quintero suddenly appeared *vulnerable*, caught by the enormity of the situation.

Several more minutes passed. The sounds of the Dead were far-gone now and Henry felt curious enough to drop the baseball bat and step shoulder-to-shoulder with Quintero. The gunman's eyes were still fixed on the blackened subway line in the distance, still not moving.

"*I've* never *seen* that before," Quintero repeated, this time accenting words that did not need accenting. His lips pursed, forcing his nose to flick in disgust as he holstered his weapons. The pistols slid heavily into their holsters, as though he meant for them to find their own way. The hollow gaze continued to fill to his expression. He seemed to be drowning in his own astonishment, yet there was now some sort of looming intensity at the front of his eyes—not necessarily replacing the vulnerability, just repositioning it. Henry did not question it, even if he thought it meant something.

He glimpsed at his watch. The dark made it difficult to see the thin hands, but Henry could read it nonetheless.

"Midnight," he whispered.

Quintero nodded, then sighed as though all hope had been rung from him like a sponge after cleaning. The street above was silent, but, both men knew the quiet was trickery, manipulating the lack of sound for a false sense of security. Rash decisions here would get them killed, *especially* in the subways.

"What we need is a distraction," Quintero mumbled, barely above a whisper. From his pocket he revealed some sort of firecracker—a small, red cylinder battered and dented by the friction of his jeans and the walk into the city. Another brief dig into his pocket—this time to the left one —revealed a small packet of matches, also with similar dents and battered marks.

"I was waiting to use these," Quintero mumbled again, "but what the hell? I figure this is a better time than ever."

The words sounded strong, but the tension in the gunman's shoulders hadn't left him. He still seemed somewhat fragile (something that truly puzzled Henry), although he was able to mask it behind his all-too-familiar expression of cynicism and darkened humor. But what Henry thought was a situation completely under control had suddenly morphed into a situation of Pandora's Box proportions, leaving the two of them at the heart of it all. And all Henry could do was respond with a quick smirk, cocking his head up against the subway exit doors to listen.

"There should be thousands of those bastards walking around out there," Quintero whispered. "This doesn't make any sense."

"Maybe they were all in that mob we saw run down the line," Henry said.

Quintero shook his head fervently. "The fact that they were even down here worries me. It's midnight for Christ's sake. What does that even *mean*?"

His eyes snapped back to Henry. Suddenly the color had returned to his skin against the moon, although the eerie, paleness of the light now shot even longer, villainous shadows across his eyes. The features that Henry had first seen outside of the city were now amplified—rough and chiseled, like the face of a god. He seemed drunk with intensified rage— a figment of himself ready to propel into the next obstacle. It was only when Henry dropped his eyes that he noticed Quintero's knuckles were a flaming white, clasping the firecracker and matches with as much force as he could muster.

"I don't hear anything," Henry whispered.

"Like I said. That doesn't mean shit."

"Think I should get a better look?"

Quintero raised his eyebrows with his shoulders, giving an I-don't-care-just-don't-get-me-killed shrug from the bottom of the stairs. Opening the doors was the last thing Henry wanted to do, but his body ignored the complaints of his mind, moving swiftly and in hunched, robotic movements. *With time there is worry. Where there is worry, there is no room for fear because there is no logic in chaos*, Henry recited through a string of harried words. He thought it must have been a vague memory from a piece of literature he had read at the university some time ago, but he could not remember from which. Out of all the things to contemplate in a moment of resistance, he wondered why he was thinking of it now.

He pressed lightly against the metal door, displacing it slightly from its hinges. New light flooded into the stairwell.

"Anything?" Quintero whispered.

Henry shifted his shoulders so that they rested against the wall adjacent to the door, methodically extending his neck so that only the top of his skull to the bridge of his nose was exposed from the street. His eyes adjusted quickly. Quicker than Quintero's, who now had his right arm up against his face, averting the pale, dry light into the subway line behind him.

"*Anything?*" Quintero repeated. The impatience in the gunman's voice grew heavy.

The cityscape was not what Henry expected to see—nothing but buildings and littered, motionless bodies scattered across sidewalks and asphalt. Even the sky stood clearer than he remembered. It shocked him to see how large the stars and the moon appeared against the black canvas of space; how the moon's ferocity contrasted against the stars' blinking, white clarity. The buildings were monsters, peering over a sea of annihilation and fear. Blocks of office lighting shone from their abandoned skyscraper windows with dimming force.

Henry took one, lasting panoramic view around the city block. An anxious pressure built in his chest. *Why are the streets so quiet?* he thought to himself. *There should be zombies everywhere, right?* Something inside of him wished for movement, for impending danger, so he could say the streets seemed unsafe, but movement never caught his eye. The city's uneasy quiet blanketed the air like a thunderstorm.

"There's nothing," Henry whispered back into the station line. His voice echoed precariously. "We should make a run for it now. We'll make it to the other side before anything even turns into the street."

As he spoke, his still-adjusting eyes noticed a large pile of darkened metal about one hundred yards ahead.

"Wait a minute," he whispered, squinting into the night.

He motioned for Quintero to stay, apprehensively extending his neck farther out into the city air. He wanted to make sure what he was seeing was real before turning back to the gunman. The last thing he needed was another act of foolhardiness. But they were weapons alright. He was certain of it. Guns—at least two dozen of them—scattered as if someone had dropped them in an attempt to flee.

"To the left," Henry said. "We could use those."

He stepped back into the station line, replaced by Quintero in a tight, quiet shift. The gunman thought, weighing their options in his head, synthesizing information behind those hardened eyes of his.

"You're right," Quintero said. "There's nothing out there. They're gone."

In a swift, calculated movement, Quintero pushed himself out, over the metal door, and farther into the cooled, but stagnant air, signaling for Henry to follow. The pistols were now loaded, safeties off, and pointing into the darkened matrix of roads. Each step felt hard against the Earth. Henry pushed up and out, not as gracefully, but kept the bat close to his thigh. Shoulder-to-shoulder, they walked cautiously, Henry watching the right side while Quintero guarded the left. They reached the scattered weapons and focused their attention to the ground.

Luck is on our side tonight, Henry thought.

He smiled, bent down, and picked up one of the bigger automatic guns in the pile. The shiny metal felt powerful against his skin, making it tingle under the weapon's weight. *Thank you, God*, he said to himself, forcing another quirky grin across his jaw. It was the best he had felt in some time.

Quintero remained still and upright, pistols up and armed. Henry heard a quick shimmy from the space next to him—an oddity in Quintero's assassin-like movements. He peered up at the gunman whose arms began to shake slightly. There was confusion for a split-second, then Henry shifted his eyes to where Quintero was pointing the pistols to see the scene he wish he never had.

The waves of Dead stared back at him with colorless, aggressive eyes. It was then that Henry's confusion flooded into fear.

3

Henry pulled back and straightened his shoulders, unable to form the words he wanted to speak. A sea of faces peered back at him with cold, numbing eyes. Teeth, dried like bone, uprooted from their nerves and gums in each dirtied, blood-soaked mouth. A blur of fists and open hands swayed to and fro with blue and green veins swiveling through degenerated arm muscles, eaten by starvation and ignorance. Time stood still. The images seared into Henry's retinas.

"Don't move," Henry whispered.

"I think it's a little late for that," Quintero replied, louder than he actually meant.

The Dead took one staggered step forward, almost simultaneously. The waves ebbed in awkward movement. To the left, Henry noticed a few rogue zombies turning their heads to the commotion, instinctively dragging their broken limbs with them. The groans to his right meant there were others he couldn't see.

"When I say run, turn and *run*. Don't look back. If you find some way to escape, I'll find you," Quintero mumbled, still unafraid of the noise his voice made. Hints of survival-mode filled the spaces between his words.

Henry's legs usually shook in moments like these, trembling so hard they lost function. The air would suddenly feel bitterly cold, forcing his lungs to empty into dead space. His eyes would water, bursting with hot tears filling his sockets to the brim. He wasn't weeping because of fear—his nerves never produced such cathartic emotions—but rather, a habit needing to be broken, an instinct caught in every molecule of his being.

It had happened over and over again during his escape from the city. He understood the feeling quite well, but something was different now. It felt almost as though he understood the concentrated panic meddling within him, as though he now chose to keep it as a deformed pet inside his chest, both separated and intertwined with it at the very same time. Only now, he could harness it, channel it into something he could use. He did not know why, nor how, but it was something remarkably useful in the moment, so he did not hesitate. He swallowed the fear threatening death and thumbed the baseball bat in slow, quiet movements in front of him, tempting the bodies to make the first move.

They did.

And Henry turned and ran as fast as he could.

He heard the whistle-like sounds of silenced bullets ringing through the air. Quintero's footsteps shuffled behind him...at least he *thought* they were the gunman's. Henry pictured Quintero running backwards, flailing bullets into the hoard behind them, but he dared not turn his head to confirm the thought. He needed to keep pace. He needed to keep going.

The Dead poured from all the city's side streets, stampeding toward them at every angle. Henry stretched his arms back with the bat in his grip and unleashed a crippling swing that collided into a thud against a matted skull. A geyser of darkened blood gushed onto Henry's chest. He flinched for a split-second, over-rushed with the sensation of the blood's liquid warmth, before continuing his sprint through the city.

The bodies closed in, cutting off every avenue of escape, lunging and stumbling wildly at the smell of warm meat.

"Quintero!" Henry yelled—a stupid idea amongst a tsunami of grunts and flailing appendages—but he had lost the gunman several streets back and worried they had outrun him. He focused his thoughts. He could still hear the whizzing streams of moving bullets above the loudening malevolent groans, so he swiveled his head. He could see the Dead continuing to funnel into the streets, almost all of them exposing their vile sets of teeth to snap and chew.

His brain cycled through a multitude of thoughts. His heart pumped vigorously. He cocked the bat once more, colliding with another *pop* of a jaw, sending a skinny-framed woman crashing to the asphalt in a flaccid whiplash of stampeding, dragging feet. Adrenaline surged through his veins.

He was alone, stuck, and out of time.

To his right was a crushingly narrow alleyway between buildings— one that would never be used in a city uninhabited by flesh-eating monsters. The walls hugged each other from a distance with narrow slits of moonlight edging in from both street entrances. Henry forced his way into the space, moving step-by-step, deeper, until he was far enough into the alley to feel some sort of temporary safety. He sucked in his chest and tried to breathe, but the motion just wasn't there. Little gasps of air gathered in his throat and temporarily satisfied his lungs, but he could feel the desire for more clouding his judgement. Before long, he would need that big rush of oxygen. For now, though, he would have to manage.

The Dead crammed their way in, but crushed themselves against the brick.

Henry could still hear Quintero's gunshots ringing through the air, but they were echoic now, as if they were too far away from real noise.

It's only a matter of time, Henry thought, *before I'm done. Is this how I'm going to die?*

Henry slid to the other side of the alley and jutted his head out into the adjacent street. Hundreds of bodies were now circling the buildings, gritting teeth, shimmying over to the smell of Henry's sweat, now dripping furiously from his forehead into his eyes. He returned to the center of the alley just before the reaching limbs of more bodies pushed from both sides of him now. He was totally trapped, pushing hot gusts of breath into the building in front of him. Only an inch of space separated him from the bricks of the adjacent building and the Dead continued closing in.

Only a few more seconds now, he said. *I'm sorry, Shanna.*

He shut his eyes tight, trying not to vomit.

Then he heard the voice above him.

"Hey!" it rang.

It was loud enough and clear, resonating with a subtle hint of smooth panic that caught Henry's attention. Henry cocked his neck as far as he could. There was a golden hue of light trickling down from the building in front of him. Someone was hanging from an open window, but he couldn't make out the figure completely.

"Hey!" the voice spoke again.

The brick walls made a response to the man in the window nearly impossible. He was already beginning to feel a sense of lightheadedness that came with the shortened, staggered breathing of claustrophobia. It was as if his vocal chords were doing their job—vibrating—releasing guttural sounds to his throat, but the emptiness in his diaphragm produced nothing but a choppy flow of hot air, so Henry did the only thing he could do. He lifted his right arm, slowly and bending his elbow to keep the Dead from ripping off his fingers.

"Grab the rope," the man spoke.

In seconds, a black, bristly cable fell in front of Henry's eyes. The

Dead were imminently closer now, cramming their useless bodies into the space in any way they could, inching forward and taking away Henry's few precious moments of hiccuped gasps. The smell of rotting flesh hit him in one potent wave, clinging to his nostrils. He bent his waist to one side and vomited, unable to hold it in any longer.

"Grab the goddamn rope!" the man yelled. "What the hell are you waiting for?"

The anxiety in his voice sounded natural, like the man had a tic or compulsive habit he could not control. Henry did what he was told, clasping his fingers around the dangling rope. It cut his hands—rather substantially, too—opening minute cuts in his palms. He gritted his teeth, forced his eyes closed, and convinced himself that the pain he was feeling was not *really* pain at all, but instead, a feeling of bliss, of knowing that the Dead, who were almost an arm's length away now, would be left empty-handed once more, left to starve without him.

"Pull me up," Henry managed to slur. He pushed the words from his throat, not sure if the man could even hear him, but the rope ran taught and Henry felt his feet lift from the ground.

"Don't let go!" the man said.

The muscles in Henry's arms began to quiver about halfway up the building's wall. The man in the window was still pulling, but much slower now, leaving several seconds of hanging time between heaves. He could hear the muffled groans of extensive labor from above backdropped by the hungry growls below. As much as Henry tried to chimney his feet against the walls on either side of him, the pain coursed like fire through the muscles in his arms. Tiny tributaries of dark red blood trickled from his white-knuckled fists as the bristled rope dug deeper into his hands. The blood was warm and comforting, though—a subtle and much needed hint that he was still alive.

With each pull, the bristles opened up larger wounds in the soft skin of his palms. The meat of his fingers began to shave at the sides, but Henry no longer cared. It was the cathartic release of propelling into safety that hid the weight of those tiny daggers. He escaped with precious, little time and was grateful for that, even amidst the pain. He dropped his gaze to the mass of bodies below. They had all but enclosed the alleyway now, reaching up with gnarly fingers at their escaping prey, crushing each other so blindly Henry could no longer decipher between faces and other body parts.

"Just a few more pulls!" the man at the window grunted.

Henry adjusted his eyes upward toward the window, suddenly returning to a familiar, empty thought: *Quintero was gone, but was he dead?* Ideas, once again, began colliding in his head like crashing waves.

Was he alone now? Of course not! He had this mysterious guy at the window now…whoever he was.

He reached the window as the last ounce of energy drained from his arms. He safely removed his grip from the cable and reached for the windowsill. The wet squish of blood accumulating in his palms forced him back into reality. Pain resurfaced, surging up and down his arms, spasming his shoulders and lower back into a mass of muscular cramps. He propelled himself from the window and fell stomach-first into the upper room, lying sprawled out and out of breath.

He pummeled into an abandoned office of some sort, with papers scattered across the floor and steel desks pushed—some flipped halfheartedly—against the interior door. The walls rose up into splatter-painted white drywall, almost too white, with varying colored tiles spread across the floor and ceiling. Light from the moon outside splashed from the window against the opposite wall just above the man's shadowed figure, but not enough to fill the entire room. Much of it remained shrouded in the blanketed darkness like a dozen sleeping ghosts with their eyes open—watching. The space felt more like a darkened chamber than an office, but Henry closed his eyes anyway, happy to be safe and away from the hoard below.

"We don't have much time," the figure said between giant gasps of air.

The cable that cut Henry's hands, he noticed, was tied around the man's waist., but he sat flaccidly against the far wall—his shadow careening against the light—with beads of sweat dripping from his forehead. His chest inflated, then deflated, in quick, laborious heaves. A curious thought entered Henry's mind: Why had the man saved him in the first place? It would have been easier just to let him die in the alley…

But there was no time to ask.

"We have to get to the roof," the man sputtered, prying himself from the floor.

"*Why?* We're not safe in here?"

Henry read the man's expressions, but the curves in his face seemed only callous and focused. He shuffled, staggering his steps through sheer exhaustion.

"We have to get to the roof!" the man repeated louder, slashing and pushing the desks away from the door in a series of noisy movements. "We have to get to the roof!"

He repeated the phrase in varying volumes, accenting alternating words each time he spoke. At first, Henry thought he was talking to him —attempting a weird, revolving conversation—but as the man kept up the sputtering, it became oddly apparent that he was talking to himself in a severely schizophrenic way.

"Get to the roof!"

The first several times the man spoke the phrase felt contrived, but this last time felt *honest*, wholly *sincere*. The words suddenly splashed into his ears like cymbal crashes, yet he still felt no need to attempt a lift to his feet. It would have to wait.

We're safe here, he told himself. *We're safe, right?*

With the weight now lifted from his legs, the glistening wounds running through the meat of his hands had become almost too much to bear. He lifted himself from the office floor to an uncomfortable sitting position, keeping his eyes fixed on the burning ridges in his skin. They pulsed with the rhythm of his heart, itching with the intensity of a man entirely consumed by fire ants. Gritting his teeth made the burning sensation subside (although more minimally than he would like), but not enough.

How am I supposed to survive now? he asked himself. *Without my hands, I'm already dead.*

"What are you waiting for? We have to leave! We have to leave *now*!" the man cried, raising his voice to match the intensity of the moment.

He stood erect at the office door and, for the first time, Henry saw him in his entirety, draped in the silk of the night's shimmering light. His face was sunken. The eye sockets dropped like craters into the bone. Short, untrimmed black hair crooked the slightly displaced part in his scalp. The color of it blended into the torn, black blazer he wore. It was ripped at his arms and sides with lines of dragged fingernails. He was of average height and average weight, although slightly soft in his midsection. He wore black slacks with muddy dress shoes that clearly had lost shine some time ago, worn and stained with blood.

The throbbing in Henry's hands continued. He distracted himself with silly guessing games—games that usually ended in downright poor predictions. *He worked in the office. Lawyer? Businessman? Cubicle space holder?*

He imagined this huddled man on the day of the Infection, taking the subway to the Hancock Street station, getting off and walking the few lonely blocks to this building, to the office in which they stood. It had felt like any other day, until the building began to evacuate. He hadn't thought anything of it, Henry imagined, watching the busy scurrying of people outside of his office door. He figured he would wait it out. *How bad can it be?* the man thought. *It's better to stay put.* But as the hours turned the sun away and the panicked sounds of people below turned to bloodcurdling screams and groans, he came to the realization that this evacuation was one he shouldn't have ignored.

And now, it was too late.

The echo of thudded footsteps shook Henry from his thoughts. The man was screaming with his arms outstretched, yelling for Henry to follow him. Henry, for a few precious seconds, forgot about his seeping hands. He pried himself from the floor in a swift push. Another wave of pain sparked through his arms and thrust him back into remembrance. At this point, he thought, his hands were borderline useless.

The man, he found, had already scurried halfway down the dimly lit office hallway, stumbling over his own feet. Henry was quickly falling behind. He wiped coagulated blood and puss from the slashes in his palms onto his jeans and hurried toward the door.

The corridor's overhead lights were off—most likely broken—but Henry could see a slew of flickering lights in the distance that opened into a large, open-design workspace. The man, draped in deep-night shadows, dragged himself through the lighting. He turned and, once again, hurriedly beckoned for Henry.

This can't end well, Henry thought. *It never does.*

He reached the end of the corridor as the space opened to cubicles. Each one was deserted, yet still eerily reminiscent of a time before now, when life was more than just escape tactics. He noticed a lone computer beeping with excited panic a dozen feet from where he stood, blinking in strobed, consistent flashes. Something about it nerved Henry. He stopped to glare at it as he passed, but only for a moment. Urgency suddenly seemed imperative, even in the otherwise silence of the hall.

Then, as if on cue, a thunderous stomping vibrated the floor. Henry contemplated it for a second in puzzlement, wondering what it could be, and suddenly realized why the man had been screaming so incessantly minutes before—the Dead were coming.

But how is that even possible? Henry thought. *The Dead don't think...*

A few more precious seconds passed and the man, still screaming and flailing his arms, vanished into a stairwell at the rear of the building, unwilling to wait any longer. He couldn't blame him. He figured that, somehow, the pain and exhaustion he had succumbed to in the alley had taken a dramatic toll on his brain function. He felt slow and terribly weak. Every movement and every thought felt so difficult to shake. Every step tore through him as he worked his way to the roof. The truth was—if he were the man, he would have left him, too.

It's now or never, Henry thought. *You don't want to die here.*

With a heavy mental push, Henry cleared the fog from his mind and forced his way to the stairwell. The thunder below him grew louder with each step he took. He thrust open the access door and nearly lost himself in the stink and surprise. The stairs, about seven stories down, writhed with stampeding bodies, flopping and squirming like salmon in a muddled stream. Mutilated arms reached upward into stretching fingers toward Henry.

Shit, Henry thought, eyes wide, panicked.

The cloud of exhaustion drained from him completely, replaced by the clarity of another surge of adrenaline. He knew he had to move—his brain screamed to do just that—but his legs stiffened at his hips, locking at the joints. He cocked his head and looked up the stairwell. The distance to the roof seemed daunting, but at this point, he had no choice. He would have to outrun the Dead if he ever wanted to see Shanna again. The man—so ahead of him now—seemed to have heard the Dead, too, because the pitter-patter of his stair climb grew fainter, but his pace quickened into a stumbling jog.

If I run, I can still catch up, Henry thought.

But the stairs felt as though they were about to collapse under the weight below him. He prayed that they would hold. He skipped stairs, stretching to gain speed as the muscles in his legs, particularly his calves, burned with tension. It wasn't long before his breathing turned to sighing, which turned, rather quickly, to exhausted heaves. He couldn't stop. He *wouldn't* stop until he reached the roof. He owed himself that at least.

The groans amplified louder through the stairwell now, but even in his weakened state, Henry still outmatched any zombie speed. He reached the roof access doors in a matter of minutes. He took a moment and breathed deep, catching his breath, peering out over the rail. Mangled limbs cracked and folded onto each other, enveloping the streets in a mess of gore. Grime caked the walls. A sour iron smell filled the air. It was as if he had entered a blood-curdling nightmare with no means of escape. They smelled him, just as he smelled them, and now they would not stop until they had him, biting him with those rotten incisors, devouring him bit by bit.

The rooftop cement landscape was, at least, clean. Rusted vents bulged in metallic openings to the right from which he entered. Across the floor rippled faint, chiseled cracks, mostly from wear and tear of years of harsh weather.

"Barricade the door," the man spoke from across the plane.

His voice carried rather quickly in the thin air. It seemed surprisingly calmer, more composed now.

Henry stood on a lone expanse of gravel opposite from where the man barked his order. His balance wavered against the unsteadiness of his shaking posture, but he swiveled his head in search of something to pry against the door, regardless. Even if his legs were failing him once again, his presence of mind was still very much alive and useful.

To his left, snaked on itself, sat a rusted chain, most likely used to keep the roof secure from trespassers, Henry presumed, before the Infection.

"I don't know if this'll work," Henry grunted, holding up the chain for the other man to see.

It clanked as it wriggled in the air, turning to a rusty powder in his hands as he shook it.

"Better than nothing," the man replied, but his eyes seemed worried, almost paranoid.

Henry wrapped the metal chain through the double door handles, weaving the links in and out of each other.

"That should hold," Henry said.

"Never mind that. It *has* to hold," said the man.

One last time, as if he refused to believe the situation, Henry pressed his ear against the doors. The thunder was there in all of its violent clamoring. It reared into a pulsating scream.

Closer now.

The man was now on his knees with his arms outstretched before him, tying something with fidgety fingers. He worked with another coil of black cable, moving quickly. Yet there was a subtle shake in his hands as he worked each braid, splaying tiny cuts into the skin with which he worked.

"Can I help?" asked Henry.

There was no answer.

Somehow, the adrenaline behind Henry's eyes kept him from the exhaustion and pain running through his hands.

"I prayed I would never have to use this, but I guess now's as good a time as ever," the man spoke.

His voice lowered and Henry reverted into a massive clash of déjà vu, remembering the first meeting with the gunman—the cool, brash clunk of the gun's barrel against his head and Quintero's sleek, tonal voice behind it. To imagine this was only a few hours ago came as a shock. His time in the subway lines had felt more like days, if anything. Guilt suddenly riddled his mind. Had he been wrong for allowing Quintero to join his blind escapade? Had he made the wrong decision befriending him? A flurry of pictures projected like a movie behind his eyes— Quintero's dead, lifeless body being ripped apart in a dark, dank alley somewhere in the heart of the overrun, a distraught Quintero caught somewhere, screaming for help, an escaped Quintero, hiding out in an abandoned building. All of these scenarios, in their own right, forced Henry to a vulnerable, empathetic state. He couldn't shake it. The rapidity of it all blurred into one block of memory.

Most likely, the voice in Henry's head whined. *It's all your fault.*

He shut off his brain and watched the man tie methodical knots in the cable.

The man reached for the butt end of the rope, carefully examining the jutting, sharp metal pick infused to its edge. In some lost corner of Henry's mind, he wondered how the man had secured this much cable and a grapple from a *retail* business building, of all places, but heard the curdling call of the Dead behind the chain-linked doors and erased his questions from his mind for the sake of more time.

"The building is far enough away that we can't jump for it," the man spoke. "But we can use this rope to climb across. Once we reach the roof over there, we can jump the rest of the buildings. The Dead are smart now, but not *that* smart. We'll lose them pretty quick. I'll go first and secure the grapple, since you're hurt, and then you can shimmy across. This is the last of the cable so let's make it count."

The night air felt comforting against Henry's aching palms. They had already developed a throb and now, faint rings of red huddled close to the skin surrounding the wounds. He wanted to ask for the man's name, ask what to do about the beginnings of infection, but the man was already taking off his jacket, preparing to drop out over the city street. Below, the streets still littered with waves upon waves of the moaning, shifting Dead.

"Remember what I said," the man repeated. "Once I'm over there, you start. We don't have time to screw around."

Henry nodded, opened his mouth like he was about to talk, but nothing came out. It was easier just to nod, appearing like he understood. There was something in the way the man was handling himself that Henry could not quite understand, almost as if the city was a playground and he was the only one with a map to its secret hideouts. Regardless, he saved Henry's life once. The least Henry could do was follow his lead.

The access doors now thundered with tumultuous, barbaric crashes behind him. The rusted chain links rattled and squeaked with nothing more than the extent of resistance they could muster. The man inhaled deeply with widening eyes, then climbed out onto the building's ledge with white-knuckled fists gripping the cable. Henry saw the grimace of pain wash over the man's face as he slid out further over the city streets. Blood tricked from his hands and dripped into lines down his arms, staining the collar of his shirt. Slowly, he placed one arm in front of the other, his legs dangling against the blackened backdrop below.

Henry held the cable as tight as he could, pulling so that the rope wouldn't give under the weight of the man's body. The wounds on Henry's palms—now almost remorsefully split again—commenced their bleeding once more, sending shards of pain like lightning to his brain. He hated the mind games of willpower, wanting to vomit to release the pressure behind his eyes, but he refused to give in, remaining as still as possible in the uncomfortable squatting position.

The chains pressed and stretched against the weight of the bodies behind it. The rusted metal seemed to be holding for a surprising amount of time, but as much as he feared the breaking of those chains, he focused on tightening his grip on the coiled rope that much more. The double doors dented with the force of constant weight, beginning to release slowly from the hinges.

"Hurry!" Henry screamed. "The doors can't hold much longer!"

It was only a matter of time before the flood spilled over the rooftop and, if one thing was certain, Henry didn't want to be standing there when the doors gave way. When the man reached the opposite building's roof, Henry reached out and grabbed the cable that draped over the street. His wounds opened for a third time in the process, spilling blood down his arms in another bout of warm, coagulated streams. The scent excited the crowds of Dead both below and behind him.

I only have seconds now, he thought.

"Your turn," the man said. "Come on!"

When Henry moved forward across the cable, he found the process excruciatingly severe. His muscles were already tired and the strain in holding himself up was nearly unbearable. It was gravity that pulled him, stretching his arms, letting only his fingers grip the rope. The aching in his hands relaxed slightly, but the spearing of the muscles in his shoulders continued. His chest expanded and stretched as he hung there, allowing him to breathe over the filth radiating below him in expanded, slow breaths. The oxygen gave him the little extra strength he needed.

The doors snapped and, what seemed like, endless currents of bodies poured onto the roof.

A mob, Henry thought.

He was far enough away from the edge of the cable that panic did not come to him. His baseball bat was stuffed into his jeans far enough so that it wouldn't fall into the crowds below, but the bulge of finished wood shifted against his thigh, chafing his skin.

The Dead filled the rooftop space behind him, angrily reaching for Henry. The man on the other roof yelled something, but Henry could not hear it over the amplified noise. He had almost reached the other side when he heard—and felt—a faint snap. A few of the Dead had filed through the rope, almost completely. It folded under Henry's weight.

The blood! Henry thought, thinking of how soaked the rope must be. *The rope is soaked with blood!*

He could see the man screaming above him, trying to tell him that something bad was about to happen. Henry could see it in the man's face. It was then, in that frantic moment, that Henry's heart sank.

The rope snapped and Henry reached for the man's hand, clasping it tightly.

"H...H...Hold on!" the man stuttered. He was gritting his teeth so hard that his jaw protruded through his cheeks like bony hills. The rope fell into the street below—grapple and all.

Henry dangled on the edge of the ridge. Memories poured through his eyes and death felt as imminent as ever. He thought of Shanna—or the *memory* of Shanna. He thought of the Boston summer breeze in August. The humid air of city living and her soft, aromatic skin against his.

"Hold on!" the man grunted for a second time.

He pulled into one, last arch of his back and rolled Henry out onto the gravel of the new building's rooftop. Henry closed his eyes, suddenly ripped back from his near death experience into reality and, almost impulsively, took in the deepest of breaths. He stared up at the clear, shattered stars. They seemed surreal, like a canvas drenched in lapping paint.

The man was screaming something at him again, but Henry could hear nothing but the pulsing of blood in his temples.

"What are you *saying*?" Henry mumbled, but the man pushes from his chest and monkey crawls toward the other end of the roof. Henry pried himself from the gravel and staggered like a drunkard, following the shadow fading into the distance..

"Who *are* y...?" but Henry couldn't spit the remainder of the question before collapsing hard on his hands. The piercing pain of exhaustion clouded everything. He found it difficult to put one foot in front of the other. As the blood filled in the spaces of his head, Henry had no choice but to listen uncomfortably to the symphony of ringing in his ears. He fell to his knees, wishing he had never entered the city in the first place. He wished he had died in the Infection. He wished he had never been born at all.

And suddenly, the weight of the night seemed too much to bear. He lost vision, then consciousness, as the world went black in the pale, early morning hours of another Boston Saturday.

4

When Henry woke, the city was quiet—*too* quiet. The unfiltered, morning sunlight hurt his eyes. He squinted against the pale blue of the sky that stretched to the East and met at the edge of the Atlantic. The blend of azure and crystal shades seemed astonishing at this time of day, especially after the dreaded black and dark reds of the night before. The air was dry and cool, but the heat his body created reeked of fever and sickliness. The pounding headache at the front of his skull and the muscular aching that resonated from his legs up into his shoulders confirmed all but the worst of his thoughts.

How the hell did I get here? he asked himself.

"I didn't want to wake you," the man spoke. He appeared much different in this lighting than what Henry could remember from the night before. "We had a hell of a time last night."

Henry pried himself from the gravel and sat up, arching his back into a slight curve. His muscles tightened and forced him to groan through the process. He stopped when he realized what the groans *sounded* like. He reached for the wounds in his palms and grimaced when he saw the purple-red of a massive epidermal infection running through his opaque skin. Red ventricular lines crept through his wrists, although the pain had lessened overnight, somehow, to nothing but a dull throb.

"I can't even remember..." Henry began. The desert in his mouth broke his voice so he could not finish the sentence he began. The process of pushing air from his lungs even seemed guttural and primitive, as if he hadn't used his throat in years.

"I know," the man said. "You passed out. Turns out this roof is pretty secure, so we spent the last few hours up here."

Henry looked down at his shirt. It was plastered with dried, dark blood, stiff with coagulation and starch.

"What's your name?" Henry asked abruptly, rubbing his chin with the back of his hand.

The man flattened his shirt and blazer against his chest. His attire, unlike the rest of feature, was just how he had remembered it—ripped blazer, mud-splattered slacks and all.

"You can call me Jones," the man spoke.

The man's eyes ventured over the cityscape as he talked, admiring the new loneliness of the buildings against the break of day. The streets were now tenuous, soaked to the core with a queasy weariness.

"What the hell happened last night?"

Henry's question was vague, but not unnecessary. He dropped his eyes to his hands once again. Jones furrowed his brow in confusion when Henry did so, but let the motion slide. His hands hurt, as well, but the scrapes had already scabbed over and started to heal nicely against the matrix of arm hair and creases in his palms. He figured the same was happening to Henry's.

"Those guns you went for?" Jones spoke. "They were a trap. They set it a few days ago. At first I didn't think anything of it, but then I realized it was more than just a random series of events. I have been underestimating them this entire time. They're hungry and they'll do *anything* to find meat."

Henry's confused expression told Jones he didn't quite understand. He kept his flipper-hands under his buttocks and blinked frequently to alleviate the brilliance of the sun.

"They're *evolving*," Jones explained, rather sardonically. "They weren't like this until a few days ago."

Suddenly the moment was filled with a cataclysmic clarity that collided with Henry's eyes like air hitting the lungs of a drowning man. He thought back to his few hours with Quintero at the start of the night, back through the *Breakers' Circle* and subway lines. The Dead—those dull gray eyes—were still staring back at him from the back of his mind. He recalled the synchronized step at the gun pile and the mob at the Hancock Street Station. Even now, with Jones' explanation, it all seemed so odd, so phantasmagorical.

"You mean they're *thinking*?" Henry asked.

The words were, once again, difficult to form in his dry mouth. He realized, for the first time, the extreme thirst his body craved. Jones nodded, then pressed his forehead into wrinkles.

"Why are you even in the city?" asked Jones.

He glared at Henry as his eyes morphed into hard fatigue. His impression in the daylight was much different now, almost paternal, much less cartoonish, more human, more exact. He was sitting on the graveled rooftop with his knees bent in front of him. His arms wrapped around at the kneecaps, linking in the front with his thin fingers intertwined like hoops. The laces flattened against the leather of his dress shoes. Henry could see Jones' ankles were soaked through his socks with a violent red. His pants rode his thigh tightly at his torso and stretched where the calves met his feet.

"My girlfriend," Henry explained. He was getting tired of defending his decisions. "She's waiting for me."

Jones giggled cynically, as if he had created this awful, brave new world and knew everything there was to know about living in it. He rubbed the stubble on his chin, displacing his jaw in the smile.

"She's gone, man," Jones spoke, lowering his voice. "I haven't seen anyone in the city since the evacuation."

Henry closed the sound from his ears. He heard this all before...and constantly, from everyone he's met from inside *and* outside of the city. Now it was Henry's eyes that ventured out over the city, watching the slow, blinking movements of the ocean in the distance. He forced his eyes to scan for Shanna's abandoned house, pretending he had replaced a pair of binoculars with his tired, squinting eyes. It came with no avail.

When he returned his focus to Jones, who was still talking to him, the man had already rose to his feet and began to brush off dust and debris from his blazer.

"...They put the walls up and I thought for sure it was too late, but the government said they caught it well before it spread."

There was a distinct smell in the air, something that Henry could not quite put his finger on.

"If you ask me," Jones continued, "I'd pack it in and get out of here before nightfall. It's too dangerous here now."

"Not a chance," Henry said, shaking his head. He lifted his eyes to meet Jones'. The man was now towering above him. "Shanna is there. I know it. And Quintero..."

"You mean the guy you came into the city with? I watched when you two were separated. He ran off into the Restricted District. It'll be a miracle if he gets out of there at all."

Henry's eyes broke to his shoes. Guilt hung at his shoulders like rocks, weighing him down. If Quintero was dead, it was his fault. Jones pulled Henry from the gravel floor, stepped back, and again, brushed the few invisible grains of sand dust off of his ragged jacket. The motion was quick and methodical, as if it was more of a habit than anything.

The man's eyes ignited into a peculiar display of exaggerated focus.

"How are you *okay* right now?" Henry asked. "I mean, I can barely walk."

Jones simply shrugged and ignored the question altogether.

"Okay," Henry continued. "Why don't we just stay here for a few hours...you know, just to catch our breath."

Jones just shook his head violently, lifting his arms toward Henry to signal for him to uncover his hands.

"Let me see them," Jones mumbled.

Henry pried them from underneath his buttocks and allowed the air to seep back into the wounds. Jones grimaced and inhaled deeply through his teeth.

"Jesus, man," he said. "We have to get you some medicine. *And fast.* Those things are infected beyond all hell."

The swollen, purple skin appeared even worse than they had been just a few minutes before. There were curving, stagnant red lines that weaved down into his wrists and tangled at his forearms. The cuts were deep and obtrusive, glistening like trenches after bloody wartime. Dirt caked the wounds along with stiff puddles of blood.

"That's blood poisoning," Jones said, pointing. "If we can't find you some antibiotics in a few hours, you can count on being one of *them* before all is said and done."

The baseball bat rested against a tattered shard of metal to Henry's right. He stretched his ailing muscles and reached for it, examining the piece of metal in the process. It appeared to be a fragment of debris from the building's rain gutter. It had rusted into a majestic golden brown color, rejected in its own little corner of the roof.

"Hey," Henry said. "This could be a pretty deadly weapon."

Jones once again shook his head.

"I'd be more worried about getting tetanus from that thing than anything. Good thinking, though."

Henry's fingers wrapped around the bat, but realized—rather quickly —that the joints in his knuckles could not bend. He decided he wouldn't try until after he had medicated the wounds, if he could help it.

"I know a pharmacy a few blocks from here that will have some antibiotics. I'm afraid if we don't get you something soon, the fever will start. And, believe me, you don't want a fever right now."

Henry's ears burned. He couldn't tell if it was primarily due to Jones' mini soliloquies or the unraveling deterioration of his health. His eyes were still adjusting to the sharp brilliance of the daylight. They watered and dilated with each attempt. It seemed as if his entire body was collapsing on itself in one, giant rush of disrupted, untouched energy. Somehow, Henry found it within himself to harness the wincing pain into a purified form of hope, trusting Jones with a sort of curious endearment, and moving forward even in the midst of easy despair.

"Follow me," Jones said, ushering Henry to the rim of the building.

The two men peered out over the edge. Their shadows stretched across the buildings in oblong shapes. Jones' eyes scoured the cityscape, mapping out the best possible course of action. His mouth moved quickly, but minimally, as if he was talking to himself, but couldn't decide if he should let the words leak out or reserve them for himself inside of his mind.

"The streets aren't safe anymore," Jones said. "There are too many of them now."

"But it's daytime. They go to the sewers during the day," Henry replied.

Somehow he knew Jones' reply before he spoke.

"It's not much of a deterrent anymore. The crazies run the streets during the day now, especially in the morning."

"Crazies?"

He had not heard this term at all during the time of the Infection. He assumed Jones had created it. Suddenly, Henry's eyes flooded into lightheadedness. *This shit always happens in movies,* Henry thought. *Not in real life.* It all felt surreal, like a perturbed delusion. *Crazies?* he continued. *What the hell...*

"You know," Jones monologued, "the ones that changed? You got the regular Dead, but these things are like those things on steroids. Those bastards will follow you until you go crazy...hence the name."

Again, Henry pretended like he understood, but Jones' vague explanations were beginning to wear on him. It seemed as though Jones knew all the secrets to surviving the city, but could only offer help encapsulated in riddles and puzzles. In any other state Henry could have put up with Jones' sly remarks and vaguely irritating explanations, but today, through pain and injury and annoyance, it was like the need for answers could easily be mistaken for helplessness.

"Ever roof jump before?" Jones asked.

Henry shook his head and followed the gesture with a small, almost indistinct frown. Jones ignored it.

"Don't think about the pain in your hands," he said. "They'll feel better when we get to the pharmacy."

Before he had finished his sentence, Jones had already propelled himself to the neighboring rooftop with surprising ease. The gap was not very significant, but enough to make Henry hesitate nonetheless. The space deceived his eyes—hazed by a fog of a pending fever—plus Jones made it seem so easy. The agility in the man's jump proved Jones' athleticism. It forced Henry's heart to pump hard in slight fear.

"What are you waiting for?" Jones egged, lifting his hands—palms up —with shoulders shrugged. Henry replied with a shrug of his own, took two steps back, and leapt over the empty space. A frightening salience wrapped itself around him while air bound—one that forced airflow to cease from his lungs. He exhaled an explosive breath as his feet hit and skid across the cement of the neighboring building.

"The pharmacy is about eight jumps away over there," Jones said, pointing east with his index finger. "When we start moving, keep your eyes level. You don't want to fall. I guarantee you won't be getting back up. And I'm sure as hell not coming for you."

Henry paused, clearly bristled by Jones' apathetic tone. The spiel was one that formed a brash sort of warmth in his voice, but simultaneously, a dark need for dominance. Jones' eyes showed no softening, no apologetic regression. It sent a squirm of shivers up Henry's spine. He decided to ignore the vile undertones, although it seemed almost unhealthy to do so. Jones straightened himself, stiffening his neck and raising his jaw so that he appeared to be facing the sun, but shifting his eyes downward into a menacing glare. Henry blinked and Jones had already turned, sprinting towards the next building's ridge.

He followed, although hesitantly, waving the breezy city air between his fingers. The oxygen sank into his wounds and attempted to heal them as best as it could, yet Henry knew the red tangles of lines in his wrists would only worsen in the next few hours. Still, the breeze felt good against his already overworked muscles.

He fell behind, but surprisingly caught up to Jones in a matter of minutes. Jones pushed gravel up into Henry's face with the soles of his shoes and Henry caught himself flying through clouds of dust for most of the journey. The man, he observed, created an incredible amount of friction with each step of his shoes and pounded his legs with each stride.

He kept his eyes level with the buildings in front of him, straying only slightly to recalibrate his balance on whatever rooftop the two men had managed to jump next. The buildings were not level in the least. Some had higher edges and ridges than others. Most of them, however, careened into steep drop-offs that he could not expect until he was already flying through the air between buildings. He found himself correcting his movements midair so that he wouldn't collide face-first with the building's side. The results usually came in the form of repeated awkward landings, although, surprisingly he remained upright and intact.

Jones stopped himself at a larger roof fifty yards in front of Henry, panting and holding his hips in need of air. Henry's knee buckled as he approached and sent him into the dirt at Jones' feet, scuffing up his wounds with more dirt and gravel.

"You were doing so well, *too*," Jones cracked through exacerbated breaths. "Get up."

Henry shook the new pain from his hands. He was used to it now, although the bits of gravel that gripped at the soft flesh of his infections enticed him into a semblance of a grimace. He picked himself off of the floor. Where he was standing, a small stain of blood and sweat marked where he fell. He was standing on the upper flood of a parking garage littered with ransacked and looted cars around its edges. Something tainted the way the space appeared. It seemed unholy, unnatural.

It looks like a...a fight ring, Henry thought.

A dizzying feeling rushed over Henry. He closed his eyes and felt the hot surges of blood run through the capillaries of his brain. The crisp morning air developed a flinching in his lungs. Mucus filled the desert in his throat, but the strings of phlegm that strung themselves against his windpipe did nothing but make it harder to take deeper, richer breaths. Jones now stood beside him, still catching his breath, inhaling hard. It steadied quickly against the rise and fall of his chest.

"A work of art, isn't it?" he asked.

Henry did not answer. The raw atrocity of the scene bellowed in hollow echoes as they talked. He felt as though he had suddenly plummeted three hundred yards deep into a cavernous abyss where only the sounds of scurrying and breathing could be heard. The sinking feeling wrenched at his heart.

"This is my masterpiece right here, Henry," Jones continued. The words seemed fatal and definite. "*This is it.*"

Jones walked to the edge of the parking garage and squirmed through a gap between two compact cars. He tilted his head down towards the building's front below and raised his hand for Henry to join him. Henry stumbled with shaky legs and fell to his knees beside the man. The baseball bat rattled quietly against the cement. Henry's eyes widened with the erratic movements that filled the street. A dozen bodies—riddled with starvation, ripped wounds, and gunshots—flailed their graying arms and legs in rigorous, angular movements. They seemed to be searching for something.

"You see them?" Jones whispered. Henry nodded, keeping his eyes pinned to one of the wild creatures. It whined and screamed, but did not look up. "They followed us here. They watch for movement and follow it. *Those* are the crazies."

There was something extraordinarily terrifying about these creatures. It was as if their bodies were the rotting carcasses of serial killers, only all of their murderous, sinister tendencies had somehow carried from their past lives and into the second. Their jaws cracked and snapped at the smell of living meat, squirming viciously and snarling their vile grins.

"Even in daylight there are dangers now. These bastards will rip you apart in seconds," Jones explained.

The man's eyes suddenly resembled those of the creatures below—dark pupils and bloodshot veins running wildly across the white canvas. The word *crazies* flooded Henry's mind like millions of canoes resting on the surface of a black water creek. He repeated it over and over, fumbling the syllables and rolling it against his tongue.

"I used to fear them," Jones explained, "but now they're just a part of living, I guess."

The world suddenly shrank into a microcosm of death, paralysis, and nausea. The disturbing images of the Hancock Street Station mob projected at the back of his eyes. His brain flooded into clarified paranoia. His heart thundered in his chest. He suddenly knew—somewhere in the darkest depths of his soul—that Jones was a type of evil that targeted its prey and never let go.

"The pharmacy doors are right there," the man whispered, now ringing his hands with excitement.

Henry's stomach dropped to a new level—like an elevator in free fall.

"This is my *favorite* part," Jones smiled. "I'll be back in no longer than five minutes. Make your swings count. They're faster than they look."

A warm bout of urine rushed to the seat of Henry's pants. This nightmare—this abrasive, new set of rules—had turned suddenly into Henry's worst nightmare.

"You can't possibly believe that I'm staying here with those *things* down there. They'll be up here in minutes when they see you jump!"

Henry's nostrils flared in fear and disgust. His forehead shimmered with sweat and radiated an unnatural feverish heat. He tried to wrap his fist around the wooden handle of the bat, but the wounds in his palms opened and began to bleed and seep. He tightened the grip nonetheless.

"This is the only way," said Jones. "*You* have the weapon, right?"

He pointed to the baseball bat. The finished wood suddenly seemed archaic, ready to split at any moment.

"Plus, I'm quicker than you. There's no way *I* could hold out. I'd be dead in minutes."

"You can stop making excuses anytime," Henry glared.

Jones' eyes exposed a glazed, but defiant focus. He rung his hands like he was running them under ice water.

"Believe me," he grunted through gritted teeth. "I wish there was another way."

Does he bring everyone here? Or just the smaller ones? He feeds the Dead... Henry thought. *At least I have a baseball bat.* But he knew the weapon would only last him so long.

"Look," Jones continued in a little more than a whisper, "I'm just trying to help you. You won't last a day out here with that type of infection."

Henry defiantly detracted his menacing stare and bit his tongue hard enough to feel his upper and lower sets of teeth nearly touch. It was true. Jones, the man he ignorantly trusted, would return with antibiotics, which could ultimately save his life, yet the feeling of being thrown to the wolves seemed overwhelming. Without warning, Jones released a loud, throaty growl. The dozen creatures below shifted their eyes upward.

"Good luck," Jones said, smiling maniacally.

Scraping and scratching filled the air. The creatures snarled and drooled, focusing on Jones and Henry at the roof's edge. They climbed—one by one—up the bricks of the building's side. The mortar chipped away at their fingertips, but they jabbed at each row of brick as though it was nothing more than a rock wall training exercise. This parking lot—*or boxing ring*—would either be Henry's throne or his tomb. There was no avoiding it now. He wished Jones would change his mind—somehow see the error in his ways—but the violent vigor in the man's grin told Henry to forget that idea. It simply wasn't going to happen.

Henry lifted the baseball bat to his shoulder. The wounds in his hands throbbed. A nasty blend of adrenaline and pain rushed to his head. He glanced over at Jones, who was now bent low, his knees stretched into an elasticized lunge. The muscles behind his tattered pants and shirt flexed with surprising force. A part of Henry desired to take Jones by surprise, batter the side of his skull with the thick of the bat, and leave him for dead while he escaped across the rooftops of the Boston morning. *Soon enough,* Henry thought, *it would be over. Either way...it will be over.*

"Once they reach the edge, I'm gone. Remember. Five minutes," Jones whispered. His voice had changed. It was thunderous and blindly malevolent. "Get ready."

Henry wanted to say something—*anything*—but words seem to cling to his tongue like burs. They deadened the air in his lungs and in his throat. The only sounds he could make resulted in the form of *screw* and *you*. Jones only chuckled at the remark. The two men waited—Henry with baited breath and Jones without—for one of the graying hands to reach up and over the metal lip.

Seconds seemed like hours.

A gray, scarred hand ran up and over the edge in crackling, jointed movement. Then another. And then another. Jones released from his trance, sprinting towards the creatures. The first of them reached up to grab him, but Jones had already gone airborne, soaring out and over, then disappeared into the street below. Henry quickly calculated the parking garage's height and wondered how Jones could have possibly landed successfully without broken bones or even fatal injuries. *It's just not possible*, he thought.

Angry, yellowing eyes emerged with broken ribs and blood stains dried against rotting flesh. Even with the gradual decay of starvation, the Dead seemed ganglier than Henry expected. Their eyes grew into a myriad of colors in the sunlight and stopped shifting at the color of the ocean at dusk. Their teeth shone with a mucus-colored tinge. Green plaque shimmered against the bone. Henry flinched with disgust, pushing bile back down in his throat.

The crazies sprinted forward with agility. The first tackled Henry with tremendous force, drooling and groaning as it grabbed at Henry's throat. He caught it with one swift throw of his fist, snapping its jaw in two jagged pieces. It whined and rolled next to Henry. He straightened himself, sitting up against the ache in his back, just in time for two others to reach for him, exposing rotted teeth. They extended with stiff joints toward Henry's abdomen. He swung another fist and caught one in the forehead. The body writhed upward and fell back onto its partner. Blood gushed from the brittle bone at its right ear and dripping ghoulishly onto the other's face.

The soft flicker of an emergency exit sign caught Henry's peripheral vision at the farthest corner to his left. It was a small sign, raised above the battered metal door access to ground level. The door craned from its hinges, wavering in the stagnant air. The stairs behind it narrowed into darkness while the walls inside the tunnel were blackened with grit. He rose to his feet and contemplated a sprint towards the stairs, but quickly came to the realization that he would never make it alive. The creature at his side was coming to, wheezing and snarling harder now while its partner growled from underneath it. He attempted a quick calculation for Jones' time since the jump, but couldn't think straight amidst the violence. He could only picture Jones' splattered body parts against the street below like a broken egg.

He couldn't have abandoned me, Henry thought. *Could he? Who would do that?*

Six additional crazies surrounded him, breathing in brash exhalations, and exposing their putrid teeth and graying gums. A toxic saliva made its way from the corners of their mouths and foamed down their jaws. Without warning, they attacked. His bat collided with one in midair, launching it backward and skidding across the concrete. Henry swung back and crashed into another, spraying blood and brain matter in a cloud of red mist. Henry tried to retreat, but lost his balance and tangled in his own footsteps, falling hard to his back.

The untouched remaining four crazies piled onto him with speed and incredible strength. He absorbed the contact by flexing his abdomen, but still, they reached for Henry in maddening, crazed screams. He flexed his leg, wriggled it free, and pushed his right foot into one of the creature's flexed knees. It snapped into a mess of spewing blood, muscle, and ligaments.

He was losing space and breath quickly in this position, using the baseball bat to pin the bodies away from him. If they collapsed, the sheer weight of dead life would kill him, let alone eat him alive. If that happened, the chance of survival plummeted to near zero. As it was, he wasn't going to last much longer in this position anyway. The Dead peered down at him with their hungry, longing eyes, breathing stale, rotten breath in his face.

He rolled a few feet to his right, somehow finding the strength within himself to pin the bodies where he had been with outstretched arms, but the Dead followed after him quickly with a resiliency of their own.

Get to your feet, Henry told himself. *It's your only chance. Get to your feet.*

So he pried himself from the cement into a push-up position and quickly back to his feet, only to be tackled by another one of the crazies just before lifting his eyes. It screamed and gurgled as the two of them hit the ground once more. Henry felt his back make contact with the cement, ripping his shirt into ragged pieces of fabric, and clawing large scratches at his shoulder blades.

Henry peered upward into the eyes of evil. Half of its face—the right side—glistened with dried bone. The skin around the wound appeared pasty and wet, sloughing from the patches of coagulated blood that held it in place. Henry reached, extending his fingers as far as they could stretch, stretching for the bat just out of arm's length. He could feel the creature's arms ripping and slapping at his torso. The face lowered towards his neck, drooling at the smell of warm meat.

"Come on!" Henry grunted. "It can't end here. It can't!"

His middle finger made contact with the wood, rolling it just enough to clasp with his weakened hand. With a blinding swing, he pushed the bat's nub-like handle forcefully into its eye. A splattering of dark blood dripped from the crater wound as its skull gave way. His hands throbbed with the infectious pain, but he refused to let up. If he didn't kill this thing now, the others would be on him in seconds, and this time, he

46

wouldn't have the strength to get back up. He pushed harder into its brain until he heard a sharp crack. Its skull caved and the body that had been scratching and scraping fell limp and lifeless beside him.

Suddenly, the air in Henry's lungs completely emptied. His body craved the oxygen his mind could simply could not give. Yet, he understood he could not surrender. Shanna was sitting scared and alone in that dark, city apartment. He need to press on. It was his job to find her.

He swung the bat to ward off the remaining creatures, yet their persistent swipes kept his arms up for added defense. He grimaced at their vile movements. He also grimaced at the growing tangle of red lines venturing past his elbow like a matrix of licorice, forcing his mind in and out of a dizzying lightheadedness. Every muscle quivered in silent whisperings as though his body had quickly fallen asleep, but his mind had not. Semi-paralysis warmed him to the bone and now, as if the determination and persistence to find Shanna meant nothing, he understood that this could very well be the end.

When he was a child, he hated the feeling of his arm falling asleep. His mother would hold him as he cried, until the blood returned to his arm and the numbing sensation disappeared. He remembered his mother's bright eyes and curled smile and wondered if, at this moment, she knew that her baby boy was on some distant, desolated parking garage in the middle of an overrun city. It was possible, Henry confessed, but he was certain that he had fled her mind a long time ago…if she was even alive. It was this feeling—the one of paralyzing limbs—that sent his mind into utter panic.

He picked himself up once more and braced himself against yet another barrage of flying bodies. This time, he threw a shoulder against the first and sent him backward against the rest. All of the remaining four, which stood behind the first, fell to the ground in a heap of useless flesh. He grunted through a rather exaggerated movement, sending a shivering pop through the forehead of a body closest to him with the sole of his shoe. He felt his foot squish against the thick resin of darkened blood. He moved and turned and Henry's foot slid against the gore. He tried to shake it out, but it was warm, squelchy and heavy, outright refusing to vacate the shoe.

Henry pelted the face of another with a jackhammer thrust of the bat. He used his entire body to propel the weapon forward and nearly fell face first in the process. An explosion of guts splayed Henry's legs. He waited for the last two to pick themselves up, which happened quickly. They were met with the last bout of thunderous clubbing. The first connected with its neck, displacing its spine with a sequence of cracking vertebrae, then a gurgling sound as its head fell from its weakened swivel. The second was a jab at the creature's nose, which broke easily and folded back into its brain. More currents of blood puddled below.

The dozen bodies that had climbed the face of the building had now dwindled to twelve severely distorted bodies splattered across cement. Skin and gore matted the wood of the baseball bat which rested heavy next to a fallen Henry. He took several deep (although not deep enough) breaths, attempting to push the pain from his mind once again, but this time, the wounds were too overpowering. His body quivered in excruciation. He wanted nothing more than to scream. Several of the crazies groaned, but were unable to move. He wished he possessed the strength to smash in every last skull, to end it now, but he decided he would rather save his energy for whatever lie ahead. *Jones,* he thought. *Stupid, goddamn Jones.*

Through the grimy stairwell, Henry watched as Jones appeared with a convenience-store plastic bag slung across his shoulder. His left hand slipped into his pants pocket as if he were on a casual stroll through the city. He noticed Henry splayed out across the cement, then shifted his eyes to the mangled bodies.

"Jesus Christ," Jones spoke. "You definitely have balls."

He said this with virtually no emotion. His eyes told the story—one of pitiful deception. Henry analyzed the white plastic of the bag that hung from Jones' shoulder, although he could not decipher what was in it. He hoped Jones had kept his word to retrieve medicine. Dark black lines—like a picture frame around his eyes—began to blanket his vision. It was only a matter of time before the fever consumed him altogether.

Henry shook off the beginnings of mild hallucinations. He couldn't believe what he was seeing. Jones jumped into a wild scissor kick, connecting the heel of his foot with the jaw of one of the fixated Dead. Its throat ripped open and sprayed another stream of blood and rotting skin into the air. He did this several times, then chuckled with his finishing work, finally redirecting his attention to Henry.

"Now," Jones said. "Let's go."

"*Wait,*" Henry bellowed. His body remained splayed out across the ground, seemingly unable to move.

He attempted a roll onto his back, but ceased the movement when a lightning bolt of pain shivered his spine. He knew he could not lay like this the entire day. The night would consume him (*literally)* with thousands of bodies if he did, but in the waning moments of his victory, Henry thought it best if he just remained still.

"*Where* is my medicine?" Henry bellowed again.

Jones opened the crinkling convenience-store bag, ripped open a sleeve of cashews, and began flicking them into his mouth one at a time. He chewed with his mouth open. Tiny shards of cashew swished against his tongue and loose strings of saliva. The slopping sounds from Jones' mouth boomed in Henry's head. Vexing anger filled him. He coughed, hoping Jones could hear the apparent frustration in the grunt.

"*Come on*," Jones spit sarcastically.

He noticed the weariness in Henry's eyes, but turned towards the stairwell in an attempt to ignore it. For a moment, Henry believed he was *really* hallucinating. Should he continue to trust Jones? After all, the exhaustion and infection running through his body was more than enough strain to throw any normal human being over the edge. But not Henry. He was weak, but not *dead*, and that, as pitiful as it might sound, was enough to pry himself from the ground and return to his wavering, unbalanced feet.

Henry repeated his unanswered question: "*Where* is my medicine?"

Still, there was no answer. Only the crunching of cashews.

It was apparent now that Jones had ulterior motives—things that he saw as maybe comical or justified in his own shifty world, but to outsiders, were evidently devilish. Yet Jones had played his hand, and well enough at that, and, still, Henry had succeeded, despite the odds.

"A chess game," Jones said, slinging the convenience bag back over his shoulder. Henry could see a medicinal label poking through the thin plastic. "Twisted, but still a chess game."

Just because you saved my life, Henry thought, *doesn't mean I can't take yours*.

Henry furrowed his brow.

"A King's gotta have a pawn, right?" Jones continued. "And I must say, you're the first pawn to make it through the trial run."

He watched Jones strut to the stairwell and lean against the grimy wall, continuing to chew with his mouth agape. He realized, to Jones at least, he must now look like one of them—a *crazy*. He fumed, ready to jump up and attack the man just like the crazies had attacked him, but waited—half by his own accord and the other with pure resilience. He craved, more than anything, those *stupid* cashews. But even more, he needed the medicine…and *now*.

"Who do you think you are?" Henry belted before he could catch himself. The words seemed to spill from his mouth like raindrops.

There was an awkward, dead time of silence that followed.

"Excuse me?" Jones spat. He stopped, cocked his head slightly to the left, and turned. The tone in his reply matched his automatic strut.

"I *said*, who the *hell* do you think you are?"

He spoke each word louder and stronger than the first. He balanced his stance now, but felt the persistence of a constant throb in his feet. His legs were no longer shaking, perhaps infinitely lost in their own eternal suffering or somehow infused with a virtuous energy. His fists clenched against the wounds in his skin. His eyes did not flinch.

"I see what this is," Jones said, smiling. "I saved you once and, just *may be* saving you *again* and *this* is how you repay me?"

Jones reached into the pharmacy bag and held up the box of antibiotics. His words were stuffed with cynical undertones and unnecessary power.

"I don't owe you shit," Henry replied.

The tip of the baseball bat scraped against the cement next to his leg. Henry swung it gently back and forth, subtly returning a bleak form of intimidation. Jones dropped the plastic bag and shrugged his shoulders, cracking his knuckles in quick, furtive movements. There was a careless aura to him that Henry despised. He had not expected the situation to escalate so quickly, but was not surprised in the least bit by where it was leading. Anger bubbled in his throat. For the first time since entering the city, he found that anger could be just as good as fuel, recharging him just enough to stand tall against the evil before him.

"You're right," Jones spoke, scratching the stubble at his jawline. "I think you guessed it the moment I brought you here. I've left a lot of people to die up here." A smile broke his lips. "But they're not *you*, Henry. *You* don't stop. *You* just keep going. I'm starting to get the feeling that you just don't die."

Jones ground his teeth hard against the words as Henry raised the bat to his shoulder. The weight did not feel like weight at all, but instead, seemed gravitationally immune. His arms flexed in sheer disgust.

"*Survival of the fittest*," Jones spoke in clear, undulating syllables. "Ever heard of it?"

There was an expression on Jones' face that Henry had not yet seen openly. It had always been there, just not as transparently clear. A familiar darkness strengthened into his sunken eye sockets, glistening in the sun, and enveloping his visage with a blinding fury.

"I apologize. I underestimated you," Jones continued. His voice was getting progressively louder. "I knew you were a fighter. Not just anybody can outrun a mob of those things. But *you...you're smart.* You figured it *all* out."

He was now rolling up his sleeves, rubbing his fingers together in impatience. A similar blinding fury raced into Henry. His heart pounded in his chest. His arms twitched anxiously. He lowered his eyes, allowing for Jones' words to soak into his ears. He savored each syllable, using them.

"This is such a shame," Jones barked. "We could've made a great team."

Suddenly Jones' frame arched more primitively now, filled with a visceral, violent dependence. Without warning, the man pounced at Henry aggressively. There was no time for Henry to defend himself, except to throw up his arms in a futile backpedal. Jones lowered his shoulder and collided with Henry at waist level, sending an additional wave of pain up through his shoulders. Henry released an amplified groan with the little air left in his chest.

On top of that, his head smashed against the pavement after falling to the concrete, sending unnatural stars twinkling in the projection of his eyes. The temporary jolt handcuffed his vision, forcing it into a darkened haze. He felt a barrage of fists thrashing his ribcage and cheekbones, but he could not see Jones behind the mix of shadows. The warm sensation of pooling blood began trickling slowly down his face. It poured into the creases of his eyes and mixed with another bout of feverish sweat. He raised his arms to defend himself, but the blows machined his body in quick, methodical strokes.

He blinked through droplets of blood. Fields of red covered his eyelashes. He caught glimpses of Jones' maddening face, swollen with anger and conviction, plastered against a canvas of a sky heaped with white clouds and furious shadows. He heard the man's lunatic shriek of laughter and undeniable gall and pictured a sinister, maniacal grin pinned to the creases of his mouth. The punches rang in Henry's ears like church bells, always louder, always there.

He likes this, Henry thought. *He really likes this.*

Henry's temples surged with pain—hot, dirty, arrhythmic pain. His back stiffens against the concrete below him.

The baseball bat had fallen an inch from Henry's right hand as he was tackled. He reached for the curled wood, clasping it between weak fingers, and clanked Jones with as much force as he could possibly summon. He felt an (unfortunately) all-too-familiar crack of wood against bone, heard the reverberating groan of pain, and sighed as the release of Jones' weight fell from him. It gave Henry a chance to rise to his feet, which he did, wiping the blood from his wounds in smears across his face.

Jones clutched the left side of his jaw, grunting violently in discomfort. Henry wanted to attack but, instead, just stood frozen with the baseball bat still clutched at his side. Jones gurgled and spat a conglomeration of blood, teeth, and saliva in a splat at his feet. He attempted to refocus, but stumbled awkwardly towards Henry with his arms outstretched, clearly affected by the strain of concussive dizziness, yelling in angry shrieks. Henry reared back, stretched his arms as far back as they would go, and unleashed a crackling blow to the left side of Jones' chest. Blood and spit ran from the creases in his mouth. He wobbled, grimacing with the pop of broken ribs, and screamed out in pain.

The crazies called back in a blood-curdling foray of noises from the streets below. Henry turned his head and listened, keeping Jones in his sights. The uproar resonated through the air in towering cyclones of sound. His stomach lurched. He knew they were climbing already. He *knew* it. It was only a matter of time before both of them, Jones *and* Henry, were surrounded by another wave of meat-eaters.

He had lost focus for only a moment when he turned back to Jones, catching a wild fist to the bridge of his nose. He fell sideways to the cement, landing uncomfortably on the palms of his hands. The violent red lines of blood poisoning had reached his biceps. Time for medicine was running short.

Jones propelled himself onto Henry, ripping his fingernails into his shoulders. Henry shrieked and heard the crazies' response surround him again. He jabbed the handle of the bat forcibly into Jones' abdomen. The man spat a burst of stale air and blood into Henry's face and fell to his side in another burst of pain.

"Is that all you *got*?" Jones growled. He pushed himself back to his feet and ground his teeth maddeningly. "*This…isn't…over.*"

Both men were beyond beaten. Jones wobbled against the strain of his leg muscles, drooling globs of blood in a spray of darkened moisture. He smeared the salivated residue against the back of his hand, wiping it away. Henry flicked the drops of sweat from his eyes. The shrieks and howls from below grew louder, yet Jones refused to stop his baiting. He howled and screamed louder now, smiling all the while. Henry glanced around with increasing worry. He proved he could take on a dozen of them, but the gurgling cries sounded fuller now, more robust than what he remembered of the first cries. And in his present state? *No way in Hell…*

Jones lunged. Henry ducked and successfully avoided the man's flailing arms, watching as Jones tried to catch himself, but stumbled and fell to his hands and knees. He released a fervent howl that boomed across the plane and all but sealed both of their fates. In the corner of his vision, he noticed movement appearing at the far side of the roof. Another slew of dirty, jointed hands reached over the lip. Their screeching, aggressive groans quickly followed. Rotting bodies ascended and hovered at the building's precipice, some still climbing while others mangled disjointedly toward the men. They sniffed at the smell of blood and sweat and licked their shattered and torn lips with vile, unearthly tongues.

Jones staggered himself, clenched his fist. and refocused on Henry. A flame burned insanity in the centers of his eyes.

"Wait!" Henry urged. He held up his hands in an attempt to apprehend Jones for a single, fleeting moment. "Look!"

Henry lowered his arms and followed Jones' eyes to the rising, degenerate bodies.

"We have to…"

Four white knuckles thrashed his face before he could make out the last of his plea. It sent his brain into a nauseating spin of bumper cars against his skull. His body faltered against the collision—struggling to remain balanced—but ultimately wavered too far to the right and collapsed against the battle-stained ground. The boxing ring had become an abattoir, illuminated with the crimson smears of both human and zombie blood. The throbbing in his face swelled, then numbed as his head hit the cement and all went black.

Jones had already crossed to the most easterly neighboring roof when Henry looked up into a concussed fog. The man was smiling and raising his hands into the air with victory. *How long was I out?* Henry thought, immediately scanning his body for bites or tears. There was nothing. *Seconds,* he concluded and ripped himself from the ground in an agonizing rush of blood from his head. He had no time to think. He would simply have to react.

The first onslaught of the Dead picked themselves onto their feet at the rooftop edge, most dragging lifeless limbs across the cement in awkward tumbling movements. A second wave, to Henry's chagrin, began their ascent over the building's lip behind the first. He could not fight all of them, which left one inextricable conclusion—*run.* He peered to his left, then to his right, and battered the badly shattered face of the first attacking crazy to his right. An eerie paralysis crept through his bones now. Fiery tension stormed through his legs and up and over his torso like a steel blanket. He inhaled deeply, sent a violent fist through the mushed eye socket of a second body, and propelled himself backward toward the buildings from which they had come the night before.

If I could just backtrack to the roof where we spent the night, I have a chance, Henry thought. Intentional optimism rang through his thoughts, although he wasn't quite sure if he believed himself.

He sprinted for the clearing when a sharp white flutter caught his eye. He stopped and turned towards it. The pharmacy bag bristled in the breeze a few feet away from him, so he shoved a third body over the edge of the garage and stepped hard with the sole of his shoe onto another. *I need that medicine*, he thought. He lunged for the bag as more bodies lunged at him. Frenzied cries lifted into the sky and Henry suddenly felt that his chances of survival were worse than he thought. Grimy, elongated fingernails reached and caught on the fabric of his shirt. The Dead scraped for anything, but found no skin. The air smelled of their putrid, sour breath, breaking like a cloud around him.

Jones called from several roofs away, still waving his hands and exclaiming in victorious bouts of unnecessary noise. The Dead ignored him, focused on Henry—the closer of the two.

It was the stench of decomposing skin permeating every inch of air that forced him into another bout of nausea. It covered him; bathed him in blood and gore and pus. Bodies piled upon bodies as Henry kicked and slashed and swung the baseball bat out in front of him. Suddenly, the world felt oddly panoptic from his view, slowing down to meet the reality of his condition. If he didn't go now, he would never go.

He found a sliver of daylight, rose, avoided contact from a few of the swiping crazies, and sprinted hard. He sprinted like he had in one of his nostalgic high school one hundred-meter dashes. Back in those days, he broke records—running just to run. *Nothing else matters,* he told himself. *Get to the finish line.* He imagined the roar of the Dead as his audience, cheering and thrashing in the bleachers as his family and friends once had. The space between the buildings suddenly came into view. He would clear it with ease.

He ran to escape.

He ran for Shanna.

He glanced up at the skyline, doing his best to visualize the route from which the two men had originally come, but it was more difficult than he thought. At this point, he had no time. He would jump to the nearest building or forget it all together. There was no choice. He reached the edge of the parking garage and pushed off with his strong foot, lifting into the air toward a smaller, slanted building. The Dead snarled and scrambled behind him, trampling their own in an attempt to catch up. As he landed he heard the thud of bodies hitting the streets below, but also felt the shaking vibrations of footsteps stomping wildly behind him.

Jesus! he thought. *They jump, too?*

He didn't look back. He couldn't. He would only be wasting time if he did. Instead, he pressed on, sprinting as though he had the energy to do so. As long as he pretended he was fine, his body seemed to move...and move quite well at that.

Don't stop, he thought.

If he did, or even worse, if he fell, it would all be for nothing. He had no choice but to forget the exhaustion, forget the pain, and build the will to keep running away from all that was behind him now. Every fiber in his body screamed with a fiery form of adrenaline. In this strange parkour marathon of sorts, the only thought that popped into Henry's mind was that of prevailing. He maintained a steady breathing, calming his heart with every long stride. After all, he still had his agility and, because of that, the Dead fell behind him relatively quickly. Within minutes, nothing but the soft echoes of falling, splattering bodies could be heard from a distance.

Henry stopped about three hundred yards into the city and caught his breath. He watched the remaining crazies attempting to catch up, mimicking his hurdling from building to building. The sight of them filled Henry with a neurotic eeriness—one of dissolution.

He remembered what Quintero had mumbled in the subway lines: *It's like they're learning…*

Their bodies—the ones still upright—were built stronger albeit their fragile, skinny frames—unlike the Dead he had effortlessly dismantled on the parking garage roof. Even from where he stood, he could see their legs wound with graying, stretched muscle, their shoulders pulling at their necks, their jaws aggressively jutting like trunks of fraying trees. They even appeared shadowy, as if they had somehow adapted to blending into night.

He counted them. At least thirty were still leaping from roof to roof far enough away, still, where he felt comfortably disconnected. Occasionally, one of the creatures tripped and fell. A dark, deepening chuckle gurgled in Henry's throat. Their movements, in his tiresome and passive state, seemed nothing but humorous. He figured dissolving the intensity of the last few days into a single, hearty laugh could only raise his spirits, so he smiled and let it come. The leader of the group—the one closest to Henry—tangled in its own gangly feet about five buildings in the distance, fell to its side, and split its skull open on a shard of drain metal. A surge of blood roared from its brain as the body went limp. Henry watched as one by one, the mob fell to its demise like dominoes.

Henry knew one thing for certain. The horizon made good company against the rubbled skyscrapers.

He squinted hard, but could no longer see Jones through the early afternoon sun. He hoped that *karma* would do the man justice somehow down the road, but the sinking feeling in his gut told him that Jones had escaped the fiasco totally unabashed. Meanwhile, the fever brought on by the nearly fatal (at this point) infection flushed his face with boiling blood, mixing with the need for vengeful anger.

A war is coming, Henry thought. *Maybe not today. Perhaps not tomorrow. But it's coming.*

Dozens of merciless growls grew closer from all directions and shook Henry from his awestruck daze. The last of the rooftop Dead continued their jumping, stopping, sniffing and snorting, and proceeded toward him.

At least Jones taught me one thing, Henry thought. *The Dead can't roof jump for shit.*

He stored this bit of information, like a microchip, in the back of his mind. He knew it would come in handy in a place like the Restricted District. He would need every bit of help he could get to make it out of there alive.

"The Restricted District is where the Infection began," Jones had explained, back on the first rooftop. "The hospital tried to take steps for quarantine, but before the steps were in place, it was too late. The Infection grew like wildfire. Most of the Dead are still roaming the hospital hallways, looking for a way out."

He owed it to Quintero to search for him. He owed it to *himself.*

Henry leapt, running again from building to building, making sure not to stop until he reached his destination—whatever that may be. Only one crazy had managed to keep its balance, but rolled its ankle, broke it in two, and fell clumsily to its death below.

Below him, however, painted a different story. The shuffling of a pack of bodies continued to worm through the city's alleys and creases. Henry had tried to keep quiet, but each movement he made set off another wave of motion below. He was certain that when he stopped—*if* he stopped—the crazies would just disappear. *Boredom*, he thought. *No distractions lead to boredom. And that's a good thing.*

He found a spacious roof about fifty jumps from the parking garage fighters' ring and collapsed. The structure itself seemed secure enough, littered with sharp barricades across the building's rim. Someone (Henry wondered if it had been Jones) had strung coils of barbed wire through the metal rails at the building's perimeter. At the center, close to where Henry had stopped, a door with padlocks and lengths of chain stood erect against a narrow access. He pulled hard at the handle, displacing the door about an inch outward, but could no more than that. It was enough to expose the flickering fluorescent lighting inside the stairwell, but, as long as the chains held stiff, there would be no entrance to the rooftop tonight.

No climbers are getting up here, Henry concluded. He fell hard to his back, partly from exhaustion and the other from clumsiness, crunching and arching his shoulder blades against the heated cement. He analyzed his hands as they oozed and bled and reeked of hard use.

When he could, he pulled himself upright and sat in the center of the roof, far from the visibility of the Dead, with his back against a deserted and already molding ventilation system. He opened the pharmacy bag with his swollen fingers and examined its contents—two full bottles of antibiotics, a sandwich bag of a dozen painkillers, hydrogen peroxide, three sleeves of cashews, two water bottles, a packet of instant coffee, bandaids, a roll of toilet paper, and a medium-sized box of crackers.

Hell of a job, Henry thought to himself, complimenting Jones sarcastically on his pharmaceutical excursion. Although there was plenty enough to share, he knew Jones would never have done such a thing. As far as Henry knew, he would have been lucky to sell his soul for even one of those painkillers. For the first time, Henry felt accomplished and deserving of what he had retrieved. He relished the feeling, soaking in the warm, heavily beating rays of the sun, ignoring the hell he was certain would return tomorrow.

His swollen fingers clasped one of the cashew sleeves, ripped, and threw the plastic top aside. He dropped half of a dozen cashews into his mouth and chewed silently behind his lips. The salt burned his tongue, but in a satisfied, euphoric way. All of this had only come from one night in the city, yet Henry had still forgotten how to chew and swallow and *enjoy*. He chewed until the saliva dissolved the nuts into a plug of mush, then allowed it all to slide harshly down his throat. He felt it scratch his esophagus walls and splash into the pit of his stomach. He followed the food with large gulps of water, which tasted mildly stale, but regardless, he drank ravenously until the bottle was empty. He contemplated rationing, but could not resist the need to feast. He had been through too much to starve himself more. He had made up his mind. Tonight, he would finish everything. He deserved it, *justifiably* deserved it.

He glared at the blood smeared watch clinging to his wrist. It read two o'clock. In a few short hours, the sun would return to its cave somewhere beyond the ocean waters, abandoning the city, once again, at the mercy of the Dead and darkness. No escape or victory would occur during the nighttime hours—at least not in his unhealthy state. Quintero, if he had not yet been eaten alive, could afford one more night. He would most certainly be holed up somewhere, closing his eyes, but never sleeping. In the Restricted District, he was sure, no one sleeps. And Shanna, if she had made it this far, would still be waiting patiently behind the thin walls of the abandoned house for Henry's return. He could afford to wait until the morning. He needed a reset.

At the first light of day, Henry vowed.

He reached into the pharmacy bag and retrieved the two plastic childproofed medicine bottles. He dropped a double dose of antibiotics and three painkillers into his badly bulging hand and pushed them into his mouth. He relished the bitterness against his tongue. With the last swig of water, he closed his eyes and felt the chemical texture grind against his throat. It forced its way into his stomach and quickly into his veins. He fell to his side in exhaustion, sighed once in a wave of hot breath, and allowed the medicine to guide him into sleep.

5

He could feel the whistling breeze against his face. The streets were empty...almost too empty, but he felt safe enough to walk the streets without caution nonetheless.

In front of him stood Shanna's abandoned house. The blanket of darkness casted shadows across its walls, making it appear gigantic. An optical illusion, Henry thought, but as he approached the front door, its measurements seemed to stretch, reaching even higher into the sky than the neighboring buildings around it. His feet sunk into the ground and covered with odd, softening mud that cracked at his ankles like glass.

He could see front door opened slightly, yet he could not remember if this had just happened or if it had been that way before he arrived. A wave of panic consumed him as the image of Shanna surfaced in his mind. If she was not inside, where could she be? Was she dead? He felt increasingly dizzy, but stepped forward towards the door anyway. He pressed his fingers against the warped wood and entered the darkened room.

He did not call for her. He wasn't even sure he could speak at all. Nothing was certain, but the incredible urge to move farther into the dark room rushing over him—an urge he physically could not control—and suddenly, before he could blink, he was standing in the center of the darkness.

From the shadows, he squinted and saw the lining of a faint figure emerge. It made no sound, yet he knew who it was. Shanna moved slowly towards him, swaying slightly back and forth. He reached out to touch her, but the darkness turned to violent sound and he was immersed in groans and panic. Her face had melted into a grotesque sloughing of skin. Her teeth rotted in cavernous holes through her widening gums. He

let her take him over, tackling him and sinking her teeth into his neck.
The pain, he thought, was nothing like the pain of losing her...

Henry opened his eyes, swinging the bat madly in front of him. He was alone, crouched into a sitting fetal position at the far end of the roof. Sweat trickled down his forehead. His tee shirt clung to his chest, lined with perspiration stains under the arms and in a dark V at his chest. For a moment, he had forgotten where he was. The medicine forced a cloud over his eyes that felt both pleasant and rather annoying. He turned his head to check the angles of space around him, but it was empty. The door in his line of sight, however, appeared different, suddenly strange. The padlocked chains had stiffened—no longer loose—against the door's opening and Henry could now see the diluted emerald glow of fluorescence stretching across the cement in contrast with the dark of the night.

A constant drone buzzed from the streets below him. He did not dare look out over the edge. He knew what he would see. Besides, he felt comfortable enough where he sat and could not trust the heavy dosage of drugs running through his system anyway. He wondered how late it was and how deep he had slept. It would be a longer night now that he was awake. He knew it, but a part of him almost felt relieved about this newfound consciousness. At least he was in control of his own destiny. He reached into the pharmacy bag and quietly opened a box of crackers, not necessarily hungry—sustenance being a relative term—but he knew if he didn't eat now, he might not have a chance later.

It was well past dark (Henry could tell by the glistening stars above him) and the scattered building lights, although fewer, were visible from where he sat. Somehow, this unadulterated moment eased the panic within him. The medicine was wearing off, but the idea of having much more comforted him in ways that pure adrenaline could not. He didn't dare move from his spot and rustle the crowds of Dead below, so every alternating minute or so, he popped a flurry of salted crackers into his mouth and chewed them softly.

The crackers tasted surprisingly pleasant, but really dried out his throat. Without water, Henry sat, with his back against the wall, swallowing the grainy powder snowballing in his mouth. It was slightly uncomfortable, but he didn't mind. If he arched his neck enough, he could accumulate just enough saliva to push it down, so like any bored and injured human being, he kept shoving the breaded squares into his mouth like an infant, refusing to stop until the whole box disappeared.

And he smiled. It was a happiness that only food could bring.

He examined the roof once more now that his eyes had adjusted from sleep. At this point, he saw paranoia as his privilege. Even in the securities of the rooftop, he felt it necessary to remain absolutely still, although his legs desperately needed a stretch. The eerie solitude did not scare him in the least bit, but instead, forced him into a strange anxiety, like he was waiting for something to happen that never would.

He ripped two more painkillers down without water, sighed quietly, rested his head against the cold metal of the ventilation system behind him, and closed his eyes to the gnashing sounds of the streets below.

Thoughts of Jones boiled in his mind. Oh, how he would kill to land a few more devastating punches to the soft spots behind the man's eye sockets. He wanted nothing more than to watch Jones collapse to the floor from a *true* beating, limp like *he* had limped after Jones' cheap shots. He wanted Jones to know what it *really* took to survive a zombie Apocalypse—sheer willpower, an unbreakable determination. And then, after all of it, he would drag Jones' body to the edge of the parapet and leave him in the midst of a dozen crazies to fight for his life, just as Henry had, to see if the man could withstand the fear, the torture, the impending evil unleashed. And when the man was ripped to shreds, Henry would feel nothing for him, because, in his eyes, Jones was not human anymore. He hadn't been since the fight, since he discovered Jones' *real* motives. The man was nothing more than a warbling coward —a scavenger feeding on the inauspicious few, the ones lost in their own bouts with death.

He shook the vengeful thoughts away and placed an aching hand on his chest. His heart was suddenly beating wildly behind the bones of his ribs. Sweat, once again, lined his shirt with spotty little lines under the armpits and down his spine. Yet it wasn't the physiological responses to these murderous thoughts that caught him off-guard. It was the way those simple feelings excited him in such a grandiose way. He took deep breaths and calmed himself, especially because his excitement seemed to spark a distinct evil inside of him—something too dark for his own good.

The light from the moon gushed over the exposed metropolitan as it slept like a silver dollar pressed against black felt canvas. It hung, perfectly balanced, in front of him with a strange energy that flooded the city and, suddenly, it felt almost as if he was being watched. He glanced around once more, cautiously, to be sure he was absolutely alone.

His line of sight, once again, led him towards the door at the center of the roof. The flickering light from within the frame sparked a delayed curiosity in Henry. Maybe, he thought, he should go check it out...

It's not worth being bitten, he concluded. *I don't know what's behind there...*

It might have been the drugs that blurred his vision, but he found himself dizzying and wishing the ground was a softer place to rest. His hands felt better now at least, but the anxiousness within him kept the tiny flame of fever alive in his eyes and in his swollen face. It would be weeks before his body fully recovered, before he was sure he would understand the meaning of the word *healthy* again, but he wasn't certain he could manifest enough energy in time to find Quintero and Shanna in this godforsaken place. Those thoughts were the fearful ones.

The rambling thoughts eventually lulled him to sleep and, once again, Henry almost forgot that the city was no place for slumber.

He woke with the early morning sunlight barely breaking over the horizon. His eyes slumped with sleep and the left side of his face pulsated with the rhythmic bursts of heartbeats from his chest. A strange, hopeful urge to move coerced him from his awkward, crunched position of sleep. He had not felt this energetic since the moments before he entered the city—the crackers couldn't have done *this* much for his system—but the sunlight was still young and fresh and he knew, if he left now, he would risk an unnecessary meeting with the angriest of the Dead —the ones that didn't know whether to stay up in the streets or hit the underground. It was something he did not want, nor need at this moment in time.

The constant drone of the bodies below had faltered a bit, but that meant nothing. Until the sunlight washed the buildings with midmorning light, the Dead would not abandon their posts. It was some kind of zombie code—an instinctual clock within all of them that catalyzed the exile underground. He thought about these things as the wind blew in from the ocean water to the East, covering the city with a sulfuric odor that lingered like ripples in the damp air. The sun, he noticed, wavered in its glow behind gray-shadowed, yet thinning clouds. He could barely see the frothy shoreline of the harbor beyond the buildings, half-glistening in the half-light.

Henry quietly wormed his way to the edge of the building and peered over the side. The crowds had dissipated since the midnight hours, just as he anticipated, but still, there were masses of gnarled Dead stumbling and mobbing their way through the maze of buildings. A sudden stew of pungent odor rose to his nostrils and he choked against a nervous slew of bile that violently rose to the center of his throat. He tasted it and lurched into a heave, but managed to keep himself together.

Keep it down, he persuaded himself. *You need every bit of energy you can get.*

It was then that he heard the faint, mousy whisper from behind him.

"*Hey,*" it said, clearly shaken by pain or fear or regret—*something like that,* Henry thought.

The voice startled Henry just enough to instigate a shuffling back from the ledge. If any of the Dead had heard him, he'd have another bout of panic to deal with, so he listened for an uptick in noise, but heard nothing swelling from below. He sighed in quiet relief. The voice, from wherever it had come, projected for such a tiny sound, so much so that Henry circled the roof, looking for a body to match the sound.

"Over here," it spoke again.

An arm jutted through the padlocked door's cracked opening, waving him closer. It was suprisingly thin and smeared with dark resinous blood, caked down to the forearm and spread through the cracks in his fingers like spiderwebbed tributaries.

Henry shuffled to the door, angling his head into the opening of the frame.

"How long have you been in there?" he asked, suddenly scared, suddenly panicked.

The arm connected to a boy of about fifteen or sixteen with dark locks of hair pressed greasily to his forehead. Blood smeared every inch of his body—*a mixture of his and others'*, Henry presumed. The boy looked down, grimacing in pain against the door.

"Couple of hours ago," the boy whispered, breathing staggered, harsh breaths that seemed to make no noise.

The door creaked, then opened only a sliver further so Henry could see half of the boy's face amidst the spreading, fluorescent shadows. His eyes were wide and blue, filled with the glossiness of innocence broken by the reality, broken by extreme violence.

Henry glared at the padlocks separating them. Even if he wanted to, he would not be able to open the door. A series of chains weaved in and out of each other in tight knots against the metal handles. Henry closed his eyes and shook his head in dismay.

Someone had made sure that this door would never open again...and had done a pretty good job with it. Sorry, kid. There's no way out from there. Not even if I tried.

More sun formed on the horizon now. Henry watched the red dawn turn to a blood orange and, finally, into a bruised lemon yellow. The Dead below hushed even more in these hours. He expected they would— a welcoming sign for a city so far lost.

"You shouldn't be in there, kid," whispered Henry.

He hadn't really meant to say that—at least not in that tone—but he pulled his shoulders back and stuck to his words. The boy adjusted again, grimacing against some kind of hidden wound, but this time with an expression of strain and contemptuous eyes. Suddenly, the conversation darkened.

"You think I *want* to be stuck in here? I had nowhere else to go. They had me trapped. This place isn't very fun at night, you know," the boy whispered through anger.

Hostility broke in his voice, but Henry disregarded it, because it was *genuinely* nice to see another living being (who was not named Jones). The vulnerability in the kid's eyes begged for help. Henry couldn't raise himself against that. He plastered an artificial smile across his face. He thought the boy could use the sentiment.

"Don't worry," Henry spoke. "As soon the sun comes up, we'll get you out of there. Another five minutes and the streets should be empty."

Sleep had diluted the strong dose of painkillers in Henry's system and the rush of localized pain accumulated once again in his hands and face. He was saving some of the antibiotics for Shanna in case something had happened, but figured, amidst the grueling stabbing and itching sensations, that he could spare a few more pills for himself now. Plus, they would be useless if he never found her. He walked over to the pharmacy bag, popped open the brown bottle, and reared his head back to help the pills slide down his throat.

"You have *medicine?*" the boy asked with a new set of empathetic eyes.

This time the whisper was a bit amplified. Henry crinkled his nose at its sound.

"Sorry, kid. It's off limits." Henry carefully put the brown bottle back into the bag and pulled out the box of crackers. "But you look hungry."

The boy nodded, reached into the box, and grabbed a handful. He shoved them into the slit of his mouth. Crumbs dribbled like snowflakes down his chin and onto the ground in front of him. He appeared consoled and a bit more relaxed as he chewed, a welcomed feeling for Henry after the brief bout of anger minutes ago.

So this is how Quintero felt when he helped me, Henry thought, which coincidentally sparked undesired Quintero and Restricted District thoughts somewhere in the back of his mind. It took a grimace of his own to shake them. He rested his hands on his hips, watching curiously as the boy continued to eat.

The sun climbed into its usual shallow bright rays of morning, now exposing the softer side of the city's buildings. Boston harbor almost appeared normal at first glance if you looked at it the right way—the skyline, the ocean, the lonely seagulls fluttering back and forth for food, a beautiful expanse of sky, displayed with colored hues often winking at the afterthought of flickering stars—yet when his eyes adjusted to the sun's rays, what was left of the Dead and grime suddenly came into glaring focus, breaking the euphoric ideas of a once pristine metropolis.

The boy dropped the cracker box and leaned against the door to keep it open. The padlocked chains rattled slightly with his gesture.

"Thanks," the boy uttered. The word echoed into a twinge of despair. "Can I...tell you something?"

Henry sank closer to the door, keeping his voice to a minimal puff of air.

"Sure," he said.

"I don't know how much longer I can take this," the boy confessed. A single tear rolled from the corner of his eye to the crease of his mouth. "I think...I think it's catching up to me."

Henry dropped his eyes to the boy's leg, which glistened with pooling blood behind a tattered shard of cloth. His eyes returned to the boy's concerned glare, then to the makeshift tourniquet, then back to the boy's worrisome visage. The boy noticed Henry's concern, as well.

"I had to stop the bleeding," the boy explained. His eyes were tired and weak. "Cut it on a sharp piece of metal on Washington Street. Didn't even see it coming."

Henry nodded sullenly, but something felt wrong in the explanation. The boy's voice resounded in an outright lie. The deepening color of blood ran hard against the cloth. And it still appeared fresh. *This boy was bit*, Henry thought.

"Please, Mister," the boy pleaded. "Could you spare just a few of those pills?"

Henry ran through the idea in his mind, counted the capsules in the bottles, and eventually gave in.

What's the difference of two pills? Henry convinced himself. *Don't be so selfish.*

"Thank you," the boy shivered. "Thank you *so much*."

And then, in the still of that omnipotent city light, it happened.

The boy reached through the sliver of space between the door and the frame and held out his calloused palm. He couldn't have seen it coming, but Henry certainly did. There was a shuffling displacement of sound behind him, then, a blurred flicker in the fluorescent lighting. Scurrying behind the boy was a shadowed, merciless body that Henry would never forget.

The boy turned, realizing what was coming, and grasped Henry's arm with a clench that made him shake. The boy wailed as the emerging body approached, revealing itself behind him. Half of its torso was missing— ripped straight from the bone like a Thanksgiving turkey. It dragged its intestines behind it in a muck across the stairs, snapping and wriggling toward the boy at the peak of the staircase. Henry reached for the padlock, uselessly pulling at the chains to release the door, but as he already knew, it did not budge. It *wouldn't* budge.

"Hang on!" Henry yelled. "Hang...on!"

The boy's eyes filled with hopeless tears as the approaching body sank its deformed, graying teeth into his neck, ripping a chunk of skin away in a mess of stretching tendons, arteries, and veins. It ripped into him a second time and a third until the shock of nerves gave way to a concentrated blinding fear—one so potent only a person near death can truly experience. The boy's cries pounded in Henry's ears, ringing hollowly and alone, until blood filled the space in his lungs and the screams turned to nothing but gurgling spurts. There was one last, rasped breath in an attempt to plea for help.

And, just like that, it was over.

The shock of the moment rattled Henry to his core. His mind screamed with repeating thoughts of anger and surprise. It was like a bomb exploded right next to him—the ringing, the surging of boiling blood to his face, the hype of adrenaline. He peered into the opened door, searching for the boy's body.

Where had it gone? he asked. It was a useless question in a faulty time.

Instead, only the corpse stared back at him with dirty gray eyes riddled with whites that housed bulging, bloodshot veins. Its mouth fell slightly opened, allowing for its mangled tongue to slide from left to right as it swayed its head. Fresh blood ran down its undulating jaw. Henry stared back, furrowing his brow in immediate confusion. There was something different about this one, something more intelligent, something bred from a level of evil uncharacterized until now.

Its eyes seemed to be branding him, searing the silhouette of his facial features in the back of its mind, *savoring* him as if to say, *I've got you now. I'll find you. I will.* Its glare sent shivers down Henry's spine.

"Fresh meat," it spoke.

Henry jumped backward.

These things can freakin' talk? he thought. *Kill it...just kill it!*

But he found he couldn't move, like watching a car accident as it happens.

The corpse kept its silent stare focused, swaying and menacing in an unwavering stupor. He had a plan. He overrode the paralysis of his legs and hesitantly reached his hand into the door, tempting the corpse to react. Its eyes roamed from Henry's face to his arm in quick shifts, then clumsily drifted itself closer. Strips of the boy's muscle still flapped between its teeth. It finally flung itself into a crazed aggression, but Henry withdrew his arm as fast as he could, pushing hard to close the door. The metal crushed the corpse's weak frame instantly, and nearly separated the entire thing in two. Its bones crunched and spurted an oozing, syrupy blood. Then the groans ceased and the rooftop returned to its usual heated silence.

Henry fell back to the gravel rooftop, put his head between his knees, and sobbed.

Late morning brought the smell of fresh rain. A dampened moisture seemed to descend over the city in warning. Henry kept his face still between his knees. The sobs were uncontrollable, yet incredibly cathartic. He seemed to need this moment of letting go, ridding himself of the pent up anger and frustration and sadness that welled up inside of him of so many things gone wrong. He had begun to worry that he was becoming something incapable of emotion (*even* after only two days), but as he sat on the roof with streams of hot tears running down his cheekbones, he was certain that all he ever was and all he ever could be was *human*. No more. No less.

He turned his head to look, once more, at the gory mess crumpled at the foot of the door. He had killed so many of them now that he felt no pain, no remorse. But *the boy*. The boy had not been given a fair shot. *No one*, Henry thought, *deserved to be ripped open like that. No one.* It pained Henry in more ways than he could count, but one thing, amidst all of this tragedy, scared him about the corpse in the hallway: It hadn't been like any other interaction with the Dead. Its eyes had burned Henry into its retinas. It had given him an *I'm-coming-for-you* feeling that, again, made Henry want to upchuck.

And it talked, Henry thought. *It doesn't matter anyway. I'll be out of here by nightfall…but it talked.*

From the stairwell, Henry heard the undead, drawn breath of an awakening. For a few moments, he felt direly uncomfortable, but composed himself and wiped away the last of the tears from his eyes. The boy, now one of them, rose to his feet in an awkward, hunched effort. He sent his weight into the door, growling at the smell of Henry, reaching for a meal he would never receive. There would be no intelligence behind its eyes like the other, nothing to even argue for a reason to live.

So Henry picked up the baseball bat, walked over like the purest of professionals, and, with the handle, sent a shattering blow to the boy's face. It growled with the contact, fell down the stairwell, and collapsed into the wall. Blood sprayed in all directions as it met the cement wall and Henry knew that it would not be getting back up. In an odd sense, he felt he had done the boy a justice and now, he could rest in peace.

He shut the door slowly and heard the pin lock snap into place. The padlocked chains jingled and quickly ceased. There was no morning breeze. A small, stagnant cloud shaded the sun, creating a magnified shadow over the city. He returned to the pharmacy bag, emptied its remaining contents into his pockets, and walked toward the edge of the rooftop.

He realized, as he stood against the contrast of the city, that this moment was his moment of clarity. He felt the chill of the metropolis as he glanced towards the Restricted District in the distance. He could barely see the hospital, but he knew that it was there, crawling with more Dead than any other place in the city. Even the shadows seemed darker there.

And that's where I'm headed, Henry thought.

The voice in his head seemed unobtrusively loud, but he was content with the idea that the voice in his head kept him somewhat entertained. He would definitely need a bit of humor to get through the mess of his upcoming days.

Henry was not sure how much more action the baseball bat could handle, but it was the only true weapon he had ever had and, after everything it had been through, he was willing to use it until it shattered in his hands. The wood was dark with a new stain of zombie blood. The handle had chipped and dulled with overuse. The thick of the bat no longer seemed like a weapon, but rather a warped piece of driftwood. He held it as if it was a living, breathing thing and kept it at his side, gripped in a weakened clasp of fingers and thumb, always close enough to feel the comfort of its visceral energy against his thigh.

He casually jumped from building to building, slowing and quickening as he scanned the streets below. He wanted no trouble with the crazies lurking below him, but he inevitably had no choice. He watched as their bodies circled and their arms flailed at the sounds of Henry's hastened footsteps above. If he kept quiet enough, he told himself, they would not be a problem.

For the first time since he entered the city, he sensed a bit of strength within himself that he had not been aware of before. Sleep had done him well and the taste of salt from the crackers still lingered on his lips—a pleasant surprise at this stage of the game. He felt an incredible urge to fight, to go to war. He wanted to kill every last one of the Dead, but instantly realized the absurdity in his thoughts. A part of his mind bordered insanity, he confessed this, yet there was no guilt in admitting it. A person fighting for survival in this city *must* be insane in some aspect of his dealings, *right*? There would be plenty of murder in the

Restricted District. He was sure of it. And that is what he was counting on.

Several minutes passed before he reached the roof of an abandoned sporting goods store. The sign at the front of the rooftop, now battered and torn by weather, read HOWARD'S SPORTS in bright gold lettering. The azure background set a contrast that forced the letters into an illusory three-dimensional plane that reached out into the city's torpid air. The banner stretched from rooftop edge to rooftop edge, running along fifty feet of granulated salt and asphalt pellets. They crunched beneath his feet.

A lone door faced Henry from across the way. Its maroon paint glittered in the sunlight. The door was foreboding and hideous, scraped in some spots that were now rusting and peeling further down its frame. Its hinges were loose and worn, frayed by overuse or, perhaps, weathered deterioration.

It had no windows, just a simple lock that had been pried and thrown to the ground. He *was* searching for somewhere to access the road safely and without turbulence, but without a vantage point into the building, however, the thought of using the door churned the nerves in Henry's stomach. Henry knew there could very well be an ambush of meat-eaters on the other side of the frame, waiting for someone to open it, unexpectedly accepting their cordial invitation into Hell. He was still at least a mile from the Restricted District and had done such a careful job in keeping the crazies at bay. It would be a shame to let all of that effort go to waste now, just because of impatience. But Henry felt, amidst all the indecision, that *this* door was one of the better doors he had passed and, because of that, weighed the decision to open it hesitantly.

Howard's Sports was a small, two-story brick building squeezed onto an even smaller piece of property at the corner of Curran Avenue and Borthwick Drive. A towering bank complex stood at its left and an Italian restaurant with a tilted-roof sat to its right. The first floor was store— racks and shelves of merchandise, a maze of fabric and tables. He tried to picture the layouts of the second floor, but his guesses were nothing but morphed representations of stores he could remember from before the Infection. He decided the best way to figure this out was to just open the door in the end and deal with its consequences.

This is a bad idea, Henry thought. *A bad...bad idea.*

He walked contemptuously over to it, his fingers touching the metal of the doorknob. It radiated warmth against the beating rays of the sun. He prepared himself for the worst, cocking the baseball bat behind his ear, readying it to swing and turned the doorknob with one, small creak, letting the whole frame swing out and open.

69

The darkness inside flooded with natural light. Henry stepped in. There was no movement, no sign of grumbling or groaning. He found he could breathe again, but the building was far from cleared of zombie wreckage, so he kept the bat raised at it shoulder just in case.

He walked by room after room of storage, peering in like a gazelle playing *cops and robbers* with a lion. He finally lowered his guard and returned the bat to its default position at his side. It rested in the loose grip of his fingers, twitching slightly with upending nerves.

He squinted his adjusting eyes and analyzed the hallway in front of him. A window at the far end of the corridor splashed light against the walls and the floor. There were stairs protruding to the right about halfway towards the window. They led to street level.

Hesitantly, he placed one foot in front of the other and tiptoed toward the spiraling stairs.

The hardwood creaked and snapped with each forward step. Henry paused and listened, but still, heard no sound from downstairs. A small bead of sweat rolled from his forehead and into his eyes. The tension deafened the air around him and clung to his ears. He attempted to control his breathing, keeping it minimal so that any movement, shuffle, or groan could be heard over his internal sounds of anxiety.

But there was nothing.

Henry was, by no means, graceful. Being light on his feet had always been an issue growing up. Each creak of loose flooring sent him back to his childhood, to the days of hide-and-seek in the backyard, where rules were just rules until they were broken, and keeping hidden and quiet meant the difference between winning and losing, not *living* and *dying*. He placed one foot in front of the other, trying desperately not to break the silence of the seemingly empty building. If there were any crazies below him in the store, he was certain that his clumsiness could very well lead to his end...and fast...if he wasn't careful.

If there is one hide-and-seek game I need to win, Henry thought, *it's this one. Somewhere in the building, they* must *be here.*

Paranoia suddenly filled his chest in weird heaves of oxygen and pockets of air. Awkward stacks of trophies and certificates littered the floor. Basketballs, footballs, softballs, and baseballs dusted the walls in the adjoining rooms, unused for however long now. A flicker of mold crept from the baseboards and reached for the ceilings. The sports logo wallpaper had all but faded now, crinkling at the corners and folding with inattention.

The owners jet pretty quickly, Henry thought. *Get out of Dodge while you can.*

The voice in Henry's mind had taken on a life of its own, which was not a bad thing, especially after witnessing—all in twenty-four hours time—Jones' antics and the stairwell boy's unfortunate melee. He wasn't going crazy—that wasn't it—but rather a gradual, decaying descension of human trust. The voice in his head mimicked his own thoughts, so, naturally, he felt no reparation of guilt, no admonition of honesty. It was the *only* voice he could trust right now, frankly.

He turned the farthest rounded corner of the dusty corridor and stopped. In front of him, the sound of running water grew louder and rumbled the pipes in the walls. The hallway floor in front of the room had flooded, presumably a long time ago, based on the rotted condition of the wood panels. To his left was a crowded bathroom. The linoleum floor concaved with the weight of overflowed water and sloughed bodily remains. The entire structure creaked with Henry's added weight as he moved forward and peered into the rot of the lavatory.

An odor of clogged pipes and wet finish made his eyes burn. It *felt* like more than just a smell. It felt like *poison*. Bloated limbs and half-eaten skulls were piled into the bathtub like a collapsed mountain. The shower head poured a constant stream of rusted water over them, slowly dissolving the remains in a pool of infection and decay. Henry hunched over at the sight of it, flexed his abdomen, and released the remaining contents of his stomach onto the floor in front of him. The sheer surprise of the scene was enough, but the *smell*...it was the smell that sent him over the edge.

The place had been cleared, and presumably, a long time ago.

But whoever did that, Henry thought, *is sick. Why would they leave the water running? Why?*

He wanted answers, but it seemed the more he desired them, the less they would come.

He retreated back into the hallway, away from the collapsing floor and into the stairwell that tunneled down into the store lobby. The wooden steps were remarkably unaffected by the watery disaster dripping through the bathroom floorboards, but it did reek of dust and damp, which worried him to the point of leaning against the wall to take the pressure from each of his steps as he descended. Each step warbled with his weight. It seemed the noises he made in this building were amplified, booming off the walls and resonating like crashing echoes. He tried to keep his composure, but was doing such a poor job.

A weakened board snapped, but Henry caught himself before he fell through. He pulled his ankle from the hole in the staircase, avoiding the worst of its splinter-teeth scraping his ankle. He peered into the gaping hole below. It was an abyss. He couldn't see anything from this vantage point, so he broke off a shard of wood from the already shattered panel

71

and let it fall, counting, watching as it turned in the black air below. A few seconds passed until it met the floor below with a less than emphatic thud.

A hundred feet maybe, Henry calculated to himself. *Quite a drop to a basement.*

He stepped out and over the wood rot until he reached the bottom step, carefully angling his shoulders against the stairwell's back wall to hide himself from first-floor sight. The retail portion of the store was a perfect square with a rectangular wooden desk stationed at the back corner of the room. Clothing racks littered the interior space and shelves piled high against each of the four exterior walls. At first glance, the space seemed cluttered, but after a longer look, the store appeared meticulous and oddly organized. The ceiling was high and painted the color of ocean waters after a thunderstorm. Two ceiling fans hung motionlessly symmetrical on either side of the room, bulging with swollen water damage from the upstairs bathroom.

Henry peered around the corner of the stairs, towards the front of the store, and out the glass entrance doors. A pair of crazies wandered chaotically in the street. They shuffled and stumbled in circles, keeping close to the other, and sometimes bumping into its partner, erupting a brief, but destructive feud between the two.

They feel no pain, Henry thought, but he already knew that. He watched as one ripped a flapping piece of graying skin from the other.

The wound seeped with chunked muscle and blood, but the exposed one didn't even flinch. Instead, it proceeded to throw its attacker to the ground and repeatedly stomp on its back. When it gave up on the beating (the fight was over before it began), the second wounded body returned to its feet, overly hunched now and swollen with a broken shoulder blade, walking as flexibly as it had before.

Henry kept his shoulders against the stairwell wall.

If I wait, he thought, *they might go away.*

The rest of the street—what Henry could see from his rigid position—appeared empty. But, as he watched, the crazies only walked in circles, never wandering farther than fifty yards from the store's entrance. A sudden claustrophobic urge of escape quickened his heart. He contemplated a sprint through the doors, out into the street, but it was a risky thought—one that might get him killed:

Just try and catch me. They have no chance…too damn slow.

But he thought better of the notion and relaxed his tense shoulders. The crazies were not slow at all. Convincing himself otherwise was a bad idea. The shadows housed many more of those things out in the many crevices of Curran Avenue. He was certain of it. *That* was something he simply could not risk. He breathed deep and shuffled low into the body of the store.

He disguised himself behind a rack of collared shirts and khaki shorts. The Dead circled hungrily outside. When they shifted focus (which seemed a rare thing), Henry took advantage, shuffling closer to the entrance, all the while hidden by the merchandise in the windows. He kept himself still by holding his breath for as long as he could. His pulse thumped heavily in his chest. It was an anchor tugging at the anxious nerves through his body.

Halfway to the glass, Henry heard the ring of gunshots from a distance. The pops were loud and clear and undeniable. For a moment Henry heard Quintero in the bangs, but erased the notion from his mind, if only for the sake of sanity. The spark of noise caught the attention of the Dead. Their shoulders straightened and their eyes perked with starved interest. From underneath the clothing rack, Henry watched a flurry of bodies propel into the sea of buildings farther in the distance, following the trail of sound.

This is my chance, Henry thought. *Go! Go now!*

He slipped through the glass doors and onto Curran Avenue.

The streets had cleared and now stood empty against the breaking winds, funneling through the alleys between deserted skyscraper buildings and retail stores. More gunshot blasts thundered in the west, so in a quick fleeting moment, Henry sprinted northeast towards the Restricted District. Pillows of clouds circled the sun, moving in a hidden current of atmosphere towards the harbor. He could see more, darkened clouds filtering in from the west. The baby blue of the sky burned into a rich cobalt that glistened the dirty Boston water with shimmering crystals. Henry only caught glimpses of the harbor between the buildings as he ran, but it looked so beautiful in contrast to the rest of the city. Curran almost felt normal with the absence of crazies, minus the streaks of blood smeared against the tar and torn pieces of flesh and bone littering the sidewalks.

He followed the street as it veered north after a quarter mile, circling back towards the hospital at the northern end of Borthwick Drive. As long as Henry could hear the bullets ringing (although the gunshots were now fading into sporadically spaced noise now), he knew there was little chance he would run into any of the crazies.

He had attempted to pace his breathing when he started, but now, his panting sat heavy in his chest. It was becoming more and more difficult by the second to catch his breath. His battering ram of a heart punched against his ribcage. Sweat dripped from his face and into his eyes and mouth. He tasted the salty rolling drops against his tongue while he pushed out longer strides. The wind felt pleasant against his overheated face, giving him a reason to stay hyper alert.

And then he saw the pack of crazies migrating at the far end of the street. His mind snapped and propelled his feet backwards against the most neighborly building. Had they seen him? He turned his head and caught a second glimpse. *No,* Henry thought. They had not seen him yet, but he was certain they could smell him. More bodies joined the mob as they passed avenue after avenue, filling the street with a viscous, rolling speed.

He had to think quickly. *Improvise. Stop shaking. Think.* He tried to calm his heavy breathing. *Go back to Central Avenue,* he thought. *Cross over to Borthwick from there.*

From where he stood, the shadows evolved into deathtraps. He sprinted back toward Howard's, but took a sharp corner well before the crazies could see him.

Central Avenue was dark with blue and black angles of light; a breeding ground for death and chaos. Henry smelled the decay before the lenses of his eyes could see hundreds of motionless bodies that littered the street. Flies and other foraging insects made the air dense and hard to breathe.

Jesus Christ. This is a goddamn war zone, Henry thought.

He plugged his nose with his thumb and index finger, but quickly surrendered the idea when he started swallowing handfuls of flies in the process. He gasped for air, but each breath felt as though he was breathing through a plastic bag. He tried desperately not to heave, but the smell burned his nostrils even as he pinched them shut. It was an odor to which he simply would never adjust.

At the far end of the road, Henry could see Borthwick Drive and, from out of the shadows, he noticed three meat-eaters on their hands and knees, dining on, what appeared to be, a pair of very fresh deaths. Their faces were covered in thickening blood and gnarled meat. One was missing an arm. The other two appeared to be as able-bodied as they came. They ceased gnawing on the feast of shredded muscle and turned their heads toward Henry's drumming footsteps as he turned the corner.

Henry threw himself against the shadows of the building to his left. He hoped they hadn't seen him, but he hadn't really thought through a plan if they had (and he knew what *usually* happened in those situations). He arched his neck to see if they had moved toward him, but they hadn't, returning to their meal instead—a good sign. The gristly sounds of chewing and smacking lips intimated and consumed him. As he stood, he tried listening without intent, but the noises seared into the storage bins of his brain anyway.

He pursed his lips and moved, hurrying across the street as quickly and silently as possible. He kept low to avoid distraction and an all-out attack, although a hunch told him that he would not leave this alley without a fight. Within only a few steps, Henry tripped over the sidewalk and nearly fell hands first to the concrete. The sound of awkward footsteps once again filled the alley as he caught himself, producing another interested turn of heads from the crazies. One attempted to get off its knees and follow the sounds, but second-guessed leaving the meal. It returned to the belly of its victim.

If I can surprise them, he thought, *I have a chance to make this an easy fight.*

The mob of bodies he had avoided on Curran Avenue passed behind him in hundreds now. The lead creatures spiraled in crazy movements. The others followed just as wildly. Raucous footsteps roared across the urban plane in a stampede-like fashion. The three alley creatures once again raised their eyes, but did not move, too focused on the rapidly disappearing, opened bodies in front of them. The mob's hands and mouths dripped with fresh blood in passing. They had killed and eaten.

He was right in the thick of it now, whether he wanted to be or not. His only hope now, he concluded, resided in quiet deception.

The street on the opposite side of the alley bodies remained empty. He questioned his decision to leave Howard's so soon. *Why had he been so impulsive?* Perhaps it was the need to find Quintero, to find Shanna? Perhaps he felt as though there was nothing else to do but run? Sometimes movement is more than just escape. Sometimes it's survival.

The sun hung in the sky almost directly above him. Time vanished quickly out here. Maybe it was the constant awareness or the imminent fear of death, but regardless, time *flew* and seemed to never return.

The alleyway bodies rose to their feet, almost simultaneously, and began shuffling south towards Henry. They had eaten almost the entirety of their victims and left only bone and remnants of what had once been human behind. They wandered closer with grotesquely elasticized torsos; their stomachs jutting into protuberant half-spheres of rotting skin. Their jaws clanked open, dripping and drooling semi-coagulated blood in streaks across their faces. Scrapped muscle-skin sloughed down their chins. Their decision to move surprised Henry and he fell back further into the shadows that covered the sidewalk. He straightened his back against the building and held his breath and body tense.

Henry grimaced. These were the most gruesome of the Dead he had seen so far. He held his breath comfortably, avoiding the monstrous stink. Flies swarmed and landed on the skin of his arms and face, scurrying and flicking their filthy little wings in patterned quavers. All around him were sprawled bodies. All were dead and lifeless.

Then he felt the pinpointed legs of a fly wriggle its way up his cheek and into his nose. The fluttering of its wings shimmied farther into his head, tickling as it moved upward into the chasm of his face. A second fly followed the first, then a third attempted to jam its fat, scaly body into his other nostril. He could almost feel them squirming in his eyeballs before it forced a brutally loud and messy sneeze into the palm of his hand. The noise shifted the passing creatures' focus to the sidewalk, where Henry lurched the bat over his shoulder, suddenly resigning the need for disguise. They rushed toward him in growling anger.

He swung the bat thrice, connecting with the skull of one and the shoulder of another. The bodies collapsed to the ground in forceful heaps. The third swing was a hard display of muscle, resulting in a shattering spray of wood splinters, separating the weapon into two disproportionate halves. He clutched the thin handle as it snapped, refusing to let go although the momentum of his swing sent him falling to his back on top of a pile of several slain and bloated bodies, crushing bones and organs on his way down. A deeper, decrepit stench filled the air in the moment. He couldn't breathe without tasting the sour smell in the back of his throat. The meat of the bat landed about fifteen feet from where Henry fell, just out of reach.

The staves at the end of the handle were still sharp and staggered enough for perfect defense, much to Henry's chagrin. One of the Dead twitched its way towards him, bending its rigid torso and opening its jaw. Henry reached up and pierced the handle of the bat through the creature's neck. Blood squirted and gushed onto his chest as the body gurgled, then went limp on top of him. He pushed it away with little difficulty and returned to his feet, preparing himself for another threat.

The first two bodies attacked a second time, but much slower now. These were crazies, but luckily for Henry, brutally mangled ones at that. He slashed the air with the shattered handle, connecting with a left eye, sending skin and brain matter in a river of blood and swabs of jelly-like skin. The last of the upright creatures ran at him in an uncontrollable rage, flung itself at Henry, but instead, collided into the wall behind him —full-force—with a sound that resembled a log snapping in a campfire. Henry turned and finished it with a final downward twist of the handle.

There was a harmonious silence, but Henry knew it certainly would not last. He had made a lot of noise and, surely, there were other crazies who had heard.

He breathed in, then exhaled deeply, releasing his momentous, shaking nerves. Hot, sticky blood soaked through his shirt and covered his skin. His clothing clung to his chest and weighed heavily against his shoulders. He peeled it from himself in an attempt to ring it out with his hands in disgusted swipes, but the blood only smeared his fingertips and stiffened. He wiped it away on his partially-drenched denim jeans and watched as the liquid turned to a dull stain across the fabric.

He stumbled back into the street, lightheaded, overtly aware of the tension that surrounded him. He gained enough composure to jog to the start of Borthwick Drive where he had first seen the three Dead. The street was a mess of mangled bodies, litter, and a few spacey Dead fumbling and flailing in crazy screeches of paranoia. Out ahead, the hospital loomed in the distance, towering like a macrocosm of death and horror. The harrowing task was finally in full view—the heart of the Restricted District.

I'm coming, Quintero, Henry thought. *I know you're here.*

He kept close to the nearest building, still immersed in the shortening shadows of early afternoon, clinging to the shattered bat handle as if something was waiting for him around each alleyway he passed. His white-knuckled grip on it produced a natural, enigmatic source of power that twitched the muscles in his forearms. The staves were now stained red and snapped in several places, but when it came down to it, he knew it was only a matter of time before he would have to use it again, regardless of how well he thought it would work. That idea grew increasingly more disparaging in his mind, unleashing another wave of ceaseless nerves like electrical currents up his ankles to his jaw.

That time might be now, he thought.

Another group of crazies wrestled only fifty yards ahead, in sight and hearing distance.

He tensed his shoulders so tightly at the sight of them that they cramped mercilessly at the base of his neck and shot ringing, painful pangs up into his skull and down into the muscles of his upper back. He opened his mouth to let out an aching groan, but caught the noise before it left his throat. His entire body spasmed for want of water...or food, both of which he no longer possessed, yet somewhere along these chaotic streets, there *had* to be something left by the looters, anything at all to curb the pangs of want within him, right? If only he had the time to sneak into a building to eat without worry of an attack of some sort.

Out of all the things to think about right now, he argued with himself, *you choose food? Get it together or you'll die out here.*

He shifted rigidly against the buildings' cool surface in slow, methodical strides. The sun shifted in the sky another several degrees to the west and hung there like a battle scar. Shadows lessened, some disappeared, and were replaced by a solar heat that bore down on the stink of the city. It mutated further into another potent, sizzling display of unbearable odor. Henry quickened his pace and pushed himself up even further against the wall, shuffling from building to building up Borthwick Drive in an awkwardly, erect position.

Only one thought invaded his mind as he came closer to the crazies in the street—if the shadows disappeared completely, he would have nowhere to hide. Borthwick Drive would no longer be an overrun metropolitan street, but an overrun insane asylum filled with lunatic, murderous patients with no one to kill but him. If he had any chance of surviving this (which he now was beginning to seriously doubt), he would have to delay exposure for as long as he could. Even then, there were no guarantees.

The shadows lessened even more. The tips of his bloody sneakers soaked in sunlight. He shuffled into a darkened spot directly across from two of the Dead. One stopped, sniffed the air in repetitive snorts, turned its balding, spotty head towards Henry and bore its gnarly, broken teeth.

It can smell me, Henry thought, *but if it saw me already, I'd be dead.*

Instead, its only intention seemed to be a not-so-thorough investigation of the area. Henry remained improbably still, so still that he reverted to an internal place of immobility within himself. Paralysis, wrought by fear, anger and courage, took hold within him, embracing him like that of an old friend. The creature lurked forward, leaning in on an imaginary railing. It grinned another sinister smirk, filled with deep brown and green teeth, laced with foul, steaming breath. It snorted once again, sending a stream of snot down its lips and neck, then, presumably bored, turned and shuffled back to the road.

For a moment, Henry felt the elation of escape—a spirit of excitement—filling his veins with lifeblood and pumping his heart in accelerating rhythmic pulses. He knew that without the bat, he was much more vulnerable than he had ever been. The jagged ends of the handle would only aid in these bloody incidents for so long. *And then what?* He would be forced to fight naked with only hands and feet, which even Henry concluded, was not the best course of action. It was only a matter of time before his lungs and weakening muscles surrendered to the cruel power of the Dead mob.

He thought of Shanna and the dwindling chances he would see her. The sight of the darkened hospital offered no relief of this, only an eerie backlash of disappointment. He thought of a Miami breeze, the Alps and their snowy white peaks, the countryside of a Michigan cabin in July—anything to displace his existence from the moments of the here and now. But there was no escape and Henry realized this when he met the face of a bloody and badly ripped, gray-haired crazy as he turned out of the shadows and into the light.

It was sloshing something in its mouth. Its eyes blurred with fiery aggression. Its fingers wrapped around Henry's neck and squeezed. He felt the pressure of a not-so-human grip, like a vice against his soft muscle. He was paralyzed with fear, his eyes widening with each squeeze from the Dead's palms—memories of childhood and days at the university. He thought of Shanna and the caress of her skin. He thought of the life he thought he could build after escaping the city with her. He thought of the children he would never have and the Sunday afternoons watching the sunset from behind the trees. He envisioned, what seemed like, *everything* in those few, lasting seconds.

Then a gush of blood sprayed like a water gun against Henry's face as he watched the attacking body crumple to the sidewalk. Slowly, fear replaced itself with a thin outline of a body Henry was certain he had seen before.

Is this a dream? Henry questioned within.

Death felt immanent, but oddly at a distance. Henry, half-awake and half-standing, doubled over with his back against the bricks of the suddenly overt buildings, gasping for air and holding his throat. His legs buckled. The long, dirty fingernails of the attacking crazy had pushed hard against his skin, but had not punctured—a brief window of fortunate circumstance.

"Get up!" Quintero screamed from across the bludgeoned street. "Get up or we die!"

Another slew of bodies ran towards the two men from the direction of the hospital. Henry pulled himself up, lightheaded and pants streaming with urine. His insides simply could not hold it in anymore, especially with death looming so visibly on the horizon. Quintero ripped at Henry's bloody shirt, forcing him into a clumsy left-right juggling of feet until his mind caught up to the awkward swinging motion of his hips and synchronized into a swift, propelled sprint.

"You son of a *bitch*!" Quintero bellowed. His voice swelled into a surge of untamed energy. He panted shallowly, as if in precaution. He turned and scattered a stream of bullets into the impending crowd accumulating behind them. "I told you I would find *you*."

"I thought you were dead," Henry sputtered. He yelled but could not explain why his voice had shrunk so soft. The feeling in his arms and feet were coming back now and he meant to say more, but his brain was caught in a fissure of fear and excitement. He spoke between breaths in staggered, chopped alternating syllables.

"It's all about patience with these things," Quintero responded. He fixed his eyes on Henry. Lines of confusion ruffled into his forehead. "Jesus man, what *happened* to you?"

"It's a long story," said Henry as he panted, speaking individual words through gasps for oxygen.

They turned the corner at Curran Avenue to be met by an even larger migrating pack of crazies. They reached and gargled at the sight of live flesh and accelerated with a spectral push of hunger. Quintero sent a blinding barrage of metal from his gun into the eyes of several mobbing bodies, but the pack only dissolved the killed crazies into rubble under their feet. Their bones crushed and organs squished and popped brashly against the weight of stomping feet. He could not kill all of them. That alone was true.

Just maybe, Henry thought, *he can slow them down.*

"The seaport!" Quintero yelled.

He spit a little as he spoke, pointing east towards the glistening, gray water. The two men stopped in the middle of the road, halfway between the seaport and Howard's Sporting Goods. The bodies behind them crashed against each other and the sides of buildings as they swam down Borthwick. They were now in overwhelming numbers, enough to return Henry to panic.

"Listen to me. There's a boat on the far dock," Quintero explained. "It's a party boat. The keys are in it. We need to get there." He tapped Henry on the shoulder hard with one of his pistols, harder than Henry had expected, then made for the water. The wave of Dead rushed closer and Henry quickly followed, as sluggishly viscous as he seemed to move.

The Dead were gaining momentum, yet the entrance to the seaport ahead seemed so close, as though he could almost reach out and grab the open gate. Henry glanced backward over his shoulder and nearly tripped himself against the clawing and scratching now only inches from the flapping of his filthy shirt. His heart fluttered into panicked patters. *Are crazies really this fast?* Quintero pushed ahead in a flurry of scissor-like strides—much faster than Henry…in fact, one of the fastest human beings he had ever seen. A few raging bullets whistled from Quintero's shimmering pistols past Henry's ear and into the senseless crowd behind him.

Oh God, Henry thought to himself, *this can't be it. Run, damn it! Run!*

Quintero was nothing but a dot in front of him now, lost in the mirage of distance and speed. He prayed he could outrun the Dead just this once, but it seemed impossible with his riddled wounds spread mercilessly across his body. His hamstrings stiffened and he wondered how Quintero had survived in the Restricted District for so long *running* and *running* and *running*. In fact, Quintero appeared just as healthy as he was when he had first met him. The more he thought about it, the more astounded he seemed with this revelation. Could he really believe Quintero was a good person? Even after what he had been through with Jones?

The bloodthirsty screams shot him back into reality. He pushed to keep distance between him and the crazies, but they reached and snapped at his heels like piranhas in waist-high water. He heard Quintero yelling something from far up ahead, but Henry could not translate the muffled words. The sound of his own harsh breathing filled his ears and echoed in the caverns of his skull.

Yet, he kept running.

The party boat rose in full view against the glistening rush of water at the shoreline. Quintero had already boarded, sloshing water up the watercraft's sides in harsh, little crests. He was untying a string of ropes from the dock and pushing the boat out and away into the rippling water. The outer edges of Henry's vision blackened once again. He was running out of breath, energy and time. His strides shortened. His legs chugged like pistons without oil. His head throbbed with rushing, arterial blood. He could see Quintero in the distance, now waving and jumping wildly. He was screaming something that Henry could not decipher.

On more than one occasion, the sweat on his arms helped Henry to slide away from the Dead's grasps. His skin glistened with dirty perspiration. He arched his back, trying to compensate for the loss of distance between them, but he lost his balance and nearly fell over twice. The first was a graceful pseudo-twirl that ended in a backpedal jab to a corpse that nearly took him to the ground. The second resulted in a large patch of shirt being ripped from his waist. All that remained was the fabric that covered his shoulders and chest—an awkward belly shirt that lined the bottom of his ribcage and fluttered in the harbor-like winds.

Henry was still about one hundred feet from the dock, but the crazies were now close enough so Henry could feel them constantly pulling him back into the horde—this time with more force than just far-reaching grabs. He tripped and caught himself once more, barely keeping his balance. The boat's motor revved, slowly at first, then in white foamed geysers back toward the port shoulder. It darted from the dock in ambient screeches. Quintero yelled something that sounded like *Jump!*, cupping his hands over his mouth like an amplifier.

The seaport smelled of sulfur and seagull feces as he crossed its open-gated threshold. Ocean liners and mounds of sand lined the untamed coastline. The water opened into a beautiful pastel of dark, choppy landscape. The sky harvested several familiar gray-black thunderclouds that rose and fell above them. A crack of thunder echoed dully from the far distance. In fact, Henry could not even be certain it was thunder at all. The sound just swelled and groaned like the crowd that continued snapping at him from behind.

He convinced himself that he could make the jump to Quintero. He would *have* to make it.

He reached the dock and felt the planks of wood bend under his weight. Each panel wobbled with the following immensity of the Dead behind him. They reminded him of the floor panelling in Howard's Sports and the floppy, mushy limbs piled to the ceiling in the molding bathroom. He could hear the splashing of bodies as they fell into the ocean water around him—another brutal memory—flailing hard and drowning as they descended to the shallow depths.

"They can't swim!" Quintero squelched. *"Just jump!"*

The dark rings that shadowed Henry's already clouded vision grew deeper and thicker, and he worried he might fall out of consciousness before he was safe enough to do so. His legs stiffened, partly because of a viscous sequence of muscular cramps and a visceral disassociation between body and mind. He felt the weight of himself lift against the *thud* of each stride and prayed that somehow—some way—he would summon enough strength to cross the finish line, to the safest spot of the moment, back with Quintero where the dull of unconsciousness could easily wash over him as he knew it inevitably would.

He neared the end of the wooden stretch and took two long, scissor kick strides, synchronizing himself with the length of the dock. The jump propelled himself over the open water and into the back compartment of the party boat. The craft reared, pushing its nose up towards the sky for a split second before splashing down sloppily against the pearly foamed, blackened sea.

Henry could hear Quintero screaming, perhaps in congratulatory *woo*'s and *yeah*'s, but his ears had stopped functioning. The intensity of the moment fled from him like a ghost and he turned in shocked gasps for air.

When the shock of safety released, he fell to his back and met his eyes with the sky. He had barely escaped death once again, but escaped it, nonetheless. He allowed the feeling of euphoric displacement to wash over his body as he glanced back, watching the crazies filter into the ocean, each drowning into the abyss of deepening water. A deep chuckle rose to Henry's throat, but somehow he suppressed it, finding, instead, the oxygen to heal his weary, tender aches and rush him into a painful, agitated unconscious sleep. He closed his eyes and fell deep into it amidst the droning of the boat's rattling engine. There would be time for laughter later, but for now, his thoughts filled with fleeting images of Shanna and a new world that seemed entirely lost.

* * *

When he woke, the first thing Henry noticed was the air. It seemed to wrap in and through everything, thick with an invisible viscosity, dripping moisture in unseen, unheard, and unfelt clumps from the sky. The temperature had dropped radically, forcing a silent chill splaying through his body. The sweat that had once lingered on his skin had long evaporated, replaced with tiny, raised goosebumps.

He had dreamt an empty dream. There was a room filled with nothing but white. He was alone and lost in the nothingness, crippled by a deep longing for color. Even the walls, which felt nothing like walls at all, collapsed into more fields of white as he touched them. There were no colors, just the absence of them. And Henry began to understand what hopelessness meant—how closely linked hopelessness and helplessness truly were.

"I'm a good man," Henry spoke. "I'm a good man."

But no one, including Quintero, could hear him.

The gunman stood at the center of the ship with his back against a padded, swinging chair, staring up into the sky.

"Looks like we're in for a storm," he spoke.

There was a tone to his voice that Henry could not find comforting.

Henry looked up and saw Quintero's foreboding words coming to life. The clouds streaked into cancerous bulbs of atmospheric explosions, shaking the boat, and pulling Henry from the fogginess that sleep had brought upon him. The cold that surrounded them was shrill and bitter.

"You see that?" Quintero asked deeply. Flickers of movement ripped through the city as his eyes caught mobs of racing bodies. A constant flow wormed their way through the streets. "We were in that goddamn mess last night."

Henry shivered and sat up into a body-heat ball. His knees rose up against his chest.

"You still think she's in there?" Quintero asked. His eyes were far away, distant from the boat. "Your girl?"

Henry shivered again, wanted to speak, but didn't. The silence evolved into a ruptured fragment of a moment.

"It doesn't matter," he said. "We'll find out soon enough. Here. Take this."

He held a thin jacket out to Henry. He took it and wrapped it around himself frantically, his teeth chattering like broken icicles falling on cement. Scattered droplets of rain fell and splattered across the coat's fabric in patterns that reminded him somehow of crushed spiders. He looked up to Quintero, who dropped his eyes and shook his head.

"We're in for a long night," Quintero rustled. Another beckoning of thunder echoed through the hollow seaside. "We just have to wait it out and try and keep warm."

"Thanks," Henry said, rather impatiently, "for saving me."

He wanted to make certain Quintero knew what it meant to him.

"Don't mention it."

The words sounded humble enough, but Quintero smiled one of his crooked smiles and brushed the water from his dark hair. The boat rocked with the short, choppy waves, each time drifting a bit farther from the seaport. A harshened, brisk wind gusted through and Henry, still chattering violently, concluded that he never wanted tomorrow to come so soon.

He would survive this, he told himself, just like he had survived everything else, but for now, Henry sat shivering against the metal railing of the boat, closing his eyes, and wishing he was anywhere else— anywhere far from quarantined Boston. He tried to think of Shanna, but a somber, shallow drowse rolled over him once again. The sounds of thunder and pattering rain sent flashes of color into his dreams like wildfire and hazy smoke. And for the few moments that reality collided with those flashing dreams, Henry was content and safe and warm.

6

The storm lasted until midmorning and rendered maddening gales of wind that gusted so relentlessly that Henry suspected the boat would tip over and into the water on more than one occasion. Henry shivered against the railing for the entirety of the night. He hadn't moved since he had fallen asleep the night before, terrified that he would not have the strength to pry himself off the floor if, God forbid, there was a reason to. The choppy water didn't bother him, but his undeniable lack of balance most certainly did. On a violently swaying boat like this, he simply did not trust himself to keep any sort of steadying composure.

Thunderclaps and watery banging noises surrounded him in deafening booms. He convinced himself that these noises were not noises at all, but instead, were nothing more than a ringing silence in his ears. This course of action worked to an extent. Shallow bouts of sleep did come to him in brief intervals, but he woke multiple times to the harsh metallic clanks of the boat clashing against its anchor and—combined with howls from the Apocalyptic cityscape in the distance—he found it even more demanding to catch a lick of useful sleep than to sit with his eyes open.

The idea of safety, however, overrode everything else that riddled his mind during this time. Even a storm as powerful as this (a storm that seemed egregiously incorrigible) offered Henry a distorted sense of well being. He was grateful for it and quavered into deep trembles under the borrowed thinly-lined jacket that Quintero had given him. He was cold, hungry, thirsty, and wet, but at least there was no worry of being eaten alive. That, alone, was enough to celebrate.

The two men endured the gusts and rainfall in silence. The effort to converse used energy they did not possess and seemed unnecessary in the least, so Quintero lowered his head and blanketed himself in the shadows, keeping quiet all the while. His eyes, as cold and piercing as they were, blended with the darkness in a mixture of chilled resonance. His hands clasped together with his fingers intertwined symmetrically in front of him, resting on his knees. The storm's ferocity drew rigid lines and rough features across his already animated face, as if he was a source of constant reckoning for Henry, preparing for the end of something that Henry could not desist. The gunman seemed to be taking in the night like a god collecting energy from the maelstrom—something like Thor would do…or the Green Lantern.

But when the rain hollowed out and the clouds retreated away into the earthen snow globe of the northern sky, Henry saw those hardened lines disappear from Quintero's face as though they had never existed in the first place. Although now, the gunman seemed transformed, reserved in a distantly pathological way. He wasn't smiling, but only gazed philosophically into Henry's weary eyes, filling the space with reciprocal shades of blues, oranges, and shimmering yellows of the vanquished lightning from the previous night.

The two men were soaked through with rain. The water rinsed their badly stained skin clean and laundered their clothes enough so that the fabric returned (tainted, a bit) to its original color. Henry's jeans, however, chafed the skin around his groin. The damp denim clung to his legs, scratching and tightening like oddly shaped boa constrictors, but the irritation had already started taking its toll. He repositioned carefully—when he did so at all—to make certain that he wasn't going to make the rash worse. Several times, he attempted to hide the look of pain, but Quintero undoubtedly knew, as he always did.

"Now that you've got your first taste of the city," the gunman spoke. It was strange to hear the gunman's voice in calm, uninhibited, rhythmic syllables. "You still want to find your girl? No one would blame you for backing out now. You did the best you could."

It was a serious question, one worth digesting at the very least. After what he had seen, was there really any chance that Shanna was still alive? Even if there was—even one so minuscule—how could he live with himself, knowing he abandoned her to those bloodthirsty monsters? He knew it would be easier to take the boat and leave the city once and for all. It would be easier to believe that there was no way that Shanna had survived all of this, that she had died a gruesome and perilous death because of him. It would be easier to convince himself that Shanna was no longer his responsibility, that he no longer had connections to the city of Boston, and that a normal life and another well-suited girl awaited him in Brazil or India or Spain.

But this was not the case.

Henry nodded, acknowledging with a firm answer to the question.

"We keep going," he barked.

Quintero half-chuckled, half-snorted, running his hand through his hair. The leather jacket he wore was dry now, only minutes after the rain had stopped, and somehow appeared newer from what he remembered of the thing, although, at a closer look, he could see streaks in the leather that mimicked strips of beef jerky—hard, chewy, impossible pieces that wrinkled and shriveled with lack of moisture. Something about the jacket made the gunman look *real*, untouched by the city.

"I have to give it to you," Quintero spoke. "You're one crazy son of a bitch."

Even the boat appeared abstract in the new morning sunlight. It was larger than Henry had remembered. Four buoy-like platoons held its platform's weight uniformly. It leaned slightly with the added weight of Henry and Quintero, but not enough to be noticed. The half-shelter that rose over the back end had ripped sometime during the night and was now useless. Someone had taken the tarp, probably in a fit of escape back at the start of the Infection, leaving only the skeleton of what it used to be.

Out of the glove box, hidden conveniently under the hard plastic of the steering wheel, Quintero revealed a slightly faded map, folded into eighths and creased at the corners. At the top of the paper someone had written PROPERTY OF THE MARY MARIE in black permanent marker, scribbling each letter in a type of cursive typography. Tiny smudged smears appeared where someone had touched the title before it had the chance to dry. The running ink looked like blood.

Quintero unfolded it, spreading his hands out over the paper to unfold the creases.

"We're here," he said, pointing to the seaport against the right side of the paper. The image of the harbor was a quaint, curved stroke of blue against a busy matrix of city lines.

"Lowell is here," he continued. "We need to find the best route of getting there without gaining too much attention from those crazies over there."

Henry nodded again in full agreement. It seemed impossible to reach Shanna without attracting a tail of bodies. Sure—they could roof jump, but getting through the harbor to a safe rooftop was something that, again, required firepower that the two of them simply no longer possessed. A lump formed in Henry's throat with the absence of a good plan.

Quintero ran his finger up the paper, following Lowell Street into the city until it met the location of Shanna's abandoned complex. He followed the coastline with his eyes, forming an invisible adjacent line where the water met the corner of Congress and Lowell Streets.

"We'll start here," said Quintero, nodding to accept the words as he spoke them.

Henry peered down at the intersection where Quintero held his finger on the map. It was located farther out from the seaport (in the direction they were heading) into strange waters that ventured outside the city limits. Henry rubbed his eyes in frustration, sighing to release an exposed lack of excitement to climb the walls yet again.

"If we go that way, we'll be out of the city walls," Henry added. "We don't have any way of climbing a wall that size. The waterfront's made the cement smoother and harder to grip. Believe me, I tried to find the best way in when all of this started."

Quintero contemplated Henry's thought in a lengthy silence, breathing slowly as if to keep his mind calm and clear. His eyes shifted, but in slow angular movements as he began to nod slowly once again, as though planning to keep his conclusions to himself.

"I know somebody," Quintero spoke through a suddenly deepened voice. "Good friend of mine for a long time. He can help us scale the wall."

"How?" Henry questioned.

The gunman glanced upward into Henry's line of sight and smirked.

"Do you *really* think I'm the only one in the city with an urge and *ability* to kill those things?"

Henry weighed his response, but ultimately said nothing.

"He lives on that side of town. He's the watch guard. Tells everyone he meets that he's the only true sniper left here. We share the ammunition bunker. He only needs a certain kind of bullet anyway. It doesn't bother me."

Quintero folded the map, hid it away once again in the glove compartment, and started the boat's engine with a roar of white foam. A dozen crazies caught its attention from the shore and flopped themselves into the water at the shore's edge. They struggled as the ocean swallowed them whole. Henry squinted into the sunlight, now far enough away from the rancid smell emanating from the city that he could breathe a healthy, introspective sigh of relief. He spat into the current and watched as the boat sped off into the open plains of water.

The *Mary Marie* chugged through the coastline with the wind raging against Henry's face. The damp air reminded him of summer afternoons spent in New Hampshire at Aunt Marilyn's house in Lake Springs. She lived on a farm with wooden shutters on each window, painted red against the aging color of its natural wooden frame, weathered by half of a century of winter snow, spring rains, and summer heat. Somehow the memory of the place had matured in his mind like a good scotch and projected itself against the back of his eyes in nostalgic images.

The farm itself, Henry recalled, had been passed down from generation to generation until its legacy hit a snag with Aunt Marilyn. She was, by no means, a farmer—not even a drop of farm life ran through her veins—yet her father (Henry's grandfather) had entrusted her to the estate in his long-winded will. Instead of selling off the land, as many thought she would, she hired a farmhand to handle the livestock while she kept to her own decorative underpinnings in the house itself. She spent the remainder of her days reading by the fireplace or gardening vegetables in the patch in the backyard or opening her doors to relatives or friends who came to visit.

About fifty paces from the house stood a towering barn constructed from planks of gray wood. It housed twelve cows, a dozen or so hens, and ten piglets (which later grew into full blown swine). Henry, as any young boy on vacation would, stayed up late into the night listening to the clucks and snorts that rustled the leaves in the forest behind the robust plains of grazing pastures. In every direction, the swollen rolling hills hugged the farm and brushed the world with the color of soft saplings breaking through hard earth. To a ten year old boy, Aunt Marilyn's farm may as well have been a glimpse into heaven.

For Henry, it was no exception.

By day, the cows grazed the land and fell to their bellies in approaching storms.

"It's a way of predicting weather," Aunt Marilyn had said. "Cows can tell you everything need to know about a storm."

Her blue eyes crystalized in the irenic sunlight and Henry stared into them with innocent amazement.

"You see over there?" she asked, pointing to a heifer about one hundred yards into the field. "The younger ones know better."

Henry watched as an older beast, with its elongated, overused utters swaying in its walk, joined its young with little hesitation. It curved its hooves inward and fell to its belly all the while keeping its stare focused into the afternoon sky.

Aunt Marilyn wrapped her arm around little Henry's shoulders in a casually intimate embrace before they walked back to the farmhouse to join the rest of the family, anticipating the sweet smell of thunder-rain accumulating in the damp threatening air. From the red painted windows, Henry loved watching the gentle summer breeze snap into violent gusting winds and cracks of thunder that shook him alive. It wasn't just the idea of extreme weather that he loved. It was the idea that he was in the knowing, that he was present in the moment when nature reared its ugly head.

He had always been fascinated with thunderstorms, but from a distance. As long as he had a roof over his head and a place to protect himself, he liked them. But in honesty, the sheer immensity of darkened clouds and that familiar, angry stillness only frightened him into a fearful curiosity. Thunder he could stand, but lightning was another animal altogether. When those jagged laser shots of electricity bolted from the sky, Henry would retreat from the windows in scared, backward steps, his heart fluttering as the thunder boomed loud just behind it, rattling the farm's antique china and hung picture frames surrounding him. To be fearful, yet absolutely amazed (in the same moment) was a mixture of feelings he might never understand—not even now, after the most exposed storm of his life—on a boat in the middle of the ocean with a stranger that now seemed like his best friend.

Henry filed these memories of Aunt Marilyn back into the yellowed anthology pages of his mind where they belonged.

The harbor docks soon ended and gave way to the outer city barricade, emerging from the rough ocean waters and rising into the etherial skyline. Surprisingly, the *Mary Marie* rode easily through the hastening currents, like an experienced horse trekking through the expanse of murky clam flats. The constant pulse of the motor whinnied in fixed equestrian-like cadences, ringing in Henry's ears and drawing him closer to a paralyzing annoyance, but Quintero continued to steer parallel with the wall where the water seemed most choppy, regardless of the motor's noises.

The walls sloped higher and steeper until only the tops of the lonely skyscrapers hovered above its roughened summit plateau. Even the spread of high-rises appeared thin and ruinous now, as if they had lost their pharaonic luster long ago.

Henry perspired softly in the heat of the morning's light. It had already begun drying his clothes and bathing him in a blanket of coruscation he had not felt in days. The chafing against his groin and the wet denim dissipated slightly. He was thankful for that. Beside him and over the edge, water lapped against the metal platoons in rugged, uneven crests. He yearned to graze the water with his fingertips—its crisp, inviting semblance was a large part of that—but he reminded himself of how dissonantly bitter it would be and ultimately decided against it.

Quintero was silent and focused, keeping the steering wheel steady, turning it only slightly to remain parallel with the barricade line. A crumpling furrow formed at the gunman's forehead. He opened his mouth as though he was about to speak, but forcibly shut it as quick as it had opened. Henry studied him, wanting to know what the gunman was thinking, but, like the gunman, withheld comment. He was sure he would find out soon enough.

Quintero finally cut the motor about a mile from the harbor and Henry felt the water catch the boat's underbelly, lurching it forward and then back in smooth sways. The gunman hopped to the starboard side of the boat and balanced himself, leaned over the lip of the railing, and raised his eyes toward the top of the wall.

Henry could see the flashes of gunmetal holstered neatly through his belt as Quintero lifted his arms in exaggerated waves.

What are you doing? Henry thought. *There's no one there.*

"Ross!" the gunman boomed.

The name bounced off the cement and echoed. He waited a few moments, cleared his throat, and scratched the top of his head as if he expected an uproarious response to the call. Again, he bellowed the name, then motioned for Henry to join him at the railing.

"His name is Rosco. He has a hot temper, but he's a good kid."

Henry nodded, although he sensed a bit of worry creeping somewhere within.

"He'll try and give you a hard time, but he won't do anything stupid. Understand?"

"What is he doing up *there*?" Henry asked. He wanted to ask a flurry of questions, but settled for just one.

"He sits up there and snipes the Dead. He's getting better than when he started. That's for sure. They get all confused and start running every which way when they hear the first gunshot and then *there's Ross* pounding bullets into their brains. I bring him food every once and awhile to keep him happy. That way, if I ever need a quick way into the city, he helps me out."

Henry probed the precipice, but saw no sign of climbing gear out over the wall. Its absence perplexed him. How could *one* man find a way to pull someone up a ledge of this height? So when Henry saw the figure look out over the edge and wave down, he kept quiet and listened as Quintero did the talking.

"Quin! You come with food? I'm starved up here."

Quintero fumbled the words in his mouth at first, swishing his tongue until he remembered the movements and shapes his mouth could make.

"I need a favor, Ross. This is Henry." The gunman raised his arms towards Henry. "His girlfriend's trapped in the city close to here. Can you get us up?"

There was a silence. Quintero bit his lower lip and waited for a response, producing a vague hint of tension in the lack of noise. Even the sloshing water below the platoons ceased its slapping of metal for a few uninterrupted moments. It worried Henry a bit.

"*Really* though? No food?"

Quintero smiled like a guilty man smiles at a mistrial. A large basket fell from where Rosco stood and plummeted to the water with airy speed. It crashed at the wall's edge and floated against the uneven oceanic currents.

"I'll go first," Quintero spoke. "I'll let him know you're alright. He won't like it if you go first."

"What's his deal?" Henry asked—a statement that seemed paradoxically comical, yet grave in the same instant. "Not a people person?"

"You don't make it this long without taking precautions. You of all people should know that by now," Quintero replied.

A brief glimmer shone in the gunman's steel eyes, perhaps a secret left untold, unrivaled by Henry's astute, but unyielding observations. There was some sort of history between Rosco and Quintero, *that* Henry knew, but he could not pinpoint it based off of conversation alone. Perhaps they had been runners together. Perhaps Quintero had saved Rosco's life, or vice versa. But one thing was certain—Quintero's eyes held the key to these secrets, locked away for some other time, yet here, in the boat, it only produced the kind of doubt that turns men into their worst fears.

Henry dropped the anchor overboard. The boat stabilized below him with its weight and suddenly felt solid. Quintero hopped easily over the metal railing and into the basket, which was near enough to cross without hitting water. He gave Rosco a stark thumbs up from the basket. A prick of momentary loneliness filled Henry as he watched Quintero slide upward, scratching the basket against the cement on its way up. The gunman reached the top lip in only minutes and flopped the basket on its side up and over the precipice. The two men met in a prolonged embrace, then disappeared over the cement tower.

There was nothing left for Henry to do, but wait.

For several minutes, all that Henry could hear was the rapping of the choppy current as it lapped against the boat and the base of the sea-caked wall. He thought of the ocean in the summer and palm trees and rope swings and jetties to keep himself occupied—how they had brought him hours of fun and sunburnt skin when he was a child. He thought of anything that took his mind off the idea that Quintero had left him on a boat without the key, stranded on the outskirts of a zombie-filled metropolis. He wrapped his arms around his chest and futilely attempted to warm himself. His clothes were still too damp to do any good.

Ten minutes passed and Henry could feel the onslaught of despair drilling into his brain. He kept his eyes focused at the top of the wall, but saw no figures or basket drop for him. He began tapping his leg in an anxious fidget. His groin continued to ache and throb with a painful, although no longer stinging, chafe. He knew there would be a rash there —a sweltering, angry red rash—but he had more important things to worry about in this moment than the pain radiating from his crotch, so he adjusted himself against his underwear and jeans until he found a comfortable position (comfortable enough to take his mind off the awkward genital throbbing).

The pain tried his patience, but he kept his eyes focused on the wall's peak nonetheless.

Then, in the fifteenth minute—yes, Henry was counting—a lone figure peered out over the wall's lip and slipped back. He could not tell if it was Quintero or Rosco, or if it was even one of them at all, but when the basket appeared and skidded its way down the side of the cement, Henry knew that he had not been deserted and could trust this Rosco kid after all.

Stop doubting Quintero, the voice in his head barked. *He's done nothing but help you.*

The voice was right. Quintero had given him no reason to doubt, yet he continued to do so anyway. It was his newfound Jones complex. It had to be—*trust no one, kill everyone.*

He flopped over the railing and into the basket, not as gracefully as Quintero had, but just as efficiently. He raised his thumb up, mimicking Quintero from before, so that whoever was pulling could start. He felt the soft rumble of rope as it tensed and pulled against the wall. Drops of water dribbled as the basket lifted from the ocean and climbed the partition one clink at a time.

Quintero and Rosco were waiting for him at the top. Once the metallic clanks of the basket crank ceased, Henry jumped out in a swivel of nervous emotion and glanced around. The top of the wall was not very wide and, in fact, the three of them took up most of its width. To Henry's right was the large rusted machine that had, he assumed, pulled the basket from below.

"Made it myself," he spoke. "Does the trick, wouldn't you say?"

Henry nodded and smiled faintly, still mildly skeptical, although holding out his hand in a casual invite to handshake.

"The name's Henry," he spoke, introducing himself. His name projected from his throat in an amplified, brassy tone, one he abjectly did not recognize. Rosco stared at Henry's hand with his own palms still stored away, each housed in their respective armpits. He was wearing a leather jacket, similar to Quintero's, except Rosco's did not fit his build. Instead, it hung loose against his body as if it was a sweatshirt rather than something made for formal attire.

Henry pursed his lips in reluctant acceptance of Rosco's rejection and lowered his hand.

He'll try and give you a hard time, Henry remembered, *but he won't do anything stupid.*

The air seemed cooler at this altitude and Henry watched the crazies swarm the streets in the distance. His eyes naturally followed the largest road in front of him. It was perfectly linear, unlike most of the streets in Boston, and clear with a cluster of buildings stacked on either side. Most of them had angled roofs, not easy for roof jumping in the least bit.

He reverted his eyes back to Rosco, who stood with his weight firmly planted against his right foot while his body leaned to compensate. He was much thinner than Quintero and seemingly uneven. Every part of his body appeared frail (although Henry agreed that this was probably not the case), except for his neck and head, which appeared muscular and disproportionately large. It was not a *deformed* disproportionality, but enough to notice a distinct contrast in the way his body was shaped. His eyes glistened a bright brown with stannic specks of green. A trimmed, but growing beard lined his jaw.

Quintero, however, appeared even more chiseled and violent against Rosco's lean frame. It seemed every time Henry laid eyes on the gunman, he aged into something more terrifying, less innocent. He cracked his neck and grimaced vainly as it popped. Somehow Quintero made Henry feel more comfortable, safer, in Rosco's skeptical presence.

"Ross agreed to help us get to your girl," Quintero spoke, breaking the silence.

Rosco released his hands from his armpits and let them fall to his sides.

"I owe him one," Rosco replied.

His voice assumed a tone of wanted defiance, yet Henry believe he sensed a bit of assurance in there, as well. It was as if Henry had just entered a strange rite of passage without even knowing he had done anything of the sort. Rosco shifted the weight of his body from his right foot to his left foot in a serene display of movement. His left hand rose to and rested on his hip.

"This is Congress Street," said Rosco.

He pointed towards the road that Henry had followed with his eyes only seconds before. He surveyed it again as it was introduced, but this time, located the vanquished, stilted house in the distance where Shanna should be. The concentrated brown was unmistakable in the midday sun, but it was impossible to see its condition from where they stood. Henry caught it in his sights, racing his heart into a shiver of excitement. He could feel it—the mystery of Shanna would be over very soon.

"Do you see it?" asked Rosco, looking out over the city.

Moisture in the form of a white, clouded mass accumulated on the horizon, past the ruinous buildings and littered city streets, past the walls far off and opposite to where they stood, rising up like steam from the world's largest furnace. Henry wondered if there was another storm approaching, which seemed to have a chance, but now, he really could not be certain where the clouds were headed.

Henry nodded, responding to Rosco's question by pointing an index finger out towards the brown complex. "Over there," he replied. "It's the brown one at the intersection about a mile down that way."

Rosco turned his head and gave Quintero an overtly diminutive glare. It was an expression that was meant for Henry's eyes, so that he knew that this mission—the mission that meant so much to Henry—meant next to nothing to Rosco. The kid was not helping because he wanted to, but because Quintero had somehow forced his hand and now, was trapped in some odd catch twenty-two, spinning his wheels against time and his own desire to push both of his guests off the side of the wall and forget this proposition had ever come to be.

And, somehow, Henry was okay with that.

"We have a plan," Quintero spoke, keeping his eyes focused on Henry.

From his pocket, Quintero pulled a small, oblong sphere and cupped it in his palm. He moved it with his fingers, revolving it like a miniature planet in orbit. Henry folded his arms and flexed his biceps against his chest while balancing questionable motives and timely schemata in his head.

"Ross was gracious enough to lend us one of his grenades. I stashed them away after the Infection started. You can never be too prepared. Right Ross?" Quintero clucked softly, but mostly to keep Rosco's temperament at bay. "We'll use this as a distraction to get us down onto the street. It should buy us a couple minutes at least." He pointed to the basket as he explained. "From there, we make a run for it. Ross can't keep all of them off of us, but he can snipe out what he can."

Rosco rubbed his eyes in a mixture of fatigue and disregard and folded his arms up into his chest once again. His leather jacket bunched at his shoulders, making him appear slightly cartoonish and a little flabby. A throaty laugh nearly burst from Henry's resisting mouth, but he caught it before it raised any flags. He could not, however, undo the gritty smirk glued to his lips. He hadn't meant to laugh, but a hearty chuckle was few and far between in this city and his *soul* apparently needed it at this moment of triviality.

It was something that Henry hoped Rosco would ignore. Fortunately, the anarchic expression blithely confirmed it in the form of Rosco's eyes, as intimidating and corrosive as they seemed, eventually shifted away from Henry in a don't-screw-with-me type of sheen.

"There's one problem," Henry spoke, trying to erase the patronizing effect from his face. Suddenly, Henry reflected back to the rooftop where he had spent the night after the battle with Jones. He remembered how dead Shanna had appeared in his dream that night. He remembered the boy in the doorway and his unfair fate. If anything, he wanted to make certain that Shanna would be safe if the plan worked. "How do we get into the house without the crazies following us?"

"Leave that to me," said Rosco.

It was a firm response and the fact that Rosco had already thought a few steps ahead put his mind at ease, so he ignored the undercurrents of irritation in the kid's eyes and averted his own back to the layout of Congress Street.

Henry could feel Shanna. He could taste her kiss on his lips. He missed the smell of her hair and how it let loose against the elastic she used to keep it out of her eyes. He wondered if those memories would ever again repopulate once the two of them were reunited. He questioned if Shanna would even be the same girl he had loved before the Infection. The day suddenly took on a bitter aura of reconnaissance and Henry shivered through it—a slave to the possibility of fate yet again.

Quintero loaded a healthy string of ammunition into a magazine at the barricade's edge and cocked his pistol.

"I'm ready when you are," he said.

Rosco walked casually a few steps past Henry and collected the long-range sniper rifle leaning against the basket-pull machine, adjusting the scope to fit his eye against the sunlight. The scope rested heavily on the top side of the weapon and reminded Henry oddly of some kind of swollen, mutant insect. What looked like dried blood had smeared and congealed on the rifle's handle. Rosco wrapped his fingers through the trigger space and lifted his eyes to his guests.

"Let's do this," he said.

Henry's ears popped as Quintero slid the pin out from the grenade.

"Here goes nothing," Quintero said.

He threw the explosive to his left and out as hard as he could. Everything blurred in the following moments, like a haze of misdirected time lost amidst a familiar landscape of space.

"Get in the basket!" Quintero yelled.

Panic riddled his words. Each syllable exited the gunman's throat with a bit of blind, rueful dependence. His hands guided Henry toward the basket until, finally, Henry flipped over its rail—with Quintero—and into its holding space.

Rosco crouched, plugged his ears, and pushed a weakly lit button that catalyzed the basket machine into its rhythmic clicking.

"Don't wait up for us," said Quintero. "We don't have a curfew."

The playful mockery surfaced a puckish grin across Rosco's face. The kid rolled his eyes and cussed under his breath. This time, though, Henry could hear the surge of honesty in the voice. "Good luck."

Then there was a distant *pop*—as if a gasket suddenly released—and a cloud of dust and fire ballooned into the sky. The explosion crippled the base of a skyscraper, sending it diagonally east towards the wall that hid the ocean from the city. The building's frame, although remaining mostly intact in its descent, creaked and bent with unnatural movement, glass shattering in a shower of shimmering shards. Henry had never seen anything like it—the version of a metropolitan Godzilla falling right in front of him. He found it difficult to even tear his eyes away.

"There must have been an easier way to do this," said Henry.

Quintero kept his eyes level with the wavering building, shrugged, remaining silent. There was a metallic *crack* and the building snapped, then shifted its weight and fell swiftly toward the wall. He could hear the chipping and cracking of the cement as the structure collided heavily with the city wall. At first, Henry thought the entire outside barricade would stop the high-rise's fall, but like a knife, the force of the building cut through the cement, sending large chunks of metal and debris splashing and sinking into the shoreline water. The ocean gulped and swallowed it all like one fantastic whirlpool.

The crazies below the basket wobbled and shuffled in the street as Quintero and Henry descended. They first perked at the grenade's heavy blast, then instantaneously began running toward it—erect and flailing— like a flock of seagulls toward a piece of bread. Noise meant fresh meat. And fresh meat meant *food*.

"Did *not* mean to do that," Quintero confessed. "Good thing those things can't swim."

Henry did not laugh at Quintero's peculiarly placed joke. He couldn't. His mind had distanced itself from things like humor and sentiment, especially since those intimate memories of Shanna sieved his thoughts. There was no longer any room in his mind for erratic, miscalculated emotions, just a necessity to finish the job he started—*finding Shanna*.

A nervous tingling in his fingers reminded him of the unfiltered excitement that complimented immanent danger. As the two of them descended, waiting for their elevator to click its final click, Henry prepared himself to waste no time when they reached the street, like a sprinter waiting for the sound of the starting gun. The rush of nerves trembled the muscles in his legs. He was ready, ready to *survive* or *die*.

The basket ceased as it met the ground and both Quintero and Henry leapt from it silently, darting into the completely emptied space of Congress Street. Ahead of them stood only open road and open skyline, but they both knew it would only be a matter of minutes before the alleys filled again with rotten bodies and that filthy smell that came along with them. It was foolish, Henry thought, to think they could reach the house without conflict, yet as Henry fell back into Quintero's brusque strides, he realized that they may, in fact, be the exception to the rule, an anomaly in an anti-anomalous predicament, and maybe—just maybe—he was on the receiving end of a break he so very desperately needed.

Only a minute passed before Henry began to feel the effects of fatigue creeping into his lungs and eyes and diaphragm. His muscles still ached from the sprint down Borthwick and, suddenly, that hopeful, elated feeling disappeared into the throes of something more realistic. He swung his arms with straight, tense hands, remembering what Mr. Goldsmith had once spoke of in high school gym class: *The more aerodynamic you make yourself, the faster you can run.* It's funny how the little memories in life somehow make big impressions. Most of what Goldsmith had taught him had been, quite frankly, a load of crap, so Henry could not understand why his mind applied this particular piece of information to such a tepid, baneful moment.

"Goldsmith," Henry muttered, attempting to clear his mind of such an officious childhood thought. "Goldsmith might save my life."

The fallen building finally settled into a bulbous disgorge of rubble against the Eastern wall. The gaping gash in the barricade, now penetrated by the welded metal of the high-rise's frame, sloshed ocean water into the city in tumescent ebbs and flows. A colossal cloud of dust flurried upward into the sky like lost butterflies swerving and diving in a shivering, malignant breeze. The smells of sulphur and seaweed compromised Henry's breathing and changed it into something more exaggerated, labored.

About halfway down Congress, a river of crazies poured into view and instinctively targeted Henry and Quintero.

"Here we go!" yelled the gunman in a sort of battle cry. He unholstered a handgun, but kept it at his side.

The vicious gnarls and snares heightened ahead of them, dismissing the chances of reaching Shanna without confrontation. *It was a futile thought anyway*, Henry reconciled. He hoped Rosco had something inventive up his sleeve to keep the crazies entertained.

What is he waiting for? Henry thought. *Do something!*

But there was no response. It was like playing a dangerous, outmatched game of chicken with no sort of reinforcement.

Henry attempted to mirror Quintero's strides, but it only seemed to slow him down, so he reverted back to his own method of running, which must have appeared even ganglier than the meat-eaters running towards him. Quintero had already gained several paces on him, veering sideways to check for skeptical movement on side streets and alleyways, and unholstering another pistol—now one in each hand.

When Shanna's complex rose into view, Henry's heart fluttered, but instantly sank when seven of the most gruesome and corrosive crazies turned the corner ahead of them. Quintero raised his gun and released a bullet that ripped into the front of one's skull. A second cartridge penetrated the pelvis of another, shredding and separating its leg from the rest of its body. It fell to the ground, leaving a trail of sloughed skin and muscle splayed against the tar. There were too many of them for Quintero to handle alone in a full-out sprint, so Henry improvised.

"Give me a gun!" he yelled. "I'll cover you. Give me a gun!"

Quintero flicked the trigger in a measured cadence and missed all but one body as he tripped and barely caught himself from falling hard to the ground. The crazy he shot fell lifeless to the street and skid across the asphalt face first. The gunman thrusted his arms out in front of him—pistols and all—and forced his feet to catch up to the rest of his moving body. Henry almost lost his breath in momentary fear as he watched. Without Quintero, he didn't stand a chance out here. No weapon. Nothing to defend himself. *And what an awful way to go, running headfirst into a pack of crazies to be slaughtered limb from limb.* Yet Quintero quickly regained his balance and Henry's eyes stabilized.

"Catch!" Quintero yelled.

He discarded an empty magazine to the street—which toppled and danced and nearly collided with Henry's shin—and replaced it with a loaded one, snapping it into the butt of its gun and tossing it to Henry so that it landed sideways in his palms; fingers fumbling in uncoordinated attempts to find its handle. When he found the trigger, he clicked back the safety and raised the barrel towards the approaching Dead. With a few quick snaps, he watched as a corpse with a missing arm and a drooping eyeball collapsed with a thick drift of half-congealed gore running from a new bullet hole in its forehead. A new elated sensation of both fear and excitement amalgamated in Henry's primal perspective of the moment. A strange ease immersed him, one that calmed the surging nerves in his arms and clarified the frenzied thoughts in his mind. The fact that the bend of his finger against a trigger could escort him to

Shanna (and to safety) erupted like surprise fireworks within him. Congress Street suddenly opened into a carnival of road kill.

They met the remaining crazies full-force in the middle of the street. Henry pressed his gun against a skull and pulled the trigger viciously, sending a hardened shoulder into another (it barreled away, smashing into the right angle of a brick building and exploding into a mash of intestines, bones, and fluids). He witnessed Quintero lead with a valiant fist into a third. The gunman's arm easily broke through the graying skin and skull as though he had punched through a bowl of gelatin, leaving a tattoo of brain matter and skin hanging from his forearm. He groaned in violent disgust.

"What the hell!" the gunman spat, shaking pads of debris from his arm. "These goddamn things *all* need to die...*All* of them!"

The words drowned in a chaotic fuel of anger that catalyzed a lightning fast barrage of bullets. Another current of bodies splayed across the street in boiling blood and tattered flaps of flesh. All lifeless.

Henry turned and locked eyes with Rosco for the briefest instant. He could hear the sequential blasts of detonated grenades to his left and right, envisioning a sly grin across Rosco's face with each pull of a pin; his cold, steel eyes glazing into calm disgust and heated focus. Bodies piled at the base of the wall—Rosco's own personal cataclysm, something to remember the moment by. Sniper rounds collided with spraying skulls in hidden alleyways to the left and right, securing the street as best he could for his runners.

Shanna's apartment building stood only a hundred feet away now, rising like a melancholy shrine in front of them, a place of both life and death, a pinnacle of Henry's upturned life. It was just how he remembered it—a lone, dark-stained cubbyhole of a living space positioned neatly between two rather large, but just as poorly maintained, apartment buildings. It loomed in the morning shadows like a dying giant. Blustering groans piled in the distance, far enough away to admonish, but close enough to recognize.

The street dulled to a frivolous peace, one to treasure as they hesitantly approached the structure.

"Well," Quintero whispered, keeping his voice muffled to make sure he did not draw attention. "Here we are."

Henry ambled to the door—the same door he had once seen in a dream —and reluctantly opened it. He mouthed the word *locked* to Quintero, who held a pistol in each outstretched hand and stood perched in a hunkered position, prepared to shoot at any sign of danger lurking in nearby alleys.

Henry fished in his pocket and found a paper clip, already bent and warm from the friction of his skin against the denim of his jeans. He untwisted it, wriggling the metal from its original position, being cautious not to wear the soft metal to its breaking point. He slid the hooked end into the latch, picking and feeling his way around the lock's internal components until he felt it catch. He pulled and heard the quiet snap of the metal bolt shift against the wood. The doorknob opened with ease.

The inner room was quiet and dark and Henry sensed the pangs of déjà vu sift through his legs. He had envisioned this all before—the ruminating quiet, the muffled groans and gunshots from a distance, the dust and dirt smearing the room. Static spasms of paralysis forced his walking into labored and bothersome stomps, rather than the graceful strides he strove for, yet the gunman followed in quick succession, disregarding Henry's lack of subtlety. A final softened explosion ended Rosco's noise as Quintero closed the door behind him. The new ruminating silence only seemed to make things increasingly tense.

Henry could barely see as it was, but now, the room was no longer entombed by the adumbral lighting of the open door. Instead, it filled with only the darkness of the unknown within. Rare droplets of sunlight seeped through the boarded windows and illuminated a slew of cobwebs swaying easily in the window frames. Dead insects crunched under his shoes. A thin membrane of dust covered the floor and walls. And Henry rubbed his eyes and squinted, apprehensive to move inward, holding the pistol out in front of him for protection's sake. He lost himself in the possibility that Shanna was no longer here.

"Over there," mouthed Quintero without sound, nudging Henry towards a slouched figure in the far corner of the room.

Henry knew it was her. The slender body slept, crouched fragilely against the corner of the room. He dropped the pistol to his side, no longer afraid of the element of surprise. He walked over to her and let the back of his hand kiss the skin of her cheek.

She's not dead, Henry thought. The amplified exclamation in his head made him smile. *Thank God. She's not dead.*

In a sweet stir of her head, she woke abruptly and pushed erect against the corner wall.

"Don't hurt me," she whimpered. "Please. Please don't hurt me."

A captivating innocence rang through her voice, almost as if a quiet, gentle breeze had somehow made its way into the building. Her eyes adjusted slowly as she sat there frozen in confusion and heightened fear.

"It's me," Henry whispered intimately. "I came back for you."

It took several seconds for Shanna to collect her thoughts. Henry caressed the skin of her ear once more and, like the rush of a drug, a

101

relay of tears formed at the corners of her eyes. She smiled and the white of her teeth shattered the darkness. Her shoulders relaxed—a weakened method of expending what energy she had left—and allowed herself to fall into Henry.

"You came back for me," she whispered.

Henry kissed her hair, feeling the warmth and let his hands probe the shape of her body as he pulled her up against him. He missed her breath, her skin, her voice. The way she seemed to stare through him. He missed it all.

"Henry," she whispered. "They're coming."

There was a small shivering catch in her voice and Henry tensed at her voice's break in timbre.

She handed Henry a small, handheld radio—the radio he left on the night he went for help. The static of the channel distorted an undulating male voice. Henry held it up to his ear. Quintero looked around the thickening room, gripping the pistols just a bit tighter, as if the next few minutes would be the worst of his life.

"What is it?" Quintero asked.

Then a dreadful silence.

"They're coming to bomb the city."

PART TWO

HELICOPTERS

7

The radio snapped and crackled as Henry turned the dial to find a receptive station. He could find nothing at first, but then settled on an AM emergency channel that replayed a looped recording in thirty second intervals. It wasn't the female voice with which he was familiar, but rather, an automated voice broadcasted in male robotic, monotone syllables. Henry listened intently: *The President of the United States has issued an evacuation order for the Boston, Massachusetts area. I repeat —an air raid has been issued for the Boston area during the early hours of Sunday afternoon. Please refer to the Center for Disease Control for other questions or concerns.*

Shanna clung to Henry, wrapping her arms around his waist as he focused, whimpering silently against him. The dark room seemed lighter now, sweeter than the dank air they had roused in their blustered entrance. It might have been the adjustment of his eyes or the relief of finding Shanna alive, but Henry sensed a euphoric kind of totality wash over him in the moment.

"We still have time to get out of here. We have a boat..." Henry said, but as he spoke, the raucous sounds of flapping helicopter blades bubbled into an unfiltered angst within him. He tried desperately to make sure Shanna did not see the expression of fear plastered on his face. He, most of all, had to be strong...*for her*.

Quintero holstered his pistols and sat down near the door with his knees against his chest.

"Ross," he whispered. His eyes widened in panic. Both Henry and Shanna heard the quaver in his voice and turned toward him. "Rosco'll have no idea what's coming. He'll assume it's a rescue mission. Or humanitarian aid. Something like that. He'll never think this. Never in a *million* years."

He pushed himself off the floor and forced a wooden plank from the window that faced the city barricades. The wood did not break, but bent enough so that he could see the street, the wall, and the helicopters all clearly. The noise stirred little movement from outside and Congress Street, Quintero noticed, laid in ruins and body parts from the house to the ocean. Open matrices of asphalt stretched forward in front of him with no threat in view, met only with the sound of the helicopters' buzzing rotor drone. He watched anxiously with panicked curiosity.

An unmoving, lifeless pile of bodies littered the area below Rosco's perch. His one-man-wrecking-crew mentality had paid off and now, he waved his arms above his head, jumping excitedly at the choppers that hovered above him, circling like vultures in the midday sun. It was an image of surreal intensity, like a painting of a perfect sky colliding with deep shades of helicopter and leather jacket blacks. Quintero had assumed correctly—Rosco had no idea of the impending raid.

Five vehicular birds swayed above the wall with the bulky weight of metal canisters fixed to their underbellies. Guilt filled the whites of Quintero's eyes. He watched Rosco's complacent unraveling, biting his lower lip so hard he nearly broke skin. The scene choked Henry into a sudden sinking feeling, not knowing what to say, as though he had just plummeted from the top of the city's highest building. His stomach lurched and a strange, sour tang riddled his mouth. What should have been a moment of euphoria had suddenly turned to moments of grave severity. He wished, with all of his mind, it would stop, but the intensity soaked his throat and lingered, burning there like a concentrated flame.

"I need to warn him," Quintero pleaded, moving towards the door.

Henry placed his hand on the gunman's shoulder, stopping him from moving any farther, empathizing as best he could. He had never heard such a sense of urgency in the gunman's voice. It made his skin crawl.

"You can't leave," Henry spoke, deepening his voice into a state of mutual gravity. "Our best shot is in *here*."

The smallest of the helicopters swayed closer to Rosco and swung its body in sleek aerial movement until its legs nearly met the plateau of the flat top. A man in black kevlar appeared from its side door. His face was stern, enough to resemble an Acropolitan statue, stiff and hieroglyphic. He carried a long-range rifle in his right hand and held the door of the chopper with the other.

The soldier yelled something to Rosco, accentuating the movements of his mouth amidst the deafening roar of the shuttering rotor blades. The clock in Henry's mind stopped and he felt the world slow to a crawl.

He knew what would happen next. He glanced to his right. Quintero was fixed, unblinkingly, to the windowpane. He chewed the inside of his cheek to calm his nerves.

Rosco stopped the excited, childish jumping and lowered his hands to his sides. Henry couldn't see his face from the window's angle—he was turned sideways—but the loosing of his shoulders and the drop of his head seemed terrifying, as if Rosco now knew there was no way out and that he would die before he had the chance to say farewell. Henry flinched. His lips moved without saying anything.

Rosco turned his head towards the apartment complex and, quickly, almost incidentally, shimmered a humorless smirk. A rush of anger flushed Quintero's face.

"Stay with me," the gunman mumbled.

The words were meant for himself—words that comforted—but they deepened and swelled desperately in their ears. Henry joined Quintero at the window glass.

Waiting.

Cringing.

The soldier raised the gun, pointed the barrel at Rosco, who now had his hands raised in one, last fleeting attempt at release, and sent a bullet through his forehead. Everything in the moment pulsed into terrifying authenticity. Angry despair drained from Henry's eyes. Shanna sobbed in the shadows behind them. Rosco's body flopped heavily towards the edge of the wall, slipped and fell into the heap of bodies below, lost eternally in the bloody, trenchant abyss of the city.

For several minutes, there was a terrible silence that filled the darkened room. It reeked of sheer anger, lost in thoughts of murder and arduous misery. Quintero re-boarded the window as if there was nothing left to see, resting his arm against the wall and gritting his teeth too hard for his own good. Behind him, Henry brushed the hair from Shanna's tear-stained face. He wanted so badly to make everything better, to show her that he had the power to make it all disappear.

But there would be none of that now.

Then the ground shook and the world outside went white.

8

"It's time," said Mr. Cass.

He was wearing a deep blue tie over a blazing white shirt. The suit coat fit him nicely, running down past his belt and mingling with his pant pockets. He was slightly balding—or thinning, as he would say—and putting on a bit of weight around the abdomen, yet he still considered himself a rather handsome gentleman. He held a clipboard with a packet of loose-leaf papers snapped to the top, filled with notes and checklists of scientific theories that he sometimes did not understand. It was over his head—this scientific jargon. That's why, he assumed, he had been assigned to the apprenticeship of Dr. Carl Norse.

"Dr. Norse?"

Behind the Maplewood desk, neatly organized and dusted, sat a man with long blond hair. His chair faced the wall so that Cass could only see the back of his head against the chair's headrest. He rarely ever felt the need to converse in person with Dr. Norse, but always felt compelled to look away before he showed his face. There was no particular reason for these actions, except his own, odd way of showing the man respect.

Mr. Cass approached the desk as though he was approaching the gallows.

"I have word from the President, sir," said Mr. Cass. "It's time."

Norse swung the chair so that he faced the door where Cass had entered. His shallow, green eyes were like needles wanting to evolve. He was a sturdy man of about fifty years with scant, little lines forming at the corners of his eyelids. Yet aside from minute and gradual signs of aging, the doctor seemed as healthy and fit as any man half his age. He wore an argyle sweater over a red tie and white shirt—an attire spilling with notions of wealth and intellectual prowess. He held a pen between his right index finger and thumb, twirling it back and forth like a pinwheel. He did not smile, just straightened his expression by pressing the edges of his mouth down and releasing before creating a frown.

"Mr. Cass," the doctor spoke with a hoarse voice—not from cigarettes or alcohol or anything manmade—just the natural wear of years. "I need you to do something for me."

Cass tilted his head slightly, attempting to read Norse's subtle cues. It was more difficult than Cass had originally thought. He had been working for Norse for some time now, since the Infection broke loose in Boston, but he still could not figure out the man's complexities. He knew next to nothing about Norse, except that he had a doctorate in pathological disease and was heading the City Sterilization Project. He placed the clipboard on the edge of the Maplewood desktop.

"Yes, sir?"

"I need you to call off the raid."

Cass nearly doubled over.

"But *why*, sir?"

"There is important research that cannot be compromised. If the city is bombed, all of it goes up in flames." Norse looked Cass in the eyes for the entirety of the explanation. "Once we have located what we need, we can proceed as planned."

Mr. Cass now looked utterly perplexed. After all, what could be more important than clearing the world from an apocalyptic disease? But Cass needed this job—more than he needed his family or his girlfriend or the air he breathed—so he nodded and smiled a disapproving-but-approving smile.

"I'll make the call," he said.

"Yes, this is David Cass at the Norse offices," he spoke, clearly annunciating so that the woman on the other end had no excuse of phonic blurriness.

"Mhm," said the woman. "What can I do for you today?"

The woman's voice was sharp and punctual as if she had been practicing the professionalism of it for years. He, for some reason, pictured a woman with a low-cut shirt, attractive in every sense of the word, with painted fingernails the color of fruit punch.

"Dr. Norse needs the raid to be called off."

There was a brief silence as the receptionist composed her response.

"I'm sorry, Mr. Cass, but the fleet is already en route."

"With all due respect, this is *not* a courtesy call. Is the President available?"

"Where did you say you were from?"

Cass let out a burst of air directly into the receiver. At first he thought it would be a good idea—a *statement*—but resolved that it had been altogether impolite. He responded by softening his voice a bit.

"The Norse offices."

"Please hold," she replied, clicking the phone into white noise.

He wondered if the receptionist felt embarrassed or if she had taken offense to his subtle antics. Her final words had seemed, indeed, a bit shaky. His mind wandered to other places, however, farther from the southern cape of Africa where he was supposed to be, when the President's voice echoed through the headset.

"Yes? This is the President."

"Yes, Mr. President. My name is David Cass from the Norse offices. Dr. Norse has asked to cancel the raid on Boston."

"On what grounds?"

"Code Blue," Cass spoke over the phone. "My ID number is 333486756."

Cass heard metallic typing on the other end of the line as the President cross-referenced his name. A female voice, somewhere in the President's room mumbled something indecipherable. Each syllable blended into a digital mirror of the words she said, just lost in the formless static of their connection. All the while, Cass waited patiently, herding his *true* judgement about the raid.

"The fleet will be called off. This better be important, Cass." The President's voice grew tense and deepened a little more. "I want this problem gone…And the only way to eliminate the problem is to *eliminate* the problem. Understand?"

"Yes, sir. I do, sir. Dr. Norse will be contacting you shortly to discuss further details of the current issue."

Cass' mind wandered back to the odd secrecy of Norse's work. How much influence was needed to overrule the President's *final* decision? He could not think of any research or publications that had been endorsed by the doctor. Not *one*. He pondered why he was working for him in the first place.

Because it pays well, he thought, *and this is the best thing that ever happened to you.*

He walked leisurely through the well-carpeted hallway, admiring the décor of the wall lights and window shades. They reminded him of academia, of his life in college before he found himself working at the Norse offices—at the only scientific pathogen research site that would hire him at this time of year. He was lucky to have even found something as practical as the International Center for Disease Control. Cass had convinced himself awhile ago that it was a dream come true.

He stopped halfway down the corridor, remembering he had forgotten his clipboard in the doctor's office.

Great, he thought. *Another awkward conversation with the man upstairs.*

He simulated the events of the interaction in his head. He would knock, then wait several seconds before hearing the *come in* from behind the oblong desk at the back of the room. He would regretfully apologize for interrupting the doctor at such short notice, then hastily grab the clipboard and leave with only the most minor of disturbances inflicted.

There, he thought to himself. *No harm done.*

Instead, Mr. Cass stumbled into a conversation he wished he had never heard. As he prepared to knock, he heard the sharp, heightened words of two men sifting through the closed door. Curiously, he pressed his ear against the pressurized wood and listened.

"I *need* that vile," said Norse.

"Why is this so important to you, Norse? The survival of the human race is in question. If that disease escapes…"

Cass did not recognize the second voice. It was not altogether booming, but not reserved, either. He pictured a middle-aged man in a suit, judging by his own insights.

"If we found a cure," Norse explained, "we could put America back at the top of scientific technology. There are *billions* and *billions* of dollars in this market. The vile is key. We need that serum."

"That's how all of this started in the *first* place," the anonymous man argued. "All it takes is one contaminate. We *cannot* be responsible for transporting such a violent and contagious disease internationally."

"This is your one shot," Norse spoke, deepening his voice into sincerity. "After today, the deal's off the table. My men are already in position just outside of Boston. This is happening whether you join or not."

There was silence. Cass thought he heard the tapping of a lone foot, possibly in thought, or a sort of pacing.

"I'll be in touch," said the other man.

Now there were footsteps approaching, coercing Cass away from the door in a panicked flurry. Eavesdropping, Mr. Cass assumed, could get him fired, so he pulled his cell phone from his khaki pants pocket and began improvising a conversation with no one on the other end. He stared at the ground and shuffled his feet slightly to affirm his complacency, leaning against the far hallway wall in a casual shift of weight.

The door opened, showing Dr. Norse with his back turned about halfway between his desk and the door, per usual, with his hands on his hips. His shoulders were tense, showing a sign of anger somewhere in him that Cass undeniably feared.

In the doorway stood a thin man (who had opened the door) of about forty years of age with black-rimmed glasses one size too large for the width of his head. The frame bulged at his ears, weighing against the bridge of his nose. His cheekbones were high—complimenting the weight of his glasses—but not overly exposing the rigidity of his other facial features.

With his shoulders shrugged, the man shot his last perturbed, antagonistic glare towards Mr. Cass, enough to radiate serious annoyance and frustration in his direction. Cass diffused the stare with a slightly strained smile, one that was meant for acquaintances, as he pretended to end his counterfeit phone call. The thin man walked away in angst, shaking his head and mumbling grunts to himself.

He pushed from the wall and knocked on the already opened door, suddenly noticing several changed attributes to the room. His clipboard, which had been resting comfortably on the closest corner of Dr. Norse's desk, had moved to the leather ottoman in the far corner of the room. The fireplace was lit and now roared yellow-orange licks of flame into its upward vent. Although Mr. Cass had not ventured outside just yet, he had a vague premonition that the temperature was, in the least bit, mild, if not damp. Summer on the Southern African Coast was delightful, but definitely not fireplace weather.

"I'm sorry to bother you again, Doctor, but I forgot my clipboard from our morning's meeting," he said. His voice seemed meek against the high ceilings and deadened space. Norse did not respond, so Cass hesitantly scrambled to the ottoman, grasped the clipboard to his chest, and returned to the doorway.

"The President is waiting on a reply regarding the Code Blue you asked me to call in this morning," he spoke. He felt that it was a better time than any for an update. The doctor's body, it seemed, had not moved since Mr. Cass had walked through the door. The fireplace roared with heated excitement.

"Have you ever read Thomas Hobbes, Mr. Cass?" the doctor asked. The man's voice was louder than he had expected. The thunderous syllables sent a twinge down his spine.

"Of course," Cass responded, again, meekly.

"*Leviathan*," Norse spoke, "is a work I've taken to recently."

The doctor bent his legs, almost as if he were about to endure a long and treacherous marathon, but extended them again after only a few seconds, walking towards his desk and reaching for a riddled, yellowed paperback book resting at the corner of his desk. Norse held it up, displaying its overly used binding.

"It's a bitter look on humanity," the doctor explained. Cass listened and watched as Norse's eyes darkened against the firelight. "We fight. We steal. We kill. Simply for power."

Cass decided to remain still. Discussion could wait.

"Hobbes speaks to the idea that we are all primitive beings attempting to gain power through social contracts and the frailties of others. Would you say that's an honest assessment?"

It was more than that, Cass thought, but nodded in hopes to stop the one-sided, awkwardly disturbing influx of information he simply had not expected from a return for a clipboard.

"We are all looking for ways to climb the power ladder," Norse continued. "Remember that."

In a small fit of panic, Cass met Norse's eyes, which gleamed with threat and vivacity. He nodded in complete paranoia and exited the office in a flurry of legs. He did not know why he felt the need to escape. There was a current of pressure that pushed at him, that scared him enough to crave absence, to satisfy the want of leaving.

Cass smiled nervously, backpedaling like a guilty man.

"Close the door on your way out," thundered the doctor.

And he did.

David Cass' funeral was a beautiful and saddening event. It took place on a mesmerizing, sun-soaked day on the African Coast. Most of the Cass family made the flight from Brazil, where they had settled after the evacuation, to pay their respects. On this day, the church was blanketed with warm, inviting sunlight that permeated the stretched stained-glass windows, producing murals of Christian belief amidst a small upturn of dust that flurried and swiveled its way to the church floor. Most of the churchgoers sat soaking in their own sweat, wishing they could have worn any other color but black.

The family had asked for a closed casket service. The wounds, the embalmer explained, were too much to disguise. Military police had found Mr. Cass washed up on the shore of the cape with several gashes in his throat and groin, directly above the femoral artery. Bruises and dents littered his face. The family wanted the killer to be brought to justice, but in times of apocalyptic disease and mass migration, the police could guarantee nothing.

Women in lacy hats and black dresses and men in suits and aesthetic ties lined the pews, some crying in remorseful sobs while others sat in silent remembrance. A gold-framed picture of a much younger, smiling David rested at the foot of the casket—a nostalgic artifact of the man he had been.

The priest finished his all too familiar gone-to-a-better-place eulogy and motioned that the service had ended. The congregation stood, and as the final hymn finished, began the slow and thought-filled descent to their vehicles. The women locked arms with the men, blowing runny snot into handkerchiefs and clanking their high-heels against the polished wooden floor.

No one noticed that Dr. Carl Norse hadn't even attended.

9

The vibrating sounds of helicopters faded into the city, humming consistently through the streets, ceasing to bomb, but not leaving altogether. Henry opened his eyes, confused that he was still alive. Beside him, Shanna kept her eyes tightly closed, shaking against the dusty floor in nervous quivers. He ran a gentle hand down her back in smooth, comfortable flows of energy, attempting to comfort her.

"It's okay," he whispered. "They're gone now."

Quintero shuffled to the window, staring out into the afternoon glare. The streets were empty, but they knew it would not be long before the sun drifted away against the power of the night and the sewers and subway lines released and filled the streets with yet another flood of damned bodies. If they were going to leave, it would have to be soon.

"Why aren't we dead?" Shanna asked.

Henry shrugged his shoulders. "Something must have happened."

"They killed Ross," Quintero mumbled. Henry could barely hear the words dribble from the gunman's mouth. "Why would they do that?"

The pain behind Quintero's eyes seemed far worse than anything Henry had seen before. It brewed and swarmed like a tempest—dark and shadowy and static. For a moment, Henry wondered if the gunman would rip a pistol from its holster, place it steadily into his mouth and pull the trigger, but Henry knew Quintero would not leave them here alone, not even in his darkest thoughts. Never.

"There's no way we're leaving here tonight," Quintero spoke. "Even if we could make it back to the wall, there's no one to work the basket." He rubbed his eyes like fatigue had riddled his vision. "And who knows where those helicopters went."

Henry nudged the gunman away and peered out of the sliver of window to three city blocks closest to the wall victims of the helicopters' explosive annihilation. Buildings had collapsed to ashes and motionless bodies were splayed across the streets. The helicopters had dropped something, then left. But why? Why would they only exterminate *three* blocks? It was perplexing, but Henry was thankful nonetheless. Maybe something changed their minds…

There are worse places to be, I guess, Henry thought.

His stomach bubbled and growled viciously. He suddenly realized how hungry he truly was. For two days, he had relied on only the sustenance of crackers to get him by, but now, the rumbling was deeper, a little more urgent. The sensation crept through him like needles stabbing blindly into his abdomen. He held his stomach, trying desperately to ignore it.

"Are you hungry?" Shanna asked through a series of soft whispers. She had always been so good at reading his thoughts.

He nodded apprehensively. She rose to her feet, still with a noticeable limp, and noiselessly walked to a dusty cupboard in the kitchen directly across from where he sat. Even in the slim-fit jeans she wore, he noticed the bruised, swollen skin of her ankle against the fabric of her sock. He felt the sudden urge to replace his ankles with hers, regretting the fact that he had left her alone in all of this—the Infection, the Quarantine, *everything*. But thinking of the past was the worst thing he could do, at least in these fragile moments before dusk settled into urban chaos. There were more important things to worry over, so he settled with nothing but the present—the *here* and *now*—on his mind.

Quintero departed from his lookout and joined Henry at the base of the opposite wall, crumbling into crossed legs with his arms folded against his chest. He didn't talk, but simply allowed his head to bob silently into a dull slumber.

Henry had seen this before. The way Quintero slept was frightening. It was not a restful doze, but merely an attempted escape from what the city had become—away from thoughts of Rosco's death and the monstrosities soon to be on their way from the subway lines and sewers. When he would finally let himself go—overtaken by the flourishes of his subconscious—he would awaken soon thereafter by the nervous, horrible nightmares his mind could muster.

Over and over this occurred until the morning when sleep was no longer an option.

Shanna scuttled around, closing the swinging cupboards and returning to the front room. Her eyes glistened with dainty light, more brilliant than they had been even minutes before. She seemed to livening up with human contact. The corners of her lips curved with a curious smirk. In her hands she held a bag of flavored rice cakes, indulging in her marked form of resourcefulness.

Quintero had weaponry. Henry wore battle scars. Now Shanna had rice cakes.

"The people who left here must've left all of their food," Shanna reasoned, ruffling the packaging in her hands. "It's mostly stuff like this, but it's food."

Henry contemplated reaching for the cakes, snapping the bag from Shanna's hands, and shoving the entirety of the bag down his throat in selfish gulps before anybody else even had the chance. But, of course, he buried these primitive thoughts somewhere behind his conscientious superego. Shanna, instead, fragilely opened the bag, cautious of the noise now, and shook a few cakes into each of their hands, saving several for herself.

The taste of onion filled their mouths in clear, artificial waves of taste. They sat on the floor, crunching like cows grazing, eating quickly, but seemingly not fast enough for how hungry they felt. Henry felt every swallow in his throat like boulders trekking in a mudslide. Occasionally the sharpened, unchewed corners of the grain scratched the soft inside of his esophagus, making him flinch with a distinct, but brief bout of pain, but he certainly didn't care. Food was food at this point, no matter what it was. He tried not to show any wincing, but his visage usually weighed on the expressive side.

"How are they?" she asked.

"A little stale, but otherwise pretty damn good," Henry replied.

Quintero kept to himself. If he felt the fear of the falling sun outside, as Henry and Shanna most certainly did, he didn't show it. He was silent, void of all emotion, yet the sounds of his chewing echoed through the room in thunderous swallowing ripples, unlike the others. He moved his jaw slowly and consistently, running his teeth against the grains and pounding them into a stew of moistened matter (much different than Henry's excited eat-everything-whole philosophy), then without thought, gulping them down in giant, smooth motions. He did this repetitively until his handful of rice cakes disappeared. He rubbed his hands together, allowing for the friction to scatter the remaining crumbs from his hands onto the floor, then looking away and closing his eyes.

Shanna watched the two men from a bit of a distance while nibbling conspicuously at the corners of hers. Henry flashed her a quick smile as if to say *I'm so glad you're here* and she returned it in a reflective grin to signal she understood, wiping the leftover flavoring from her fingers onto the denim of her jeans. He could not help but think of how adorably attractive she was, even with her slightly matted hair and weakened frame.

Quintero finally broke the silence.

"I'm out of ideas," he whispered. "I thought the basket was a surefire thing. Without it, we're just a bunch of goldfish in an aquarium waiting for the piranhas to find out they've got easy dinner."The gunman's eyes lowered to his feet, which stretched outward in front of him, flexed and pointing towards the ceiling. His words caught Henry and Shanna by surprise.

"What about the *Breakers' Circle*? We can find our way back to the subway and out that way." Henry was thinking out loud at this point, but instead of the enlightened response from the gunman he expected, Quintero simply wrinkled his nose and shook his head arduously.

"You saw those things," he said. "They're evolving…and *quickly*."

Shanna gaped with widening eyes.

"You should've seen them in the Restricted District," Quintero continued. "They were *talking*, man. *Talking*."

The thought of this didn't scare Henry as much as it should have. He, too, lowered his eyes and stared at his bloody shoes.

"There's a broken ladder on the other side of the city," he brainstormed. "I used it to escape during the Quarantine. It's pretty well hidden and sturdy, too."

Quintero lowered his head even more.

"What if the helicopters come back this way? I can still hear them in the distance. Those bastards will just shoot us on the spot…like Ross."

A depressive quality seeped into the gunman's voice—a kind of negative depreciation for the reality of the situation. Henry swallowed the bit of aggravation that swelled in his throat. For the first time, he could see the light at the end of the tunnel. He could see *salvation*. He needed Quintero to see it, too, even if the loss of his friend seemed a little erroneous.

"He's gone," Henry murmured. The words propelled from his mouth a bit harsher than he expected. "And there's nothing we can do now, except find out why."

Suddenly Henry felt his back collide hard against the wall behind him. Quintero had thrusted to his feet with incredible speed. A fist wrapped into the collar of Henry's shirt. The gunman's other arm reached behind his waist, then snapped back into place. Tears formed in the gunman's eyes as the barrel of his pistol pressed furiously against Henry's forehead. His lower lip quivered mercilessly while Henry lifted his hands, surrendering. The fury behind Quintero's eyes, glazed with those hot tears, seemed blinding, fueled by hurt.

"Don't you *ever* say that again!" Quintero screamed. The words were clear, but slightly augmented. "Don't you *ever* say that again!"

The barrel of the pistol pressed even harsher into Henry's skull now. He grimaced against the metal while Shanna whined and covered her face with her arms.

"This can't be happening," she mumbled with quivering lips. "Please God. *Please*."

"It's okay," Henry muttered. The low strings of sound didn't seem to catch her attention. His mouth could not form any other words, so he continued to repeat them, hoping they would somehow catch. "*It's okay. It's okay.*"

"How about I kill *your* girlfriend right now and see how *you* feel? I bet you'd want to put a gun to my head too, wouldn't you?"

Another forceful push against his forehead nearly sent Henry to the ground. He thought he heard the stretch of a trigger click against the gunman's index finger.

"He was my *brother*!"

The sentence released from Quintero's throat in a burst of cathartic air. The pistol fell to the floor at the gunman's side and rattled as it settled. Tears flowed now from his eyes in streams of hot saline and dripped to his leather jacket, rolling and sliding down his chest. He stumbled to the opposite side of the room, rested his hands against the wall and sobbed— a vulnerable moment for an invulnerable type of man.

Henry stood in horrible shock, glancing back and forth between the sobbing gunman and his frightened girlfriend. The windows filtered the final few rays of the day's sunlight as he stooped over and picked up the fallen pistol, feeling the true weight of it in his palms. Its shimmer disappeared in the waning light, but in its wake, the aesthetics of a dull black block behind an array of darkness.

He walked slowly towards the gunman, careful not to ignite the situation for a second time. Quintero only wiped the last swell of tears against his sleeve.

"Here," said Henry. He handed Quintero the pistol. "I'm sorry."

"We're screwed, Henry," he said through wandering sobs. "We're so *goddamn* screwed."

"We'll get through this. We have to."

Henry didn't expect to be the voice of consolation, but, in a moment when he found he must, the aura of sympathy came rushing in like a beautiful resistance. He rested his hand on the gunman's shoulder. Quintero turned, wiped a bout of fresh tears from his eyes, and returned the favor.

It was then that a knock at the back door (through the kitchen) startled them all. Shanna, alone and still arrested by the gunman's furious burst of anger, barked a horribly feeble whimper and wrapped her arms around herself even tighter.

"This can't be happening," she whispered.

Henry kissed her forehead, another act of consolation, and motioned for her to push farther against the wall and out of sight.

"I need you to be strong right now," he whispered to Quintero. The gunman nodded, following with the pistol raised through bloodshot eyes. A darkened figure silhouetted the crack at the base of the door, standing firmly against the backdrop of the twilight outside. Henry considered prying back a panel of the boarded wood from the door's window to catch a glimpse of whom he would be dealing with, but ultimately decided against it. Whoever this was, they meant to come in, regardless of whom was inside.

"I think they heard us," Henry whispered. The gunman nodded.

Another knock, this time, with force.

Henry glanced back once more at Quintero, nodded in preparation, and swung open the door.

A long, curved blade cuddled against Henry's neck. Chains rattled and he could already feel the warmth of a new body press against the back of his. It was petite, but solidly defined. He raised his head to tighten the skin at his neck, to try and create a little more room between blade and skin, but the metal inched closer, drawing trickles of blood down to his collarbone.

Quintero held the pistol steady, although unable to aim at the figure's shadowy movements. Henry let out a groan, and then forced his body to relax. If he moved anymore, the blade would surely cut into his neck.

"Let us in or I kill him," the figure spoke. The voice was rough, but clearly feminine.

The gunman lowered the pistol and backed into the room, away from the open door and into the shadows where Shanna waited. The woman released the blade with ease from Henry's throat, allowing it to hover about an inch from his skin as they entered the dark apartment space. He could still feel the heat of her chest burning into him like a furnace. She was sweating, smearing streaks of it across the back of his shirt.

"Walk," she demanded.

Henry did as he was told, slowly, hoping to keep his footing across the linoleum kitchen floor. He heard the door close and clamp behind him.

There are two of them, Henry thought. *Someone just locked the door.*

They approached the kitchen and Shanna whimpered as Henry came into view. He wanted to tell her not to worry, that no matter how all of this ended, she would be fine, but he could not collect the air from his chest to form words, nor could he find it within himself to lie to her in the midst of blinding uncertainty.

"We don't want no trouble," the woman's voice spoke. It was a half-whisper. "Usually folks don't take too kindly to people like us invading their space, but on a night like tonight, we don't have much of a choice. It's getting dark out there." A tense silence filled the murky air, then, almost as if to clear it, her raspy voice reappeared. "So what do you say?"

Henry babbled a hesitant, bullied yes. Quintero nodded bitterly. Shanna did not answer.

The blade loosened and Henry felt the rush of air return to his lungs. He turned and saw the two new bodies for the first time.

The woman was short, but built with rigid muscles from her neck to her legs. Cornrows moved sideways against her scalp into a ponytail that fell to her shoulders. She held two long, curved scythes—one in each hand—attached to jingling chains that wrapped around her palms in tight, rope-like strings. She mouthed a genuine *sorry* to Henry but he wasn't sure he accepted her apology, not just yet. And even if he did, it wouldn't be because he *wanted* to, but because he would *need* to. Those scythes were sharp, large, and provocatively intimidating.

Beside her stood a towering, dark-skinned man wearing a white, cutoff tee shirt holding the longest bladed sword Henry had ever seen. Hanging from his back were two holsters in the shape of an X. One holster was empty (presumably used for the blade he held). The other holster (the left-handed side) housed another sword with a handle that appeared identical to its twin. He had deep, brown eyes (which were difficult to see in the dark) and a quiet, serious demeanor that made Henry flinch.

"I'm Harro. And this here is my husband, Fender."

The rest of the group took turns introducing themselves, most in quivering attempts to seem smooth. Harro sensed the hesitation in their voices almost immediately and smiled from the corner of her mouth. It raised her left nostril so that it flared with noiseless abandon.

"Listen," she said, dropping the timbre of her voice into a blissful, conversational tone. "That whole scene over there was just precaution. You seem like good people…honestly. We won't hurt you. You have our word."

She raised her hands as if being arrested, forcing that already waning smile to stay for as long as it could. Fender holstered the sword to his back and sat clumped against the wall by the second-floor stairs.

"We were caught," he started. "Dumbass helicopters brought all the crazies to us. We had to fight them off. Took us forever. It was getting dark and we heard the commotion in here, so we figured there were people. We decided to join."

"Hell of an *invite*," mocked Quintero. A good amount of suspicion still housed in his eyes.

"You would do the same thing if you were about to be mauled to death. There's too many of them after sunset. We had to do something."

Harro cracked her neck, rubbing the palms of her hands against it, as if they held a magical cure for stress tension.

"If you really want us to leave in the morning," she spoke, "we'll leave. No harm done, but we *have* to stay here tonight. We can't go back out there."

She was right. Before any of them could respond, the demonic groaning and hissing erupted from outside the door. Bodies stumbled over each other as their shadows traveled across the shades. By now, Henry had learned to grit his teeth and ignore it. They were hidden and, for once, comfortably housed. A good situation, despite the company, to find one's self in.

He made eye contact with Harro and nodded coldly, smiling all the same. She sat and rested her head against the wall, closing her eyes, breathing deep and long. Henry shifted silently against Shanna, who had returned to her quiet softening doze, accepting the warmth of Henry's body with an arm that wrapped around his. Her head rested, bobbing gently at his shoulder.

It wasn't long before he felt the true weight of sleep take her, but Henry forced his eyes open, looking out into the room's darkness in front of him. Somewhere at the far end sat Quintero, resting motionlessly, staring, too, into nothing. *We'll find out why this happened*, Henry thought. *Ross' death will not be in vain.*

And then he fell deep into sleep.

He woke well after the sun climbed its ladder into day. Harro and Fender were already awake, talking and laughing with each other, speaking quietly enough so that Henry could not understand the dialogue between them. Quintero kept watch through a chipped hole in the boarded front window, monitoring the sky and the street simultaneously. For the first time, the gunman truly looked weak, pale and exhausted.

"The helicopters left last night," Quintero said, craning his neck so that the entire group could hear him.

"They *did*?" asked Henry.

Quintero turned and furrowed his brow to show a mild bout of puzzlement.

"You didn't hear them? They shook the whole goddamn house."

"Guess not," he replied.

Harro stood up and stretched, arching her back and pushing out her small breasts. Henry tried to turn away in respect, but honestly, found the attraction to her harmless. Fender, fortunately, had his back turned away from Henry, sharpening his swords soundlessly against a jagged fragment of rock. Sparks splashed downward as he did so, disappearing as they hit the floor.

"So," said Harro. "Why are all of you in the city anyway?"

When no one answered, she added a curt, but curious, "If you don't mind me asking."

Henry shot an innocent glance toward Shanna. Her breathing—long and slightly exaggerated—meant she was still fast asleep beside him.

"She broke her ankle during the Infection," he explained. "I went to look for help outside the city, but there was no one. I came back for her after the Quarantine and met Quintero on the way in."

The gunman continued his watch from the peephole, ignoring the mention of his name. He watched for movement, finding a slew of newbie zombies in the distance, but disregarding them as they passed.

"And you?" Henry asked, mostly to be polite. "What's your story?"

"Our nephew lived up here before the first of the outbreaks," Harro spoke. A sudden sadness filled her eyes. It darkened her face, but softened her features. "No one else was going to save him, so we figured we would give it a shot."

Henry could see the tragedy wilting in her eyes. This story, he sensed, would not end with a *happy-ever-after*, so—humanely—he offered a mumbled *sorry* and an apologetic, semi-diverted half-smile.

"He was dead before we even reached him. He was a smart kid, too, you know? Went to Boston College and everything," she continued. "We've spent the last couple of days trying to get out of the city. It's harder than it looks."

"Tell me about it," Quintero affirmed.

"Tell you what," Henry spoke. Something about their story confirmed an authenticity about these people. "We're all trying to escape, why don't we all just stick together. The more numbers the better, right?"

Harro smiled, almost as if to say *I knew you'd come around.*

But Quintero flinched.

"Thank you," Fender spoke. The first time he had this entire time. He dropped the sharpening stone into his pocket and holstered his swords. "Harro, let's search the upstairs. There could be something up there the group can use."

"Good idea," she replied. And the two of them creaked up the stairs and out of sight.

Shanna shifted from her sleep, opening her eyes, but squinting into the changed morning light. She ran her hands through her hair groggily, but stopped halfway when she caught her fingers in a knot, instinctively pulling them out in an irritated tug and combing through the entanglement from the outside. She was sweaty, dirty, and distant because of sleep, but her aura never changed. The attraction between her and Henry still seemed as fiery as ever.

"I had the weirdest nightmare," Shanna told the two men at each of her sides. "A short woman with scythes and a giant man with swords barged open the backdoor. They murdered you." She pointed to Henry and continued. "They slit your throat and watched you bleed out on the floor, then they targeted *you*." This time, pointing to the gunman. "You shot six bullets into the man but his chest only absorbed the metal. He laughed and then decapitated you in one fell swoop with one of his blades."

She shivered harshly, wiping a smear of feverish sweat from her forehead. Henry wrapped an arm around her.

"Then the giant man turned towards me and wasn't a man anymore, but a horrible, mucous-colored ogre. It drooled, not moving, just meeting its eyes with mine. The girl with scythes laughed a hideous cackle behind it. '*You're no match for ussss,*' she hissed. Her teeth were rotting. Half of her skull was missing, too."

She thinks last night was a dream, Henry thought.

The floorboards creaked and snapped above them, but Shanna didn't seem to notice. No one stopped her.

"I felt a warm shower of blood running down my chest...like this." She ran her hands down her shirt to mimic the action. "My neck unhinged and I fell to the floor. The bloody scythe she was holding glistened in the moonlight and I looked up into the eyes of a dozen of the Dead smiling down at me. The ogre was laughing behind them all. '*Eat up boys!*' it yelled. And then I woke up."

Harro and Fender reappeared from the stairwell and Shanna gasped.

"There's nothing up there but rats," Harro cawed.

"Shanna? Look at me," Henry said, turning the girl towards him. "Harro and Fender are joining us. It seems they're good people after all."

Her eyes showed a disapprovingly, concrete glare. Quintero's showed the same.

"We don't even *know* them. I mean, they held you at knifepoint!" she exclaimed.

"They're *human*," Henry said, attempting to persuade Shanna. "Just like us. We help our own, right?"

She couldn't speak, nor wanted to at this point—just shook her head.

"They won't kill us," Henry assured.

"I won't let them," said Quintero, through the dark. The shadows of midmorning blackened his face to char.

Fender turned, recognizing the obvious suspicion, but Harro raised a palm to her husband's arm. "It's okay," she said. "It's normal."

Quintero craned his neck once more and lifted the window plank. "The streets are back to normal," he said. "Plenty of crazies to kill, though."

"You mean jumpers? That's what *we* call them. I absolutely hate those things," Harro interrupted. "It seems like they just don't die."

"Crazies?" Shanna asks. "I...I don't know what those are."

She listened in earnest curiosity. *Crazies? Jumpers?* She had only seen the flailing bodies from the window at night and, even then, she was too scared to look at them for any span of time. She would catch a glimpse of them—only a glimpse—and then immediately fall back, retreating into the shadows to hide and wait for the hissing to disappear from the porch. She feared they could smell her or, even worse, *feel* her in some weird way and, before long, she would be nothing but bloody, helpless dinner meat.

"Let's just say you're lucky you've never encountered one."

Harro looked up as she explained, cleaning the nightmarish scythes until they gleamed. "They're quick and strong—the ones that have been infected since the beginning. They'll rip into you before you know it, if you're not careful."

"I'll tell you what," Fender said. "There's something fishy about those helicopters. They killed someone up on the wall."

Quintero flinched, suddenly gripping at his pistol.

"I don't know what they're up to, but I don't like it," finished Harro. "Whoever it was up there, he was waving them down. They shot him in cold blood."

Henry ran a hand against his throat and Harro suddenly grew silent. The gunman clutched at the windowsill, fighting back the urge to boil over once again. He kept his eyes on the street, never tearing them away.

"It was my brother," Quintero mumbled. "They killed my brother."

His head dropped slowly, then swung back, snapping into place like a boulder on a plateau, strong enough to balance its own weight.

"I'm sorry. That's...*horrible*," Harro relented.

Her words were honest and the gunman certainly appreciated the gentility. He boarded the window and let the rage within him dissipate, then reached and unsheathed each of his pistols, resting them on the side table in order. There were nine guns all together. The first originated from a sling under his leather jacket, then his sock line, two against each of his triceps, and several hanging from his belt.

"You can never be too prepared," Quintero muttered with a sly, joking upturn of his lower lip.

Henry peered around, catching glimpses of metal from all points of the room—Quintero's guns, Harro's scythes, Fender's long swords—feeling naked without any means of defending himself now that he wasn't in possession of his well-suited baseball bat. It was no longer useable (and he was alright with that, considering its surprising frailty against the Dead). It was not enough to rely on the others, however. With Shanna in the picture, he would need something more than just two fists. *That* he was certain of.

He turned to Shanna. "Are there any knives in the kitchen?"

She shrugged.

"I don't know. I never thought to look."

Henry pried himself from the floor and walked to the kitchen. The cupboards and drawers were mostly made of unfinished wood—the kind with an abundance of splinters through each surface—all the while oddly complimenting the darkened, musty room. It was brighter than the front room by a long shot which, fortunately, shielded his movements from passing the closer crazies outside.

He ran his palm against the roughened wood and searched, opening each cupboard, finding nothing but Shanna's limited buffet of perishable foods and a few curled and dead spiders, wallowing in their own messes of web. He opened each of the drawers at his waist next, finding nothing but a small roll of string and a battery (which had no use for the group, at least not now). He opened the last of the drawers—a dingy collapsible thing—expecting nothing, but there, in the sepia lighting of the morning, Henry looked down on three silver butter knives. He balanced them between his fingers and slowly returned to the group.

He handed one to Shanna.

"Keep it safe." His voice clambered for seriousness. "In case I can't help you."

He kissed her forehead and plopped down beside her, then slipped his hand into his pocket where he had stashed the remaining two knives, feeling the rough ridges of each blade. He wondered how long they would last if forced into use. He wondered if they would do any damage at all. Either way, he felt more at ease knowing that Shanna had *something*, even if it was next to nothing.

He opened his ears to a discussion between the other three of the room.

"So it's settled then. Today we rest," said Quintero, scanning the room, looking each person in the eyes. "Tomorrow, we'll leave." His hands hung only inches from his pistols, fingers ready to pounce if needed.

A unanimous agreement rose from the group, even Henry, who seemed to think nothing would do him better than one more day of true rest.

10

Burlington, Massachusetts
The Day of the Infection

The alarm rang its annoying little ring when the clock hit 6:00 AM. William heard it, but, as always, refused to press snooze. Instead, he waited until he couldn't take the beeping any longer and reached over and ripped the clock from the wall. It let out one last dying, erratic drone and fell quiet into the sunlight peeking through the shaded bay windows.

For William, this happened daily. The clock performed its only task (and with a certain flare, he might add), waking him from a disorganized sleep, and then consequently suffering an unexplained outburst of abuse because of it. Of course, he reconfigured the clock when he returned home the following night, but always wondered why he felt so barbaric in the morning hours. It was a curse he simply could not break.

He was a very deep sleeper, but the past few nights had been nightmare after nightmare, shrouded by very shallow fits of rest. He found himself opening his eyes in the middle of the night with his sheets and clothes drenched with perspiration. He would lie there, soaked, for hours until the lake of salt felt too clingy and gelled against his skin. Then, when he couldn't take it anymore, he would change into a clean shirt and a new pair of underwear, replace the bed sheets with something fresher, and repeat the process.

As if it was not already one of those strange, merciless mornings, William remembered that today was the second day of the workweek. He sighed. Tuesdays were always the worst work days. Not only had he made the worst decision of his life in accepting the Charles Swarley Grant in front of hundreds of prestigious and well-to-do doctors and

127

scientists this past year, but also, Tuesdays were media days. He was to present any advancements in academic progress to them during the day. The grant required him to make a useful, scientific discovery that would serve some purpose in the medical community in future years. He was already three months into the project and, honestly, felt like an abject failure. "You're one of the brightest minds of the twenty-first century!" his colleagues proclaimed. "There's not many like you out there!", but in his mind (and the upper echelon of the scientific community), he had clearly not lived up to the heightened expectations that came with a Swarley Grant winner.

The silent alarm clock now sat on the floor at the base of the nightstand staring at William like a guard of the morning. He wanted nothing more than to sleep, so he allowed himself to slip back into the blankets and pillows that surrounded him, guiding his tired mind back into the confines of his unconscious world.

He awoke, now feeling remarkably well rested, but strangely disjointed by the newfound brightness streaming in through the bedroom shades. It told him that he was horribly late…and on *Tuesday* no less! He reached for his cell phone, turned it on, and watched as the voicemail messages piled into his inbox.

There were two from Laura—the pretty, blond-haired assistant at the pathogens clinic. She spoke clearly into the phone, but the roar of the backdrop machinery blurred out half of what she recorded.

"Will, where *are* you? Please call back. You're…the…waiting…"

He listened to the messages for a second and last time, but couldn't decipher any more words of importance, so he flipped to the other messages from people he recognized.

Jamie Ludder's messages, however, were much clearer, although he preferred Laura's voice to his. The man had never smoked a cigarette in his life, but talked as though he smoked a pack a day. He was certain his supervisor would have something cleverly acerbic to say, so he held up the receiver to his ear and listened.

"Will, it's Jamie. Listen. Don't know where you are right now, but you better get here. We're not shelling out a million big ones for you to screw this up. You got me? Call me as soon as you can."

William jumped out of bed, literally propelling to the bathroom, where he pushed the toothbrush against the lines of his teeth for a few miserable seconds before considering it a job well done. He ran his fingers through his hair, felt the bent locks turning every which way, but ultimately decided it was of little importance in his hurry out the door. He licked his hand and tried to press the hair down, but only added to its greasiness.

And to top off his flinging tardiness, he skipped breakfast, tripped down the stairs, and grabbed his coat from the hanger (sending the stand flopping against the hardwood floor). He slammed the front door as he brushed by it to his car.

The nine o'clock traffic was nothing like the seven-thirty Hell to which he was accustomed. For one thing, there was much less honking, but he was still cut off several times on the far end of the four-lane highway. He gripped the wheel with both hands, ringing the leather to release the quickly surmounting stress within him and tried desperately to erase the thought of the punishment he would soon be awarded when he arrived at BPM.

Boston Public Medicine stands in the shadow of the city—a monstrous building amidst architectural suavity in the heart of downtown Boston. He had, on more than one occasion, admired the beauty of the hospital with its pipeline bridges connecting from one wing to another, its revolving front doors and affluent lobby entrance, and the copious amount of windows. If you count the lines of them, as William had on one of his many slow research days, you could count thirty-two stories to this public high-rise. If you were *important* enough to know about the pathogens clinic in the basement, you would know that the building was, in fact, not thirty-two stories, but actually thirty-eight.

William stormed into the parking garage, something he never did, paid the thirty-five dollars up front, and walked with his carrier bag slung over his shoulder in sways of bulky gesticulations. The commotion of the city streets was enough to make him sick. If BPM had not offered a hefty salary to join their medical staff, William would never have moved to the city. He would never have accepted the Charles Swarley Grant and he would never have lost his now long, lost wife of five years.

"Work is important to you," she had said. William, being all too familiar with the it's-not-you-it's-me speech, had felt the rush of daggers piece his heart in these final moments with her. If there was one thing he had learned about his ex-wife over the years, it was that she loved to watch him bleed (metaphorically, of course), but she had had her share of screw-ups over the years. Like a protective husband, he forced himself to keep silent in the name of love.

"We're just two different people looking for different things in life," she had lied.

True, but not true, William thought. They could've made it work.

She was having an affair with a convenient store clerk. The same clerk he had caught her with the year before. He sometimes wished he could see her now, not talk to her, but just watch. He wondered what she was doing. He wanted to believe that she woke up every morning wondering what life would be like if she had stayed with him. He wanted her to apologize. He wanted her to miss him in every sense—mentally, spiritually, *physically*. *Definitely* physically. But it would never happen. Never in a million years.

William continued swinging his bag back and forth like an oddly shaped pendulum. It helped maintain his quickened stride. The main entrance to the hospital was littered with coughers, visitors and doctors in white lab coats. Every so often, he would lose focus and bump someone, who would turn and flash a disgusted, overly annoyed glare. William would wave, apologize, and keep forward.

Boston is such a strange place, he thought.

He opened the main entrance doors, waved to the security guard, who waved back nonchalantly.

"Late start today, Dr. O'Malley?"

The guard had a certain brashness to him that skewed the humor.

"Car troubles," William responded, clearly lying through his teeth, but shuffling out of sight before any other questions could be asked.

He walked down the hall to the unmarked entry to his right. William pressed his eye against the green scanner. It flashed a brief blinding spark over his iris, held it for another second, and cleared William for entrance. He despised the eye scanner for the only reason that it twisted the rest of his day into dull pain and aches. His right eye glistened with, what looked like, empty-channel television snow, showering his vision with metal-tinged fireflies. It usually resulted in a headache, which always forced him into a gloomy, passive-aggressive mood.

The hidden elevator opened and William rushed in quickly, avoiding witness from the lobby. He pressed the metallic button that read LEVEL 1 and watched as the door closed on its own, clicking into place. He felt the tiny lurch as it slid down the shaft, which never helped his anxiety. He exhaled a deep, nervously daunting breath. The elevator door opened to a slew of people, one of which was Laura, who smiled and breathed a sigh of relief with her shoulders.

"Rough morning?" she asked.

She wore a thin set of glasses, which she constantly and affectionately pushed up the bridge of her nose. She smiled, which was always infectious. William couldn't help but return it convincingly.

"Are they here yet?" William asked. If the Board of Trustees had already arrived, he was in *big* trouble. She nodded and bit her lip, almost to ask, *what do we do now?*

"They said they would like a demonstration of what we've been working on," she said. "I stalled them with coffee and donuts." Her eyes were clear and honest. "Is that bad?"

William smiled and shook his head.

"Not at all. In fact, you might have just saved my life."

Without thinking, he reached upward and touched her arm in a gesture of gratefulness. Instead, what he felt was a surge of sexual energy. He found her incredibly attractive, but they worked together, and she was five years younger than him. To diffuse the flirtatious spark, he whispered a *thank you* and walked off toward his office. Laura watched, standing still, half-smiling in the hallway.

"I'll tell them ten minutes?" she yelled from down the corridor.

William raised his thumb in the air and nodded. With confirmation, she walked toward the meeting room, opened the glass doors, and cleared her throat.

"Dr. O'Malley will see you in about ten minutes for a demonstration on his work." She had said it with a smile and an air of professionalism that surprised even herself. The men and women nodded and returned the smile. She adjusted her blouse—the one that showed her delicate, thin curves—and went, once again, to find Dr. O'Malley.

William estimated that the demonstration would only last about ten minutes. He would explain the viral composition, how he intended on producing a cure, and how containing the virus meant that it never left the hospital walls. He asked Laura to gather the Board of Trustees and meet him at the LEVEL 5 demonstration room. She nodded and left.

When the Board arrived, William had already sterilized, dressed in a biochemical suit, and began handling vials that contained several strips of a red substance.

"Welcome," he projected. His voice rang clear through several speakers in the showing room where the Board watched. "Sorry for the inconvenience this morning. I seemed to have had trouble with my vehicle. But everything is fine now, so, shall we get started?"

William despised group conversation of any sort. Public speaking forced him into a shaky nervousness that he could not break. His voice quivered. He lost the feeling in his toes. Usually, his mouth ran dry. Even now, separated by a glass barrier, he felt the early onset of anxiety start to take effect. He attempted to cover it, but Laura's expression told him, rather bluntly, it was not working.

"You are at LEVEL 5 of the Pathogen Containment Clinic here at Boston Public Medicine. What I am handling is the only virus to ever break the LEVEL 5 barrier. It is a super-virus that houses itself in the brain, creating a zombie-like resurrection of the body. It is *very* contagious and *very* lethal."

When William finished talking, he looked up from his work and saw the widened eyes that peered in. The emphasis on the *very* seemed to amplify interest. Laura smiled.

"Dr. O'Malley," spoke a scrawny, thin-haired member of the Board. "Are we talking about an apocalyptic virus?"

William nodded.

"We are indeed," he confirmed.

There was a collective gasp and William knew he had caught their full attention. For the first time in a long time, he felt in control and professional enough to carry on. He opened the vial and placed the red substance under a magnified electron microscope.

"You can see here that we are talking about one of the most profound super-viruses ever discovered. It travels through contact of bodily fluids —a scratch, bite, or anything of the sort."

The virus, floating in a hazy liquid, shot from corner to corner under the microscope, consuming other molecules around it. William moved the specimen slightly so that the picture was made clearer.

"What I can do, with today's medicinal technology and *your* generous funding, is create an antidote that not only stops this virus from ever touching the human population, but help stop viruses like these from ever happening again."

The members of the Board were astonished and confused, mystified. Until now, the zombie virus was merely an idea for science fiction novels and video games. Now, Doctor William O'Malley held the world's deadliest virus in the palms of his hands. A few Board members were queasy. Others grew pale.

"Where did you *find* this virus, Doctor?" one of them asked.

"That's a good question. Dr. Carl Norse of the International Center for Disease Control headed a very private, very isolated mission trip deep into the African jungles for Ebola research. He stumbled across a village that had been completely overrun by the Dead. Luckily, several of his men had weapons and, because it was a relatively small and isolated village, the disease did not spread. He took a few samples of the deceased, which now rest in my hands. As long as it stays here in LEVEL 5, it is completely containable."

The projector that showed the virus flickered as William turned it off. The sensation of success washed over him. He even contemplated asking Laura out to dinner that evening in celebration of a job well done. His mind buzzed with endorphins as he smiled, picking up the vial and red substance from the microscope.

As he turned, William stumbled over his own feet, falling to the edge of the table. The sound of shattered glass filled the room as the doctor landed hard against the ground.

"Everything's fine!" yelled William. He was shaken, but pulled himself up with hands raised.

"Doctor!" Laura yelled.

It was not until he looked down that he noticed the shattered glass vial had somehow penetrated the biochemical suit, lacerated his forearm, and seemingly intermingled his own blood with the virus.

"It's...It's not what it looks like!" the doctor spoke. His voice continued its violent quivering now. "Remain calm. Everything is fine!"

The Board of Trustees gasped collectively once more, this time in nightmarish fashion. Laura pressed the security button to her left, initiating a loud and piercing siren. The Board members ran for the elevator like a stampede, pressed the up indicator, and waited with their hands over their ears and mouths like children in a haunted house.

Laura had already run through the sterilization room and bypassed clearance. William tried to call out to her, yelling to stay back, but the siren was too piercing, the glass between rooms was too thick, and he was too weak to even pick himself up. The wound in his arm was deep and dripping blood methodically in a pool at his side. He was losing blood too quickly. Soon he would be lightheaded, then unconscious, then who knows what if the virus had really infected him.

The nearest airtight door snapped open and Laura chaotically reached for him.

"Don't," William said, louder than the siren. His face was already growing pale. Laura brushed the back of her hand against his cheek, bending to one knee in front of him. He smiled curtly because he knew what she was saying.

"You're going to be fine," she mumbled, reassuringly. "You *will*."

William shook his head.

"The virus," he said, but that's all he could muster.

Laura could hear the thunder of decontaminant specialists' footsteps hustling through the LEVEL 5 chambers. It would be mere seconds before they pried her away. She reached out, turned his head slightly toward her, and kissed him passionately, more intimately than she had ever kissed another man, then released.

He squeezed her hand with his good arm and smiled.

"Good to know you felt the same," he said.

Almost on cue, the men in biohazard suits filled the laboratory, screaming over the piercing howl of the siren. One pushed Laura out of the room. Another dragged her to the elevator. She watched as they swarmed the doctor in a cloud of white, then closed the elevator doors, leaving her there with another man—this one stern and openly lackluster.

"Are you scratched, bitten, or otherwise exposed to the virus in question?" interrogated the man in the suit.

She thought of the kiss, not about contamination, and how blissfully real it had felt. She could still taste him on her lips, wishing it would never go away. A single tear fell from her eye, but she quickly wiped it into nothing more than a smear of moisture.

"Ma'am, you need to answer the question. Are you scratched, bitten, or otherwise exposed to the virus in question?"

"No," she answered firmly, refocusing.

"Get out at LEVEL 1. Wait for one of us there. We have to evaluate you."

Laura nodded, sniffled three tiny sniffles, and relocated to LEVEL 1, where she sat in a chair, awaiting specialist clearance.

The specialists never came and Laura began to feel a bit nauseous. Several people passed her and stared at her wearily. Their eyes told her that she had lost her healthy appearance. She glanced around and found a mirror in the reception area, but dared not look at herself through it. It had been several hours now since the incident on LEVEL 5 and she feared that something terrible had happened in her absence. She contemplated returning to see if everything was all right, but then realized the naivety of her thoughts and brushed them aside. She had always been one to second-guess herself.

Something turned inside of her, suddenly and furiously, that she could not explain. She felt it tug at her organs and pinch her spine.

Something is seriously wrong, she thought.

A tingling sensation ran up and down her. It slowly morphed from a tickle into a sharp sting. She knew it was the virus. It couldn't be anything else. But paranoia began to set in and instead of seeking help in the Pathogen Clinic (which would not have helped anyway), she set out to find help in the upper levels of the hospital.

More strange sensations washed over her. She felt lightheaded and extraordinarily unaware of her surroundings. She bumped into walls, shuffled her feet into vending machines, and pushed people away who walked too close to her. Her legs were weak, but overwrought as though they were about to explode from the inside. She began stumbling over herself, sweating profusely, towards the Emergency Room.

The halls to the Triage Wing seemed endless. The fluorescent lighting radiated in waves across the hospital space. She breathed hard, feeling the acute *schwop* of her heartbeat, like a subwoofer against her eardrums. It hurt to think. It hurt to move. And the tugging inside of her grew increasingly worse, like the sharp end of a hammer digging harder into every part of her.

She reached the reception desk with virtually no energy left, gazed into the receptionist's eyes, and tried desperately to formulate the words to ask for help. Warm foam dribbled down the side of her mouth. She had lost control of her face, which hung against the rest of her head in a mess of sweaty skin. Her jaw dropped slightly.

There was a scream from the receptionist before Laura slipped to the floor, closed her eyes, and let the last of her breaths slip from her mouth. All thirty or so patients in the room fell silent, mostly in fear. The receptionist screamed for a doctor.

"She just came out of nowhere, started foaming from her mouth, and fell over," the receptionist explained.

She was a heavyset woman in a flowery scrub top. She wore a pair of pants that may have been a size too small and sneakers that rose at the tips. Everyone watched the doctor examine the body.

"Poor girl," one of the patients said from across the waiting area. "I'm getting out of here before anything else happens."

"Wait a minute," the doctor said. "I still hear a heartbeat."

He ran the stethoscope to Laura's chest and listened intently. The sound was so minor that the doctor squinted his eyes and leaned in closer. The waiting room was as tranquil as midnight on Christmas Eve.

Then, it exploded.

Laura jumped up and sank her teeth into the doctor's neck. He screamed in pain and fell to the ground, reaching for the spurting blood gushing from several ripped arteries and veins. The crowd of patients began sprinting towards the Emergency Room exit in typical mob fashion. Laura reached out and grabbed the receptionist by the leg, pulling her down to the floor. The woman cried, too helpless to escape as Laura ripped a chunk of meat from her calf, chewing and spitting with stained red teeth.

The receptionist pried herself away and behind the desk before Laura could take another bite. Instead, her body rose to its feet and shuffled toward the exit where several elderly women and severely injured men sat screaming in waiting room chairs, trying to pull themselves away from the carnage. She ripped into a man with a broken leg and a woman who had just had a seizure at the waiting room chairs, filling the walls with the spray of arterial blood.

The screams of the Emergency Room patients down the hallway caught her attention—the transformed doctor now shuffling behind her. They stumbled down the Triage Wing, leaving only smeared, bloody footprints in their wake. Within seconds, the sounds of chaos rose from a distance. The Triage survivors could only sit in silence, blood everywhere, praying for a quick death.

The receptionist, who barely held on to her consciousness, waited until the bodies had disappeared down the hallway, reached for the phone at the far end of the desk, and dialed 9-1-1.

The pain in her leg burned—an inevitable, lonely burn that drained all the life from her in a brutally short amount of time. She watched as the air around the room began to melt away.

"What is your emergency?" a woman on the other end of the line asked.

"Zombies," she managed to say. "*Zombies.*"

11

Norse rested his hands on the surface of his desk, spreading his fingers so that he could see the wood surface behind them. The burning logs in the fireplace crackled and snapped. They had burned all night and now were covered in a thick layer of blackened ash and sulfur that filled the air with earthy, robust aromas. The flames projected an orange lick of light against the office walls, blending with the morning rays of the sun that shone through the rectangular office windows. It was a brilliant azure day outside and Norse knew it. But he felt most comfortable behind his desk, as he always did, so he immersed himself in the shadows of the room's farthest most corner.

He was waiting for a call—a very important call—that would launch his plan into immediate action. His hand lingered only inches from the office landline, feeling the electricity in the space between the receiver and his hand. It tickled the tips of his fingers with excitement and a curious, anticipatory tautness. He closed his eyes and pretended to hear it kick, but the room remained calmingly soundless, except for the roaring flames of the fireplace.

Norse could see the sky from where he was sitting and wondered if it ever rained in Africa. He'd been here for months now and, to his amazement, he couldn't remember if he had seen even a single raindrop fall from the sky. To be fair, he spent most of his daylight hours inside these four walls, conceding that the humid, African daytime weather did not exactly suit him well, but on days like this, he wished he could take a stroll outside, inhale and exhale deep breaths of the dense, heated air and allow his body to relax against the beauty of the coastal morning. Instead, Norse made time by never sleeping, but taking long walks in the dead of the night, when the air cooled to more mild temperatures and he was alone and undisturbed.

On occasion, the African twilight snapped a batch of rogue heat lightning bolts into the accumulating clouds in the distance. The oranges and yellows and greens were something of a marvel and Norse felt the heat of their power as they unleashed pure energy into the atmosphere. He had always felt that he connected with lightning on an uncommonly intimate, personal level, possibly more than human beings should, but his mother had attested to it, and that made it fine.

When he was just a child, Norse ran away from home after an incident with his father. The man—surly and uncommonly strong—had returned home one night with the bitter stench of alcohol on his breath. He plopped himself down at the kitchen table, almost taking the furniture to the ground with him and smiled languidly at his wife sitting at the other side. He began with playful, touchy swipes, reaching for her hands, but in the discomfort of the moment, Mrs. Norse retracted her arms and turned away, disgusted.

Carl listened from his bedroom as passive disagreements between his parents quickly evolved into steaming, verbal quarrels. These were uncomfortable enough, but like most drunken arguments, those dissonant quarrels rapidly mutated into a lurid scene of fists and flailing limbs. Father pushed his mother to the ground, pulsating a sinister crash from across the room. *Crash* after *crash* lured Carl from his bedroom, gritting his teeth with nervous and furious reckoning.

Without thought, Carl pushed open his bedroom door, ran into the kitchen and stepped in front of his father. His mother lay bruised and hurt at his back.

"You better back off, boy," his father slurred. Even at the age of ten, Carl knew the smell of liquor meant demons were close. He was terrified, shivering mutely with fear.

"You can't hit, Mum," Carl quivered. Tears filled his eyes.

A lone backhand struck the soft skin of his cheek and his mother bellowed a piercing scream, pleading for her husband to stop.

"You. Can't. Hit. Mum," Carl sniffled.

He grabbed a black-ink ballpoint pen from the kitchen table and swung his closed fist into his father's arm. The man shuffled, groaned the deepest, defiantly painful groan he could muster, and fell back onto the closest chair. Blood and ink dribbled from his skin.

"You stupid boy," he whispered. "You stupid, *stupid* boy."

With nothing but a sack over his shoulder, filled with an extra set of clothes, a granola bar, and his uncharged mp3 player, Carl left the house and vowed to never return. He felt adventurous and independent and rebellious all at the same time. He had left that night with the exposed stars still shining and sparkling in the gray-dark sky. The night felt like a friend, comforting him in a way that his father, or even his mother, could not.

For that alone, he was appreciative.

Young Carl walked about five miles before he realized he was making a childish and dangerous mistake.

An Icelandic thunderstorm—one that shook the houses and washed away the roads—overtook the land. The wind pelted him with sharpened blades in the form of rain. Thunder hurt the most sensitive parts of his eardrums.

Carl, not knowing what else to do, curled himself into a makeshift crescent on the side of the flooded street. And just when he thought it could not get any worse, young Carl stood up and collided with a bolt of electricity that shook every fiber of his being. He lay there, on the side of the road in a puddle of muddy water, half-breathing and half-awake, wondering if that was what death truly felt like.

A lone passerby discovered Carl's twitching body a half an hour later, scooped him up (seeming as though Carl weighed close to ninety pounds soaking wet), and transported him, as quickly as he could to the nearest hospital. He spent the next week trying to shake the pins and needles from every inch of his body with little to no avail.

Sometimes, even now, the feeling still erupted in his hands and feet.

"That's why you're so smart," his mother would say. "The gods gave you their power. You're meant for big things, Carl."

The phone in his office rang in loud, obtrusive tones. It jolted him from his vivid, abrasive memories like whiplash. He picked up the receiver and held it to his ear. There was a messy jumble of noises from the other end of the line, including the sound of heavy breathing.

"Yes?" Norse asked.

He spoke through hardened teeth and no signs of a smile.

"Sir, the vials are safe. All of them. We are nearing the helicopters now. The hospital is a goner, sir. We lost three…"

Norse interrupted, changing his tone from concerned to brash. He shifted the phone from his right ear to his left ear, trapping it between his shoulder and his hairline.

"Good," Norse spoke. "Bring them to me as soon as you can."

There was a silence tainted by Norse's apparent disregard for body counts.

"Right away, sir. One more thing," the voice spoke. "There was a man on the wall. We couldn't tell if he was infected. We elected to kill him."

The voice was lost in more hard breathing and, what seemed like, gunfire.

"Why do you bother me with such petty technicalities?" Norse questioned in unmistakable conceit. "Do what you have to do. If that means murdering every last human in that *goddamn* place, you do it."

"Yes, sir," the voice responded submissively.

The sound of helicopter blades rustled the air into a cyclic chaos of wind against the microphone. Then the noise ceased and all went quiet.

Norse clicked the phone back onto his desk and closed his eyes, rubbing the skin under his eyebrows.

The vials, he thought, smiling for a moment, then pushing his mouth back into a straightened line of lips.

He pushed himself from the desk and walked toward the windows. The sky stretched out over the ocean and glistened the water like millions of shattering stars.

"I'll think I'll take a walk today," Norse said, mostly to himself, intermingled with a sigh of relief and morning weariness. "It's a good day to be me."

12

"Did you hear that?" Shanna whispered to Henry, who dazed in and out of yet another exhaustive state of sleep. Besides the usual shuffling of footsteps and rustling of brush outside, there was a growing drone at the window. It started slow and soft, more like a whistle, and grew to a vibrating hum that woke her from her drifting fatigue.

"Hear what?" Henry opened his eyes, drearily at first, and then wider to show her that he was awake and listening, somehow taking this seriously. "I don't hear anything."

Shanna rubbed her eyes and sunk back against the dusty wall.

"I thought I heard someone humming," she said.

Henry shook his head gently. He breathed deep, stuck out his chest for a brief stretch of his torso, and allowed the air in his diaphragm to rush from his chest in one, drawn out burst of air.

"Go back to sleep," he whispered, then wrapped his arm around her and returned to the place behind his eyelids.

She tried, but couldn't shake the feeling of discontent. The moonlight seemed oddly bright against the boarded windows. And the constant groaning had all but ceased from the street. She heard Quintero adjust and snort from his crouched position opposite her.

Sleep finally took him, she thought.

Harro and Fender were asleep, too, not wholly letting themselves fall deeper, but enough. Their breathing was short and nearly soundless, listening with passive ears for anything out of the ordinary.

The whistle-hum began again and Shanna's heart raced. She pinpointed where it was coming from, contemplated waking Henry again, but decided against it. Slowly, she rose to her feet and took the few steps toward the window. The moonlight filtered through the cracks in the wooden boards. It reminded her of her childhood in the Midwest—plains of grain blanketed with the silver glow of a vast, inviting moon.

She hesitantly touched the window with shaking fingers. The night had cooled the air enough to shiver, but a shiver laced with a pleasant appreciation for comfort. Just outside, the hum continued, filling the street with the sounds of a nursery rhyme. She could not decipher which one specifically, but the innocent combination of jumbled notes and rhythmic meter couldn't be mistaken for anything else. It *was* a nursery rhyme, and suddenly, Shanna felt herself losing sanity, scared to proceed any further in her exploration. She backed away from the window, catching herself quickly.

What am I doing? she asked herself. *There's nothing out there scarier than what you've already witnessed. Just take a look.*

Henry's bravery had apparently already had an effect on her because she suddenly enveloped herself in the quiet need to proceed. As the others slept, she wondered if she was catalyzing something she shouldn't be, or if her mind was merely playing tricks on her. She inhaled one, deep breath, controlled the panic that threatened from within, and cautiously moved the peephole board once again, widening her right eye to look out into the night.

The strip of asphalt she could see was virtually empty. In the distance, past several shaded buildings, a few shuffling Dead meandered about. They veered their heads, but in rigid displays of movement and disregard. Just to be safe, Shanna double-checked, moving her eyes from the skyline, to the left of the house, and to the right. Still, she found no reason to panic, except for one, large apparent miscue.

In the middle of the street was a child, probably three or so years old, sitting in a dirtied shirt and colorless underwear, splayed out onto the cold asphalt. In her arms was a ragged doll to which she sang *Humpty Dumpty* in a cute and bouncy bout of imagination, swaying her upper body to put the doll to sleep.

"Oh my *God*," Shanna whispered.

Her eyes grew wide. She turned to the others and motioned for them all to wake. There were slow movements and grumblings, but Shanna's persistence drew a need for hasty attention.

"Now!"

The one word seemed strangely definitive, wrapped in a bit of pent-up annoyance.

Shanna pointed her index finger to the peephole and mouthed the word *look* to Quintero, who was the first one up. One by one, the group pried themselves from the floor and lumbered over to the front of the room. Shanna stood waiting, pressing herself up against the wall with her hands outstretched.

"What the hell, Shanna?" Quintero grunted. "What's so important that you had to wake all of us up in the middle of the night?"

Henry, like the others, wanted to see what the commotion was about, but his mind only seemed to drag him furher and further into sleep. Only seconds had passed, but he found it excruciatingly difficult to separate what were dreams from what was reality and, instead of fighting the need to be a part of what was happening outside, the need for sleep felt even more potent, consuming him like a drug that amplified the haze of imagination. He fell back into a deep slumber.

"Holy shit," Quintero whispered. "How the hell did *she* get there?"

He was still trying to shake the exhaustion from his eyes, but the child shook his attention.

The child continued smiling and giggling at the doll, still swaying it in a rocking motion at her chest.

"I *love* you," she said to the doll, as a mom would say to her newborn baby just after birth.

Shanna welled with tears. The child fell to her back, rolled a few times, and crawled on her hands and knees about two feet to her right.

"We have to help her," Shanna whispered. The motherly features shone bright in her eyes. "Before it's too late."

Fender placed a hand on her shoulder. His eyes told a story of forbearance that any woman had the heart to follow.

"I know we have to do something," Fender spoke with gravity, "but something feels off about this."

There was a bit of déjà vu that stung Quintero like the pinch of a wasp. He had seen this scene before, somewhere not too long ago, which he could not quite pinpoint. It made him shudder.

"We don't have much of a choice," Harro spoke, reasoning with Fender. "She's just a little girl."

Fender paced the darkness. Quintero watched.

Don't do it, Quin, he told himself. *Something's not right here. Figure it out first.*

The already immense task of finding a way out of the city had just become even messier. The gunman gritted his teeth, looked down to his feet, felt the distinct jolt of metal against his waist and made a quick and, possibly overzealous, decision.

"I'll do it," he said. "I'll get her."

He spoke as if it was a definitive decision, but everything in him told him otherwise.

"You don't have to do this alone," Fender spoke, shaking his head in disapproving waves.

"The less of us that go out there, the better, right?" the gunman asked. The question seemed to scatter throughout the room.

"I'm not letting you go alone," Harro said. "And that's final."

Fender stepped closer now.

"You can't…"

"Don't tell me what I can and cannot do. This is *my* choice."

Fender bit the fat of his bottom lip, cringing at being interrupted by such a free and abrasive tone. He scratched at his chin just to keep his hands busy. If there was one thing he understood about his wife, it was that she was a strong and stubborn woman. It was why they were in Boston in the first place. She had coerced him enough, manipulated his thoughts even more, and tugged at his conscience, ripping open a flood of guilt that finally broke the dam of *no*'s and *absolutely not*'s.

He ripped a sword from the holster slung to his shoulders.

"Looks like we're all going then," he said.

"No," Shanna interrupted. The conversations stopped immediately. The group looked over at her, who had turned and now faced them. "*I'll* do it."

The men were puzzled. Harro sensed a bit of heroism in her voice.

"Let's be honest," she continued, "I don't have guns. I don't have swords. I'm the one with the least to lose."

They all kept quiet to digest her words.

"You *can't* be serious," Harro blurted. "I'm not letting you go out there alone."

Shanna shook her head and wondered if her shortened speech were words of uncontrollable impulsivity or courage.

"Fine," Quintero surrendered. "The three of us will cover you from the sides. Fender, you take the right. I'll take the left. Harro, you shield the house."

"Where's Henry?" Shanna asked.

They shot their eyes across the room, looking for any signs of movement. His body was spread out across the floor in the corner near the kitchen. Deep breaths stirred the dust and cobwebs in tiny microbursts around him.

"It's better if he sleeps," Quintero spoke. "Poor kid's done everything he can just to get here."

The gunman took in a deep breath and sighed. "Quick and painless."

He unsheathed two pistols, clutching one in each hand, tilting his head like a man suddenly aware of immortal danger. He felt the unmistakable burst of adrenaline release into his veins, but somewhere deep inside of him, amidst the necessity and urgency to save the child, he knew this would not end well. Nothing in this place ever did. Their hopes of leaving the city unscathed would soon be a hope that dwindled into nothing but a waning glimmer of light in the far off distance.

Fender curved the edge of his mouth into a faint smile. With a fleeting bit of strength, he opened the front door.

The air was crisp and bitter as they made their way to the street. Fender faded to the right. Quintero countered to his left. Harro stayed back against the shade of the porch while Shanna nervously fluttered out to the little girl, who hadn't even noticed the new commotion around her, still immersed in her own make-pretend world.

Shanna bent a leg, kneeling at the child's level, and looked into her eyes. They were the color of a summer sunset.

"Come with me, Sweetie," Shanna whispered.

The girl ignored her and kept murmuring to the doll in high registering pitches. Her skin was pale. A bulging, blue vein traveled from the left side of her forehead past her cheek to her neck. Against her skin it rose, but not enough to venture beyond its opaque contrast. Something strange careened over Shanna in this moment of observation. What the rest of the group had seen as a playful bout of innocence, Shanna now recognized as a searing display of pain. The toddler twisted and rolled, aching for her infection to stop.

"Help me," she pleaded. "Help *me*."

Shanna reached for the girl's arm, noticing a small slit near the elbow the width of a dime. The edges of the wound were jagged as though made by a fingernail or sharpened incisor tooth. It was not bleeding, but the small stains of red around its edges told Shanna the wound had coagulated and been there for some time now. With a little body like hers, the infection had already made its way through her.

Heartbreak riddled Shanna's frame. She glanced up into the child's eyes once more, which were now the color of burnt caramel, changing quickly, devolving. Her pupils enlarged, then tightened as she breathed, until she produced a small flood of foam from her mouth.

"Stay with me," Shanna whispered.

But she knew it was too late. Whatever or *whoever* had done this, timed it perfectly. It was a trap.

"Hurry," Harro whispered, clutching tightly to the scythes in her hands.

The baby girl arched her back, let out a violent and terrible scream, and went limp. Her final breath gurgled against the lathered foam running from her nose.

There was a not-so-distant laugh, followed by a voice that projected terribly deep, swelling into the night.

"Trick," it said. "Trick!"

From above Harro, a hardened figure appeared on the roof of their apartment. It was half-clothed, gray-skinned, and horribly mauled. Its lower lip hung against its jaw, now unusable, displaying two rows of disproportionate teeth, enlarged and rotten. Strands of long greasy hair flopped against its face, leaving streaks of something as it slapped. It looked like fresh blood.

Quintero wasted no time lifting his pistols and shooting three well-aimed bullets into the figure's abdomen to slow it down. It staggered, gushing blood, but remained upright and sturdy, disregarding its wounds and pain entirely. It smiled, then propelled from the roof, hitting the street with tremendous power.

Harro swung a chained scythe in front of her and clipped at the figure's torso. It roared, in a mixture of surprise and pleasure, turning slowly towards her. Its smile appeared more like a widened glare— metric, like the stare of gathering information, not the emotional upheaval that the sensation of pain usually brings. She swung the scythe from her left hand in a release of the chains. The figure ducked and charged Harro, who now found herself caught in limbo, attempting to furiously gather back the scythes before it was too late.

"No!" Fender yelled, clanking his longswords in a metallic battle cry. He held both blades out in front of him as he sprinted towards the porch. The figure grasped Harro by the neck with tremendous strength and lifted her from the ground. It opened its mouth and cried mercilessly into the sky.

Fender swung the blades at thigh level. The figure turned at contact, despite the new monstrosity of a gash the swords had sliced into its body, nearly separating its torso from its legs. It walked, although tenuously, towards him with his wife still clutched in its grimy hand, roaring and grimacing and sliding against its own bodily fluids. Fender attempted another swing at head level, but missed. The corpse simply reached out, grasped the sword blades with its free palm, and smiled again. Thick, black blood spewed from its hand, drizzling to the ground.

Just as Fender felt the blades bend, almost snapping both of them under its profound pressure, a shimmer of metal flashed from behind him that forced the creature to its knees. The handle of a crooked butter knife stood immersed in blood, penetrating the creature's softened skull. Henry stood there with hand over handle, panting. The body continued to fidget, uttering encrypted Dead talk, but they all knew the fight was over. A knife to the brain meant the end. It reached at Fender with a disgusted, monotonous stare and finally released Harro from its maniacal grip, who gasped for breath and held her neck in security.

Like a sledgehammer, Henry hammered the knife with full strength farther into its skull until the body fell limp and mangled.

"I'd *really* appreciate a wake up call next time," Henry said in a tone of semi-seriousness.

Fender nodded, turning to his wife.

The street to the left, Quintero's side, suddenly mobbed with the Dead.

"Time to go!" he yelled. "It's time to go!"

Shanna was still hovering over the body of the girl, which began to convulse, snapping its jaw and breaking teeth.

"She's one of the them now," Fender spoke from over her shoulder. "We need to go. Forget her."

Shanna nodded, wiping the tears from her eyes. She tried to hold them back, but the injustice of the situation wrenched her heart into a void of emptiness. Her bottom lip quivered. No matter how hard she tried, she felt the warmth of more tears forming behind her lids.

Fender helped Shanna from the street and gently pushed her away from the snapping, toddler body. He ran his blade against the girl's neck, separating the skin and muscle. In one motion, the convulsive groans stopped. It was over.

"Look at this," Henry said.

The onslaught of groans grew imperiously beyond them. They needed to act fast.

"This guy was a doctor."

Henry pulled an identification card from the body's breast pocket and scanned it quickly: *William O'Malley, PhD, MD, Boston Public Medicine.*

"Jesus," Fender spoke. "Good lookin' guy, too."

Quintero barreled through the street with his guns in his hands, reaching back and firing a few shots into the wave of bodies behind him. Several times, he tripped over his own legs as he pushed himself back to the group.

"Time to go!" he yelled again. "Run!"

Henry reached his hand into Dr. O' Malley's breast pocket once more. There was a bulge there he hadn't noticed the first time and, even with his escape time dwindling, he did not question the urge to do so. Fender bent his forehead in confusion, wondering why Henry would be so infatuated with such a little find. Where the fabric of the shirt met the seam, Henry revealed a small, hidden glass container the size of a thumbnail. At first, Henry thought about discarding it, but as he analyzed the red fluid within, he decided against it and dropped it in his pocket.

"What was that?" Fender asked.

Henry shrugged his shoulders, grabbed at Shanna's arm and started to run. Harro had wrested herself and joined Fender's side.

"Follow me," said the gunman.

The mob of dead had already doubled their numbers in the short amount of time it took to regroup and Henry suddenly feared the worst. A mob this big could finally be too much to handle.

Henry tried to keep a similar speed with Shanna at his side, but Quintero, as Henry already knew, was agilely fast. Fender and Harro bolted ahead just behind the gunman with long strides, while Henry pulled Shanna from the back, trying to take her mind off of her pained ankle. The mass of bodies gained, though, and Henry felt the weight of sheer vulnerability wash over him.

"You can do this," he said, speaking to Shanna, but all he heard were the gasps of fatigue and little *umphs* of pain.

She was gulping for air. Sweat poured from her forehead. She wiped it away with her empty hand and kept her stride, hobbling against the break. No matter how much she wanted to, Henry did not let her stop. He pulled, even when she reared back for rest.

"I won't let you go!" he screamed over the onslaught behind them. "I won't! Keep running."

Quintero turned a corner out of sight, then Harro, followed by Fender. Henry and Shanna were quickly losing ground about a hundred yards behind the rest of the group. The potent, rancid smell told Henry the waves behind them were close, but he refused to admit it. They were going to make it, he told himself.

"Keep running!"

Sometimes the simplest remarks turn out to be the best motivators.

Shanna pushed, landing several times hard on her already swollen ankle, cringing in pain, letting loose another string of tears. The bones crunched on impact, finally buckling and nearly falling headfirst to the ground, but Henry felt her twinge first and without thinking, picked her up in his arms and continued his sprint. Suddenly, an untapped spurt of energy surged through him that he could not explain. His legs hardened with unforeseen power and, remarkably, the screeches behind him started to disappear.

For one unequivocally brilliant moment, Henry felt invincible.

He turned the corner in a hard push of feet. He couldn't find where the others went, but searched the dark landscape for any signs. Straggling bodies swiped at them, but were far enough away to avoid any contact.

"Here!" he heard.

The voice seemed distant, but not out of reach. He maintained speed, adjusting his arms underneath Shanna as he pushed. This was it—the final stretch. His biceps ripped under his skin. His forearms began to lose circulation. And Shanna continued to cringe. She kicked a violent body that surprised them from a nearby alley. It nearly sent both of them toppling over each other, even then, he refocused just in time.

Up ahead, amidst the swarming bodies approaching them from all angles, Henry focused only on Quintero, hidden behind a batch of gnarly bodies. The gunman held out his two pistols—one in each hand—up and parallel to his eyes. One by one, the approaching bodies splattered and fell to Henry's left and right. A narrow, but clear path opened. Bullets whizzed.

Keep it straight, he told himself. *Let Quintero do the work.*

So he did, and the bodies around him fell like rag dolls in a puppet show. Brain matter and blood splattered in every direction. He felt as though he was running through a tunnel that would never end.

Fender held the door open of a strange building and Henry squeezed in, sending Shanna skidding across the lobby. She let out a silent whimper and pulled herself up.

"Are you okay?" Henry asked.

He hadn't meant to throw her, but he, too, had lost his balance and scrambled across the tiled floor. The entrance was far from graceful, but they *had* survived because of him.

"I'm okay," she replied, brushing herself off and hobbling to grab hold of something for balance.

Only seconds passed before the Dead pressed up heavily against the glass, spewing and exposing rotten teeth like feral animals. Quintero locked the door, but backed away hurriedly.

"It won't last long," he said. "We have to hurry."

Shanna wrapped a nervous arm around Henry and managed to hobble on one foot behind the rest of the crew. She whispered a solid *thank you* in his ear, placed her hand gently in his, and followed Quintero down a dark set of utility stairs.

"You could've just left me," she said. A bashful glow rose to the skin of her cheeks—one even Henry could see in the dark of the stairwell. "I'm the broken wheel, Henry. We won't make it out alive if…"

Henry turned, interrupting his girlfriend mid-sentence.

"Don't you dare talk like that," he said. He held her safely in his arms. "I came for you. I *will* get you out."

A ghoulish dripping of water could be heard from somewhere, but it echoed as if it were everywhere. Above them, the sound of shattering glass reverberated through the walls. Footsteps and groans pummeled through the entrance, but the noise seemed distant now.

"We're far enough away. Just keep moving," the gunman whispered.

They did as they were told, skipping stairs in stride as they descended farther into the depths of the mysterious stairwell. They did not ask questions. Shanna grimaced on the weight of her ankle. Henry held her up as best as he could, while Quintero finally felt it safe enough to holster his weapons.

They reached the basement and hustled through the blocked entry. Quintero ushered the group inside, then shut the door, wrapping chains around the double-handled access and snapping a rusty padlock into place with a heavy, anchored *clank*. A stained couch, a badly warped desk, a ceiling fan, and a shaky wooden chair filled the limbo room. They all contemplated a rest here, but again, knew it would be best to just keep going.

The footsteps had faded from above them. It was tranquil and strange to be in a room so secure after such a brawl. Yet Quintero sighed heavily, running his hands through his sweaty hair, then onto his pants. Shanna shivered in the unnatural lighting.

"Wait," panicked Henry. "Where are Harro and Fender?"

Suddenly a flash of alarm surfaced in his mind and, for a brief moment, Henry considered going back to find them, but the gunman pointed to another darkened entrance on the opposite side of the room. Shanna hobbled over to the next room, let go of a stymied yawn, and hunched over into several dry heaves. What had only smelled like sitting farts a moment ago in the furniture room, suddenly grew to an even stronger odor in the empty space. The stagnant air hovered and trapped the group in filth.

"Guys, I don't think you're going to like where we're headed."

He wiped sweat from his hairline. It smeared across his forehead in a streak of moisture.

Both Henry and Shanna seemed oblivious as to their location. The smell alone should've given it away.

"It's our best chance to get out of here. There're still a few hours before sunrise and we sure as hell can't go back up there." Quintero pointed back to the door as he spoke. "We never should have left the house. We had a plan."

"We had no choice," argued Shanna. "What were we going to do, leave that poor girl in the middle of the street? We had no idea she'd end up like that."

"I can't believe it was a *trap*! I should've *known*. They pulled something like that on us on our way in. Remember, Henry? How could we be so *stupid*?"

"He was a doctor," Henry spoke, not sure if Quintero knew where he was going with his words, "the one that almost killed Fender. The one that talked."

150

"The big guy? I shot him three times square in the chest and he didn't even flinch."

"He had this in his pocket," said Henry, revealing the vial. The red substance within the glass moved slightly, like a timer, as Henry tilted it. The gunman leaned in and looked at it with wearisome eyes.

"What the hell is it?" he asked.

Henry shrugged his shoulders, returning it to his pocket.

"I don't know, but I couldn't leave it there. It seemed kind of... *important*."

Shanna wandered over to the adjacent room and peered in. It was similar to the room that they were standing in except for a heavy amount of chipping paint peeling from the walls, bare ceiling space, and a desire to vomit due to the rank, sour smell. Darkness clouded anything beyond that.

"Thank God you found us. I thought we left you for dead," Harro spoke up. Her eyes were genuine.

"Pretty damn close," Henry replied.

There was a bit of extenuating sarcasm, but only enough for a fit of playful smiles. Henry stretched out his arms, feeling new tension in his swollen biceps. They throbbed, but like the rest of his body, the stinging had lessened, leaving room for something far worse—a dull, aching soreness.

Harro shifted her line of sight to Quintero.

"It's clear back there for the most part. Once we hit the line, we couldn't see a foot in front of us, though. Not sure what's down there."

"It'll have to work," the gunman responded. "We don't have much time."

Henry noticed the expression of reluctance plastered on Shanna's face. He suddenly realized he was still very much in the dark on the group's new plan.

"Where are we exactly?" Henry asked.

He rubbed his aching muscles.

"The city's sewage treatment facility," said the gunman. "Just think of it like the subway lines, except *shittier*."

Shanna sighed and hobbled over to the rest of the group. She folded her arms in front of her against her breasts. Henry took delight in the way she slunk her weight on her good foot and nudged out her hip. A little attitude emerged from her suddenly vivid expression.

"Then what are we waiting for?" she asked. "Let's get this over with."

Quintero smirked, delighted in Shanna's sparked commitment. Harro reached into the pocket of her jacket and exposed two small flashlights. She handed one to Fender and the other to Shanna.

"Found these back in the utility stairwell. Don't know how much battery life we have, so we have to move fast. Without any light in the sewage line, we're as good as dead," she said.

Quintero unsheathed two loaded pistols and held them at his sides. Fender mirrored the action by ripping the right-handed sword from its holster and gripping the flashlight in his left. The gunman met eyes with everyone. They all knew it was time.

Without another word, the group ventured into the darkness.

13

Southern Africa
Monday Evening

There was a biting chill in the after-dark air, but Norse thought nothing of it. The moon illuminated the sky, like a smiling silver dollar set placidly against the blinking stars. Norse rested on a park bench, drizzled with the early onset of dew. Soon it would turn to frost against the grass, but for now, Norse admired the way the moisture felt cool against the warmth of his body.

In front of him sat a quaint, rectangular floral garden filled with blues, yellows, and greens. The ocean rumbled against the coastal rocks as its backdrop. Norse crossed his right leg over his left and exhaled a sigh of comfortable relief. In the far distance, he heard the choppy thunder of helicopter blades rumble and ripple the air. A brief, faint smirk slid across his face, like an expression that should not have been there, but refused to vanish.

A light breeze brushed Norse's face, shimmering his eyelids enough to force him into a fit of blinking. His eyes watered, but only enough to enhance his vision, refreshing the exhaustion from his eyes. From behind him, he heard the rustling of dust and overhung vegetation that tunneled the dirt path. He glanced over his shoulder and saw a thin, soft man walking toward the bench. His black-rimmed glasses and thin hair glistened in the moonlight.

"There will be no more negotiations," Norse spoke. "I told you. My men were en route the entire time."

"I'm not here to negotiate. What you're doing," the man rebutted. "It's *vile*."

"What I'm doing," Norse continued, "is brilliant. I will be the single most recognized scientist on the face of the *planet*."

"If you continue with this, I will be forced to report you."

Norse burst into a hearty, sinister laugh. It thundered from the depths of his chest and rocketed through his teeth. He unhooked his crossed leg and leaned forward, resting his elbows on his knees. He looked up into the man's eyes. The figure stood cryptic against the waning sky.

"I will not hesitate, Dr. Norse," the man continued. "I am beyond reservation."

Norse slowly rose to his feet, groaning almost habitually to show his age, motioning with his fingers in a delicate, swaying motion.

"Walk with me."

The man, hesitantly at first, found his stride next to Norse, shivering in the bitterness. The floral gardens looked wet against the dew.

"You see," Norse spoke. "This is more than just an isolated event."

He interlocked his fingers in front of him as though he was giving a lecture without the comforts of a podium. He swiveled his hips slightly to convey a certain casualness while he talked. Although Norse appeared relaxed, the bitter cold stung the man's lips as he breathed. It was a peculiarly well-lit night with a breeze that shot like daggers through skin.

"You of all people must understand the magnitude of such a breakthrough, Dr. Welnik," Norse spoke. It was a compliment that came and went entirely unnoticed. "That's why I came to you in the first place."

"It isn't the breakthrough that concerns me," Welnik replied. "It's the means in which you intend to reach that goal."

"I see," Norse said. He bowed his head only enough for Welnik to observe the slight change in appearance.

Welnik straightened his posture against the wistful breeze.

"There is no way around it," Norse explained. "The virus *only* affects the human population. In order to test it and find the cure, we need a strong specimen."

"And I simply cannot allow human testing on such a volatile disease."

The two men strolled to the edge of the garden, which halted against the vivacity of the African coastal cliffs. The ocean slapped against the rock five hundred feet below. The moon watched in tranquil solemnity. Welnik gasped at its beauty.

"I take it you've never been this far from the facility before?" Norse asked. His voice balanced a curious mixture of affability and enmity. Welnik gazed out at the crystal shards of ocean water, shaking his head in response.

The helicopter thunder was closer now. Norse thought he could see

154

them in the distance, but the darkness of the evening only clouded his perception. The expression on Welnik's face changed from an aestheticized daze to a fit of clarity. He sighed against the wind, watching as his breath crystalized in front of him while Norse stood unforgiving behind him.

"My plan only works if I have the full support of the staff," Norse spoke. His voice was calm, but excruciatingly deviant. "If I find that the support is not there, I rid the staff of its incongruities."

Norse shifted quickly and grabbed the meat of Welnik's arm in a fit of excited fury. The moonlight burned in his eyes. A hint of fear washed over Welnik. Norse delighted in it. He dragged Welnik's body over to the cliff's edge. The white foam blasted against the rock. Large shards of sharpened crag pointed like spears up at the men.

"You don't have to do this, Norse," Welnik pleaded. He tried to break free, but Norse's grip was unbearably tight. "We can find a way to work this out."

"You've made it quite clear," Norse spoke. "Farewell."

And with no sign of guilty recompense, Norse watched as the man let out a blood-curdling scream, collided with the rock below, and fell silent against the rushing waves. He wiped his hands on his neatly ironed pants, as if ridding some grimy dust from his fingers, and walked amusedly back through the wilting floral gardens.

"Sir," the soldier spoke clearly. "I have what you are looking for."

"Come in," Norse spoke.

It was well past midnight now and the sounds of shuffling feet and scientific conversing outside of his office had completely disappeared. It was the time of night that a lonesome feeling ignited within him—one that could not be rid without ripping a hole in his already fragile soul. But along with that craving for company was a biting need for quiet reflection, which was the emotional avenue he always, without a doubt, chose to follow.

The soldier was a strongly built, young man with a childish face. He wore entirely black with an automatic weapon slung to his side. He maintained a posture that arched his back and jutted his shoulders enough to emphasize the muscular stability of his frame. In his right hand, he held a metallic case that rested against his thigh.

Norse noticed the case immediately.

"I will be the first to congratulate you on a job well done," Norse spoke, looking the soldier square in his tired, but unreachable eyes.

Norse ran his hand over the top of the case, savoring the feeling of accomplishment it brought. He slipped his fingers under the two latches and snapped them into place. He heard the airtight compartment release as it opened. Four small vials rested comfortably against fitted, black foam. One vial was missing.

Norse's eyes rose to the soldier in a deep loss of gratitude.

"What is this?" Norse asked.

The soldier folded his hands in front of him and raised his chin in mild indifference.

"The vials, sir," he spoke. "What you asked for."

The doctor cleared his throat and rose to his feet. There was no animosity in the way he circled his desk, but a strange puzzlement wrestled with his unusual silence. He flipped the case so that it faced him from the other side of the desk. The soldier heard quiet tinkling as Norse picked each of the vials into his hand one-by-one.

"There's one missing," Norse spoke calmingly. "I *need* all five."

"Sir," the soldier replied as professionally as he possibly could, "we could not locate the fifth vial. The Dead were closing in. We had to get out while we still could."

Norse kept his back to the soldier, who now grew increasingly weary of the doctor's doings. The sound of metal against metal filled the office.

"I understand," Norse spoke. A bit of sarcasm rang through his voice.

The soldier reached for the gun at his side apprehensively.

"At ease soldier," said the doctor. He had yet to turn and face him, yet the tension that filled the room was unmistakable. "I just want to understand the part in my objectives where I was—how shall I put this—unclear."

"You were not unclear, sir," the soldier spoke once again in his professional, soldier-turned-scholar voice. "I was forced to make a decision and I chose to retreat to spare the lives of my men. I was not aware of the importance of the fifth…"

"That *vial* is worth more than your life!" Norse screamed in vehement anger. He spat as he yelled. The soldier remained uniformly direct, even as the doctor turned and locked stares. The tips of their noses were millimeters from contact.

"You have two choices. I *suggest* you choose wisely," Norse explained. A small, unintimidated smirk slipped from the corner of the soldier's mouth. "You gather your men, board the helicopters, and find that vial, or…"

"Or *what?*" the soldier interrupted. The professionalism had vanished now replaced by a man unfazed by fear.

"Or I find someone who will."

The soldier reached for his gun, tilting it enough to catch Norse's attention. The doctor's hand reached and caught the metal of the weapon in an awkward display of quickened movement. His grip bent the barrel of the gun away from him, snapping the base in half. A single vein formed at the base of Norse's neck, fluttering and pulsating with disheartened and feverish disappointment. It was strength the soldier had never seen.

"Wrong choice," Norse whispered. In his unused hand, the doctor revealed a small syringe. The soldier flailed his arm in one last attempt to ward off Norse's assault, but felt the thin needle slide into the skin of his neck despite his attempts of escape. There was a distinct pinch and a moment of desperate realization.

The soldier fell to his knees, still holding the dysfunctional weapon. He clicked the trigger, producing nothing.

"What have you done to me?" he asked. His eyes were that of a child, aware of helplessness, desperate for help. "What have you done to me?"

"Relax," the doctor whispered. "It'll all be over soon."

With a violent fist, Norse struck the soldier at the jaw. His body flailed with the force of it then fell, without grace, to the office floor. Norse returned the syringe to the metallic case where it rested with the three remaining vials. He dropped his gaze to the empty slot where the fifth vial should have been and grimaced in vicious frustration.

After securely tying the soldier's wrists, neck, and ankles to the armchair in the corner of his office, Norse returned to his desk, resting his arms against the cool surface of the Maplewood counter. He rubbed his eyes, finally feeling the pull of sleep lure him away. It had been a long day and an equally exhaustive evening. But his plan was just beginning and there was no time for sleep.

Norse picked up the receiver and dialed the front office, twirling a business card between his index finger, thumb, and middle finger. He heard the sound of a digital ring and then, almost immediately, a woman's voice answered.

"Yes, please have Mr. Antonio Devolds call me as soon as he is available," Norse spoke. The woman's voice complied and clicked off.

Norse leaned back in his chair. The fireplace had burned to a dull ember and glowed orange against the walls. The soldier squirmed, foaming, like a river, from his mouth, and once again, fell limp and irreversibly quiet. It would not be long before the tests were run and the beginnings of an antidote could be made. Norse smiled, closed his eyes, and waited for his phone to ring.

The hours of the early morning were always the hardest. While the rest of the world slept, Norse kept awake—sometimes closing his eyes—but never sleeping. When the phone finally rang, a sluggish, half-awake voice answered.

"Yes," spoke Norse.

"This is Devolds. You wanted me to call," the voice spoke. It was deep and heart stopping.

"Yes, yes…Devolds. I have a small favor to ask of you."

There was no answer, so Norse continued.

"There is something in the city that I need retrieved. I heard you are the best of the best."

"So they say," Devolds spoke. "What happened to your men?"

Each word was splayed in monotony sprinkled with a drizzle of sarcasm.

"The job was too big for them," Norse explained. "They did their best, but I relieved them of their duties."

Norse could hear the sounds of quiet breathing. He broke the irritating silence once again.

"So I can count on you then?" Norse asked. There was a vivid impatience in his voice.

"What's the pay?" Devolds asked.

"More than you can fit in your pockets," Norse snorted.

There was nothing from the other side of the line.

"There will be a helicopter waiting to retrieve you. We will discuss financial compensation afterwards. My men will fill you in with what you need to know."

"I'll be waiting," murmured Devolds.

The phone clicked and Norse cracked his neck loudly. The groaning commenced from the armchair. The soldier, who was no longer a soldier at all, heard the conversation and began writhing at its restraints. Norse, scalpel in hand, rose from his desk and walked patiently over to the Dead. It widened its jaw and snapped at the air to no avail. In some ways, Norse felt the company of the Dead felt a little less obtrusive than human company. As long as they were controlled—*like pets*, Norse thought— they were uncannily mild. He smiled at his quirky thoughts.

He watched the body stare and shift, trying in every way to escape, but fail time and time again. He slid white latex gloves over his hands, placing each sizeable finger in its proper place. The bands stretched across his wrists. He reached in and began slicing a section of graying skin matter from the soldier's face.

"Now hold still," Norse spoke, emphasizing each word as if he was talking to an infant. "This will only take a minute."

He sliced another section of skin from its bicep and yet another from its chest, placing each cut into its own container, away and secure. As he ran a syringe into its arm, the soldier groaned into a scream, not out of pain, but of boredom. Its restraints rubbed and irritated the skin at his wrists, ankles, and neck. A good amount of molasses-colored blood filled the plastic, rising like viscous currents.

"Intriguing," the doctor muttered, analyzing the contents of the syringe.

He ripped the gloves off in a loud elastic snap, discarded them into the waste bin, and returned to his desk. The phone rang and the woman's voice at the front desk offered a good morning.

"Shall I tell the boys to head home?" she asked.

Norse envisioned a dozen or so black-suited soldiers waiting in the lobby.

"On the contrary," Norse bellowed. He forced his voice into a spell of shakiness. "I need one or two of them up here immediately."

"Right away," said the receptionist. Her voice faded into the click of dead space.

When the soldiers arrived, they knocked politely. Norse invited them in.

"Sir? You called?" one of them asked. His eyes darted to the unrecognizable soldier in the armchair. Both men backed away and raised their weapons.

"Please," Norse spoke, signaling to lower their weapons with his hands. "I have already done the hard work."

They lowered their weapons, but demanded an explanation in a pseudo-hostile sort of tone. *He was my friend*, they said, *Our brother.*

Norse pretended to empathize and work through an imaginary concoction of a story in his own mind.

"He must have been scratched or bitten or *something* in the city," Norse described. "He walked in here stumbling. I asked what was wrong, but he wouldn't reply. I sat him down in the armchair. Offered him some water. But as soon as he started changing, there was nothing I could do. I knew you would want to pay your respects."

Norse bowed his head, almost believing his own story. The soldiers looked on him with a sense of clarity and slight suspicion.

"Should I?" the second soldier asked. He exposed a long dagger from a sheath on his waist, pointing it towards the Dead.

Norse nodded and raised his eyebrows.

"If you wish," he replied.

The soldier jabbed the dagger into the Dead's skull. The groaning and writhing ceased. The body fell limp against the armchair.

"We'll make sure he gets the proper burial," the first soldier explained, cutting the restraints with the dagger. "Thanks, Doctor. Was there anything else you needed?"

"Now that you *ask*," Norse spoke, "I need one last favor. Then, as promised, you can go home."

The soldiers sighed quietly, attempting to disguise their disgust with yet another mission to the city. The two soldiers took a few, uninhibited steps towards the desk.

"If it's entering that hellhole of a hospital again, it's out of the question."

"No, no," Norse corrected himself, waving his hand to disregard the thought. "I need you to transport someone to and from the city. That's all."

The soldiers stopped, looked to one another, and nodded. For the first time, Norse noticed that the men's attire was streaked in high volumes of blood and dirt. The expressions on their faces showed an attack of fatigue, but never fear or surrender.

"We can do that," the second said. "When do we leave?"

"Get some nourishment, then leave right away. The sooner you leave, the sooner you return to your families."

Norse smiled a convincingly brutal smile.

"Yes, sir."

Norse handed them a small binder, filled with a packet of freshly printed papers.

"Give this to Antonio Devolds. His address is printed on the first page of the objective."

The first man nodded and slid the binder into a backpack, which wrapped around his shoulders like a black snake. Then they departed, carrying the graying body of their fallen comrade in their arms, slowly and cautiously towards the door. It clicked as it closed. *I can do anything*, Norse thought. *The world is mine.*

And it was true. The world waited anxiously, including the President, who delayed his decision to bomb the city, for Doctor Carl Norse and his lost vial of the undead city of Boston.

14

Providence, Rhode Island

The helicopters battered the ground in a display of chaotic wind. Antonio Devolds leaned against his house as if he had no care in the world. The sun was shining, but there was always the threat for thunderstorms during this time of the year, so he carried a rain jacket just incase he found himself stuck somewhere where he could not control the weather, let alone his own fate.

He was a middle-aged man that talked and held himself like a man well past his years. When he struck conversation (which was hardly ever), he made certain the dialogue *meant* something. He made certain his voice boomed with emphasis. Most of the people he interacted with were men infatuated with themselves, obsessed with scholarly words and infinitely terrible intentions. He had learned, many years ago, to avoid asking questions. Get the job done and nothing else mattered.

There were gray streaks that ran along the sides of his scalp, contrasting against the rest of his hair. They made him appear sophisticated, but utterly intimidating. The rest of his hair was a thick brown jumble, patted down with the help of combs or brushes. At first glance, Devolds might have appeared as slovenly, but that was never the case. The delicate blend of French and Italian bloods that ran through his veins gave him a slick appearance. They should not, according to him, be mistaken for slovenliness.

He took pride in the power of his eyes. They were also a delicate brown, mingled with specks and shards of hazel and mint green. His irises were devastatingly involved, prodding everything they came across. His pupils enlarged with things he liked, especially young and

161

curvaceous girls, although he was reaching the volatile age that would convey him as a pedophilic monster. He shied away from those interests.

The helicopter propped itself against the ground in one thudded landing. One soldier—a young man—hopped from the helicopter cabin and out towards Devolds.

"Devolds?" he asked. "Antonio Devolds?"

Devolds nodded, released from the wall, and met the soldier with a stiff handshake.

"I'm Private Smith. Doctor Norse asked to transport you to and from the city. Do you understand the circumstances of the situation? This is no ordinary task."

It was an honest question that demanded an honest answer, so Devolds opened his mouth and spoke.

"I do."

"Okay," Smith said, yelling over the sound of thundering blades, "Let's get going then."

Smith reached into the backpack that hung tightly against his shoulder blades. With a swift unzip, the bag's flap fell open, exposing the black binder from Norse's office.

"This is for you," Smith continued. "You can read it on the way into the city."

He motioned for Devolds to follow him and he did. The cabin of the helicopter was larger than Devolds thought it would be, judging by its limited space from the outside. He climbed in with ease and strapped into the farthest seat from where they had entered. The door closed, but the sound of the blades did not cease. It deafened the air around him and pulsed the inside of his ears. He pretended that it did not hurt him and, eventually, the pain dissolved into nothing but an annoying noise.

The binder wriggled as the helicopter propelled from the ground in several large vibrations. Devolds opened it and read the first page:

Confidentiality Notice:
The contents of this objective are highly confidential.
Attn: Antonio Devolds

Devolds flipped to the second page. The helicopter wind, even with the doors sealed on either side of the cabin, rustled the pages into annoying wings that would not stop flapping. He pressed his hands against the pages to hold them down against his lap. He felt that he was trapped in some awkward meditative posture, but let the thought slide as he began to read:

Your objective: There is a glass vial somewhere in the city of Boston

*containing a very small, but very potent amount of the Boston super-
virus. Be aware. It is highly contagious and 100% fatal once digested or
mingled with bodily fluids. It was last seen on the sixth floor of the
pathogens clinic at Boston Public Medicine with a Doctor William
O'Malley. There is no guarantee it is still there. Because this objective is
time sensitive, it is asked that you work within the time frame given. A
bonus financial reward will be offered for exceptional timely mission
success.*

A picture of the glass vial filled the rest of the page. It was a small, cylindrical container the size of his middle finger. It glistened in the glossy black and white colors of the ink. A box enclosed the time—48 hours—to which hung towards the top right corner of the page. At the bottom was a barely noticeable second notice. The italics camouflaged the lettering against the image. Devolds squinted and read:

*Note: You have complete government clearance to retrieve the virus.
Eliminate any and all obstacles in your path.*

Devolds snapped the objective shut and smiled. The words hung at the tip of his tongue in sweet, undeniable delight.

"Murder," he mumbled. The sounds of the helicopter blades drowned out his voice. No one heard him speak. "I can do murder."

15

They climbed out of the rooms and descended underground. The sewage line dropped into a cavernous tunnel of liquid feces, snaking through valleys of manmade underground pipes. The walls lined with mold and streaks of other bacterial growths that simply could not be identified. It was not the stagnant fear of disease and illness that scared the group, but the fact that the darkness was not just the obscurity of invisibility anymore, but a deep, jet-black daze that seemed eternally morbid and outright dangerous. The darkness consumed the stench.

There were echoic noises that reverberated against the cavernous walls —click after scrape after splash and noises that went unidentified. All seemed demonic and maniacally taunting from where the group stood, hovering over the edge of the entryway like ghosts entering the confines of Hades for the first time. A rusted, auburn ladder clung to the wall at their feet. It creaked against the cement tiles and the hinges that held it up. The rungs were narrow and fragile. They sat suspiciously against the metal sides.

"This is a bad idea," Fender whispered. Harro shushed him quietly, although the look in her eyes meant exactly what Fender had said. Shanna sighed, and then coughed at the potency of the stench. The guttural hack bounced down the cavern in an ugly parade of sound. Somewhere in the far stretches of the underground pass, they thought they heard the sound of angry groans, but in their already jumpy states, they tried to push it from their minds.

Henry descended first. Shanna fixed the light against the sewage line, which proved empty. Lumpy water passed in a steady tributary of brown and green. Ladder rung after ladder rung, the smell grew almost unbearably strong. It was no longer filterable through his mouth rather than his nose. The lack of oxygen, replaced by the extreme humidity of excrement and urine, forced Henry into panic. He sucked in more wind, but only felt the pull of bile against his throat.

He leaned over and heaved. The splash erupted against the current of dirty water below, washing the vomit away with the rest of the septic current. A rush of a better feeling blanketed, him, almost as if he was a new man, changed by the empty contents of his stomach. The stench grew deeper, inhabiting every part of his body, but not enough to send him into heaves again. He continued to climb down the rickety ladder, praying that each rung held him up as he descended.

He let himself fall waist-deep into the murky sludge. He waded, pushing to keep himself stationary in the stream. The flashlights shimmered two thin rivers of light down the ladder and at Henry, who silently conducted, maintaining a steady weight against the water. He watched as each body made their way, cautiously, into the decrepit tide.

As a team, they waded through the stream of feces, keeping their arms and chest above the water. Quintero kept a single pistol aimed ahead into the unknown. Fender held a sword at shoulder level toward the front of the group. Harro carried her scythes, watching the space from where they had come. Henry helped Shanna maintain her footing, which did not always work. Besides the fact that they were swimming in a river of sewage, the loneliness of the current became a comforting time to wallow in the quiet of trickling water. It calmed Henry's beating heart.

"How much longer?" Harro whispered, directing her question towards Quintero.

Everyone waited for a response that did not come.

Harro tried again with just a bit more force. "Quintero, how much longer 'til we're out of here?"

"There's no way of knowing," Quintero spoke after a sigh of frustration. "These sewage lines are a goddamn labyrinth."

He directed his attention to his wristwatch that glowed dimly against his arm.

"All I know is that we have an hour and a half before this shit gets real."

The formality of walking slipped back into an eerie, familiar urgency of stress and despair. Their footsteps hastened. Weapons arched into cautious awareness.

The septic waters rose and fell at different places in the cavern. The group followed the current as best as they could. There were tunnels that separated and flowed in different directions, penetrating them farther underneath the city. Quintero kept fingering his watch, gritting his teeth as the minutes passed and, still, no progress had been made. Even without direct access to the city sky, they knew that morning was quickly approaching.

"What happens if we don't make it before morning?" asked Harro.

"You don't want to know," Quintero responded. His voice was solemn and tense.

An intense sensation of claustrophobia ran down Henry's spine. He knew what would happen. The manhole covers would pop open and thousands of shuffling dead bodies would begin flopping and descending into the sewage line—exactly where the group waded through the cloudy, indescribably putrid water. There would be nowhere to hide, left to be eaten alive with nothing but the ease of Death to look forward to.

"We have to hurry," Henry said. "Make the best time that we can."

"We don't even know where we're going," Shanna interrupted. There was a distinct feeling of unavoidable panic in her voice. "How much time do we have?"

Quintero glanced long and hard at his wristwatch. The glowing display illuminated an orange glow against the gunman's skin. He let his body shiver in silent disgust.

"Half an hour," he said.

There was no end in sight. The cavernous darkness extended in endless paths. The sewage line forked into odd, narrow passageways and, sometimes, large, amphitheatric rooms that stretched the murky waters into a thin film at their feet. Just when they thought they reached an end, it reverted back into winding tiled rivers that opened into more septic waters. Hope drained from their eyes and panic settled in.

Up ahead, the faint sounds of splashing echoed against the walls and rang in their ears like a monstrous roar. All five stopped, clicking pistols and scythes into place as if to deter some sort of barrage from ahead. The splashing stopped for several seconds, then grew louder and clearer until it seemed to be directly on top of them. Shanna clung to Henry, shivering in both disgust and frigidity.

They stared into the darkness, awaiting answers. A figure appeared from the shadows, raising his arms as if to present an air of innocence.

"Don't shoot," the figure spoke, clearly male and fatigued to some degree.

Quintero lowered his pistol. Harro lessened her gripped scythes. Fender dropped back. The figure waded through the waters with small, scissor-like strides, swaying his hips with the turning of the water against him. He was small and sleek against the currents. Henry knew the voice. It fluttered his heart into irregular pumps.

"I'm stuck," the voice said. "I've been lost in here for hours. Can you help me?"

"We're just as lost as you are," Harro replied.

The man approached, still with his arms raised, and came into view. Henry nearly stopped breathing. Jones smiled a particularly feigned smile, making eye contact with each of his new acquaintances and nodding to show that he was no threat, simply a passerby in the need for company and a bit of assistance.

"Can I drop my hands now?" Jones spoke, rather sarcastically.

No one seemed to know how to answer.

Jones noticed the perplexity in the group and dropped his arms anyway. He let them splash against the excremental water. He lifted his eyes and met glances with Henry, who gritted his teeth and jutted his jaw in fierce bulges of bones. There was a maniacal sort of grin, maybe it was not a grin at all, and a few seconds of motionless contempt. Neither man planned to break the silence.

Quintero finally noticed the oddity of the situation and bent his eyebrows.

"You two know each other?" he asked both Henry and Jones simultaneously.

Henry nodded, unable to formulate words in the fury of anger that bubbled inside of him. He stared, now clenching fists into rock at his sides. The water rushed past his waist, naturally drawing him closer to Jones. He was able to mutter a few, almost indecipherable words, "It's Jones."

"*This* is Jones?" Quintero asked. "This shit just keeps getting crazier and crazier."

"Hold on," Jones spoke, trying to incite a benign calm within the group. "If you know what I know, we need to get moving, regardless of how much you want to beat the life out of me. Twenty minutes."

He was right. As much as Henry wanted to start a riot, they had no time to do such a thing.

"Let's work together to get out of here and then, I *promise*, we'll work this out," Jones said. The tone was demeaning. Henry's blood boiled even more.

"Your promises mean nothing," Henry said.

He had let his voice project. Shanna gripped his arm tighter to keep his inner rage at bay. All eyes were now focused on Henry and some, after awhile, suspiciously set their eyes on Jones.

"After," Quintero spoke like a true mediator. "I'll make sure of it."

He pointed a pistol at Jones' chest, which brushed the devious grin from Jones' face, and then walked past him, wading in the dark waters again.

"This way," the gunman said. "It's the only way we haven't tried."

With Jones at the front of the group, navigating and swiveling his hips in the water, Henry lost all focus. He remembered the rooftop battle with the crazies. He heard the crunching of cashews from Jones' overtly obnoxious chewing. He heard the dictatorial slew of demands he expected Henry to follow, whimpering and groveling like a dog. If he had had his bat—even the sharp, shattered nub of a handle—he would have finished Jones in a fiery swing of adrenaline. It would have ended there.

But there was Jones, alive and well-equipped with the heart of a true villain, waiting for his chance to pounce. In Henry's already fragile mind, it was not a matter of *if*, but simply a matter of *when* Jones would attack. So he kept his eyes fixed on him, analyzing his every move and every word. Quintero glanced back and winked, signaling that all was right, but the gunman did not know Jones like he knew him, and because of that, he worried for all of them. He worried that this was a wrinkle in the plotline that simply could not be ironed out.

"Five minutes," Quintero mumbled. "We should probably prepare ourselves for a fight."

Choppy breathing commenced and the group fidgeted with their weapons. Jones cracked his neck. He wielded no weapon to fidget, but still appeared comfortably secure with nothing but his own fists and legs. Ahead, about one hundred feet from where the group stood waist-deep in the murky water, a small inlet of light scattered the dust and methane back into the darkness. Jones lifted his eyes and pointed.

"Look," he said guilefully, "We can pigeon hole them there and try to escape that way. It'll be tough, but it's doable."

With no other option, Quintero nodded and looked for reassurance from the rest of the group. Hesitantly, each of them nodded, except for Henry, who widened his eyes and remained in silent suspicion.

The drain was at street-level, which hung above another rusted ladder clinging to the bacteria-ridden, tiled wall. This ladder, Henry thought, appeared even more unstable than the first one, which they had used to descend into the sewer hours before. He shivered at the nearing sounds of groans.

Reluctantly, he joined the rest of the group at the base of the ladder. Quintero handed him a pistol.

"I've got a plan," the gunman said. "Fender, you climb first. As the Dead expose themselves, take 'em out. Once the initial wave stops, I'll find a way up onto the street. I'll cover the rest of you. Henry, kill any of the Dead that fall through the cracks. Fender might miss some."

Henry nodded and Fender began to climb. The drain rattled with thunderous footsteps. Slimy, sloughing hands reached for the drain cover, ripping at it, roaring in discomfort from the burning sun. The sound of metal friction against its sheath rang true against Fender's back. In the beckoning sun, the metal of the sword blades shone brightly into the sewer. Quintero hung from the ladder rung below him with his left hand, clinging to the railing, and his right hand pointing a pistol up towards the city.

The drain ripped from above them and burning, disarrayed bodies began flopping headfirst into the sewer. Fender sliced as they fell. Quintero shot at one of the Dead that reared an open jaw at Fender's arm, spraying skin and blood against the tiled wall. The assault seemed to maintain a steady flow for an eternity. Fender carved. Quintero covered him. Henry shot at anything that got through, which did not seem to be much at all.

Sounds of splashing and flailing in the sewers began to surround them, so Quintero propelled himself up and out of the drain, firing silent bullets into the too-close-for-comfort Dead that ran and hid from the pain of the warm daylight. Fender followed, signaling a furious *Let's go!* to the group down below.

From the street, Fender helped Harro climb into the early morning, then Shanna. He then peered into the darkness of the sewer, watching Henry climb the rungs in quick succession.

"Where's Jones?" Fender asked.

"He's right behind me," Henry replied.

It was then that Fender met Jones' fiery eyes. He wished he had listened to Henry all along. Jones smiled, showing a line of straight, rectangular teeth. There was hatred that harbored behind them, slithering with his tongue. Fender reached for Henry's hand, but there was still a break of distance between them. In what seemed like no more than a split second, Jones wrapped his arm around Henry and pushed from the ladder. The two bodies shoved from the wall as Fender screamed, reaching for Henry in one, last ditched effort, but he and Jones were now airborne and careening straight down towards the sewer water and far from the rest of the group.

As he fell back, Henry looked up at Fender, whose eyes spilled with regret. He knew he should have let Jones climb before him. He knew there was some sort of disgusting evil twitch in Jones' polite *after you* motion. He wondered if he even had a chance of survival now. In midair, Jones wrapped an arm around Henry's neck and squeezed. Henry tried to breathe, but found it extremely difficult under the pressure of Jones' arm. He squeezed harder.

The splashing of the Dead in the far dimensions of the sewer lines turned from growling to screeching sounds of intrigue. Above the noise, however, Fender could still hear Henry's panicked flailing and the angry laughter of Jones against the acoustic walls. The Dead were camouflaged by the darkness, which was a blessing for Henry at this point. Fender averted his eyes to the psychopathic sounds of crazies attacking from street-side. He lost Henry when he turned and sliced at the bodies with his wielded swords. There was no longer time to think—only to survive.

They hit the septic water with force, creating a splash that morphed into another loud upheaval of approaching groans and screams. Both of them surfaced from the water in agonizingly disgusted gasps for air. They were covered with excrement and thick globs of things. The smell lurched Henry's stomach back into the need to heave. He felt his throat close like a vice, but he forced it open and continued to breathe in long, drawn out pants.

He flipped his leg up and into the groin of Jones, who buckled and winced in the enormity of the pain. Jones let go of the grip he had on Henry's neck and shot back into a stance, punching Henry hard enough to crack his jaw several times over. Henry felt the joints at his cheeks snap with the momentum, but not break. He fell back, clinging to the wall and the currents, disoriented with the darkness and the throbbing of his face.

"*No one* makes a fool of me," Jones screamed. "I *own* this city!"

The psychopathic rhythm of his voice shook the insides of Henry's eardrums. He almost willed himself to jump for the ladder, but knew that Jones was much quicker than that. He would be met with another bout of pain before he was able to defend himself.

"You left me to die up on that roof," Henry spoke. "What the hell was I supposed to do?"

The groans grew louder against the reverberating, echoic walls.

"I'm going to leave you down here to die," Jones said, dropping his voice into a demonic whisper. "Like you should've died on that rooftop."

Jones revealed a knife the size a household kitchen steak knife, pointed and ridged on one side and flatly parallel on the other.

"If you move," Jones said, "I'll slit your throat faster than you can scream for help."

At the base of the ladder—up onto the ledge and a few feet from where the two men stood in the currents—rested the pistol that Henry dropped when Jones took him down to the waters with him. *If only I can reach the gun*, he thought. *I could get out of here.* He heard Shanna screaming from the street from fear of the crazies. From where he stood, Henry could see the Dead appear from all angles, surfacing in the darkness.

"You found your little girlfriend I see," Jones puckered. There was a sour and angry twinge that erupted inside of Henry. "You *know*, I'd love to keep her for myself. She looks like a *catch*."

"I'll make sure you never touch her, or anyone, ever again," Henry replied.

Jones followed Henry's eyes to the pistol and smiled.

"Try," he spoke, waving the knife like a rattle at Henry. "I *dare* you."

Without thinking, Henry propelled himself from the water, allowing his arms to harness the weight of his torso as he pushed out and onto the tiled edge. Jones slashed the knife wildly, running through the brown waters, and catching Henry in the hip with a sharp and incredibly precise gash. The skin at Henry's side opened with the cut, pouring with an initial rush of blood. Henry reached for the gun, screaming in pain, but clasping it in his hands.

Jones flung another wild swing at Henry, who rolled out of the way. The knife collided with the metal tiles of the sewer edge, glowing sharply against the darkness. The collision of the knife and the tiles sent violent vibrations through Jones' hand. He grimaced and dropped the knife into the water, then looked up to see Henry. He was bleeding heavily, but holding the pistol at eye-level, pointing it directly at Jones. His hands were shaking nervously, quickly growing pale.

Jones laughed, cackling.

"You'll never make it out of this city alive. I bet you won't even be able to climb the ladder with that gash in your side."

Henry didn't care. All that mattered was that he was holding the gun and Jones stood useless in a running stream of urine and shit.

"Don't move," Henry managed to say. He felt the rush of blood leaking from his hip. His lip quivered.

Jones laughed again, manically and utterly ear piercing, and propelled himself towards Henry. One bullet was all it took, sending Jones back into the water, streaked with blood and a sudden display of surprise. The bullet collided with his shoulder—anything but a fatal shot—but enough to knock him back against the far wall. Jones clutched the wound in surprise and glared into Henry's determined eyes.

From either side, Henry noticed, the Dead surfaced from the shadows. The water splashed as they flailed towards them. Henry knew this was the only chance he would get to escape, so he turned and wrapped his arms around the third rung of the ladder and tried to pull himself up. It was harder than he thought, but he did not think of the pain or the exhaustion or the fear. All he thought of was Shanna. He was up and out of reach before the Dead crowded the tunnel space.

As he climbed, he continued to hear the cackling from below. Jones sat against the back wall with blood careening from the wound in his shoulder. It was an open invitation for the Dead. He applied pressure with his left hand, although he knew it would not do much. The Dead collapsed around him. Jones' eyes were numbing spheres of terror and madness. He looked up at Henry with them, smiling with nothing but pure acceptance that somebody had *finally* outwitted him. He watched as Henry climbed, reaching the top, before the Dead blanketed him with the ripping sounds of his own skin. *Strong kid,* Jones thought, *but he won't make it much longer. He won't.*

The last things Henry could hear from the sewer tunnel were the groans and tears of human flesh and the hushed obscenities of a man finally reaping his just sowings. He watched the Dead pile onto Jones. The vibrant screams and laughter of a man past insanity slowly turned to the gurgled plea for death, which finally dissolved into the maddening fury of the Dead eating their fill.

He reached his hand out and over the drain opening, clinging his fingers to the tar. He pulled himself up and out of the sewer, covered from head to toe in filth. The city was a quiet and eerie place without the sounds of monsters clogging his ears. The street was virtually deserted— no crazies for miles—but the group had left him, probably out of their control, but nonetheless, disappeared into the city once again. He sighed, thought of how to find his friends, and decided to limp north towards the city wall. He took a deep breath, ignored the pain at his hip, held his ailing wound tightly in the grip of his fingers, and pushed himself to place one foot in front of the other down the motionlessly sunlit city street.

16

"We have to go back for Henry!" Shanna screamed. The crazies were still far behind them, but Fender angrily shushed her.

"He's a big boy," Fender said. "He can fend for himself until we can go back."

Shanna did not notice in the fury of the moment, but Fender's voice lacked conviction. The anger convoluted the absence of sincerity. He had seen what happened with Henry in the sewer. He had seen Jones' demonically-set eyes fix on him as he grabbed Henry's waist and pulled him down. He had watched them both fall back into the watery currents, sending a dynamic display of splashing excrement, like a geyser, into the damp sewer air. His heart wanted to believe Henry could survive something like that, but his mind told him otherwise.

"Our best chance is the northern wall," Quintero managed to speak through exhausted pants. "Henry said there was a ladder."

The rest of the group nodded and fell behind him.

Shanna's ankle throbbed and flared with sharp, unyielding pain. She continued to run despite the crunching of bones and the awful sounds of cracks and snaps that overwhelmed her with each and every scissor kick step. She stretched her strides so that the momentum might disperse the force of her sneakers, but the continued wear of gravity did nothing but accentuate the problem. She wondered when the pain would cease. She wondered how long she had before her ankle surrendered to the weight of her body and threw her to the ground in a splay of limbs and flesh.

Ahead, before the turn onto Washington Street, stood a wall of swaying bodies. Some appeared more ghoulishly erect than others, but all stood with the look of insanity plastered lazily to their faces. Quintero wondered if the wall of the Dead had been there the entire time or if they had heard the commotion at the sewer drain and came running.

"How did we miss them?" Harro asked. "You think we would have heard them from a mile away."

Quintero shrugged, leveling his pistols and aiming.

Shanna gasped when she noticed the tsunami for the first time. One loud, collective hiss rose into the air and the sounds of bouldering movements began to edge forward toward the group. They stopped, collectively swiveling their heads, looking for empty openings in alleyways or buildings for any means of escape.

A second wave of crazies turned the corner to meet them from the south. The doors of the closest buildings were padlocked, tightly secured by city dwellers before the evacuation, attempting to protect the little assets that remained inside. It was a futile attempt that Quintero cursed heatedly. Another smaller wave filtered through the alleyways to their left and right. In a matter of seconds, they were trapped from all directions and forced to push together, back-to-back, in the lonely Boston street.

"Check mate," Harro said, beyond worries and shakiness. She spoke through panicked, choppy neurosis. Fender sighed and continued to scan the landscape for anything useful. Quintero grunted in frustration and swung his guns at his sides.

"Damn it!" he screamed. The roar of the Dead screamed along with him. "This is *not* happening."

A body broke from the wave, spraying and spewing new and old blood from its mouth. It had gruesome wounds at its waist and chest. Harro felt the chain in her right hand drop. The scythe glistened in the sun. The rest of the group watched.

The body drew closer as she swung the scythe above her head in cyclical swings, timing each thrust with the Dead's paced lumbering. Just as it dropped its jaw and opened its arms with rigid fingers, Harro swung the chained scythe, cutting into the soft, gray skin of its neck, and releasing its skull from the rest of its body. The scythe boomeranged back to her hand, swiveling until it tightened against her palm.

"I can't keep that up," Harro said, peering out over the mob collapsing on either side of her. "I'm not *that* good."

They fought off as many of the Dead as they could, but it still wasn't enough. The bodies enclosed on them even further, forcing them back into an even tighter retreat.

"I can't hold them!" Quintero screamed.

"Get down! Brace yourselves!" yelled Harro.

They were finally trapped, spared so many times just to die like the rest of Boston.

Then, when hope had all but vanished, in that indescribable moment of fear and near-death, there came helicopters.

They flew in. The underbellies were the same shimmering metal as the aircrafts they had seen before, carrying the weight of carbon-rich bombs and the fuzzy weaving of strapped fabric that held them in place. The Dead stopped and lifted their eyes into the morning sky, forgetting, for a split-second, about the group they had already surrounded.

Fender took advantage, slicing into a few more gurgling throats while the bodies remained distracted. Harro swung and connected with a few of her own. It was a moment of sheer vulnerability—a moment that felt both jarringly daunting and equally surreal, as if the helicopters that hovered above them were a strange mix of angel and demon, here for nothing more than to settle the aftermath of both salvation and damnation once and for all.

A lone helicopter broke from the rest and swooped down nearly onto the group. The remaining four choppers fell back into the bleeding blue sky, whirring away to hover in the distance. The pulsating wind pushed down on them from every direction. Countless Dead growled and edged even closer, lumbering just to get a taste. Shanna closed her eyes and prayed that the end would be painless, but Harro, Fender, and Quintero kept their weapons splayed out in front of them like true warriors. They were hoping for the best.

Quintero flailed his arms, yelling for help from whoever the aircraft was carrying, switching between motions of waving and violent downswings to ward off the broken, scraggly teeth of a particularly nasty body.

The helicopter found a slice of open street as the cabin opened. There was a moment of mysterious confusion, then a man in a raincoat dropped gracefully to the south side of the group, holding the largest weapon any of them had ever seen. The man's right hand gripped a large, metal trigger connected to the weapon's butt, which hung like a hornet's stinger against his chest. His left arm stretched across the middle of it, allowing for his hand to stabilize the barrel at its far end. The man pointed it at the crowds of the Dead and snapped the trigger. A thick stream of flame propelled through the cylinder, burning the first dozen rows of the mob, which repelled with the force of the flames. The survivors watched on in complete astonishment as the bloody oranges and reds ascended like a gasoline-induced explosion.

"Hold them back from the other side!" the man yelled over the helicopter blades. His voice was deep and raspy.

Quintero emptied the rest of his ammunition and began whipping the butt of the pistol hard into the skulls of oncoming bodies. Harro slashed the air with both scythes, cutting in dizzying cyclic patterns of gore. Fender sliced and jabbed with his monstrous swords. But Shanna only opened her eyes at the smell of burning flesh (which no one seemed to notice), wondering why she had yet to feel the pain of her own ripping skin from the bone. It was then she witnessed the chaos surrounding her for the first time—and the strange man invoking it.

He was built with muscular tones. His arms tensed at the power of the flamethrower in his hands. His shoulders were square, but his neck rippled with the presence of tension veins protruding from his skin. He smiled coyly when he noticed her staring. Her cheeks flushed instantly with the sensation of embarrassment.

We're surrounded by hundreds of flesh-eating monsters and this guy smiles at me? she thinks. It's a creepy thought, but one that rose instinctively to the forefront of her mind.

She pulled out the butter knife in her pocket simply as a precaution, but held it close to her, hoping to avoid attacking with it at all costs. Fear washed over her as she watched the group lose ground towards the north and east. The strange, jacketed figure held strong against the south.

"Almost there!" the man yelled.

The group, which seemed to be collectively panting now, kept swinging and cutting, but slower now and riddled with exhaustion. They peered over their shoulders and watched as the ashes and burning, lifeless limbs of the Dead blanketed the city streets. Waves of the Dead were now diluted to a few stragglers, somehow lucky enough to veer away and avoid the flames.

"Switch," the man yelled. "I'll finish them off."

In a half-turn, the flamethrower snapped off and then on once more, finishing the last of the bodies still hobbling toward the group. Shanna tried holding her breath during this part, but the stench of burnt flesh found a way to trickle into her nostrils anyway. Ghastly smoke drifted into the air, mingling with the other stagnant odors of gasoline and heated tar. She gagged, but somehow held herself together—a sure sign she had been in the city far too long. Shanna turned to Quintero, who met eyes with Harro, then Fender. She was sure they were all thinking the same thing. This man was as professional as it gets.

For good or for worse, we don't have a choice, she thought.

And she was right.

The Dead were no longer a threat when Quintero approached the man (who coincidentally towered over him by a handful of inches), offering an expression of puzzlement, but fitting gratitude. He watched as the man angled the flamethrower in front of him, diagonally from the group.

The barrel smoked, reeking of gasoline fumes.

"If you don't mind me asking, who *are* you?" the gunman asked. The helicopters maintained a constant whir in the sky above them, far enough away now so that it did not interrupt the normal volume of conversation. "And why are you here?"

"Antonio Devolds," he spoke. His usual quiet and stern demeanor covered the benign resistance in his expression. Quintero took note of the man's quick and apparent change in mood. "And we will get to that."

Quintero pointed to each member of the group and spoke their first names as a way of introduction. Each nodded as their name was called. Shanna, still wary, continued to clutch the butter knife with awkward sincerity.

"And I'm Quintero," he finished, looking past the man's eyes, analyzing every aged line, every bit of hesitation, twitch, response. Something felt coerced. Something felt ultimately wrong. He simply could not let go of the mild volatility in the man's appearance. *He's hiding something*, Quintero thought. Devolds feigned a curt smile. He understood it with familiarity, because it was an expression he used himself. *He* knew what it *really* meant. And it worried him greatly.

"Let's get to the point, shall we? I'm looking for something," Devolds confessed. "It's something small, but *very* important."

Quintero knew the object before Devolds could even begin to describe it. It filled his mind like a thundercloud. *There's a storm coming*, Quintero thought. He didn't know where the words had come from, but they rolled off of his tongue in a violent, inaudible whisper.

This man was not a friend. The way his shoulders flared and tensed. The way he held the flamethrower at his side, ready to strike. Even the formal way he wore his raincoat. Each of these things suggested that they were in trouble, deeply and insurmountably in trouble.

"Our friend," Quintero spoke. "He may be in trouble about a block that way." Quintero pointed in the direction from which they came. "We'd be glad to help if you help us."

He pursed his lips and listened, wishing he had not already used all of his ammunition.

He glanced at Fender, then at Harro.

"It's a vial of liquid," Devolds continued. "Time sensitive, too."

The group quieted, suddenly under the impression they had just walked into something much bigger than an escape from the city. Quintero gripped the pistols in his hands, tensing his forearms. Devolds waved the flamethrower at their feet in a subtle warning sign. The motion forced Quintero to flinch.

Silence.

"Have you seen it?" Devolds asked.

One by one, the group denied any knowledge of the vial.

"Nothing?" Devolds asked again.

The group continued to shake their heads.

"Well," Devolds said, dropping his eyes, "then you are no use to me."

Predictably, the man raised the flamethrower to attack, but Quintero was quicker. He had forced himself behind the man, planting a gun at his temple and another at his back. Harro, Fender, and Shanna retreated. Devolds smiled, as if absorbing the cool power of the gunmetal barrels.

"I knew there was something wrong here. Why do you want the vial so badly?" Quintero prodded.

Devolds shifted his eyes, stretching his demonic grin even further.

"I'll ask one more time. Why do you want the vial so badly?" This time the question was direct and loud. Quintero felt his grip push against Devolds' skull even harder and with blinding strength.

"It's not *for* me," Devolds spoke. "My employer, on the other hand..."

Quintero jabbed the barrel of his gun hard against the curve of the man's high cheekbone.

"Who do you work for?" Quintero asked.

"That's none of your business," Devolds spat.

Quintero, aggravated and pumped with adrenaline, shoved the barrel of the pistol into Devolds' mouth—hard and without hesitation. The gun raked against a tooth, breaking it in half. Devolds instinctively groaned, then forced out a miserable, soul-rendering laugh. The gunman jutted a second pistol into the man's side. The movements were quick, efficient, and blunt.

"This would be much more threatening if your weapons were actually loaded." Devolds muttered the words through a mouthful of blood. "Excuse me if I'm being too brash. It's just that I can't take you seriously."

Quintero took another thunderous shot at the man's jaw, sending him to his knees. The flamethrower hit the ground and wobbled a few feet from Devolds' outstretched hand. The gunman kicked it away, far enough so that it rattled against the curb of the sidewalk and into the shadows of the buildings.

"My turn," Devolds whispered.

The man jumped to his feet and peeled off his raincoat. Quintero couldn't shoot. As Devolds had observed (correctly, at that), his pistols hadn't been loaded, and now, whatever this man was planning to do, they were helpless in stopping it. Underneath Devolds' jacket were slings and belts housing guns of all sizes. He unsheathed one—a long, sleek handgun, raising it to Quintero.

"On your knees," he said angrily. Quintero, without fear, dropped and watched as Devolds walked to him and pressed the gun intimately to his forehead. The rest of the group watched in silence. It was as though they had been freed from one nightmare and propelled headfirst into another. "Any last words?"

Devolds usually never did this (the whole assassination without mercy thing), but the mysterious strength in Quintero impressed him. He *wanted* to break him, watch as the fear filled his eyes like tears, and then —and *only* then—would he send a bullet through his brain. For now, though, he would settle for the groveling whimpers of people lesser than himself. He clicked the safety and cocked the weapon.

"Yeah," Quintero said, loud enough for the other three to hear. "Two things."

"Quick," Devolds replied through a fit of harnessed giggles. He found this entire situation humorous. He swallowed blood from his gums, shaken by Quintero's abrasive jaw hit. "I don't have all day."

The northern wall was a mountain in the distance. It stood against the rest of the city like a prison sentence. Quintero could barely make out the movement that scrambled at the top. It was Henry, holding his side, and fumbling to keep his balance. *That son of a bitch*, Quintero thought. The gun applied a bit more pressure and brought him back to the actuality of the moment.

"Those two things?" Devolds said. "Thirty seconds."

"If you kill me...or any of them," Quintero explained, pointing to the group. "You'll never get that vial. I know where it is and without us, you don't stand a chance. You'll be searching for weeks, months, *years*."

The fit of humor that had so courteously shimmered in Devolds' eyes and lips vanished at the sound of Quintero's voice. Confidence rang true within each word. Devolds pressed harder now.

"And why should I trust you?"

Quintero thought of what Henry had told him in the sewer. *He was a doctor...* Quintero thought hard, swerving in and out of the capsuled memories in his brain. The stress of the moment was wearing on Devolds. And Quintero loved every, insoluble second that passed as he continued to think...*A Doctor O'Malley*. The gunman smiled, showing his teeth, and taking a deep and uninhibited breath.

"We found it on Dr. O'Malley. He had already changed into one of them. He came after us, we killed him, and found the vial in his shirt pocket."

Devolds scanned the objective in his head. He remembered the doctor's name vividly. It sent a shock of validity through him. There were no more giggles. This man—Quintero—had pulled too many strings. The anger sent a blow to the side of Quintero's face. He fell over, but was quickly returned to his knees by two of Devolds' twitching fists.

"Where is it?" asked Devolds. The impenitence in his voice was alarming.

Quintero grinned in a silent victory.

"Let's make a deal."

Devolds pursed his lips, forcing them to go white. He clicked the gun back and holstered it at his waist. He liked bargaining—almost as much as he liked killing—but if he were going to get paid on his return, he would have to return with the vial. Devolds was sure Quintero knew where it was. The name *Dr. O'Malley* triggered it.

"Okay," Devolds said, gritting his teeth just a little. "Let's play hardball. Name your price."

The street still twitched with barbecued bodies. Devolds snickered at the destruction. It was a common sight now, almost a formality.

"We get a free ride out of the city," Quintero demanded. He spoke each word with precise clarity as if he wanted the helicopters to hear him, as well. His eyes ascended to the metal birds that hovered and quivered in the air.

"Done," Devolds replied. *The easiest bargain I've ever done*, he thought. *That pretty little girl will most certainly do.* He was looking up and down Shanna, who flinched and took one more step backwards behind Harro. "Now where is it?"

Quintero blinked and let the smile drain from his expression.

"Don't you want to hear the second thing before you *shoot* me?" His voice was beyond sarcasm, borderline mockery. He looked so deeply into Devolds' eyes that he thought he could see his stinging soul.

"What would that be?"

Quintero straightened his back, pretended like he was getting to his feet, but instead, brushed a few flecks of dandruff or, what looked like, flakes of dried, burnt flesh from his leather jacket. Only then did he revert his eyes back to Devolds' and raise the middle finger on his right hand.

"Screw you," he said.

Quintero peered out to the northern wall again, pointing towards the skyline. The powdery blue appeared almost perfect against the dingy cement of the city barricade. He could not see any of the crowded suburban neighborhoods that stretched for miles on the wall's other side, but knew they were there. Quintero wondered how long it would take for another thunderstorm to come rolling in. As the skies foretold, there would be none in the near future. He didn't know how he felt about that.

"He has it," Quintero spoke. Devolds averted his eyes to the shadowy figure that flopped and scrambled across the wall. "Without a doubt."

"If he doesn't," Devolds threatened, "I'll make sure that every last one of you wished you were dead. I'll skin you alive, then feed you to these things. Understand?"

"Clear as day."

Devolds motioned for the nearest helicopter. It hovered lower, starting a string of chaotic, chilling gusts against the still-sturdy mess of vandalized buildings and startling a few restless, burned bodies down the street. A young man in soldier attire watched the group from the cabin with a rope ladder in his hands. Devolds motioned for it anxiously. He began to climb, but Quintero grabbed his arm, shaking his head and pointing toward the others.

"Us first," he mouthed.

Devolds ran his tongue against the front side of his teeth with distaste, then reluctantly accepted, climbing down from the rungs with pistol in hand. Quintero waved to the others with his fingers. They piled in one behind the other until the latter swung with escaping bodies, nervous of what was to come. The man helped them up into the cabin holstering the rifle at his back.

A few crazies appeared in the distance, flailing and running toward the men. Devolds sighed. Quintero climbed. When he was about halfway to the top, he glanced over his shoulder and watched Devolds pull several hooked blades from his shoulders. Now there were a dozen of the Dead sprinting and screaming. For a fleeting moment, Quintero wondered whether he should jump down and help, but was confirmed with an astounding *no* when he saw the swift, agile movements that Devolds put on display. With five abnormally wide swings, the pack of Dead fell motionless against the asphalt.

It was something Quintero had never seen before—the perfect slashes, the synchronized swinging of blades—but honestly, he was not surprised in the least bit. Devolds was mysterious and threatening. This he knew, but what else was he? Quintero allowed questions to seep into his brain until he could not think of anything else. He turned and continued to climb.

Nerves shot up and down Quintero's sides. The way Devolds had taken care of the crazies made Fender's blade technique look like an infant swinging his rattle at a wall. He forced his nerves to calm almost instantaneously, but the fear of wondering if a bargaining tactic was that great of an idea in the first place lingered like a migraine in his head. This man—Antonio Devolds (he spoke the name in his head hundreds of times so that the frailties of his mind would not forget it)—was a man of horror. A feeling of looming regret replaced the suspicion behind his eyes. *Behind every man like him*, Quintero thought, *is another man that sits behind a desk and wishes he could do the same thing.*

Quintero reached the lip of the helicopter cabin, climbed up to the others, and peered out over the edge to watch Devolds swing with the ladder, moving his legs like propellers against the fidgeting city breeze. When he had had enough, he sat back against the cold metal, took a deep breath, let it out, and met eyes with Fender for the first time in a very long time.

"Be careful," the gunman mumbled. Fender nodded innocuously.

Devolds appeared over the lip and hopped up, clinging to the raincoat that had been flung over his shoulder. He whispered something to the young soldier, who collected the ladder by the rungs, nodded, and pointed to Henry at the northern wall. Devolds gave him two pats on the back and took a seat at the far end of the cabin. Quintero flickered his eyes to watch him in his peripheral vision, but figured that there was nothing to watch at this point.

Everything depended on Henry. Without the vial, without ammunition, they were all as good as dead. If anything, Devolds would make sure of it. Quintero thought about Rosco, prayed that he had somehow made it past the pearly gates of Heaven, kissed the crucifix he kept hidden underneath his tee shirt, and allowed his body to relax against the cold metal of the helicopter cabin. It might be the last bit of recourse he would ever have the chance to use.

Henry tried to keep himself on his feet, but the numbing feeling in his legs made it difficult to stand, let alone walk. He stumbled hopelessly, looking for anything or anyone to help. The wound at his side was still seeping blood. It felt warm and slippery against his hand. He tried to ignore it all, but was afraid that if he stopped applying the pressure, his insides would fall out and splatter against the ground.

It wasn't like him to feel weak and deathly ill. He had been through worse than this. The world turned around him like a giant, magnified snow globe without the snow. Blood pulsed through his eye sockets and under his teeth and in his ears. Things resonated in his jaw and behind the curves in his skull with sounds he could not replicate if he tried. He wondered how much longer he could take the dirty growling at the base of the wall. The Dead were circling.

He wondered if time was even moving at all. The flexibility of reality was like nothing he had ever known before. It was like a drug that never crashed. *So this is what death feels like*, Henry thought. None of it mattered anyhow. White lines began forming at the perimeters of his vision. He felt the lightheadedness of the moment before losing consciousness. It rushed into him like something he could not control.

It was then that he heard the helicopters cutting the air in the distance. He squinted through the blurriness of his vision, watching the bulbous choppers sway in the upper-city winds. He thought he saw bodies, as small as ants, climbing up a ladder to one of them, but his mind was beyond believability. He thought he was hallucinating and then knew he was when the helicopters mutated into large spiders, crawling through the air and hissing at Henry from a little ways off. They inched closer. Henry panicked.

"Stay away," he mumbled. His heart fluttered with fear. "Stay away!"

But they did not. The spiders crawled closer, opening their mouths as if to swallow Henry whole. He shifted backward, stiff against the imbalance of his injured right side. He kept his hand there, pressed to stop the bleeding.

In no time at all, the spiders were towering in front of him, their legs whirring and moving around them. The one closest opened its mouth wider. Instead of a ghastly insect-like tongue (which Henry believed he would see), a figure appeared. He was wearing a raincoat.

"...is it?" the figure asked. "Where's the..."

Henry could only make out bits and pieces of the questions the figure asked. The man wore a raincoat and held a gun to his forehead.

The white lines of unconsciousness began creeping in again. Soon he would be lost in his own comatose-filled dreams, away from the pain in his side, away from the spiders that hovered above him, away from the man who rudely pointed a gun at him and screamed questions to which he had no answers.

"He's in shock," he heard the man say to someone farther back, *probably* somewhere in the spider's throat. He was harshly pulled into the spider mouth (the cabin), but found that it was rather comforting and padded. Henry shivered at the blurry people around him. He knew most of them, but his brain would simply not connect the dots and give him names. They were strangers that somehow held acquaintance.

"Can you hear me?" a sweet, petite voice asked. The timbre of the voice made him melt. A thin, intimate hand brushed his hair. A shard of pain ran up his side when he tried to move to meet her gaze. The gash in his side started to bleed again.

"We're getting you help," the voice said. He recognized it and smiled. "Stay with me."

The helicopter lifted even higher and Henry felt everything swing with speed. They were on the move somehow and to somewhere he could not be certain. The pain kept him mute. He could no longer open his eyes. He was falling deep into the confines of unconsciousness, lost in his own brain. He had finally lost too much blood. He had met his breaking point and had no choice but to give in.

"Found it," said a man with a voice he did not recognize. "You weren't lying."

There was a fit of clearing throats and the sound of metal-against-metal, like swords scraping against each other.

"Where are we going?"

Quintero, Henry thought.

"Somewhere safe," the unrecognizable voice replied. "Don't worry. I won't be killing any of you. You've helped me out greatly and I... *appreciate* that."

Henry could almost feel Quintero grimace.

Who is this guy? Henry asked, mostly rhetorically. None of the passengers could hear him. He screamed inside his head while his body shut down.

"Besides," the voice continued. "Your friend needs medical attention. Where we're going, there's *plenty* of that."

There was a violently stable laugh and then the helicopter cabin went silent. Henry allowed his body to shrug and then go limp. He veered in and out of consciousness for a few moments, then, without hesitation, dropped into the darkest and deepest sleep of his life.

17

At first, he thought it was all a dream, or at least a figment of his imagination, but as he walked through the field, running his hand through the stacks of tall grain, he was no longer certain that it was that simple. In the distance, a giant and archaic willow tree stood against a backdrop of dark forest. The darkness was not evil, only temporary, Henry thought. It reminded him of the kind of darkness needed for a good, restful sleep. He smiled at the thought of resting, but knew, it was not time to do anything of the sort just yet.

The sky was colorless. Henry still believed it to be an apparition, slithering into digital chromosomes above him, but as he approached the tree, everything rushed to him in a moment of clear revelation. There was a spiritual power that Henry could not account for, nor did he have the ability to outrun, so he soaked in the shivers it brought. He felt the tips of his fingers tingle with a curious excitement. It filtered in and out of him, penetrating every pore and every part.

He walked even closer, allowing his legs to carry him without the forceful need to push. It just felt right, pristine and extraordinary at the same time. He touched the tree's bark and felt its rustic swivels and turns. He could sense how alive it was, how it breathed, how it touched him as he touched it. He heard whispering in the back of his head, meekly at first, but it grew, not in volume, only in lucidity. He heard and *felt* every word. Each syllable fluttered his heart into palpable beats that rocked his entire body. He ebbed and flowed with the heartbeat tide within him.

There is more, a whispered voice spoke. Henry was not sure if it was his own voice or that of another. *There is more to be done.*

He let his hand reluctantly separate from the bark. The sensation faded into the back of his head. He tried to catch it, keep it and hold it there for as long as he could, but it vanished before he could focus enough energy to grasp it. Suddenly, the darkened forest dispersed in an explosion of glittery confetti, taking the willow tree with it. What could have been something special, quickly changed to a deep, brutal loneliness.

The landscape in front of him morphed and wriggled from all angles. Henry took a few hesitant steps backward, squinting through the ache of watching his vision disperse into particles. He was now surrounded by falling pieces of glitter. They entrenched him, tickling his arms and legs. It was then that he realized there was no gash at his side, the bruises on his face had vanished, and the scarred skin in his palms had healed. He stood completely healthy and *happy*, which he could simply not comprehend. No matter how much he tried to counter the joy, the fleeting moments of suspicion and depression dissipated into the nothings of dead space.

He was *happy* and nothing else.

Piece by piece, the glitter began to glue itself into a memory, like a mirror made of gelatin. It pulled him into a bedroom. The sun shone lushly through the window curtains. It was morning—he knew that—one of the most beautiful mornings he could remember. It was why he had stored the memory in his brain in the first place. He wondered if there would ever be another morning with such vivacity. He scanned the room and sighed in nostalgia.

The glitter dispersed, leaving him to watch Shanna sleeping in the bed next to the window, shifting silently and opening her eyes.

"I hope this never changes," she spoke.

Under the blankets, he could see a former image of himself. Her leg wrapped around his waist.

"Me either," younger Henry said.

The mattress squeaked as he turned to meet her eyes. They were blue and glossy, like rain on a windowpane. He had always enjoyed the way she looked at him. It made him feel like the only person on the planet, at least the only one with a girl like Shanna.

Older Henry walked to the window, ran his finger down the wooden frame, and smiled, letting a burst of air release through his nose.

"Promise me something," she said. Henry remembered this perfectly. "Promise me that you will always be you. Never change."

Younger Henry looked at her with deepening romantic sentiment. He took her hand and squeezed it gently. "I promise," he said. They smiled, curled up closer, and lost themselves in the golden hue of the streaming, unfiltered sunlight.

The memory fissured and dispersed again. The glitter sprinkled the air.

This time, the joy he felt slowly twanged and switched into a melancholy awareness of trepidation. He saw the ancient tree in the distance once again, but this time, far enough away almost to be forgotten. It swayed in the breeze. The colorless sky met the stacks of grain and collided into a blend of violent sounds and calming hands. The landscape was no longer tranquil. The branches of the willow pushed heavily to one side.

There's a storm coming, he thought.

The words baffled him until the landscape vanished all together and he was left in nothing but the eternity of blank space.

The touch of her hand confused him at first. He felt her fingers run through his hair.

"Stay with me," she whispered. *"Stay with me."*

She was crying. He could tell by the way her fingers quivered slightly as they met the nape of his neck. The texture of his skin, he noticed, was rough and cold. His heartbeat was faint, calculated. He tried to let her know he was all right, that everything would soon be okay, but his eyes could not open. His throat was too dry to speak.

Please, he tried to say. The words reverberated against the walls of his head. He did not know if he would ever wake up, or ever talk again. He decided not to think about that possibility. *Please know that I love you. Please...*

Shanna held Henry in her hands. His pale skin had grown even paler. His eyes were hidden behind his thinning eyelids. She wanted nothing more than to see them flicker with life, like they had in the apartment, when she saw him for the first time (again) since the Infection, but somehow, she knew that this time was different. The wound at his side had dried and was beginning to crack and peel. The skin around it lined red with a furious infected. Shanna had asked for a medical kit several times, practically screaming for it, but the young soldier at the front of the chopper only shrugged sympathetically.

Devolds grinned as though this was his plan all along.

"He's dying!" she spoke with commanded emphasis. "He needs something to counteract the infection!" She pointed to Henry's side, where his motionless hand still clasped the wound. She thought about removing it and nursing the wound herself, but was afraid of what more bleeding might do to his already fragile state.

"Stay with me," she whispered. "Come on, Henry. *Stay with me.*"

She repeated the same words over and over again, hoping the act of redundancy might somehow bring him back to life. She kissed him passionately, moving her lips against the lifelessness of his. She believed in fairy tales, after all, even after everything she had witnessed in the city. But nothing happened. Henry remained still, lifeless.

For several minutes, she panicked. She felt no pulse in his chest. She whimpered quietly against the whirring of the helicopter's blades.

"Don't do this to me," she said. The sounds of her own voice scared her into choppy breathing. "Please, Henry, don't…"

But then she felt the faint bump in his chest and released the pent up horror that collapsed in her brain. It vanished with the terror of dying at the hands of the Dead. He breathed erratically in a way that, blatantly, did not even seem like breathing at all. But this was a sign of relief. He was alive. She brushed the back of her hand down his face, making certain to feel the breaks at his ear and jaw.

He loved it when her hand met those places.

"How much longer?" Quintero asked, directing the pointed question at Devolds. It took a second before the man registered that Quintero was, indeed, asking him.

"Not too much," he replied, shifting. The sound of weighted guns and knives rattled underneath his raincoat. "But when we land, you do as I say."

It was not a question. Quintero simply nodded, accepting enough to humor him.

Scythes moved and clinked as metal hit metal. Harro had had enough of the mystery game. She looked into the eyes of Devolds, who stared back, excited with the fury that erupted in her face. She let her left nostril twitch in an obviously frustrated state.

"Where the hell are you taking us? We asked for a ride out of the city, not a trip halfway across the world. Henry is dying. He needs help."

Fender wrapped his tree trunk arm around his wife in a gesture of support. His other hand clasped one of his swords, which clung to the cabin floor. He did not move it, but considered a quick swirl of the blade, thinking that it might offer Devolds' a bit of authenticity in the type of people with which he was dealing.

"His name is *Henry*, you say? Interesting," Devolds answered.

He dropped his eyes, fixing them on Shanna. No one seemed to notice that his intentions were quickly dissolving into lustful temptations of the flesh. His mind wandered, but never too far to be reeled back. It was clear that the girl had some distinct infatuation with Henry, but he was not sure to what extent, maybe boyfriend? Fiancé?

The first step, he convinced himself, *is getting rid of the boy.*

It would be somewhat of an easy task, knowing Doctor Norse's precocious, immoral sentiment.

He'll have some use for him.

"And where are we going, you ask?" Devolds continued. He arched his back in some sort of disjointed stretch and raised one finger, as if to motion for Harro to wait as he adjusted comfortably. "To meet the boss."

"Look," Shanna said, motioning to the window. The purity of the sky and upper-cloud levels dispersed, giving way to clear air and a large building that towered monstrously across the lush, neatly mowed landscape. It glistened with liquefied frost. The shoreline, in front of the building, collided with a sharpened cliff, eroded over time by the crashing of powerful waves. The scene induced a strange sensation of fear, more like intimidation than anything. The azure blue of the sky only intensified the radiating power of the building.

"Ladies and gentlemen," Devolds spoke. His hand gestured towards the window. Everyone but Henry fixed their eyes on the African coastline and gasped quietly. "Welcome home."

18

The helicopter blades heightened their gravitational pull as they slowed and came to a halt. The chopper rested gently against the lawn at the front of the building. Henry was stiff against Shanna's legs—still pale and deathly. Devolds pushed himself from his sitting position and picked Henry up from under his knees and behind his neck. The deadweight was more than he had expected, so he adjusted by shuffling the weight to his elbows and taking the body outside.

"Follow me," Devolds said. "There's nowhere to go now but up." His face was stern, lifting to the towering building in front of them, then shifting to Shanna. "And *I* have your boyfriend."

A creeping anxiety flooded Shanna—something in the way Devolds spoke those last few words.

The group walked through the entrance. A restless blonde sat behind a circular desk. She wore a headset that combed her hair back behind her ears and fell to her shoulder blades in almost perfectly straightened strands. When she caught the eyes of Devolds and the rest of them, she perked up and stuck out her push-up bra chest. She radiated a feigned smile of welcome and asked, pleasantly, for identification.

"Antonio Devolds. Doctor Norse is expecting me," he spoke.

His voice was very matter of fact. Henry's body flopped in his arms, which rang a hint of suspicion in the girl's eyes.

"Excuse me for one second," the receptionist spoke, smiling a highly professional, yet equally hesitant smile. She picked up the phone and dialed a three-digit extension. There was a pair of short dial tones before a strong voice answered.

"Doctor Norse, I have an Antonio Devolds here. He said you're expecting him?"

She nodded and bit her lip as if she was scolding herself for even picking up the phone.

"But... There's more... *Right away, sir*."

She clicked the phone back to its original place on the desk and lifted her eyes.

"Doctor Norse knows you're here. He told me to send you right up," she spoke.

Her demeanor had deflated, clearly affected by the candid Norse response, but she managed to maintain that perfectly professional smile.

There was a *click* as the magnetically locked doors snapped open to the right of them. Devolds mumbled a thank you and strolled briskly to the elevator beyond the glass. Quintero was the first to follow. Shanna huddled behind him. Harro and Fender brought up the rear.

The elevator lobby was chilled, conditioned by cold air that filtered through a blowing vent above them. It whipped cyclonic bouts of air down onto their heads. The girls shivered under their blood-stained clothes.

An electronic beep catalyzed the sliding elevator door as it folded in on itself. Devolds managed to hit level nine despite the added weight of Henry's body in his arms, using his rugged knee to prop the body up, releasing his hand for the split second needed to snap at the plastic button. He curtly smirked at Shanna, who had been nervously watching his every move since the helicopter. He couldn't tell if he liked the added attention or not.

"When you meet him," Devolds explained. His eyes lacked any sort of emotion. "You want to be to the point. Nothing else. He does *not* like small talk."

Devolds disguised his deception all too well. Norse, he was sure of it, had his own plans for the rest of the group. It was a satisfying feeling to know that he had completed the objective, not only in record time, but also, through defiantly remarkable conditions.

Now the plan had changed. It was simple. Use the group as hostages—*especially* Henry.

He snuck another brief glance at Shanna, who had her arms crossed against her chest. The expression on her face was certainly one of disdain. She did not notice that Devolds was looking at her, but he wished she had. He wanted her to watch him wrap his hands around the curves of Henry's jaw and snap his neck just to prove a point. He wanted to see the hope of reuniting with her lover drain from her eyes as he stole her away. Only then would he be free to take her in as his own.

"Here we are," Devolds spoke.

The elevator doors opened to a corridor flooded with architecturally sound half-pillared décor and lush academia-style carpeting. Although the stubborn air-conditioning continued to gust, the hallway felt warm and comforting—*slightly too comforting*, Quintero suggested.

The sun drifted through the sizeable windows like birds flapping their wings against the pulled curtains. Devolds' face grew properly stern. Quintero noticed this as a purposeful act, so he scrunched his face into a similar expression. The others already had their faces prepared, either noticing, like Quintero, that staying in character may be the single most important tactic in surviving this mess.

Either way, Devolds knocked on the wooden doorframe of thick wood treated door. For one fleeting moment, Quintero had the incredible urge to stay in the hallway and leave everyone to deal with this without him. He wished he could just close his eyes, think hard of his favorite place in the world (it was, in fact, a beach somewhere on the south side of Mexico. He had had the vision of lapping waves and crystal blue waters stretching), and leave here once and for all. All of this was beginning to be too much.

And to be honest. What did he owe to these people? *Nothing.* Let the others figure it out.

But that fleeting moment evolved into another image—one of his superego and the hero he knew he always had the potential to be. At least to avenge the memory of Rosco.

As they waited for the invitation to enter the room, Quintero knew— *believed*—that this was exactly where he was supposed to be. Somehow he knew that, behind that door, was a man he would ever regret meeting —a man that wanted everything, that *had* everything, but will never truly be content until the entire world bowed to him. He would understand, of course, that acquiring these things was a futile cause, because he is looking for more than just earthly things. He is looking for the means to control the world. He is looking for a way to live forever. In some strange afterthought—behind the spew of his words, the gunman's brain decided to corrugate into philosophical thoughts.

The man behind this door was looking for *immortality.*

"Come in," a voice spoke from inside.

"Remember," Devolds reminded with sharp, unquestioning eyes. "Business. That's all."

As the door opened to a neatly kept office, Quintero remembered, frantically, that he was no longer carrying any ammunition. He had nothing to protect himself except unloaded pistols, which would do no good against men of this caliber. Thoughts of the inevitable circulated his mind. He watched as Devolds carried Henry like a ragdoll. He wondered if Henry was somehow alive behind those lifeless, closed eyes of his. He wondered if Henry could ever forgive him for all of this.

Then he remembered.

He watched as an elongated bulge in Henry's jeans swiveled against Devolds' angular movements. The butter knives did not clink, but merely rustled against the fabric. He wondered if he could somehow reach over and steal them. It was possible, but would take extreme stealth and a bit of separation to pull it off.

"Devolds," the man behind the desk spoke. "What have you brought me?"

A rugged man with long, tidy locks of blond hair sat with his swivel chair away from them, facing the far wall. He swiveled around and met eyes with the group, scanning each face until he locked with that of Devolds. A brief flicker of fire ignited in the man's irises, only to extinguish before most could see.

Quintero twitched, however, in his subtle response. Outside, the sounds of thunder and flickers of lightning began to form against the African coastline.

There's a storm coming, Quintero thought.

A sweet, but strange taste filled his mouth, like flat soda burning in the sun for hours.

"I see we have company," the man spoke. "Let me introduce myself."

He stood and bent his hips with a bow that seemed more sarcastic than anything, then returned to his chair almost immediately. A broad streak of lightning cascaded from the sky, spilling yellow and orange electric light across the water. Thunder roared as a way of introduction.

"My name is Doctor Carl Norse. Pleasure to meet you all."

No one returned their names. There was a silence that filled the room with a violent form of contempt, making the group rightfully nervous.

"I have what you're looking for," Devolds spoke, only to Norse.

"Ah! In good time, too," Norse replied, grinning in excitement.

"I also have something else you might be interested in," Devolds continued.

He raised Henry slightly to present his offering. Only Quintero noticed the slighted gesture. Norse raised his eyebrows in intrigue.

"We still have the matter of payment to discuss, don't we, Mr. Devolds?"

Devolds grinned a demonically curious half-smile.

"I have already given this some thought," he spoke.

Norse waited for the suggestion.

"In exchange for the vial and the boy," Devolds continued. "I take the girl."

He glared at Shanna, who now backed into the wall in morbid terror.

Devolds kept his eyes focused on her for several seconds, watching the fear envelope every inch of her, before reverting back to Norse. The doctor slid his tongue against his teeth, then ran his right hand through his illustrious blond hair. Fender unsheathed both swords and Harro dropped the scythes from her hands.

"Now, now," Norse spoke with uncomfortable ease. "Let's not hasten the moment. Lower your weapons."

They did not.

"Mr. Devolds is somewhat of a lush. I've known this for some time now. But one thing that I've learned throughout this entire mess of a situation is that you do *not* go against your best employee." Norse looked to Devolds, who grinned once more. "You have yourself a deal."

In the time it took Fender to inhale, he noticed a small peephole in the front of Norse's desk. It shimmered in the pale lighting, amplified by the frequent bursts of lightning resonating from the windows. The sound of a click registered a streak of horror within him as he came to realize what was behind it.

"Goodbye, all," Norse spoke with strenuous delight.

Fender pushed from his stance, colliding with Harro and driving her to the ground. The sound of a trigger snapping exploded in the form of gunpowder. The cylindrical clot of metal streamed through the air and met the muscle of Fender's shoulder in a distinct squish of muscle. He grunted with the initial sensation of pain, grimacing against the metal. Harro widened her eyes with shock and anger from under him.

Quintero scrunched, luckily avoiding the stream of bullets that followed the snapping of the Norse's finger against the trigger. Devolds dropped Henry's body to the ground in a heap of limbs. He flopped hard and came to a rest. His eyes remained closed and unaware, truly immobile against the hustle of the moment. Quintero splayed adjacent to Henry and reached into his pocket, wrapping his fingers around the knives.

"Sorry, buddy," he whispered, wondering if Henry could hear. "I'll be back for you."

Shanna screamed from the doorway. Devolds dragged her through the hallway and to the elevator. There was a snap and Quintero watched Norse jump from his seat behind the desk with a sawed-off shotgun in hand, pointing it towards him. The rage in his eyes had reached cataclysm.

The gunman scrambled for the door. He was able to shuffle out of sight and into the hallway with enough time to see the elevator doors close. Norse turned and fired a healthy barrage of ammunition, taking a block of doorframe with it.

Shanna screamed for help.

The shotgun pellets had barely missed the gunman, but he could feel the dizzying after effects of the amplified *pow*, which deafened his ears into an annoying ring.

With little time to flee, Harro and Fender climbed quickly out of sight. Fender was bleeding profusely, but refused to holster his swords. His knuckles burned white with vehement anger.

"He tried to kill you," he mumbled. "No one gets away with that."

He ignored the pain and the trickling of warm, dark blood down his shirt, trying to stand with his swords cocked to swing.

There was another maniacal spray of pellets, an angry burst of groaned anger, a shuffling of feet from the other side of the office, and then silence.

Quintero was the first to peer in. Norse had suddenly vanished with Henry's body. A half-open door stood pressed at the far end of the office, behind the desk, which led to a dark hallway. The sound of heavy footsteps echoed through its brick walls while the gunman searched the room. He found no weaponry, nothing to defend himself in the wake of a loaded shotgun. In the back of his mind, he thought he would have found *something* to use, but the room was deserted and now demolished.

Louder cracks of thunder began relaying the lengthier flickers of lightning through the office windows. They shook the building, vibrating it from top to bottom.

"Harro and I will get Shanna," Fender whispered. "You work on the doctor. I *knew* it. From the moment Devolds offered him up, he was planning something with Henry. I don't know what, but you need to get in there."

Quintero mustered a nod and watched as the couple sprinted towards the elevator. They broke the corner and headed for the stairs.

This is the storm, Quintero thought. *This is it.*

"You know," Norse said, locking the door from the doorknob, then reaching up and snapping three oddly specific, manmade deadbolts into place from the door's right corner. They were now, in what looked like, an operating room from a greasy hospital reality show. "It didn't have to end this way."

Henry's eyes were still closed—externally shut down—but his brain relayed every sound the doctor made. It was like being in a soundproof closet where the walls are mirrors, while the speakers exposed everything.

"I've been waiting for this moment for a *very* long time. Oh! And if you're wondering about your friends down the hall, they won't find you.

This door was made for people like them. I know your kind...always looking out for each other. It *disgusts* me."

Who are you? Henry asked from the confines of his brain. His body rested against the cool of an operating table. His back touched the sterile tabletop, but his arms fell backwards due to lack of room. They hung motionless in an awkward stretch and the new tension at his shoulder blades tightened. *What are you going to do to me?*

"It could've been anybody. It didn't *have* to be you at all, but the fact that you're here and you're *already* unconscious just gives that added treat I was looking for."

Henry heard the rustling of metal against another table across the room. Norse fidgeted with something, screwing metal against metal, preparing. The room and the hallway outside were otherwise quiet.

Quintero, where are you? he thought. *I can't move. I can't move at all.*

"You see, there were five vials all together. I'm guessing *you* had the fifth. It only takes four to make a proper antidote. I needed enough specimen to make a viable amount for duplication. But the fifth vial," Norse sighed and shook his head as though the information he was about to divulge would tear a hole through the universe, "was even more important than that."

There was a silence again as Henry tried to scream. Panic began settling in the caverns of his mind. The metallic sounds of Norse's tabletop rang and tinged, then ceased, finally finishing in long, approaching footsteps. Norse overlooked Henry's body, towering and hovering above him like the tallest tree in a forest.

"Without the fifth vial, there's no point in this whole social *experiment* we find ourselves in." He grinned because he could. "Because there's no way to test that it *really* works."

It was clear now that Dr. Norse was holding a syringe. The needle was thick and spurted a small bit of liquid from its opening at the tip. The doctor swayed as he held it up to his eyes. His pupils enlarged with satisfaction. He was a man of conviction and dedication who took time to relish in the lasting moments that came before success.

"There's a part of me that wishes you were awake," Norse continued, "so that I could hear you scream. But I have to say, this *is* rather peaceful."

No, Henry thought.

The faint sound of footsteps began scrambling from the other side of the hallway.

It all came down to this.

Henry could feel the syringe closing the space between his hip and Norse's hand. The temptation to stab it into the bone, making it

196

impossible for Henry to squirm (not that he would), flooded the doctor's thoughts. Norse wanted it to ache, to burn, to linger in his body like an itch that simply could never be scratched. His hand did not shake as the syringe grew closer, but the quivers of excitement wavered the needle only enough for Henry to feel it as the metal penetrated skin.

"This might pinch *just* a bit," Norse smiled. He inched the syringe farther into the fat of Henry's leg at a slight downward angle.

It felt cool, even cooler than his skin, which was exceptionally pale and chilled from the loss of blood. Henry grimaced without grimacing and distanced himself from the paranoia that riddled every inch of him. He felt helpless and completely vulnerable to the coursing venom in his veins. He knew what the liquid in the needle was. He knew what would happen to him. It wrestled each and every healthy particle and consumed every moving part of him. The virus writhed in his legs and sent irregular flutters into his heart.

Norse laughed. He pushed the last of the virus into Henry, then slid the syringe from Henry's skin. It was an odd tickling sensation that made Henry chuckle. A subtle grin stretched the corner of his lips.

Norse noticed the movement and stepped back.

"What is *this*?" Norse asked. "Could he be waking up?"

He had rested the shotgun at the base of the far wall, which was too far to run for now, but too close for any means of comfort. He reached and wrapped his fingers around a small capsule filled with yellow liquid. He squeezed it in his fist to hide it away.

"Come on," Norse spoke. "Wake up!"

Then, without notice, Henry jumped up and was alive again—weak and drunk with the feeling of the virus. It tugged in him like unbreakable chains digging into his skin. His intestines suddenly came alive and slithered inside of him. They were boa constrictors swerving around his organs. He heard Quintero's voice from behind the door, slamming his fists against the metal and screaming. He thought about running over to it and unsnapping the deadbolts, but his legs would not bend. They were asleep, paralyzed enough to constrict the muscles.

Henry shifted his eyes to Norse, who came into view for the first time. The doctor admired Henry with his hands folded in front of him. A strong, proud smile filtered through his eyes and resonated against his teeth, which stuck out from his lips like little, white stones.

"Well look what we have here," he said.

There was a capsule in the doctor's hands, Henry noticed. The golden liquid sloshed inside the container, synchronized with Norse's swaying movement. The virus continued roaring inside of him, threatening to crawl up into his throat and to the base of his brain. He bowed with the pain and listened to Norse applaud with halting entertainment.

"You are *quite* the fighter," the doctor noted. His finger stretched out in front of the others, pointing to Henry mockingly. "I put enough of it in you to increase the turn. Let it take over. You'll feel *much, much* better."

But Henry refused, deciding to, instead, focus on the clamor that Quintero made on the other side of the door. He kicked and screamed and punched, but the door wouldn't budge. The boiling feeling in his lower back lurched and shimmied up into his shoulders. He pushed it back down.

"Let's make this a little more interesting, shall we?" the doctor asked in a smooth display of patience. He was enjoying Henry and his struggle to stay conscious.

Henry grunted, closed his eyes, and pushed the virus down and away from his neck. He had all he could do to focus on that. The pain was unbearable. He wanted nothing more than to let it take its toll, allow for the effects to consume him, and finish this horrible process once and for all. But he did not give in. He kept his focus on the door and nothing else.

The doctor walked to the far wall and wrapped his left hand around the base of the shotgun, pointing it towards the door.

"Your little friend out there," Norse said in an exceptionally sarcastic fashion. "I would very much like to put a bullet in his brain. That annoying noise he *insists* on making out there is *really* getting to me. Plus, if I kill him off, there's more a chance you'll just give in. Am I right?"

Henry did not answer. He couldn't, although he was not sure he would have even spoken if he had the ability to formulate the words with his mouth.

"I'll take that as a yes," the doctor continued.

He snapped back the safety, pointing the shotgun at the metal door. He unlocked the three deadbolt locks and snapped open the handle. Henry watched Quintero's eyes scan the room, meeting with Norse's, then the shotgun, then Henry.

The gunman was not holding pistols.

Norse snorted to catch the gunman's attention.

"I can only assume that you're here to rescue your *dear* friend," said Norse.

Quintero nodded in anger, also a bit of surrender at the sight of the pointed weapon.

"What's your name?" the doctor asked.

"Quintero," the gunman replied, subdued enough for Henry to question the response.

"You do realize I *will* be killing you, don't you?"

Silence.

"We'll see about that," Quintero replied.

Another silence.

"I'm enjoying this," Norse said. "I really am, but I think it's time to finish."

Norse lifted the shotgun, leveling the barrel with Quintero's chest. He wanted to believe that there was a stilling calm in the air, but the adrenaline that rushed in his ears was too loud to conclude any sort of volume projecting through the room. Henry pushed from the table, still resisting the urge to surrender to the virus, falling to the tiled floor. The sound of the falling body distracted Norse for no more than a split second, but was enough for Quintero to pull a butter knife from his pocket and throw it overhand towards the doctor's shoulder. With luck, it stuck at the topside of his left pectoral muscle, driving into his collarbone, forcing the doctor to drop the aimed weapon from shoulder level.

A terrible pain grew in its place.

"Very good, very good," Norse spoke, ignoring the metal that jutted from the bloodied skin below his neck. "Maybe I'm underestimating you, Quintero."

The doctor pulled the knife from the wound and produced a wild swing of the shotgun, which nearly collided with the gunman's chin, but he managed to avoid the butt of the gun and jump away frantically as the shell dispersed into the wall near the door. He disguised himself behind a clunky apparatus across the room, scrunched with his knees wrapped close to his chest, waiting. The spray from the gun produced violent dents and jagged chips in the tiles. The broken flakes of concrete rattled as it fell to the floor.

Henry was losing the grip on the raging sickness inside of him. He squirmed belly-down on the greasy floor, gritting his teeth. It would not be long before it took control, regardless of his efforts.

Norse stepped back, closer to Henry, as he scanned the room, waiting for Quintero to present himself. Any flicker of movement heightened his senses. He cocked the shotgun and blasted another round at the door's adjacent corner—the only one where Quintero could have fled. He laughed when he heard Quintero's sighs of escaped near-injury, wondering if he had even thought this through—the fact that he was alone in a room with a shotgun and a seriously infected boy.

"Come out, come out, *wherever* you are," Norse sung.

His voice hung in the air in eerie drones.

Henry felt the cells in his brain changing. The space behind his eyes boiled and begged for release. He could no longer focus on Norse or Quintero's lucid movements. He focused on his own breathing, which pushed on his chest and closed his airway as though he was breathing through a straw. Every few seconds, he gained a bit of composure, clearing his eyes before the pain returned.

Norse stood over him with the shotgun. Quintero hid himself behind the table at the far side of the room. Then, in Norse's eyes, Henry saw the leather jacket shifting and shuffling against the table. The doctor smiled. This was the moment he had learned to adore so much—the moment right before a kill, right before a murder.

Quintero leaned into the furniture and peered around the edge of it. He was staring directly into the shotgun barrel.

"I'm sorry, Quintero, but this has to be done. Enough of this cat and mouse game."

Henry reached out with all of his strength and clutched at Norse's leg. He pulled hard and watched as Norse lost his balance. He fell in a heap with the shotgun at his chest, appearing genuinely shocked to see Henry still conscious. It was as though he was looking into the face of a miracle worker—or a *really* convincing magician.

"It isn't supposed to take this long!" Norse yelled, slapping at his foot.

Henry began to hallucinate, foaming at the mouth. Norse was now a basilisk producing long, bending horns and searing, ruby eyes. Now more than ever, he wanted to let go, but clutched the doctor's leg in a fit of determination. He tried to yell to Quintero, but forgot how to speak. Suddenly, he forgot how to think. He forgot how to breathe. The ruby eyes turned to black. Its teeth dripped with blood as his vision deepened into darkness. It closed in until there was nothing left.

He sighed, released his last attempt to subdue the virus, and, finally, surrendered.

"You can't beat loyalty. Even in his last breath he made sure I would have a chance to kill you," Quintero whispered into the doctor's ear in hot, bursts of air.

His hand held a butter knife to Norse's throat. The rigid side ran close to his skin. Norse dropped the shotgun. Quintero kicked it away.

"This isn't over," Norse replied. "Once he wakes up, we'll both be in trouble. *You* know that. *I* know that."

"Then give him the antidote," Quintero blurted. "I heard everything from the door. This knife is, by no means, sharp. It'll take a few slashes to open your throat, but believe me, if you don't inject that antidote into Henry, I will make sure you feel everything on your way out. *Give him the antidote.*"

Quintero's emphatic words spilled from his mouth along with small, stringy strands of saliva. The knife blade inched closer to Norse's trunked neck. He wanted so badly to finish this—once and for all—but resisted, knowing that the only person in the room who knew how to inject the antidote was the doctor. As much as he wanted to kill him, he knew he simply could not just yet.

"What a *predicament!*" Norse screamed in a crazy fit of emotion. There was no fear in his voice. "Administer the cure...which was my plan all along, or let Henry die as *you* watch."

Each word defiled into violent anger. The word *watch* somehow lit a spark in the gunman. The very essence of it invoked every ounce of fury that could possibly rage through a human voice.

The crazed look in the doctor's eyes turned to vengeance as he broke from his assailant's stronghold. Quintero stabbed the butter knife in Norse's hip and listened to him scream in agony. The knife had cracked bone and slashed through nerves, but the doctor ripped it from his side and threw it to the ground, absorbing the throbbing pain that emanated up and down his right side. It was as though he embraced it, allowing it to become a strengthened part of him, transforming him into a bigger and better self.

Blood spurted from the wound while he ignored it. Thunder, again, began roaring from the office down the hallway. Rain poured from the clouds in sheets, ripping against the windows. The sounds caught both of their attentions.

And to top it off, Henry's body rolled and groaned at Norse's feet.

The virus was coming to life.

"It's too late now," the doctor said between bouts of anger and pain. "The antidote only works before the change is complete."

Norse took a few stuttered steps forward, closing the space between Quintero and himself.

"Don't move," Quintero spurted. The movement in Henry's body was a reminder of the danger both of them were in.

"You think you have the balls to kill me? You think you have what it takes?"

Quintero reached for the shotgun, but Norse lunged at him, meeting him before he was able to grab it. The doctor's hands wrapped around Quintero's neck, raising him up against the wall. The gunman felt the tremendous pressure against his throat, crushing his windpipe. It made it difficult to breathe, nearly impossible. He pried at Norse's hands for a bit of relief, but could not muster enough strength.

"I will *not* stop until every bone in your neck snaps. How *dare* you try and kill me!"

The doctor gritted his teeth, grinding them in sheer power and arrogance as he looked into Quintero's fading eyes. It was a moment filled with violence, disappointment, and horror. The gunman wished it didn't have to end this way. He prayed for a second chance.

And he would get it.

Henry's body wobbled and reached for the closest body, sinking its teeth hard and fast into Norse's shoulder. The doctor screamed in horror, shocked that he had forgotten about Henry's change, and released Quintero. The gunman fell to the ground, holding his neck, and coughing at the sudden expanse of his airway. He watched Henry shuffle drunkenly, rearing his head back and attempting another bite at Norse's wounded hip. He missed and slammed into the wall, slumping and struggling to get to his feet.

"The antidote..." Norse mumbled.

His voice shook.

He fumbled for vial. The yellow liquid rested in the canister about two arm's lengths away. He reached and wrapped his fingers around it, bringing the glass close to his body. Henry groaned, still tripping over his own feet to meet Norse at the wall. The doctor prepared the syringe, shaking in his work, watching Henry stumble, but rise to his feet. He was running out of time and he knew it. He placed his thumb on the base of the needle, squirted the liquid to release the air bubbles inside the syringe, and turned the needle to push it into his arm.

It was then that Norse heard the click of a cocked weapon and heard the sound of a trigger. He felt a blast of shotgun pellets sear into his skin and blow open the right side of his face. Pieces of his skull bent and stabbed at the soft tissue of his brain. He saw nothing but white light as the pain evolved from aching nerves to warm, undulating submission.

The gunman watched the doctor's body slump in expiration. The shotgun smoked at its barrel. He dropped it, but immediately regretted doing so. Henry's body turned, distracted by Quintero's sudden movements, and scrambled towards him in awkward, vicious strides.

It's too late now, Quintero's mind raced. The doctor's words flooded every cavern and every empty space of his mind. *The antidote only works before the change is complete.*

"Let's hope your wrong, Norse," Quintero muttered.

The gunman braced himself as Henry's body roared, tackling him to the ground. His eyes were gray and bloodshot, but in some odd way, they still reminded Quintero of the old Henry—the one he had met outside the city walls on that fateful night. There was a glimmer of character that hid somewhere in that livid, blinded expression. It offered hope and a real sense of clarity. Henry reached to pry into Quintero's skin, but was too slow. Quintero reached for Henry's arms and pushed with considerable force. His jaw slid open, instead, and bent towards Quintero's face. He could smell the vile mess of blood and stale bacteria harbored in his gums and behind his teeth and tongue, averting his eyes in an attempt to escape the smell.

The doctor's lifeless body pinned against the wall in a sitting position. Blood and skin and muscular matter served as a backdrop to the body, dripping from the tiled wall in a mural of gruesome finality. In his open palm rested the prepared antidote. He could see the yellow liquid slosh in viscous waves within the vial. It was the color of sunlight-infused honey on a clear, undisturbed summer day.

Quintero reached. The tips of his fingers wrestled for contact, but the cylinder only rolled in place. Henry pushed the most impossibly searing noise from his throat. It was the most revolting thing Quintero had ever heard. His ears pierced with amplified terror. It invoked another bout of inconsolable, deathly strength from Henry's arms as he strained to make contact with the gunman's body below him.

The weight was enough to drain the strength from Quintero's body. He couldn't breathe and could barely control the impulsivity of the moment. Yet, the gunman never considered any other plan but retrieving that cure. If he was going to leave the room alive, he wanted Henry to have that same chance, no matter how slighted it seemed.

His arm reached. His other arm warded Henry away with shaking muscles. He reached, stretching his arm as far as possible toward Norse's lifeless hand, feeling his own ligaments and joints separate in microscopic cuts.

Just when the ache of fatigue was about to buckle his arms, Quintero's middle finger caught with friction against the glass vial, rolling it towards him. He wrapped his fingers around the cylinder, clasped the glass in his palm, bent his thumb against the base of the syringe, and stabbed it into Henry's neck, watching the amber liquid flow out of the vial and into his bloodstream.

There was no response. Henry continued groaning and screaming in abhorrent hunger. The gunman tried desperately to cling to the hope that the medicine took time, that all he had to do was wait and Henry would return to his normal state. But as the seconds passed into minutes, there was no change. Henry's gray eyes remained that way. His vicious stare remained uncontrollably inhumane. His hands splayed rigid fingers that needed to kill, to feed. It was in this moment—the moment that everything was supposed to return to what it was—that Quintero lost all signs of hope.

"Sorry, buddy," he mumbled. He shoved hard at an upward angle, releasing Henry from his position and sending his body backwards into the wall. "I did everything I could."

He turned, grabbed the abandoned butter knife from a shiny puddle of Norse's blood and drew it back in a concerted effort to swing.

"Wait," Henry spoke, meekly and through weird, gurgled noises. "*Don't.*"

Quintero dropped back and into the wall as if a strong gust of wind had thrust him there. His eyes widened. He dropped the knife and straightened his shoulders.

"Henry," he whispered. "You're here?"

Henry nodded, but in monotonically robotic movements. It appeared as if every inch of him needed oiling, creaking under the weight of the virus that threatened to break him.

"It *hurts*," Henry managed to speak. His body seized.

"Fight it, Henry. Shanna needs you."

"It's strong. It won't..." His voice trailed off, then crackled back into the air. "...give *in.*"

He reached and ripped the syringe from his neck, staring at it for a moment, then dropping it. It smashed into large shards of glass at his feet.

"The antidote!" Quintero said. "It's working!"

There was bravery and undeniable pride in his voice.

Henry squeezed his abdomen with contracted muscles and screamed again, roaring as if it helped. It was not a Henry scream, but the same kind of morbid yelling that had crushed his eardrums a few minutes earlier.

"It's everywhere," Henry gurgled. "It *hurts.*"

"FIGHT IT!" Quintero yelled.

There was a moment of surreal power as Quintero watched Henry fall to the floor, cringing and flailing as the virus threatened to take control again, this time, for good. The gunman contemplated restraining him, holding back his erratically moving arms, but decided to avoid it all together. This was Henry's battle. Not his.

Then Henry's body went limp. Quintero ran to his side. His eyes closed and went still. His mouth was plastered in a permanently contorted grimace, which sent shutters through Quintero's spine. His face was still sunken and had already aged a bit with death. No movement, not even for breath.

"*No, no, no, no,*" Quintero screamed. "Come on, Henry."

But the body hardened at Quintero's incessant poking.

"Damn it!" he yelled.

He pressed two fingers against Henry's neck, but felt no pulse. The room was cool, but filled with the effects of stale, potent tension.

First came anger, which the gunman exerted by kicking Norse's already bludgeoned and bloodied body several times in exuberant, overworked strength. Then came sadness, which arrived in the form of weakened knees buckling to the ground at Henry's side. Finally came the withdrawal. It was during this time that Quintero picked himself up, mumbled a few, scattered obscenities and made his way to the door.

Fender, Harro, and Shanna would be waiting for him outside. They would leave this place—and Henry—forever.

He clasped the heavy, metal door in his left hand and turned, one last time, to Henry's abandoned frame.

This is how he'll be remembered, Quintero thought. *What a damn shame.*

19

"You're a monster," Shanna muttered through a locked jaw and a quivering voice.

Devolds had a firm grasp on her arm, dragging her out of the elevator, through the glass doors and into the lobby.

"Have a great night," the blond receptionist spoke without looking up.

It was an automated response from her brain while she complacently maintained focus on the keyboard, typing in front of her. Shanna attempted to plea for help, but Devolds wrapped his free hand across her lips, muffling the sound before it was too noticeable. By the time the receptionist glanced at the fleeting their figures, it was far too late. She watched them push through the exit doors and walk out into the threatening weather, which had darkened the sky into a black, swirling blanket of clouds.

"Wherever you take me, Henry will find me," Shanna threatened.

Devolds laughed and tightened his grip. Shanna sucked wind through her teeth to show the pain of Devolds' grip. She was certain there would be a bruise where his fingers wrapped around the meat of her arm.

"Are you sure about that? Do you want to know what *I'm* sure of? I'm sure Norse is dissecting your little boyfriend *as we speak*," countered Devolds.

He stretched the last three words for added intimidation.

Shanna did not respond. The image of Henry's unconscious body on Norse's office floor surfaced in her mind and she was overcome with a potent amount of despair.

"Don't worry," Devolds said, admiring the finality in Shanna's face, "I'll take care of you."

The helicopter came into view from a distance. Five soldiers, dressed in their usual black army garb, stood disguised against the shimmering black of the chopper. Only two soldiers had their backs turned toward the coastal cliffs at the far end of the floral garden. The not-so-distant thunder and lightning shook the ground and flickered light into the air. Raindrops pattered against his face and jacket. It felt refreshing, actually, like shower water before the heating system powers up.

The soldiers noticed the two figures walking impatiently towards them.

"Hey!" one of the soldiers shouted. "We're parking it for the night. No travel tonight."

Devolds flapped open the left side of his raincoat, unsheathing an automatic rifle, planting his aim at the soldier to the far left, held down the trigger, and, panoramically, splattered a healthy display of automatic bullets into each soldier. In a matter of seconds, all five were dead with puddles of fresh blood pooling at the base of their wounds. Shanna gasped at the sheer brutality in Devolds' actions.

To him, it was just another annoyingly simple means to an end.

For Shanna, it was the murderous underpinnings of a sociopath.

"Why did you do that?" Shanna cried. Her hair was now damp with rainwater.

Devolds looked at her with calm eyes.

"We need the chopper," he replied, as if that was a dutiful explanation.

He hustled to the helicopter with Shanna in his tensed arm. Devolds' grasp was now cutting off circulation to the extremity of Shanna's arm. She felt that all-too-familiar sensation of pins and needles seeping through her muscles and the odd numbing sensation in her fingers and hands. She tried to rip her arm away—and did—averting her eyes from Devolds' untrusting stare. He walked behind her, smirking and quickening her pace.

Instead, he pushed Shanna into the helicopter. She tripped and fell to her elbows, squirming into the cabin and struggling to avoid Devolds' strange touch. He propped his leg up onto the metal step and lunged into the cabin with ease. He closed the door and shot another aggressive stare at her with his peripheral vision.

"You'll stay in here if you know what's good for you," he said, as if his eyes were the only point of emphasis worth noting. "And jumping won't do you any good once we're over the ocean."

Shanna looked down at her feet. Her ankle was still swollen, but not throbbing anymore. The pain seemed to be a part of her now.

She rested her forehead against her kneecaps, feeling the bony joints against her head, and letting her thoughts dissolve into a muddled, dull ache. The sound of the blades above circled and cut the air in fierce circles as Devolds started the twin engines. The quickened noise hurt her ears, so she covered them with her hands and pretended that it was only a temporary thing, when she knew—very well—that it was not.

The helicopter began its ascent, hovering in the air and swinging slightly with the weight of the wind. Shanna glanced ahead into the cockpit. Devolds straightened his shoulders and kept his eyes ahead of him. Somehow she knew Devolds was watching, without his eyes, but instead, with every fiber of his being. There was nowhere to run.

She suddenly understood that this could very well be her fate—a fragile girl whisked away by a monster, never to be seen or heard from again.

There was a quiet *clank* (one that would have been a louder *clank* without the rush of helicopter blades drowning any form of noise within a one-hundred foot radius) that vibrated the metal floor for one brief moment. Devolds didn't seem to notice a thing, keeping his hands on the steering console and his eyes ahead. She wondered if he had actually heard it or if this was just another one of his ways of keeping her in line.

She rolled to her side and bent her knees so that they touched the cabin floor, peering out through the glass side window, and looking down. The landscape was now fluttering away in a downward spiral as the helicopter turned. The greens of the manicured lawns, the grayish-blue paneling of the shadowed building, and the pastoral shades of the floral gardens dissipated under the swirling masses of immersing black clouds.

The sky that surrounded them suddenly grew dark. The sounds of thunder shook the helicopter. Shanna prayed that God would somehow spare her life from the mess she found herself in. She prayed that the helicopter could somehow lift higher into the air, away from the clouds and pounding rains and shattering currents of lightning that threatened their destruction. She clasped tightly to the armrest of one of the flight chairs so firmly that her knuckles nearly fledged from her skin.

It was then that she noticed the scythe that wrapped around the landing skids of the helicopter. The chain coiled around itself enough times to pin the blade into a stationary position, jamming itself safely against the aircraft's underbelly. Shanna followed the chain with her eyes, although she already knew where it led. Harro dangled in the wind—her eyes straining at the onslaught of air and rain, clinging to the helicopter's side door.

Just when she had convinced herself that this tale was a hopeless, continuing feud of battles lost, she smiled at the glimmer of hope that dangled from the landing skids.

That is, until Devolds turned and realized the two of them were no longer alone.

When Fender and Harro came sprinting through the lobby of the International Center for Disease Control, the blond-haired receptionist followed the sounds of their footsteps with her eyes, making contact with the two of them as they slipped through the glass elevator doors (that connected to the stairs) and into the reception area.

The receptionist's thin, manicured eyebrows slipped into a concerned furrow. It was not every day, she thought, that sword and scythe wielding men and women came running through the room. She did not speak—only questioned, behind her eyes, how she could possibly react to such an odd chronology of events.

"Which way did they go?" bellowed Fender. He ran as he asked the question, wanting an answer while in mid-stride.

The blond receptionist hesitated, then pointed towards the entrance doors. Normally, she would have not known how to answer such a vague question. So many faces passed through those doors on a daily basis, but during the night shift, there were never any guests. Tonight seemed to be the exception to the rule.

The swords and pointed blades forced her heart to jump in fright. Her legs simply did not work, or else she would have tried to run in escape.

Halfway through the lobby, Harro and Fender stopped and quieted their breathing. A distinct splattering of gunshots ran clearly from outside.

Shit, Fender thought.

All of this time, they had disregarded the fact that Devolds was a mercenary. He had played the part for some time, especially during their first introductions in the city, but recently, as in the confines of Norse's office, he acted only as a master of his own fate at the hands of Norse. Both Harro and Fender had entirely forgotten about the display of weapons he housed under that anomalous raincoat of his.

"This just got much more difficult," said Fender. "We'll have to do this in stealth unless we want bullets in our brains."

Yes, they had thought about leaving Shanna. Norse was the bigger concern, after all, but clearly that would never have been the appropriate response. They were decent people, and it was about time they proved it.

Besides, Quintero could handle Norse on his own. They were sure of it.

"What the *hell* was that?" the receptionist asked, clearly overcome by an overdosed mixture of panic, chaos, and fear.

Harro raised her hand, exposing the scythe's handle wrapped with a multitude of insatiably feminine fingers. It told the receptionist not to worry without the use of words.

"Just stay here and stay low," she said.

The receptionist began breathing choppily, like a child with asthma, flopping from her chair and disappearing under the security of her circular desk.

Harro and Fender turned and walked cautiously to the doors, opening them in a distant quiet.

It had starting to rain. Thunder rolled in from the lathered ocean waters in the distance. The sky was angry, but the two of them knew that these clouds carried much more than anger in their lumpy, black appendages. They carried fate, death and possible doom.

Yet there was no fear in the couple's eyes. They walked out into the fragile African temperament and fixed their eyes on Shanna and the hurried Devolds as they approached the base of a military helicopter in the distance.

"Listen," Harro spoke, making sure each word carried over the sound of pattering raindrops and thunderous bellows. "If they get into the air, I don't think we have any other choice."

Fender understood what she was saying, as cryptic as the comment was. She possessed scythes and chains that very well could be used as ropes, but the feeling of leaving her *alone* and dangling from the landing skids of a helicopter left a distinct and regretful doubt in Fender's mind. There were many events that could end in demise, but only one that had potential to end the right way. In his mind, bad vastly outweighed good.

"No," Fender said, shaking his head. "I can't. I won't leave you alone up there with him."

"We don't have *time* for this!" Harro screamed. "Shanna *needs* us."

She dropped the scythe from her right hand, releasing the grip and letting it fall. She reached out, brushing the palm of her empty hand against his jawline. Tension built in his chest, but drained in one, powerful wave of neurotic intimacy.

"I promise you," Harro continued. "I will come back."

If it was not for the way she pursed her lips tightly against her teeth or the fact that he saw salvation in her eyes, he would have never let her go, but something felt increasingly perfect about this moment, more perfect than he could ever attempt to explain, so he nodded hesitantly, and looked outward towards the helicopter.

The blades began swinging above its cabin. The twin engines roared. Lightning crashed, illuminating the landscape and the shimmering black paint that disguised the chopper in the dark of the storm. Harro grasped the dangling scythe in her hand and smiled.

I love you, he mouthed to Harro.

The blood in his veins seemed to course with undying courage.

We're coming, Shanna, he thought. *We're coming.*

They took off, running toward the helicopter. Fender scampered in enormous strides, pushing hard and fast against the earth, sprinting ahead of Harro. The swords swung as he moved through the air, cutting at nothing. He pushed even harder when he saw the helicopter lift from the ground, swaying in the incessant wind.

The chopper gained speed and lift, faster than they expected. It now hovered about fifteen feet above his head. He wondered whether this would work. He threw the swords to the ground and waited for Harro with his hands cupped in front of him.

"Hurry!" he yelled.

The rain was pouring in sheets now, obstructing his view as Harro came tumbling towards him. He kept his hands intertwined at his waist, giving her a place in which to aim. He tried not to think of what could happen in the helicopter if she, indeed, did make it up there. Instead, he forced himself to focus on this moment and nothing else. He would leave the horrible sensations of worrying for later, for when he was alone and living in silent, excruciating anticipation—the kind that can break a man.

Harro lined up her steps and, smoothly, slipped her right foot into Fender's cupped hands. With his overdriven thrust, she had timed it perfectly, propelling herself into the air against the whipping raindrops and swirling, stormy winds. She felt the burden of gravity lift as he she opened her eyes against the pelting water and quickly located the swaying helicopter above her. She threw a quick scythe in the direction of the helicopter's landing skids and connected in a quick, wrapping *clank*. The chains settled against each other and pinned the scythe securely against the metal.

The jolt of the helicopter's movements threw her against the tumultuous air to her left, then right. She held tightly to the chains and, with tremendous energy, began pulling herself to the cabin above her. She was completely drenched now and felt a bitter chill running through her limbs. The blinding gusts of wind did not help.

The thunder she heard distended against the expanse of sky, but even Harro could not mistake the low-drone of thunder with the fiery *click* of an automatic weapon. She shifted her eyes up into Devolds' I-have-already-won stare and, for the first time, wished she had taken Fender's advice.

She stopped her climbing, holding herself in the air with her fingers wrapped around the chain, staring into the barrel of Devolds' gun.

If this was the last moment that she would ever know, she wanted it to be remembered with Fender at the forefront of her mind.

"What is it *now*?" Devolds asked in an angry drone. He swiveled his head from the cockpit to the side door several times. He reached under his raincoat and ripped a gun from his waist. "We're getting out of here, even if that means I kill every last one of your little friends."

Shanna ripped her eyes away from Harro in an attempt to disguise her thoughts, but Devolds already knew there was something or *someone* outside the helicopter cabin.

He wouldn't take any chances. Not now.

Shanna felt the aircraft kick and lift higher into the blackened clouds. The thunder and scattered bolts of lightning lessened with the elevation, but the rain continued to pour and smash against the chopper's gaining force.

"We should be fine up here," Devolds spoke, rising from the driver's seat in the cockpit and venturing to the passenger cabin, over to Shanna. The helicopter leveled in the rain and buoyed against the wind. "As long as the lightning doesn't pick up, this thing will fly itself. Now, let's see what we've got here."

Shanna begged for Devolds to stop, to somehow have mercy, but with the flick of his wrist, she fell back against the floor and whimpered as he opened the sliding door and dropped his eyes to Harro. She looked up at him through a water-stained plea, fixing her vision on the barrel of the gun pointed at her forehead. Devolds leaned against the side of the helicopter and pointed towards the dangling body.

"I don't know how you even *got* here," he yelled. The words dissolved into the air. Harro could not hear what he was saying, but assumed that it was anything but polite. "But it's time. Farewell."

As Devolds squeezed the trigger, the helicopter lurched to the right, swinging everything in that direction. The barrage of bullets missed Harro by several feet, deflecting off of the far end of the landing skids and away into the night.

The helicopter's lurch gave her the chance she needed to climb the rest of the way. She grunted and pushed her arm muscles to the limit, lifting her torso little by little until she reached the lip of the cabin's open door.

He dropped the gun to his waist, suddenly out of bullets, and reached for the door's handrail with his empty hand. When he found it, he pulled himself up and glanced over his shoulder at the controls in the cockpit. The unattended buttons and knobs blinked furiously and then shone steady with a multitude of colors, signaling another stabilization.

"Must've been the wind," he said calmly, as if nothing had even happened. He let the words spill from his mouth. The thunder and lightning rose and met the aircraft, pushing the blades that held them stranded.

Shanna did not say a word.

"She can wait," said Devolds, pointing to Harro.

He left the cabin door open, walked back to the control panel, flicked a few switches, and returned with another gun cocked and ready for a final display of ammunition.

"Now," he said rhetorically, "where were we?"

This time, there would be no farewell speeches, casual eye contact, or wasted time. Shanna knew that expression on Devolds' face. It was the same one he had seen just before the flamethrower incident in the city. He had every intention to pump Harro full of bullets, to let her taste the iron running cold in her organs, and leave her hanging off the side of the chopper like a symbol of death, a symbol of *don't mess with me*.

He lifted the gun to his shoulder, resting it there in an outward motion, pointing it at Harro. She was now only a few feet from making an attempt into the cabin. Devolds pressed his left eye closed as if to use it as a means of aim and wrapped his finger around the trigger.

Shanna knew what she needed to do. It was clear and justified. She slid the butter knife from her pocket—the one that Devolds had seemingly forgot about (or disregarded as nothing but a petty excuse for a weapon), stared at it for a moment, analyzing its shimmers as her destiny.

This would be her moment.

She raised herself to a standing position, crept forward with the knife's handle, clutching the inverted weapon in her fist. The ridges pointed down and away from her body as she extended her arm in attack, tensing her muscles and swinging hard and fast.

Devolds caught the movement at the very last second, turning and blocking her with the thick metal of the gun. The ricochet broke the grip in Shanna's hands as she let the knife fall from her fingers and out into the open air. Gravity pulled it down toward the ocean currents below.

The momentum of the swing carried her out to the edge of the helicopter door, balancing at the lip of the cabin. She felt the rush of air batting down from the blades above her, wobbling and flailing her arms as if it would help her gain some sort of lost balance. But her heels slipped against the metal and a horrible feeling of desperation came over her as she toppled out the hatch, screaming.

Devolds merely watched, but did not try and help. Instead, he smiled and taunted her with a flinch of his fingers, as if he was debating whether saving her would be to his benefit.

Harro reached out her hand to help, but Shanna was just too far away.

Shanna turned so that her back was against the air and her shoulders squared with that of Devolds. She ripped the space in front of her for anything to grab, snatching at the hem of Devolds' jacket as a last resort. He tried to shoo her away, but felt her weight tear him from his stance. She clasped the fabric tighter and pulled harder, taking note of Devolds' smile as it morphed into a vague form of surprise. He tumbled out of the cabin with her, ditching the bulky weapon and grabbing at the landing skids before it was too late, before they both careened to their death below. Shanna slid down his torso, losing her grip, but wrapping her arms around the base of his leg until she clutched tight enough to catch herself. He kicked and wriggled to pry her from him, but the movement only forced her to hold tighter.

Harro continued to brace herself for the stream of bullets she was certain was still coming, although Devolds had completely switched his attention to the severity of his situation. Her fists were numb, now wrapped as tightly as possible around her scythed chains. She hung, like the others, from the landing skid several feet over, thinking of a way to fix this.

Get to the controls, she thought. *Land it.*

A different kind of horror washed over Harro. To her right, she watched as Devolds swung from the landing skids. His arms wrapped around the metal base from his elbows. He shook his legs harder to kick Shanna away, but she clung to it in a maddening display of fear. They were both screeching in high-pitched, quarreling notes that rang heavily through the thunder and helicopter buzz.

The cabin swerved and Harro's stomach heaved with the movement, like the moment a roller coaster dives in free fall. She watched the cabin equalize against the chaotic winds once again, but she knew it would not last for long, not with someone behind the controls.

She was struggling to maintain her position at the chains. Her body shifted with the wind, making it virtually impossible to gain any semblance of balance. At this altitude, the rain felt like tiny ice daggers against her skin that transformed themselves into tributaries that ran down every inch of her. Her clothes clung to her body in strands of damp fabric.

"Harro!" Shanna screamed.

Her grip was slowly slipping from Devolds' leg. He continued his violent shaking, but she adjusted and dug into his skin with her fingernails. He screamed and tightened his arms against the landing skids. The helicopter shook once again with its angled weight of the bodies, but this time, did not stabilize as it had before. It hung in the air, tilted, as if the sky were suddenly repelling the blades.

Harro loosed the chains in her hands, but Shanna was too far away to simply reach out in an attempt to rescue. The helicopter pulled Harro away from them—her chains sliding across the skid's slippery surface. She tried swinging towards them, but the aching her in biceps was nearly unbearable at this point, so she hung there, battling with herself whether to take drastic measures or let the dilemma take its course.

She shivered in the rain and wished that these sorts of things were not so complicated.

Something inside of Harro moved—something emotionally gripping—only enough to recognize why she was dangling there in the first place, telling her that this was not something to walk away from. This was a moment that would live on forever, regardless of her decisions. This was no longer a moment tinged by the sincerity of life and death, but a moment that defined a personal legacy—simply knowing that evil could, indeed, be conquered and the small glimmers of hope could still somehow shine for others to see.

She witnessed all of these thoughts, vividly, in this moment of sudden clarity. Her mind instinctually fluttered with bravery and reached out, clasping the landing skid with her free hand.

Devolds noticed the movement and snickered in an odd attempt to diffuse Harro's newfound courage. He thought about holding himself up with one arm, reaching into his jacket for one of his blades, but could not muster the strength to release his arms from the metal rail above. Even he struggled with his own weight. His arms were tired now and, even a bit of exertion at this point could force him to his death.

The helicopter lurched and Harro's grasp on the landing skid faltered, slipping against its smooth surface. Devolds laughed as she balked.

"This is the end for all of us," Devolds spoke. "Stale mate."

He adjusted his arms and met his eyes with Harro's. The sounds of the helicopter made it difficult to converse, so he screamed over the pulsating noise.

"Even if you make it to the controls, you'll never land this thing. It'll be your grave. I promise you, Sweetheart."

"I don't think so," Harro replied. Her mouth was drier than she would have liked—mostly because of the prominence of her nerves, which made her heart feel like a million shattered pieces in the center of her chest, each beating with its own distinctive heartbeat. "I can make it."

She spoke those last words under her breath, so that Devolds would not hear them. She wanted her courage to be her own, not derived from the manipulative schemes of a sickened individual like the man in front of her.

Harro reached back and unsnapped the other chain from her wrist, releasing her scythed arm that held her there. She now held the bar only with her own muscles, like Devolds, who watched obsessively. He

215

stopped shaking Shanna and dropped his jaw in awe.

"Don't come any closer!" he threatened. His arms were shaking. His face was turning pale. "I'm taking her with me. I can't hold on any more. *My arms…*"

Shanna screamed for help, but the initial falling sensation took over and her eyes widened with immeasurable terror. She reached out a bloodied hand to Harro, who screamed, and swiveled an unattached scythe chain towards her in a moment of sheer reaction. Shanna reached up and took hold of the bottommost link, grasping it at the meat of her fingers. The sharp edge of the scythe bit into her wrist and sent a searing pain down her side. Still, she did not let go.

Devolds attempted to lurch back and cling to Shanna as she did to him, but missed. He was in free fall now, but all he could think of was the feeling of freedom—a release from the aching that tore at his biceps moments before. Even in his downward spiral, he did not fear death, only how he could stop Harro from winning, from rescuing Shanna and living another day. He fell with his back against the upward winds, staring back at the hovering helicopter in the cloudy skies. For the last time (and he knew it would be the last time), he ripped a long-barreled pistol from his right side and pointed it towards the helicopter.

Harro and Shanna were barely visible from where he was. They were dots against the dark. Yet he steadied his arm, raised the barrel and used the top of the cylinder as an imaginary scope, shooting one final bullet in a straight line into the sky.

He relished in the moment—the weight of the gun, the recoil, the cold shimmer of the metal in his hands. When the clouds swallowed the chopper, he squinted until he knew that it was useless to do anything else. He traveled as the rain traveled, watching the droplets slow to meet him in the rushing air.

Yet, at the very last moment, before he met the water in a violent collision, Devolds thought he saw a poof of a spark where the helicopter had been.

He smiled, knowing that the bullet had somehow made its way to the girls. There was a moment of sheer, cynical bliss, then nothing but a blinding, stabbing pain that ran through every inch of him.

As his body hit hard against the choppy ocean, he lost himself in the moment, losing all focus against the primitive sounds of exploding brain cells and the end of his miserably torrent life.

Harro held tightly to the landing skid, but her grip released, slowly, due to the added weight of Shanna and the watery film accumulating atop the landing skids. Her fingers numbed with the weight of the two bodies. She closed her eyes to shake the rainwater from her vision, clearing her vision, then opened them only when she felt the helicopter lurch again, threatening to tip sideways into the air. Luckily, it shakily balanced itself once more, but it was becoming achingly clear that the girls' luck was severely running out.

The lurch felt more powerful this time, as if the helicopter had suddenly grown anxious.

She screamed a primal grunt—one that allowed for another strong, bout of energy to restrain Shanna from under her. She focused all of her thoughts on thinking of a new plan—something that could get the both of them into the helicopter cabin safely.

Their chances were bleak, but Harro forced herself to believe that situations like these were never inevitably futile. She remembered what Fender used to say when she thought the world was collapsing in around her (back when Boston was not infested with the cannibalistic, groaning Dead she had reluctantly become accustomed to): *There's always a way out, no matter how bad it seems.*

The familiar doses of courage and adrenaline coursed through her system and, again, she felt alive enough to give it a shot. It was a feeling she wished everyone had a chance to live through—a moment worth savoring.

Harro glanced around in a panoramic scan. Above her, there was nothing but the smooth metal of the helicopter's underbelly. Shanna hung from below her, clawing at the chains and trying not to think of her slit wrist that cut deeper each time she clasped harder to the unavoidable scythe. Blood trickled down her arm and mingled with the rain. From where Harro hung, Shanna's gash was a nasty one. It was only a matter of time before Shanna lost too much blood—*another* twist in the game.

To Harro's left was the scythed chain that still hung from the skid where she had released. It slithered in the wind and chimed against itself several feet away.

It was then that the idea came to her like a cyclone, picking her up and carrying her away: if Shanna could somehow reach the chains, Harro would be free to climb up and into the helicopter. She tested the links that connected her arm to Shanna's. It buckled enough so that she could gently rock the rope at soft, rounded angles.

Shanna noticed the movement and panicked.

"What are you *doing*?" she yelled.

It was a chaotic jumble of words that felt rushed and full of uncontrollable fear. Harro turned her eyes towards the bodiless chain, then back toward Shanna. She watched as clarity streamed into Shanna's eyes.

"Oh!" Shanna yelled over the whirring of the blades, nodding in inspiration.

Fresh blood stained her shirt in a 'V' at her chest. She clutched both her cut wrist and the chain against her breasts to make certain she would not let go. She reached out for the dangling chain with her empty arm, still too far to gauge the proper distance. It was an awkward sight, but the best plan the two girls could muster.

Harro swung Shanna harder. The chain tightened back and forth like a pendulum, increasing speed with each sway. A *clink* buckled the chain. Shanna's weight had finally become too much. A *pop* resonated up Harro's arm. The links were giving way. Soon, they would shatter— breaking under the pressure—and there would be too much guilt to watch Shanna fall to her watery grave.

Unless, she thought, *one more push.*

Her thoughts strained against her conscience. She understood the consequences of her decision, if this plan should go wrong. It was no longer her life she was dealing with, but that of another's—an innocent one at that.

Harro reared back and swung Shanna as hard as she could in the direction of the chain. Several links broke in the movement, but Shanna had already released, floating towards the opposite side of the landing skid. Harro watched intently, gasping as the helicopter dipped, forcing Shanna to nearly miss her target. Her limbs extended to snatch at any part of the dangling metal rope.

She clutched at the links in a lucky rip of her right hand (the wrist with the open wound), then the left, wrapping her fingers around it and pulling herself up enough to hold on.

Harro screamed in excitement and pulled herself up and over the skid so that she could wrap her arms and legs around it like a log. She crawled slowly, shimmying her torso towards the cabin entrance, pulling herself up in a few final muscle contractions.

She was the first to reach the lip of the open doorway and reached up to pull herself over the cabin edge. She outstretched her hand to signal for Shanna to reach for it and the girl reached with her bad arm, exposing the wound. The slice was gruesome, cut open almost to the bone. Harro wondered if it was even salvageable at this point, yet Shanna never seemed to realize the fatality of her situation, reared up, and grasped Harro's hand.

The helicopter swerved into a furious tailspin. Shanna gripped Harro's arm in fury.

"Don't let go!" Harro yelled over the blades. "I've got you!"

The grip was faltering in the wet of the rain, but Harro only squeezed tighter. She pulled until Shanna was able to grab hold of the cabin lip and pull herself up into safety.

It was then that the helicopter jerked backward, faltering against itself in a mess of machinery.

Harro looked around the cockpit, amidst the confusion, and wondered what could have made such a succinct, but damaging blast to an aircraft of this caliber—clearly not a rock (at this altitude) or a bird or hail of any kind.

But a bullet, she thought.

At the far end of the cockpit—where the windshield met the sheet metal—was a small, circular hole about half an inch thick. The force of the bullet cracked the windshield and damaged the furthest expanse of control buttons, dipping the helicopter's nose quite dramatically. From where she stood, now leaning over the expanse of machinery, she observed the situation, sighed and shifted her focus to the functioning buttons and levers that remained.

Devolds, she thought. His imaginary laughter haunted her mind. *You good for nothing bastard.*

First, she checked that both engines were still intact, jutting her head from the blasted windshield to check the tail rotor and the main rotor blade. All seemed fine.

The momentum of the contact shifted the balance of the chopper, sending the nose of it deep into a mass of thunderclouds. She reared a lever back, hoping it would ease the aircraft back into a stable state, but instead, it fell harder. She pushed a few more blinking buttons and the helicopter reverted to an upright position, wondering how long it could truly be maintained.

She ran over to the open cabin door and looked out to Shanna, who clung by her last breath at the helicopter lip. In the inside corner of the cabin was the black rope ladder. Harro flung it out of the doorway. It flopped heavily down just a little ways.

"Grab the ladder!" Harro yelled.

Shanna raised her eyes, exhausted, quickly shifting her weight to it.

"Quick!" Harro continued.

She reached the lip of the doorway and used the ladder to climb in, hugging Harro with weak limbs.

"It's okay," Harro said, patting her on the back. They both felt like crying. "We're fine now."

"We got lucky on this one," Shanna spoke, but she didn't know about the controls just yet.

"We're not out of the clear just yet," said Harro, returning to the cockpit.

She jogged back over to them and placed her hands on the central levers. She pushed forward and the aircraft moved with her. She reared back and the helicopter dipped into reverse. She edged the nose of the helicopter forward, testing the controls with her initial movements.

"So far so good," said Harro, but Shanna had already ventured away.

The thunder was now only in its most fragile form, relieving itself in the wake of summer sun. She lessened the power of the spinning blades and dipped back so that the African coast came into view. The gray building in all of its haunting dominance grew as they descended towards the cliffs.

It was a moment filled with the horrors of what could have been. Somehow, they had all survived. At least that's what she thought. It was a moment lived in the doomed presence of danger, but rightfully overcome. It was a moment that Harro would forever remember as a moment of sheer brilliance.

Shanna couldn't speak, only rested against the floor. The loss of blood took control of her body, creating a strange feeling of lightheadedness that filtered into hallucinogenic thoughts of childhood memories. They filled her brain like paintings that flickered in and out of warm lighting. Her ears picked up on a chilling laughter that haunted her to the core. She was not sure whether it came from the helicopter or her mind, but regardless, it scared her into shivers. She thought of Henry in watercolors, but could not grasp the details of his face as well as she would have liked to.

Henry? she called. *Are you alright? Henry?*

It frustrated her into a muted scream. Only the beating of the helicopter blades replied.

She allowed herself to drift into sleep. If she was about to die, she embraced it.

She thought that maybe Henry would meet her at Heaven's Gate, holding out his hands and smiling like he used to, as he had before any of this ever happened. Maybe Heaven was a place that could make her forget about Boston and the dusty apartment and her violently damaged ankle and wrist. Maybe death was the only true form of recompense after all.

She slid deeper into her thoughts, but felt nothing but the true confines of sleep, so she dozed and felt comfortable enough in the dreamscapes she entered, knowing she could very well wake in a few hours to the same uprooted world she had left or die here in the cabin of a rogue aircraft.

Goodnight, Henry, she thought, wondering if she would ever see him again. *Goodnight, World.*

20

"He's dead," Quintero said in a deepened slew of words. "I was too late."

Fender, who picked up his blades from the grass below him, sheathed them behind his shoulders, shook his head and looked over his shoulder at Quintero.

"I'm sure you did everything you could," he replied.

He could tell it was the last thing the gunman wanted to hear in the moment, but it was the most consolable phrase he could find within himself to say.

Quintero nodded, attempting to accept Fender's words as truth, but deep within himself, he still felt the twinge of despair wrench his insides like a gnome trapped in his stomach. The pain turned to exhaustion and the gunman closed his eyes, wishing he could keep them closed, but there was a concerned tension that filled Fender, too, and the gunman knew that the only courteous reply was an attempt to console his woes, like Fender had tried with him, whatever they may be.

"Where's Harro?" he asked, afraid of the response.

Fender pointed towards the sky. The clouds had passed along with the blasts of rain and could now be seen over the distant oceanic horizon. A random crack of thunder resonated quietly, but never truly boomed like it had before. If there was any lightning still housed in those black clouds, it was no longer visible.

"The helicopter took off before we could reach it. Devolds had Shanna. He killed all of these soldiers."

Fender pointed to the littering of dead bodies around them. Each one glistened, but Quintero assumed it was the rainwater that made their lifeless skin glow. It was clear where the puddles of blood had been—stained circles of light red amidst lush, green lawn.

"Harro was the only one that made it up onto the helicopter. She was hanging from the landing skids last time I saw her. I was trying to keep an eye on her, but I lost it in the clouds."

His voice shook enough to be noticeable, but not enough for emotional instability. Quintero patted him on the back twice with a brotherly type of condolence.

"If there's a girl that can take care of herself," Quintero argued, "it's her."

Independence had always been a strong point in Harro, anyone who knew her agreed, but still, Fender's heart felt like it was being ripped from his chest in quick, surgically precise tears. He kept his eyes glued to the distant clouds, even as he talked.

He wanted his wife back.

"So that's it? We sit here and wait?" Quintero asked.

"That's all we *can* do," Fender replied.

His voice was weary, but still remarkably understanding and collected.

"Alright," the gunman said, folding his arms and shifting his weight to his left leg. "Then that's what we'll do."

Even before the gunman could spit out the final words, he noticed a figure falling from the sky. He could tell by the expression on Fender's face that he saw it, as well. From where they stood, there was no way to tell who or what it was, but it fell and jutted out its arms as if it were reaching upward. They heard a small *pop* a second later and then the smack of it clashing against the water.

Fender couldn't speak. He didn't *have* to. Quintero understood what he was thinking. Thoughts of fishing Harro's broken body from the water filled his mind and he bent his knees into a catcher's stance, resting his elbows on his upper legs, scratching nervously at the stubble that grew from his chin. He closed his eyes and moved the scratching to his forehead, breathing out a sigh filled with disgruntled stress and a strange sound of pleading that Quintero had never before heard escape from his mouth.

"I'm sure it wasn't her," the gunman consoled, or at least attempted to.

But Fender was beyond nerves now, reaching the realm filled with a paranoid stream of thoughts that seemed to paralyze any other form of living.

Quintero walked away, unable to help Fender any longer. He thought of Henry and his lifeless frame up in Norse's unnerving layer behind the office. He returned to the feelings of guilt and inevitability. He remembered vividly the pain that coursed through him as he looked into Henry's horribly lifeless face. Pain like this was what made him human. It was what made him strong.

The gunman thought of Shanna and how her life would be changed now in the absence of the man who saved her from the overrun city. He wished he didn't have to be the one to tell her about Henry, if she even made it from this predicament alive, but after all they've been through, he had no doubt she would make it, regardless of the obstacles in her way.

He turned to Fender, who hadn't moved from the crouched position since he had turned away. Harro was his strength. He needed her to survive. What would happen if the falling body was his wife? Would it mean the end for him? A new sense of loss and abandonment?

Quintero breathed, shut off his thoughts, and closed his eyes. All he could do now was hope that the falling figure was not the fallen angel of Fender's worst nightmare.

All he could do was stand and wait.

Wake up, said the hissy voice. *Wake up, you.*

But he didn't. He was stuck somewhere between unconsciousness and sleep. His ears burned with a strange heat. His eyes felt like searing charcoals scorching the front part of his brain. He tried to raise his arms to ease the burning, but his muscles refused to lift.

It was then that he remembered what happened.

He remembered *everything*—the prick of the infected syringe, the feeling of the virus ripping at him from the inside out, and the way Quintero's eyes dropped when he fell to the ground for the last time. He remembered Shanna and her sparkling eyes. He remembered her vividly intimate touch. He even remembered his name.

Wake up, it said. *You will wake up and walk. Wake up!*

But he couldn't. His body felt like a thousand pounds. The tiled floors were bloody and smeared and slippery. There was a putrid taste in his mouth that could not be avoided. It seeped through every crevice, snaking in and out of his gums and teeth. It tasted of metallic iron and a potent tangy rottenness, something like decaying, half-eaten apples. He decided he would try and ignore it all, but for some reason, it would not leave his thoughts. It was locked away in some sort of mental prison within him. It screamed and suppressed itself.

Slowly, he gained control of his fingers, then his hands, and then his arms. He squeezed his fingers into a fist on both hands without opening his eyes. He took pleasure in the way they moved—the way he controlled them again. It was as though he regained some sort of mysterious superpower that had been taken from him some time ago. He smiled, but his face did not move.

Something screamed inside his head.

When his eyes finally *did* open, his vision was a blurry yellow-orange that fizzed at the corners of his eyes. The sepia filter scared him for only a minute, but slowly, dissipated into the normal, everyday colors he had seen before he passed out in the city. He never felt more alive than in this moment. He felt pain-free and awake—two things he forgot even existed in this world.

Then he found he could move his neck, so he stretched and lifted his head away from the swimming floor. First, he stared at the wound in his side. It had not healed in the least bit, but the blood had coagulated and hardened the skin and muscle around its opening. He touched the corners, but felt nothing. He made a mental note to get it looked at when he returned home, so that Shanna could be reassured that an infection of any sort would not start creeping into his veins and murder him in his sleep.

Henry laughed at the thought. He had, indeed, been infected with the most fatal and violent of viruses known to man and survived, but Shanna would want to make sure that *this* wound would be properly medicated and rid of any deadly impurities because, as she said it: *even the littlest of scrapes have the deadliest consequences.*

"Always so thorough," he mumbled. "That's why I love you."

But no one answered and he remembered he was alone. He pushed himself up from the tiled floor and listened to the vertebrae snap and crack in his back. The popping felt good and he closed his eyes and stiffened his spine to initiate more, but he cracked enough and he stopped, slouching and resting his arms on his legs. He never liked the sound of popping bones and joints, but for some reason, the way his bones were realigning put him at ease. It was a strange type of ease, though, almost as if he was a different person—one that knew himself exactly like he had before, but awoke with a few added eccentricities to his genetic make-up.

He felt the circulation return to his legs. He wiggled his toes and watched the movement. His knees snapped loudly when he shifted them for the first time, coupled with a flash of discomfort, but then evolved into a distinct form of pleasurable catharsis, just as his back had done seconds before. Every inch of him felt new and responsive, but appeared, still, wounded and frail.

"Why do I feel like this?" Henry asked openly.

That's a good question, someone answered.

He bent his legs a bit more and pushed himself onto his feet. It was then that he noticed the body pinned between the floor and the wall on the other side of the room. Half of its face had exploded against the tiles in a messy array of body mass, exposing the brain. The untouched side of his face was marked with a horrid expression of pain and surprise. The untouched eye was gray and specked with a crème-colored white. The other was indistinguishable. There was no motion in his limbs. Henry, after careful analysis, noticed that the disfigured body was that of Norse's.

He shook his head, wiped his face with a horribly dirtied hand, and walked towards the door.

I know you better than you know yourself, said the voice caged in his brain. *I'm not going anywhere. I'm bigger than you think. I've been waiting for a host like you.*

The voice sounded like his, but the thoughts were not. They came from somewhere else that Henry could not control. It laughed, and then disappeared. *Am I going crazy? A virus can't talk,* he thought, chuckling it away.

Oh, yes I can, it said. *I most certainly can.*

A shiver ran down Henry's spine. He felt an incredible urge to flex his arms and make fists with his clamped fingers. There was an anger that settled in the pit of his stomach. It slithered and worked its way up from his lower back to his chest, hovering and clinging to his ribs. He suppressed it and let his breathing overtake the need to kill. He reached out and leaned against the wall for support, closing his eyes for only a second, then opening them and regaining composure.

Did you feel that? the voice asked. *Just a little taste of what life is going to be like from here on out.*

There was a snap, like a microphone clicking off, and then his head went silent. No voices or laughs or hisses rumbled through his ears. There was nothing but silence.

Henry convinced himself that it was only his imagination that had concocted such a vile voice. He had been through a lot, after all. When he added the fact that his mind tended to play tricks on him anyway, even before the Infection broke out, it was apparent that this was just another silly scheme his mind created to get him through to this point.

And nothing else.

He taught himself how to walk again. His legs were crooked and felt backwards. His ankles inverted slightly, pointing the tips of his sneakers towards one another.

"Strange," Henry spoke to no one.

Step by step, he ventured towards the door. He should have never come here, he thought to himself, but he hadn't really had much of a choice. It was Quintero's idea. It was everyone's idea...except for his.

He opened the laboratory door and walked down the darkened brick hallway. He could see the mangled remnants of an office in front of him.

Henry tried to remember what had happened in this room, but couldn't. Everything seemed chaotic and strained in the unconscious state in which he was trapped. He remembered the big things, like the name *Doctor Norse* and the loud *pops* of gunfire, but never details.

The office, unfortunately for him, was a part of the details, which remained hidden far away, possibly to never be uncovered again.

He climbed through piles of shattered polished wood from a desk and splintered bookshelves, working his way to the bay windows that overlooked the front of the building. Already, he could see the clouds of a distant thunderstorm traveling out of sight, farther out where the ocean meets the sky at the horizon line. It took him several minutes to step over and around all of the ruin, especially with his buckling legs, which were the one thing—out of all this situation produced—that bothered him. He wished his body could somehow be normal, revert back to what it had been before Norse had changed him.

He knew, though, this would never happen.

His eyes peered through the bay window glass. He searched, scanning the floral gardens and the African coastal cliffs in the distance. He scanned the area near the building, where the entranceway, grass, and asphalt met with a sign that said: WELCOME in large, curvy letters against a white-colored backdrop and gold borders.

But all of this paled in comparison to where his eyes went last.

Henry placed the fingers of his right hand against the windowpane, pressing to feel the cool touch of the glass against skin. Outside, towards the outer limits of the facilities, stood Quintero and Fender—two large men that seemed like figurines from where he watched, each with their own, distinct body language. Fender was in a catcher's stance with his knees bent in stretched angles, resting his elbows against his groin. Quintero had backed away with his arms crossed, looking down at his feet.

Henry knocked heavily to catch their attention, but it was useless. The distance and height of Norse's office was just too much.

Then, a sort of nervousness blanketed Henry's chest. The sound of hard flapping resonated against the sky and Henry knew what it was. In the distance, pummeling from the clouds out near the horizon, roared a black helicopter, wobbling slightly as it approached. Henry peered down at the two men, who screamed with their hands above their heads, celebrating. Fender pulled a sword from its sheath just to be certain, but the smiles pinned to their face said it all.

"I have to get out there," Henry thought. "I have to let them know I'm alive."

He tried to judge what floor he was on, but found it too difficult of a task.

The microphone voice clicked on again.

You can't do it, it said. *See? They're already landing the chopper. You know what that means, right? Time's...almost...up.*

Henry sprinted, as best as he could, down the hallway to the stairs. He fixed the form in his legs one more time as he ran, then reached for the railing that led to the roof.

When the clouds parted and the metal bird rose from the ashes of the thunderstorm, Fender's heart nearly leapt from his chest. Quintero noticed it only after Fender burst out in celebration.

"It's them!" he yelled. "I *know* it."

"Wait a minute," Quintero said, deepening his voice, trying not to dilute the excitement of the moment. "What if it's not?"

Fender thought for a second, running each scenario through his mind like it was a calculator.

"Tell me this—would Devolds come back?" Fender asked, half already knowing the answer.

The gunman shrugged his shoulders, but couldn't give a definitive answer—only waited for Fender to come to some sort of general conclusion. The helicopter was getting closer and louder, wobbling as it streamed forward through the now crisp air. Fender unsheathed both swords and tossed one to Quintero. He held it in front of him, upright and still.

"Just in case," Fender said, smiling.

The gunman returned the grin, wishing he had some sort of weapon for himself that was not associated with too-close-for-comfort warfare, and turned his eyes toward the sky, watching the black of the aircraft shimmer in the late afternoon sunlight as it approached in waves of wind. He thought he heard tapping from somewhere above him, but misconstrued it with the battering of the helicopter blades in mid-flight. He did not even bother to look back at the building. As far as he was concerned, that place was nothing but Hell built on earth.

The helicopter slowed and buckled as it approached the grassy knoll of the African cliff. The motors scuffled, blubbering and stuttering with Harro's unabashed flying skills, before the landing skids hit hard against the land and the rotors stopped turning, smoking with the intensity of their flight.

The cabin door was already open and Quintero ventured closer to it in hesitant, long strides. Two feet dangled from the opening in the final blasts of rotor winds. He noticed they were Shanna's—her red boat shoes tied in elongated bow ties—dangling there immobile, like an unused puppet. He sprinted to her side.

No one else is going to die on my watch today, the gunman thought. *No one.*

Fender trailed him by a good thirty feet. He reached the door and quieted his heavy breathing, inching closer.

"Don't swing," Harro spoke. "It's me. Devolds is gone."

Quintero released the sword to the grass and hopped in, kneeling beside Shanna and her caked, dark wounds. He placed his ear next to her mouth, listening for breathing. It was faint but still there.

"What happened?" the gunman asked.

Harro crossed her arms as though she was fighting a chill that swept across her skin unexpectedly. She chattered her teeth as she stood in front of him in damp, clinging clothes, absorbing the warmth of the still air and standing content with her feet touching land.

Her expression, however, showed no signs of contentedness, yet Quintero looked past the physicality of her body language and even further past the way her eyes gleamed in the sun, revealing a spot of pride that swelled somewhere in her soul—the way she peered down at Shanna, the way she wished the girl could have avoided the pain Devolds had put her through. But, despite their nearly impossible obstacles, they both made it. And that's all that mattered.

At least she's alive, Harro thought.

She scratched the back of her head in fidgety strokes.

"It's a long story," she mumbled through chattering teeth. "Devolds fell. He tried to kill us, but he didn't."

It wasn't the best explanation, but Harro's mind was racing with terrible thoughts. She wanted nothing but sleep at this point, to relax enough to fall into a sort of comatose for hours and hours and hours.

"Come on," Fender ushered, waving his arm in front of him. "Sit."

She did and, immediately, began to drift away into the wading waters of slumber. She wrapped her arms around her chest to seal some sort of warmth within her.

"Is she alright?" Fender asked, scanning Shanna's weak frame from where he sat.

"I don't know," Quintero mumbled. "She's unconscious."

He wrapped his leather jacket around her shoulders and grimaced. He held Shanna's wrist where the cut had smeared into a slice of darkened blood.

"What do you say we get out of here?" he asked Fender. "Shanna needs medical attention now. She's lost a lot of blood."

He dropped his eyes to his feet and folded his arms. The thunderclouds were now scattering into blue skies over the brisk ocean waters. He wondered if he would ever see a storm like that again. He wondered if it had even been a thunderstorm at all, shaking his head, displacing the ubiquitous supernatural urges he may have been feeling, and returned his thoughts to the helicopter.

"Do you know how to fly one of these things?" Quintero asked Fender, fidgeting with the controls in the cockpit.

Fender shook his head and shrugged his shoulders only enough so that Harro's head bobbed slightly against his muscle and fell deeper into sleep.

"Well then," Quintero continued, "I guess I'll give it a shot."

He stood over the controls, blinking at the multitude of buttons, switches, and levers. Each possessed its own, mysterious task. He flicked a green button to the left with his index finger and heard the sound of sucking wind as an engine roared with power. He flicked another switch that resembled the first and yet another engine puttered and then growled with excitement.

"I could get used to this," he murmured.

Fender smiled in the cabin behind him.

The tail rotor flapped vigilantly along with the main rotor blades, which sliced the air like ancient albatross wings. They reassured safety and a homeward path that they had lost somewhere amidst the turmoil and destruction of such recent events. The landing skids lifted from the ground and the cabin wobbled slightly, but Quintero steadied the aircraft and lifted it higher into the air.

"It's lost a lot of steam," said Quintero, "but it's got enough for one more trip."

As the girls slept against the day's late afternoon sunlight, Fender and Quintero let their minds drift away into silence, knowing that they had escaped the impossible and, somehow, lived to tell the tale. There was not a doubt in their minds that, in however long it would take to find Norse's office as it was, Boston would soon be erased and renewed to start fresh. No more zombies. No more perilous antics through mobbed city streets. And this nightmarish vision of an evolving race of the Dead, a broken city defiled by everything evil, and a menacing scientist willing to take extreme measures to keep the virus alive, would soon fall by the wayside and be forgotten against the beauty of a fresh, new beginning.

Henry heard the whooshing of the helicopter as it ascended into the air. His knees cracked and wobbled as he took to the stairs in triples. He was almost there.

The stairwell narrowed into a metal door, locked from the inside. He used the power within him (which scared him enough to ignore until this moment) to shoulder the door like a battering ram. The first contact only produced a series of heavy dents, but forced no budge. The second, however, cracked the frame, propelling the door into a skid across the cement rooftop. It was a moment that made his heart race.

Feels good, doesn't it? the voice in his head asked.

He refused to reply. To answer meant to acknowledge it existed, which sounded crazy, but he wanted nothing to do with his new mental state. It frightened him, wore him down.

Just think about it, the voice continued. *You're strong now—stronger than any other person on the face of this planet. Imagine the power. Imagine the feeling. That door you just pile-drove into the ground? That's nothing. Imagine that feeling forty times bigger. All you have to do is…*

"Stop!" Henry yelled.

The voice rang like a megaphone in his ears, almost loud enough to incite a riot in his skull. The fluttering helicopter came into view across the rooftop. He scanned the cabin—Fender had his arm wrapped around Harro, who slept against his shoulder, and Quintero manned the controls.

Shanna? Where was Shanna?

"Wait!" Henry yelled, but the fluttering metal blades were too loud for the group to hear his fleeting voice.

He sprinted across the rooftop. The late day hours scorched his eyes with golden light. He squinted and grimaced as he ran, screaming to catch any sort of attention he could, but Quintero shifted the body of the aircraft towards the oceanfront in a slow, hovering movement.

Anxious nerves bubbled in his stomach and in his throat.

There's no chance you make it, the voice said. *Go ahead. Jump.*

The taunting ridicule of the sound of his own voice made him shiver. His knees felt disjointed and unused. He wished he could just run faster, but the hitch in his gallop kept him from increasing speed. The helicopter wobbled with its own movement, then began a slow dip forward.

He was only a few feet from the ledge now and had already made his decision.

He was going to jump. It was an easy choice, closing his eyes and lunging, arms outstretched in front of him.

You jumped, the voice screamed in his head. *You actually jumped!*

There were several startling moments of disarray that scattered Henry's thoughts. He coasted through the air, feeling the cool breeze against his skin as his feet left the cement and drove him out into free fall. The aircraft hovered away, distancing itself, while Henry's depth perception undoubtedly failed him. He could not tell if he was about to slam face-first into the outside metal of the cabin, veer into the slicing blades of the tail rotor, or simply miss the entire compartment all together. Everything appeared to him as if he was looking through a very thick piece of scratched and treated glass.

He reached out his arms in an attempt to cling to anything that would save him.

Thoughts, words, and phrases circulated through his mind—things to which he had never given the slightest thought before. He thought of home—not his apartment in Boston, not his childhood home, but a new home, filled with fresh and invaluable memories and things that could never be replaced. He thought of a woman, his wife, (he presumed her be Shanna) in a sunflower summer dress, soaked in the afternoon glow of light. He thought of his unborn children—the kids that needed him to survive this moment to carry on the Walters legacy.

He smiled, presently not afraid.

He jerked back into reality, quickly gaining control over his wandering brain. His perception hadn't cleared, but he was no longer concerned with it. If he was going to make it, it would happen.

He stretched his arms as far as they could possibly reach, aiming for the lip of the open doorway. There was a *thud* as Henry's body collided with the landing skids. His arms wrapped around the metal bars and clung as forcefully as possible, barely holding on.

The helicopter swayed with the momentum of his body. He heard Quintero belt a distinct *What the hell was that?* as he scrambled to level the aircraft.

Fender swiveled his head hard at the noise, as surprised as Quintero. Harro woke with Quintero's twitch, partly because of the unexpected swivel. Her eyes widened with labored sleep and sudden acute awareness of the situation.

The sun broke the oceanic plane in the distance, bursting with a constant splash of golden fireworks as Fender crawled to the base of the door and peered out over the side. His eyes widened at the sight of Henry, clinging to the metal with his knuckled fingers. Everything about the boy seemed to have changed in an odd, faltered way. And the fact that it was him!

"But..." Fender began. "You're *dead*."

It wasn't exactly what he had meant to say, but the words crossed the threshold of his lips anyway like bad tasting food. He considered calling for Quintero, but the sounds of the main rotor blades were too much to challenge.

The boy's eyes were different than what Fender remembered—now a hazel color with scattered flecks of orange. They seemed frightened, but frightened in a way that exuded more than just fear. They pleaded for acceptance and courage, as well. The angles of his face and jawbone had shifted somehow, making him ghostly and sunken. His legs and arms were gangly and lengthy and wafted in the aircraft's brash gusts of wind like a tattered flag. He was certain this had something to do with the administering of the virus and antidote, but still, something wasn't sitting right with this situation. Fender could see that, at least.

"Fender, it's *me*," Henry spoke. The words woke Fender from his strange internal struggle. "Pull me up."

Fender wrapped his hand around Henry's wrist and pulled him upward into the cabin. He wasn't quite sure this was the best decision, surprisingly, but it *was* Henry, regardless of his strange and conflicting appearance.

"I…I didn't even recognize you," Fender said, slighted by confusion. "How the hell did you even get here?"

"It's me. It really is," he replied. "I don't know what happened. I woke up and everyone was gone. I saw the helicopter from Norse's office and figured I only had one chance, so I took it. Seriously. That's all."

"You…don't…*look* good," Fender said in hesitation. It was an honest observation. "You sure you feel alright?"

Fender was worried that Henry, although he claimed he was, was not himself, perhaps taken over by a strange force none of them could identify just yet. Harro watched with caution, hiding it well in the midst of him. She breathed slower, calming her pattering heart.

"Hi," he said, noticing the slight change in her eyes. He made sure to keep space between them.

She returned the acknowledgement and shifted her eyes back to Fender. Henry felt an even stranger bit of apprehension flood the cabin. It felt controlled, but slightly abrasive, as if he had committed a crime that he was not aware of.

He stepped back and away from the group, resting his hands on his hips. He felt the crusty opening of the wound at his thigh. There was no pain, but a significant opening now from the jump, and an eerie textural cognizance.

"*Guys*," he said, knowing that no matter what he attempted to say, the tension wouldn't lessen, "it's really me."

Fender nodded with hesitant believability. Harro bit her lip.

After a few awkward seconds, Henry bent down to one knee, standing over Shanna in an overtly concerned, intimate posture. He had seen her body the moment his feet had hit the cabin floor—she had been the first one he looked for—but the newfound apprehensive tension threw him off-guard. Harro and Fender continued their stares, ready to step in if Henry made any brash movements.

"What if it's not *him*?" Harro asked her husband. "What if he's something else now?"

Fender kept his eyes on Henry, who seemed to hear the question from where he kneeled.

Oh, but you are, the voice in his head spoke. It sounded distant, as if it had spoken from down an echoed hallway. *You are more than just Henry now.*

He closed his eyes, pushing hard to rid his thoughts of that vile voice, but it grew as it walked down the metaphorical hallway and whispered heatedly into the deepest part of his brain.

Tell them about me.

"No," Henry spoke out loud, again acknowledging the voice he vowed he wouldn't.

He shot a concerned look towards both Harro and Fender, then shifting his eyes back to Shanna.

"She's alive," Harro spoke through fragile tones, "but unconscious. She's lost a lot of blood."

"She needs a hospital," said Henry.

Harro nodded, finally turning away.

He noticed Shanna's torn wrist, the way her breathing caught in shallow hiccups, and the swollen ankle resting against the cabin wall.

I could've stopped this, he thought.

You know you did the best you could, the voice within him replied. *Some things are just meant to be. Fate, Henry. Besides, she'll be fine.*

How do you know? Henry replied.

I know a lot of things. More than you probably think I should.

"I'm here," Henry whispered. "Stay with me, Shanna."

After all, it was her voice, saying those exact words, that kept him going all along. He clung to them like an infant clings to a pacifier, like a toddler clings to his thumb. Returning the favor was the only logical thing he felt he could do, so he kneeled over her, and repeated the words over and over again.

He knew, in this moment, that his life would never be the same. And he was okay with all of it—as long as Shanna was there.

Quintero turned and caught a glimpse of the new passenger in his sights. He let go of the controls, stabilizing the helicopter to a floating position, buoying in the air. Fender replaced him, noticing the gunman's sudden notice. He wrapped his hands over the control levers, pushing the helicopter into a dip and then a forward leap against the morning sun.

The gunman took slow steps towards Henry, balancing against the speed of the traveling aircraft, letting his eyes fill with shame. In fact, he couldn't say a word—his mouth malfunctioned in complete surprise—

merely taking short, stumbling steps until he opened his arms, consuming Henry in a hearty, brotherly embrace.

"I'm sorry," said the gunman. They were the only words he could manage to say, so he spoke them again. "I'm sorry."

Henry returned the embrace, shaking his head simultaneously.

"No," he replied. "Thank you. I wouldn't be here without you."

Quintero released his arms and backed away, confused at Henry's response. He expected anger, sadness, perhaps a sense of betrayal. He *had* left him in a bloodied room to die, alone with a villainous counterpart rotting away with half of his face splattered against the wall. Yet Henry wanted to *thank* him for that?

"You saved my life, Quin," Henry continued. "You gave me the antidote."

The helicopter swayed to the side, but no one seemed too frightened at its movement. Fender raised his hand to signal everything was fine.

"I remember everything," said Henry. "You did all you could."

Henry raised his arm and rested a dirtied palm on Quintero's shoulder. His eyes were more than honest. They were joyful.

"Don't beat yourself up about it," Henry said. "I understand."

The gunman looked into Henry's hazel-colored eyes and wondered what could really be behind them. Like Fender and Harro, he noticed an indecipherable augmentation toying somewhere deep within Henry's true character, but having the boy back was an elated feeling of relief that outweighed everything else. He reached out his hand. Henry returned the gesture, clutching Quintero's fingers in his, and squeezing gently in a firm handshake.

Both smiled.

Life suddenly filled Shanna's lungs and she inhaled in deep, heavy heaves. Henry turned as her eyes opened in a slow seep of energy. Her vision was blurry, but she recognized Henry's presence and smiled faintly with a singular, comfortable warmth. He returned to her side, one knee pressed against the floor, running his fingers through her hair. She breathed in with the movement of his hand, exhaling as he caressed her forehead. There was no need for words in a moment like this. They simply relished in its entirety.

Quintero returned to the controls and Fender joined his wife at the front of the cabin.

All was well.

"Let's go home, shall we?" Quintero spoke over the rotor blades.

They all nodded.

PART THREE

EPILOGUE

There was a stinging sensation in the pit of Henry's stomach. It had been there for days. He wished it would just go away.

But it didn't.

He could not eat. He could not sleep. He could not do anything without feeling that uncomfortable tugging in his abdomen.

I know what it is, the voice spoke.

It was soft and barely there.

"I don't want to know," Henry said, ringing his hands against his skull. "Don't say it. I don't want to know."

You need meat. You need it bad.

When they returned to the States, the first thing they did was find a hospital. They had barely made it to the coast of Florida before the empty tank of gas gave way. Henry admitted Shanna first, then himself. They dressed her wounds and put her ankle in a cast. Within a day or so, she was looking much better.

Harro and Fender said their goodbyes and returned home. Henry sometimes wondered if that would be the last time he saw them or if, by some divine miracle, their paths would cross again.

Either way, he knew he would sure miss them, more than he ever thought he would.

Quintero decided to stay in the area and let his mind wander. He visited a local funeral home and paid for a proper service for his brother.

The service was scheduled for a few days out and, nervously, was not certain if anyone would come. He didn't have many family or friends, but regardless, Henry and Shanna promised they would be there, sitting in the front row.

Henry sat in Shanna's care room, feeling the tinge in his stomach, wishing there was a way to satisfy it…without *satisfying* it.

Shanna was napping in the bed beside him.

You need meat, the voice rang.

He pried himself from the plastic chair and walked toward the hallway wing. A sign hovered above him, displaying an array of building directions. On the right, the letters ONCOLOGY illuminated the space in bright white lettering. To the left, SURGERY did the same. And in the middle, the word MORGUE caught Henry's attention. Even the word itself sent a powerful urge through him.

His feet carried him down the hallway, passed white-coated physicians and scrubbed nurses that greeted him with a smile. He grinned back at them all the same.

He reached the elevator and pushed the button labeled *M.* He watched as the elevator moved passed the second floor, then the first floor hospital lobby, and finally, entered into a dungeon-like, grayed brick reception area below ground.

A middle-aged man sat behind a metal desk reading a newspaper dated with yesterday's date. He looked up as Henry entered.

"Can I help you?" the man asked.

Henry's heart was beating heavily, battering against his ribcage.

"My mother," Henry lied. "She's in there."

"Visitors are not allowed in the autopsy room. I'm sorry."

The man lowered his eyes and scanned the words on page three of the opened paper. Henry inched closer, leaning to the desk with his palms down.

"My *mother*," Henry repeated.

"And I'm *sorry*, sir, but you're going to have to step away. There's nothing I can do."

Without thinking, Henry lunged from across the table with a closed fist. His hand collided with the side of the man's face, sending the sound of crackling through the air. The body splayed across the cold, cement floor, completely unconscious. Afraid, Henry hid the body underneath the desk, away from the elevator's line of sight.

I didn't know you had that in you, the voice chimed.

Henry grimaced with each and every word.

I like this new side of Henry.

He fixed his collared shirt, adjusting the fabric so it fell onto his shoulders in a more comfortable way, and walked into the autopsy room. It was twelve noon and the Floridian sun was at its highest peak. Most pathologists despised this time of day—adapting to such a dark and ominous work setting for most daylight hours—but not the pathologist at *this* clinic. A sign hung in the doorway, saying: *Gone to lunch. Be back in one hour.*

A body, in perfect posture, lay helpless on the operating table. A large incision had been opened in a vertical line down her chest, exposing organs and coagulated blood.

Henry salivated, widening his eyes.

If you're going to do this, he thought to himself, *you have to be smart about it.*

Now you're thinking, the voice continued. It laughed, undulating into a dull, full headache.

A small electric saw rested on a table to Henry's left. He raised it to his eyes, turning it on. The edges spun in circular streams of air, aching to slice.

"Perfect," he said. "This will do."

Henry lowered the saw to the girl's neck and turned it on. Skin, muscle, and blood spattered to the floor. He didn't stop (*couldn't* stop) until he cut through the entire neck and watched as the girl's head rolled off of the operating table and onto the ground below.

It's the only way for this to happen, he thought. *She can't come back. Without her brain, the virus can't...*

She can't hear you, the voice interrupted. *Don't worry. You're doing the right thing.*

Henry hovered over the incision in the now headless girl's chest and gazed at the glossy organs inside. His brain ached for food. His mouth watered. His heart fluttered. Slowly, he lowered his mouth into the incision. She was cold, but it didn't matter. His teeth met the muscle of her heart, ripping a large chunk, chewing it, and swallowing. The stinging in his chest immediately began to dull.

He ate more and more until he felt entirely satisfied.

And then he finished, wiping his mouth with a handkerchief, worded an apologetic string of words to the dead girl on the table, and fluttered out the door.

Shanna would be waiting for him upstairs.

The elevator doors opened, then closed as he entered.

It was only then he realized he was alone to wallow in the guilt of what he had just done.

There's no way to avoid it, the voice said. *This is the new you.*

Henry closed his eyes, picking at the remnants of tissue in his teeth, and vowed to never do it again.

Promises are useless, the voice said. *Just wait. You'll see.*